the PROBLEM with FOREVER

JENNIFER L. ARMENTROUT

the PROBLEM with FOREVER

Recycling programs for this product may not exist in your area.

ISBN-13: 978-0-373-21224-8

The Problem with Forever

Copyright © 2016 by Jennifer L. Armentrout

This edition published by arrangement with Harlequin Books S.A.

For questions and comments about the quality of this book, please contact us at CustomerService@Harlequin.com.

Inkyard Press
22 Adelaide St. West, 40th Floor
Toronto, Ontario M5H 4E3, Canada
www.InkyardPress.com

Printed in Italy by Grafica Veneta

For everyone who is still finding their voice, and to those who have found theirs.

PROLOGUE

Dusty, empty shoe boxes, stacked taller and wider than her slim body, wobbled as she pressed her back against them, tucking her bony knees into her chest.

Breathe. Just breathe. Breathe.

Wedged in the back of the dingy closet, she didn't dare make a sound as she sucked her lower lip between her teeth. Focusing on forcing every grimy breath into her lungs, she felt tears well in her eyes.

Oh, gosh, she'd made such a big mistake, and Miss Becky was right. She was a bad girl.

She'd reached for the dirty and stained cookie jar earlier, the one shaped like a teddy bear that hid cookies that tasted funny. She wasn't supposed to get cookies or any food by herself, but she'd just been so hungry that her tummy hurt, and Miss Becky was sick again, napping on the couch. She hadn't meant to knock the ashtray off the counter, shattering it into tiny pieces. Some were shaped like the icicles that clung to the roof during the winter. Others were no bigger than chips.

All she'd wanted was a cookie.

Her slender shoulders jerked at the sound of the wall cracking on the other side of the closet. She bit down harder on her lip. A metallic taste burst into her mouth. Tomorrow there would be a hole the size of Mr. Henry's big hand in the plaster, and Miss Becky would cry and she'd get sick again.

The soft creak of the closet door was like a crack of thunder to her ears.

Oh no, no, no...

He wasn't supposed to find her in here. This was her safe place whenever Mr. Henry was angry or when he—

She tensed, eyes peeling wide as a body taller and broader than hers slipped inside and then knelt in front of her. In the dark, she couldn't make out much of his features, but she knew in her belly and her chest who it was.

"I'm sorry," she gasped.

"I know." A hand settled on her shoulder, the weight reassuring. He was the only person she felt okay with when he touched her. "I need you to stay in here, 'kay?"

Miss Becky had said once that he was only six months older than her six years, but he always seemed so much bigger, older than her, because in her eyes, he took up her entire world.

She nodded.

"Don't come out," he said, and then he pressed into her hands the redheaded doll she'd dropped in the kitchen after she broke the ashtray and rushed into the closet. Too frightened to retrieve her, she'd left Velvet where she had fallen, and she'd been so upset because the doll had been a gift from him many, many months before. She had no idea how he'd gotten Velvet, but one day he'd simply shown up with her, and she was hers, only hers.

"You stay in here. No matter what."

Holding the doll close, clenched between her knees and chest, she nodded again.

He shifted, stiffening as an angry shout rattled the walls

around them. It was her name that dripped ice down her spine; her name that was shouted so furiously.

A small whimper parted her lips and she whispered, "I just wanted a cookie."

"It's okay. Remember? I promised I'd keep you safe forever. Just don't make a sound." He squeezed her shoulder. "Just stay quiet, and when I...when I get back, I'll read to you, 'kay? All about the stupid rabbit."

All she could do was nod again, because there had been times when she hadn't stayed quiet and she'd never forgotten the consequences. But if she stayed quiet, she knew what was coming. He wouldn't be able to read to her tonight. Tomorrow he would miss school and he wouldn't be okay even though he would tell her he was.

He lingered for a moment and then he eased out of the closet. The bedroom door shut with a smack, and she lifted the doll, pressing her tearstained face into it. A button on Velvet's chest poked at her cheek.

Don't make a sound.

Mr. Henry started to yell.

Don't make a sound.

Footsteps punched down the hall.

Don't make a sound.

Flesh smacked. Something hit the floor, and Miss Becky must have been feeling better, because she was suddenly shouting, but in the closet the only sound that mattered was the fleshy whack that came over and over. She opened her mouth, screaming silently into the doll.

Don't make a sound.

CHAPTER 1

A lot could change in four years.

Hard to believe it had been that long. Four years since I'd set foot in a public school. Four years since I'd spoken to anyone outside a very small, very close-knit group of people. Four years of preparing for this moment, and there was a good chance I was going to hurl the few bites of cereal I'd been able to force into my mouth all over the counter.

A lot could change in four years. The question was, had I?

The sound of a spoon clanking against a mug pulled me from my thoughts.

That was the *third* spoonful of sugar Carl Rivas had tried to inconspicuously dump into his coffee. When he thought no one was looking, he'd try to add two more. For a man in his early fifties, he was fit and trim, but he had one mean sugar addiction. In his study, the home office full of thick medical journals, there was a drawer in his desk that looked like a candy store had thrown up in it.

Hovering near the sugar bowl, he reached for the spoon again as he glanced over his shoulder. His hand froze.

I grinned a little from where I sat at the huge island, a full cereal bowl in front of me.

He sighed as he faced me, leaning back against the granite countertop and eyeing me over the rim of his mug as he took a sip of the coffee. His dark black hair, combed back from his forehead, had started to turn silver at the temples just recently, and with his deep olive-tone skin, I thought it made him look fairly distinguished. He was handsome, and so was his wife, Rosa. Well, *handsome* wasn't the right word for her. With her dark skin and thick, wavy hair that had yet to see a strand of gray, she was very pretty. Stunning, really, especially in the proud way she carried herself.

Rosa had never been afraid to speak up for herself and others.

I placed my spoon in the bowl, carefully, so it wouldn't clang against the ceramic. I didn't like to make unnecessary noises. An old habit I'd been unable to break and that probably would be a part of me forever.

Glancing up from my bowl, I found Carl watching me. "Are you sure you're ready for this, Mallory?"

My heart skipped unsteadily in response to what felt like an innocent question, but was really the equivalent of a loaded assault rifle. I was ready in all the ways I should be. Like a dork, I'd printed off my schedule and the map of Lands High, and Carl had called ahead, obtaining my locker assignment, so I knew exactly where everything was. I'd *studied* that map. Seriously. As if my life depended on it. There'd be no need to ask anyone where any of my classes were and I wouldn't have to roam around aimlessly. Rosa had even made the trip with me to the high school yesterday so I got familiar with the road and how long the drive would take me.

I'd expected Rosa to be here this morning since today was such a big deal, something we'd been working toward for the last year. Breakfasts had always been our time. But Carl and Rosa were both doctors. She was a heart surgeon, and an unplanned surgery had called her in before I'd even pulled myself out of bed. Kind of had to give her a pass for that.

"Mallory?"

I gave a curt nod as I pressed my lips together and dropped my hands to my lap.

Carl lowered his mug, placing it on the counter behind him. "You ready for this?" he asked again.

Little bundles of nerves formed in my stomach and I really wanted to puke. Part of me wasn't. Today was going to be difficult, but I had to do it. Meeting Carl's gaze, I nodded.

His chest rose with a deep breath. "You know the way to school?"

I nodded as I hopped up from the bar stool and grabbed my bowl. If I left now, I would be fifteen minutes early. Probably a good idea, I guessed as I dumped the leftover cereal in the trash and placed the bowl and spoon in the stainless-steel dishwasher.

Carl wasn't a tall man, maybe around five foot eight, but I still only came up to his shoulders when he moved to stand in front of me. "Use your words, Mallory. I know you're nervous and you've got a hundred things going on in your head, but you need to use your words. Not shake your head yes or no."

Use your words.

I squeezed my eyes shut. The therapist I used to see, Dr. Taft, had said that phrase a million times over, as had the speech therapist that had worked with me three times a week for two years.

Use your words.

That mantra contradicted everything I'd been taught for nearly thirteen years, because words equaled noise, and noise was rewarded with fear and violence. *Used* to equal those things, but not anymore. I hadn't spent nearly four years in intensive therapy only to not use my words, and Rosa and Carl hadn't dedicated every moment of their free time to erasing a past full of nightmares only to watch their efforts fail.

Words weren't the problem. They flew through my head like

a flock of birds migrating south for the winter. Words were never the problem. I had them, always had them, but it was plucking the words out and putting a voice to them that had always been tricky.

I drew in a breath and then swallowed drily. "Yeah. *Yes.* I'm...ready."

A small smile tipped up Carl's lips as he scooped a long strand of hair back from my face. My hair was more brown than red until I stepped outside. Then I turned into a living, breathing crimson fire engine of auburn awkwardness. "You can do this. I completely believe in that. Rosa believes in that. *You* just have to believe in that, Mallory."

My breath hitched in my throat. "Thank you."

Two words.

They weren't powerful enough, because how could they be when Carl and Rosa had saved my life? Literally and figuratively. When it came to them, I'd been at the right place at the right moment for all the wrong reasons in the universe. Our story was something straight out of an *Oprah* special or an ABC Family movie. Unreal. Saying thank you would never be enough after everything they had done for me.

And because of everything they had done for me, every opportunity they'd given me, I wanted to be as perfect for them as I could be. I *owed* that to them. And that was what today was all about.

I hurried to the island and grabbed my book bag and keys before I broke down and started crying like a kid who'd just discovered Santa wasn't real.

As if he read my mind, Carl stopped me at the door. "Don't thank me," he said. "Show us."

I started to nod, but stopped myself. "Right," I whispered.

He smiled then, crinkling the skin around his eyes. "Good luck."

Opening the front door, I stepped out on the narrow stoop

and into the warm air and bright sun of a late-August morning. My gaze drifted over the neatly landscaped front yard that matched the house across the street, and was identical to every house in the Pointe subdivision.

Every house.

Sometimes it still shocked me that I was living in a place like this—a big home with a yard and flowers artfully planted, with a car in the recently asphalted driveway that was mine. Some days it didn't seem real. Like I'd wake up and find myself back...

I shook my head, pushing those thoughts away as I approached the decade-old Honda Civic. The car had belonged to Rosa and Carl's real daughter, a high school graduation gift given to Marquette before she'd left for college to become a doctor, like them.

Real daughter.

Dr. Taft had always corrected me when I referred to Marquette that way, because he believed it somehow lessened what I was to Carl and Rosa. I hoped he was right, because some days I felt like the big home with the manicured yard.

Some days I didn't feel real.

Marquette never made it to college. An aneurysm. There one minute and gone the next, and there had been nothing anyone could do. I imagined that was something Rosa and Carl had always struggled with. They saved so many lives, but couldn't save the one that meant the most.

It was a little weird that the car belonged to me now, like I was somehow a replacement child. They never made me feel that way and I'd never say that out loud, but still, when I got behind the wheel I couldn't help but think about Marquette.

I placed my bag on the passenger seat. My gaze crawled over the interior, landing on the reflection of my eyes in the rearview mirror. They were way too wide. I looked like a deer about to get slammed by a semi, if a deer had blue eyes, but whatever. The skin around my eyes was pale, my brows knitted. I looked scared.

Sigh.

That was not how I wanted to look on my first day of school.

I started to glance away, but the silver medallion dangling from the rearview mirror snagged my attention. It wasn't much bigger than a quarter. A bearded man was engraved inside a raised oval. He was writing in a book with a feathered pen. Above him were the words *SAINT LUKE* and below was *PRAY FOR US*.

Saint Luke was the patron saint of physicians.

The necklace had belonged to Rosa. Her mother had given it to her when she entered med school, and Rosa had given it to me when I'd told her that I was ready to attend public school my senior year. I guessed she'd given it to Marquette at some point, but I hadn't asked.

I think there was a part of both Rosa and Carl that hoped that I'd follow in their footsteps, much like Marquette had been planning to. But becoming a surgeon required assertiveness, confidence and a damn near fearless personality, which were three adjectives literally no one would ever use to describe me.

Carl and Rosa knew that, so they were pushing me more in the direction of research since, according to them, I'd displayed the same aptitude in science in my years of homeschooling as Marquette had. While I hadn't protested their urging, spending forever studying microbes or cells sounded as interesting as spending forever repainting the walls in my room white. But I had no idea what I wanted other than to attend college, because until Rosa and Carl had come into my life, college had never, ever been a part of the equation.

The drive to Lands High took exactly eighteen minutes, just as I expected. The moment the three-story brick building came into view beyond the baseball and football fields, I tensed as if a speeding baseball was heading for my face and I'd forgotten my mitt.

My stomach twisted as my hands tightened on the steering

wheel. The school was enormous and relatively new. Its website said it had been built in the nineties, and compared to other
schools, it was still shiny.

Shiny and huge.

I passed the buses turning to do their drop-off in the round-
about and followed another car around the sprawling structure,
to the mall-sized parking lot. Parking wasn't hard, and I was a
little early, so I used that fifteen minutes to do something akin
to a daily affirmation, and just as cheesy and embarrassing.

I can do this. I will do this.

Over and over, I repeated those words as I climbed out of
the Honda, slinging my new bag over my shoulder. My heart
pounded, thumped so fast I thought I'd be sick as I looked
around me, taking in the sea of bodies streaming toward the
walkway leading to the back entrance of Lands High. Different features, colors, shapes and sizes greeted me. For a moment
it was like my brain was a second away from short-circuiting.
I held my breath. Eyes glanced over me, some lingering and
some moving on as if they didn't even notice me standing there,
which was okay in a way, because I was used to being nothing
more than a ghost.

My hand fluttered to the strap of my bag and, mouth dry, I
forced my legs to move. I joined the wave of people, slipping in
beside them. I focused on the blond ponytail of the girl in front
of me. My gaze dipped. She was wearing a jean skirt and sandals. Bright orange, strappy, gladiator-style sandals. They were
cute. I could tell her that. Strike up a conversation. The ponytail was also pretty amazing. It had the bump along the crown
of her head, the kind I could never replicate even after watching
a dozen YouTube tutorials on how to do it. Whenever I tried,
I looked like I had an uneven growth on my head.

But I said nothing to her.

As I lifted my gaze, my eyes collided with a boy next to me.
Sleep clung to his expression. He didn't smile or frown or do

anything other than turn his attention back to the cell phone he held in his hand. I wasn't even sure if he saw me.

The morning air was warm, but the moment I stepped into the near-frigid school, I was grateful for the thin cardigan I'd carefully paired with my tank top and jeans.

From the entrance, everyone spread out in different directions. Smaller students who were roughly around my height, but were definitely much younger, speed-walked over the red-and-blue Viking painted on the floor, their book bags thumping off their backs as they dodged taller and broader bodies. Others walked like zombies, gaits slow and seemingly aimless. I was somewhere in the middle, moving at what appeared to be a normal pace, but was actually one I'd practiced.

And there were some who raced toward others, hugging them and laughing. I guessed they were friends who hadn't seen each other over the summer break, or maybe they were just really excitable people. Either way, I stared at them as I walked. Seeing them reminded me of my friend Ainsley. Like me, she'd been homeschooled—still was—but if she wasn't, I imagined we'd be like these kids right now, hopping toward one another, grinning and animated. Normal.

Ainsley was probably still in bed.

Not because she got to goof off all day, but because our mutual instructor did summer break a little differently. She was still on break, but once her year got going again, her homeschooling hours would be as strict and grueling as mine had been.

Shaking myself from my reverie, I took the stairwell at the end of the wide hall, near the entrance to the cafeteria. Even being close to the lunchroom had my pulse spiking, causing my stomach to twist with nausea.

Lunch.

Oh, God, what was I going to do about lunch? I didn't know anyone, not a single person, and I would—

I cut myself off, unable to really think about that right now.

If I did, there was a good chance I might turn around and run back to the safety of my car.

My locker was on the second floor, middle of the hall, number two-three-four. I found it with no problem, and bonus, it opened on the first try. Twisting at the waist, I pulled out a binder I was using for my afternoon classes and dropped it on the top shelf, knowing that I was going to be collecting massive textbooks today.

The locker beside mine slammed shut, causing me to jump and tense. My chin jerked up. A tall girl with dark skin and tiny braids all over her head flashed a quick smile in my direction. "Hey."

My tongue tied right up and I couldn't get that one, stupid little word out before the girl with the short hair spun and walked off.

Fail.

Feeling about ten kinds of stupid, I rolled my eyes and closed my locker door. Turning around, my gaze landed on the back of a guy heading in the opposite direction. My muscles tensed again as I stared at him.

I didn't even know why or how I ended up looking at him. Maybe it was because he was a good head taller than anyone around him. Like a total creeper, I couldn't pull my eyes away. He had wavy hair, somewhere between brown and black, and it was cut short against the nape of his bronzed neck, but was longer on the top. I wondered if it flopped on his forehead, and there was an unsteady tug at my chest as I remembered a boy I used to know years ago, whose hair always did that—fell forward no matter how many times he pushed it out of his face. A boy it kind of hurt my chest to think about.

His shoulders were broad under a black T-shirt, biceps defined in a way that made me think of someone who either played sports or did a lot of manual labor. His jeans were faded, but not in the expensive way. I knew the difference between name-brand jeans that were designed to look well-worn and jeans that were simply old and on their last wear. He carried a single notebook in his hand, and even from where I stood, the notebook looked about as old as his pants did.

Something weird moved through me, a feeling of familiarity, and as I stood in front of my locker, I found myself thinking of the one bright thing in a past full of shadows and darkness.

I thought about the boy who made my chest hurt, the one who'd promised forever.

It had been four years since I'd seen him or even heard him speak. Four years of trying to erase everything that had to do with that portion of my childhood, but I remembered *him*. I wondered about him.

How could I not? I always would.

He had been the sole reason I survived the house we'd grown up in.

CHAPTER 2

One thing I quickly learned after my first period was that the row of seats in the back of the classroom was prime real estate. Close enough to see the chalkboard, but far enough away that there was a good chance the teacher wouldn't call on you.

I got to each of my AP classes before anyone else and snagged a desk in the back, blending in before I was even seen. No one talked to me. Not until just before lunch, at the start of English, when a dark brown–skinned girl with sloe-colored eyes sat in the empty seat next to me.

"Hi," she said, smacking a thick notebook on the flat surface attached to the chair. "I hear Mr. Newberry is a real jerk. Take a look at the pictures."

My gaze flickered to the front of the classroom. Our teacher hadn't arrived yet, but the chalkboard was lined with photos of famous authors. Shakespeare, Voltaire, Hemingway, Emerson and Thoreau were a few I recognized, though I probably wouldn't recognize them if I didn't have endless time on my hands.

"All dudes, right?" she continued, and when I looked back at her, the tight black curls bounced as she shook her head. "My sister had him two years ago. She warned me that he basically thinks you need a dick to produce anything of literary value."

My eyes went wide.

"So I'm thinking this class should be a lot of fun." She grinned, flashing straight white teeth. "By the way, I'm Keira Hart. I don't remember you from last year. Not that I know everyone, but I think I would've at least seen you around."

Sweat covered my palms as she continued to stare at me. The question she was throwing out was simple. The answer was easy. My throat dried and I could feel heat creeping up my neck as the seconds ticked by.

Use your words.

My toes curled against the soft leather soles of my flip-flops and my throat felt scratchy as I forced the words out. "I'm... I'm new."

There! I did it. I spoke.

Take that, everyone! Words were totally my bitch.

All right, perhaps I was exaggerating my accomplishment since I technically only spoke two words and repeated one. But I was not going to rain on my own wow, because talking to new people was hard for me. Like as hard as it would be for someone to walk naked into the class.

Keira didn't seem to notice my internal dumbassery. "That's what I thought." And then she waited, and for a moment I didn't get why she was looking at me so expectantly. Then I did.

My name. She was waiting for my name. Air hissed in between my teeth. "I'm Mallory...Mallory Dodge."

"Cool." She nodded as she rocked her curvy shoulders against the back of the chair. "Oh. Here he comes."

We didn't talk again, but I was feeling pretty good about the sum total of seven words spoken, and I was totally going to count the repeat ones. Rosa and Carl would.

Mr. Newberry spoke with an air of pretentiousness that even

a newbie like me could pick up on, but it didn't bother me. I was floating on a major accomplishment high.

Then came lunch.

Walking into the large, loud room was like having an out-of-body experience. My brain was screaming at me to find a quieter, easier—*safer*—place to go, but I forced myself forward, one foot in front of the other.

Nerves had twisted my stomach into knots as I made it through the lunch line. All I grabbed was a banana and a bottle of water. There were so many people around me and so much noise—laughter, shouting and a constant low hum of conversation. I was completely out of my element. Everyone was at the long square tables, huddled in groups. No one was really sitting alone from what I could see, and I knew no one. I would be the only person sitting by myself.

Horrified by the realization, I felt my fingers spasm around the banana I clenched. The smell of disinfectant and burnt food overwhelmed me. Pressure clamped down on my chest, tightening my throat. I sucked in air, but it didn't seem to inflate my lungs. A series of shivers danced along the base of my skull.

I couldn't do this.

There was too much noise and too many people in what now felt like a small, confined area. It was never this loud at home. Never. My gaze darted all over, not really seeing any detail. My hand shook so badly I was afraid I'd drop the banana. Instinct kicked in, and my feet started moving.

I hurried out into the somewhat quieter hall and kept going, passing a few kids lingering against the lockers and the faint scent of cigarettes that surrounded them. I dragged in deep, calming breaths that really didn't calm me. Getting farther away from the cafeteria was what calmed me, not the stupid breaths. I rounded the corner and jerked to a stop, narrowly avoiding a head-on collision with a boy not much taller than me.

He stumbled to the side, bloodshot eyes widening in surprise.

A scent clung to him that at first I thought was smoke, but when I inhaled, it was something richer, earthy and thick.

"Sorry, *chula*," he murmured, and his eyes did a slow glide from the tips of my toes right back up to mine. He started to grin.

At the end of the hall, a taller boy picked up his pace. "Jayden, where in the fuck you running off to, bro? We need to talk."

The guy I assumed was Jayden turned, rubbing a hand over his close-cropped dark hair as he muttered, *"Mierda, hombre."*

A door opened and a teacher stepped out, frowning as his gaze bounced between the two. "Already, Mr. Luna? Is this how we're going to start this year off?"

I figured it was time to get out of the hallway, because nothing about the taller boy's face said he was happy or friendly, and the deep scowl settling over the teacher's face when Jayden kept walking made him look like he wanted to cut someone. I hurried around Jayden and kept my chin down, not making eye contact with anyone.

I ended up in the library, playing Candy Crush on my cell phone until the bell rang, and I spent my next class—history—furious with myself, because I hadn't even tried. That was the truth. Instead I'd hidden in the library like a dork, playing a stupid game that only the devil could've created, because I seriously sucked at it.

Doubt settled over me like a too-heavy, coarse blanket. I'd come so far in the last four years. I was nothing like the girl I used to be. Yeah, I still had some hang-ups, but I was stronger than the shell of a person I'd once been, wasn't I?

Rosa would be so disappointed.

My skin grew itchy by the time I headed to my final class, my heart rate probably somewhere near stroke territory, because my last period was the worst period ever in the history of ever.

Speech class.

Otherwise known as Communications. When I'd registered

for school last spring, I'd been feeling all kinds of brave while Carl and Rosa stared at me like I was half-crazy. They said they could get me out of the class, even though it was a requirement at Lands High, but I'd had something to prove.

I didn't want them stepping in. I wanted—no, I *needed* to do this.

Ugh.

Now I wished I had employed some common sense and let them do whatever it was that would've gotten me excused, because this was a nightmare waiting to happen. When I saw the open door to the class on the third floor, it gaped at me, the room ultra-bright inside.

My steps faltered. A girl stepped around me, lips pursing when she checked me out. I wanted to spin and flee. Get in the Honda. Go home. Be safe.

Stay the same.

No.

Tightening my fingers around the strap of my bag, I forced myself forward, and it was like walking through knee-deep mud. Each step felt sluggish. Each breath I took wheezed in my lungs. Overhead lights buzzed and my ears were hypersensitive to the conversation around me, but I did it.

My feet made it to the back row and my fingers were numb, knuckles white, as I dropped my bag on the floor beside my desk and slid into my seat. Busying myself with pulling out my notebook, I then gripped the edge of my desk.

I was in speech class. I was here.

I'd done it.

I was going to throw myself a freaking party when I got home. Like an eat-fudge-icing-straight-out-of-the-freaking-can kind of party. Hardcore.

Knuckles starting to ache, I loosened my death grip as I glanced at the door, sliding my damp hands across the top of the desk. The first thing I saw was the broad chest draped in black, then the well-formed biceps. And there was that tired notebook that looked seconds from falling apart, tapping against a worn-denim-clad thigh.

It was the boy from this morning, from the hallway.

More than curious to see what he looked like from the front, I raised my lashes, but he had turned toward the door. The girl from the hallway, the one who stepped around me, was walking through it. Now that I was sitting and sort of breathing, it was my turn to check her out. She was pretty. Very pretty, like Ainsley. This girl had pin-straight, caramel-colored hair that was as long as mine, past her breasts. She was tall and the tank top she wore showed off a flat stomach. Her dark brown gaze wasn't focused on me this time. It was on the guy in front of her.

The expression on her face said he gave great full frontal, and when he laughed, her pink lips split into a wide smile. Her smile transformed her from pretty to beautiful, but my attention swung away from her as tiny hairs rose all over my body. That laugh… It was deep, rich and somehow familiar. A shiver crept over my shoulders. *That laugh…*

He was walking backward, and I was rather amazed that he didn't trip over anything, actually somewhat envious of that fact. And then I realized he was heading toward the last half circle. Toward *me*. I glanced around. There were only a few seats open, two on my left. The girl was following him. Not just following him. Touching him.

Touching him like she'd done it a lot.

Her slim arm was extended, her hand planted in the center of his stomach, just below his chest. She bit down on her lower lip as her hand drifted farther south. Golden bangles dangling from her wrist got awful close to the worn leather belt. My cheeks heated as the boy stepped out of her reach. There was something playful about his movements, as if this dance was a daily routine for them both.

He turned at the end of the desks, stepping behind the occupied chair, and my gaze tracked up narrow hips, over the stomach the girl had touched, up and up, and then I saw his face.

I stopped breathing.

My brain couldn't perceive what I was seeing. It did not compute. I stared up at him, *really* saw him, saw a face that was familiar yet new to me, more mature than I remembered but still achingly beautiful. I *knew* him. Oh my God, I would know him anywhere, even if it had been four years and the last time I'd seen him, that last night that had been so horrible, had changed my life forever.

It was too surreal.

Now the reason why he'd popped in my head this morning made sense, because I'd seen him, but hadn't realized it was *him*.

I couldn't move, couldn't get enough air into my lungs and couldn't believe this was happening. My hands slipped off the desk, falling limply into my lap as he dipped into the seat next to me. His gaze was on the girl who took the seat next to him, and his profile, the strong jaw that had only been hinted at the last time I'd seen him, tilted as his eyes moved over the front of the room, across the wall-length chalkboard. He looked like he had back then, but bigger and with everything more…more *defined*. From the eyebrows darker than the mix of brown and black hair and thick lashes to the broad cheekbones and the slight scruff covering the curve of his jaw.

Goodness, he'd grown up in the way I'd thought he would when I was twelve and started to really look at him, to see him as a boy.

I couldn't believe he was here. My heart was trying to claw itself out of my chest as lips—lips fuller than I remembered—tilted up, and a knot formed in my belly as the dimple formed in his right cheek. The only dimple he had. No matching set. Just one. My mind raced back through the years, and I could only think of a handful of times I'd seen him relaxed. Leaning back in the chair that seemed too small for him, he slowly turned his head toward me. Eyes that were brown with tiny flecks of gold met mine.

Eyes I'd never forgotten.

The easy, almost lazy smile I'd never seen on his face before froze. His lips parted and a paleness seeped under his tawny skin. Those eyes widened, the gold flecks seeming to expand. He recognized me; I had changed a lot since then, but still, recognition dawned in his features. He was moving again, leaning forward on his seat toward me. Four words roared out of the past and echoed in my head.

Don't make a sound.

"Mouse?" he breathed.

CHAPTER 3

Mouse.

No one but him called me that, and I hadn't heard that nickname in so long, I never really thought I'd hear it again.

And I never in a million years dared to hope that I'd see *him* again. But here he was, and I couldn't stop staring. None of the thirteen-year-old boy he'd been remained in the guy in front of me, but it was *him*. It was those warm brown eyes with golden flecks and the same sunbaked skin, a trait from his father who'd possibly been half white, half Hispanic. He didn't know where his mother or any of her family had come from. One of our... our caseworkers had thought that his mother might have been a mix of white and South American, maybe Brazilian, but he would most likely never know.

Suddenly I saw him—the *him* from before, from when we were little and he'd been the only stable thing in a world of chaos. At age nine—bigger than me, but still so small—he'd stood between Mr. Henry and me in the kitchen, like he'd done too many times before, as I'd clutched the redheaded doll—*Velvet*—he'd just retrieved for me. I'd held her close, trembling, and he'd puffed out his chest, legs spreading wide. *"Leave her alone,"* he'd growled, hands curling into fists. *"You'd better stay away from her."*

I pulled myself out of the memory, but there were so many of him coming to my rescue for some reason or another until he couldn't, until the promise of forever had been shattered, and everything...everything had fallen apart.

His chest rose deeply, and when he spoke, his voice was low and rough. "Is that really you, Mouse?"

Vaguely aware of the girl on his other side watching us, I saw her eyes go as wide as mine felt. My tongue was useless, which for once was strange, because he...he had been the one person I'd never had any problem talking to, but that had been a different world, a different lifetime.

That had been forever ago.

"Mallory?" he whispered. Turned completely toward me, I thought for a second he might climb out of his chair. And that would so be him, because he wasn't scared of doing *anything.* Never had been. As close as we were, I saw the faint scar above his right eyebrow, a shade or two lighter than his skin. I remembered how he'd gotten it and my chest ached anew, because that scar symbolized a stale cookie and a shattered ashtray.

A guy in front of us had twisted around on his stool. "Yo." He snapped his fingers when he didn't get a response. "Hey, man? Hello?"

He ignored the guy, still staring at me like a ghost had appeared right in front of him.

"Whatever," the kid muttered, twisting toward the girl, but she, too, ignored him. She was focused on us. The tardy bell rang, and I knew the teacher had entered, because the conversation in the room was quieting.

"Do you recognize me?" His voice was still barely above a whisper.

His eyes continued to hold mine, and I spoke what turned out to be the easiest word I'd ever said in my life. "Yes."

He rocked back in his chair, straightening as his shoulders tensed. His eyes closed. "Jesus Christ," he muttered, rubbing his palm against his sternum.

I jumped in my seat as the teacher smacked his hand on the stack of texts piled on the corner desk, forcing my gaze forward. My heart was still acting as if an out-of-control jackhammer had gone off in my chest.

"All right, all of you should know who I am since you're in my class, but just in case some of you are lost, I'm Mr. Santos." He leaned against the desk, crossing his arms. "And this is speech class. If you're not supposed to be here, you probably should be somewhere else."

Mr. Santos continued to speak, but the blood rushing through me drowned out his words, and my thoughts were too caught up in the fact that *he* was sitting next to me. He was here; after all these years, he was right beside me like he'd been since we were three years old, but he hadn't seemed happy about seeing me. I didn't even know what to think. A mixture of hope and desperation swirled inside me, mixing with bitter and sweet memories I'd both clung to and longed to forget.

He was… I squeezed my eyes shut and swallowed against the lump lodged in my throat.

Textbooks were handed out, followed by a syllabus. Both sat on my desk untouched. Mr. Santos went over the type of speeches we'd be writing and delivering throughout the year, everything from an informative speech to one that would be based on interviewing a fellow classmate. While I'd been seconds away from full freak-out mode when I'd walked into the class, the prospect of having to give multiple speeches in front of thirty people was now the furthest thing from my thoughts.

I stared straight ahead, realizing that Keira was also in this class, sitting in front of the guy who'd tried to get *his* attention at the beginning. I wasn't sure she'd noticed me when I entered the class. Then again, maybe she did and didn't care. Why would she have? Just because she spoke to me in one class didn't mean she was lining up to be my BFF.

My lunch fail seemed like it happened years ago. Each breath I took I was aware of. Unable to stop myself, I tucked my hair back as I glanced to my left.

My gaze collided with his, and I sucked in an unsteady breath. When we were younger, I could always read his expression. But now? His face was completely impassive. Was he happy? Angry? Sad? Or as confused as me? I didn't know, but he didn't try to hide the fact that he was staring.

Heat infused my cheeks as I averted my gaze, and somehow I ended up looking at the girl beside him. She was staring straight ahead, lips pressed in a thin, firm line. My gaze dropped to where her hands were balled into fists, resting on top of the desk. I looked away again.

Maybe five minutes passed before I caved and peeked at him again. He wasn't looking in my direction, but his jaw was working, causing a muscle to thrum in his cheek. All I could do was gawk at him like a total idiot, incapable of much more.

When he was younger, anyone could tell he'd grow into someone with heart-stopping looks. He had the framework for it—big eyes, expressive lips, and defined bone structure. Sometimes that had been a...a really bad thing for him. He had received all kinds of attention. It seemed like Mr. Henry had wanted to break him like he was fine china. Then there were the men that roamed in and out of the house. Some of them had... They had been too interested in him.

Mouth dry, I shut those thoughts off. I shouldn't be so shocked by how attractive he'd turned out, but as Ainsley would say, he was stupid-hot.

While Mr. Santos was passing out index cards for some reason I'd missed, the guy in front of us turned around again, his sea-moss-colored gaze direct. "You good for after school?"

I couldn't help it. My gaze flickered to *him*. Lips taut and arms folded across his chest, he nodded curtly.

The guy raised dark brows before he glanced in Mr. Santos's direction. "We need to talk to Jayden."

Jayden? I thought about the boy I'd almost plowed over in the hall.

The girl looked over, head cocked to the side.

"Got it, Hector," *he* replied, voice clipped, and I was struck by how deep his voice was now. A moment passed as his chin tilted toward me.

Flushing, I looked away, but not before I caught Hector's curious green gaze flicker to me. The rest of the class was an exercise in stealing glances at *him*, as if I needed to see him to remind myself that he was seriously sitting there. I wasn't really good at being furtive, because I was pretty sure the girl on the other side of him, the girl that had been touching him quite familiarly on the way into the class, caught me about half a dozen times.

As the minutes ticked by, my stomach began to churn around the ever-increasing knots that were forming. Anxiety circled like a viper waiting to attack with its crippling venom.

Pressure closed my throat, a steel vise squeezing until it eked every last breath out of me. An icy burn crawled up the back of my neck and then splashed across the base of my skull. My next breath hitched, and I felt *it*—the flash-flood feeling of losing all control.

Breathe.

I needed to breathe.

Curling my fingers into my palms, I forced my chest to rise and fall evenly and willed my heart to slow down. When I had been in therapy, Dr. Taft had drilled into me the fact that I wasn't losing control of my body when this happened. It was basically all in my head, sometimes triggered by a certain loud sound or a scent that would throw me back in time. Sometimes, I wasn't even sure what was triggering it.

Today I knew.

The trigger was sitting right beside me. This panic was real, because he was real, and the past he symbolized wasn't a product of my brain.

What would I say to him when the bell rang and school was over? Four years had gone by since that night. Would he even want to talk to me? Or what if he didn't want to talk to me?

Oh, God.

What if my being back here wasn't something he'd hoped for or even thought about? He had... He had taken a lot of crap for me, because of me. While there were good moments over the course of our ten years together, there had been a lot of bad. A lot.

And it would... Yeah, it would suck if he got up and walked out of class without saying another word, but that would be better in a way. At least now I knew he was alive and appeared to be physically unscathed, and he seemed to be familiar with the girl on his other side. Maybe she was his girlfriend. That meant he was happy, right? Happy and whole. Knowing he was okay meant I could officially close that chapter of my life.

Except I'd thought I'd already closed the chapter. Now it was reopened, flipping all the way to the beginning.

When the bell rang, protection mode kicked in, like it had oh so many times in the past. I wasn't even aware of what I was doing. An old instinct reared its head like a sleeping dragon, an instinct that I'd spent four years beating into submission, but had already caved to once today.

Standing, I scooped up my book and grabbed my bag off the floor. My heart slammed against my ribs as I darted around our seats, and I didn't look back, didn't give him a chance to walk away first. My sandals smacked off the floor as I hurried down the hall, easing past slower-walking students as I shoved the textbook into my bag. I probably looked like an idiot. Well, I felt like an idiot.

I burst outside and into the hot sun. Chin down, I followed the path to the parking lot, hands trembling as I opened and closed them, because it felt like the blood had stopped at my wrists. The tips of my fingers tingled.

The silver Honda gleamed up ahead, and I drew in a ragged breath. I would go home and I would—

"Mallory."

My pulse spiked at the sound of my name, and my steps faltered. I was feet from my car, from escape, but I turned around slowly.

He stood beside a red truck that hadn't been there when I parked this morning and that I hadn't even noticed on my mad dash to my car. In the sunlight his hair was more brown than black, and his skin deeper, his features sharper. There were so many questions I suddenly wished I could ask. What had he been doing for four years? Did someone finally adopt him? Or was he moving from one foster home to the next?

Most important, was he safe now?

Not all group homes were bad. Not all foster parents were horrible. Look at Carl and Rosa. They put the *awe* in awesome. They'd adopted me, but before them, this boy standing before me and I had not been lucky. We'd been fostered by the worst kind of people who somehow managed to pass inspection. Caseworkers were underfunded and understaffed, and most did the best they could, but there were a lot of cracks to slip through, and we'd fallen right through one in the worst way.

Most foster kids didn't stay in the system or one house longer than two years. Most kids were reunited with parents or adopted. No one besides Mr. Henry and Miss Becky had wanted us, and I still couldn't figure out why they wanted us and yet treated us so badly. Our caseworkers came and went with the frequency of the seasons. Teachers in school had to have seen what we'd been going through at home but none risked their jobs to step in. The bitterness of being overlooked and stepped on for so long in an overburdened and broken-down system still clung to me like a second skin that I wondered if I'd ever shed.

But there was good and bad in everything. Had he finally found some good?

"Really?" he said, his fingers tightening around the old notebook he held. "After everything, after four years of not knowing what the hell happened to you, you just show up in fucking speech class and then run away? From me?"

I inhaled sharply as I lowered my arms. My bag slipped off my shoulder, hitting the hot asphalt. Shock flowed through me, but in the back of my mind, I wasn't surprised that he'd caught up to me. He never ran. He never hid from anything. That had always been me. We had been yin and yang. My cowardice to his bravery. His strength to my weakness.

But that wasn't me anymore.

I wasn't Mouse.

I wasn't a coward.

I wasn't weak.

He took a step forward and then stopped, shaking his head as his chest rose and fell unsteadily. "Say something."

I struggled to get the word out. "What?"

"My name."

I wasn't sure why he wanted me to say that, and I didn't know how it would feel to say it again after all this time, but I drew in a deep breath. "Rider." Another breath shuddered through me. "Rider Stark."

His throat worked and, for a heartbeat, neither of us moved as a steamy breeze tossed strands of hair across my face. Then he dropped his notebook to the pavement. I was surprised it didn't burst into dust. His long-legged pace ate up the distance. One second there was several feet between us, and in the next breath he was right there in front of me. He was so much taller now. I barely reached his shoulders.

And then his arms were around me.

My heart exploded as those strong arms pulled me against his chest. There was a moment where I froze, and then my arms swept around his neck. I held on, squeezing my eyes shut as I inhaled the clean scent and the lingering trace of aftershave. This was *him*. His hugs were different now, stronger and tighter. He lifted me clear off my feet, one arm around my waist, the other hand buried deep in my hair, and my breasts were mushed against his surprisingly hard chest.

Whoa.

His hugs were most definitely different than they were when we were twelve.

"Jesus, Mouse, you don't even know…" His voice was gruff and thick as he set me back on my feet, but he didn't let go. One arm stayed around my waist. His other hand fisted the ends of my hair. His chin grazed the top of my head as I slid my hands down his chest. "I never thought I'd see you again."

I rested my forehead between my hands, feeling his heart beat fast. I could hear people around us, and I imagined some were probably staring, but I didn't care. Rider was warm and solid. Real. Alive.

"Hell, I wasn't even planning to come to school today. If I hadn't…" His hand unclenched from my hair, and I felt him draw a strand out. "Look at your hair. You're no longer a carrot top."

A choked laugh escaped me. When I was younger, my hair had been an orangey-red mess full of ratty knots and unruly waves, and thank God, the tone had calmed down somewhat. A visit to a hair salon had helped. The knots and waves were still up for debate whenever it was humid.

Rider drew back just enough that when I blinked my eyes open, I found him studying me. "Look at you," he murmured.

"You're all grown-up." His hand left my hair, and a fine shiver danced along my spine as his thumb swept across my lower lip. The touch startled me. "And you're still as quiet as a mouse."

My spine stiffened. *Mouse.* "I'm not..." Anything I was about to say died a fiery death, because his thumb had tracked its way across my cheekbone, the pad of his finger callused and rough, but the caress tender.

My gaze tracked up to eyes I'd never thought I'd see again, but he was really here. Oh my God, Rider was here, and so many thoughts bounced around. I could only grab hold of a few of them, but memories surfaced like the sun cresting a mountain.

One night I'd woken up, frightened by the booming voices coming from the dark downstairs. I'd snuck into the room next to mine, which had been Rider's, and he'd let me crawl in bed with him. He'd read to me then, from a book that I'd loved, a book that Rider called "the stupid rabbit story." It always made me cry, but he read to me to distract me from the shouts filling up the small, broken-down row home. I'd been five, and from that moment on, he'd become my entire world.

Rider suddenly stepped back and grabbed my right arm. As he lifted it, he turned it over and pushed the sleeve of the thin cardigan up. His brows knitted as he frowned. "I don't understand."

My gaze followed his, to where his hand circled my wrist. The skin near the inside of my elbow was a deeper pink, as was the skin on the inside of my arms and both my palms, but it was barely noticeable.

"They said you were burned badly." Lifting his gaze, he searched my face. "I saw them taking you out on the stretcher, Mouse. I remember that as if it happened yesterday."

"I... Carl..." I shook my head as his frown deepened, realizing he had no idea who Carl was. I focused, took a few moments and then tried again. "The doctors at Johns Hopkins. They...did skin grafts."

"Skin grafts?"

I nodded. "I had...the best doctors. There're...barely any scars." Well, my backside, where they had grafted the skin, was also a different pink, but I doubted anyone would be seeing that anytime soon.

His thumb smoothed over the inside of my wrist in a slow swipe, sending a bolt of sensation up my arm. He didn't say anything for a long moment as his gaze held mine. The golden flecks in his eyes were brighter now, making them more hazel than brown. "They said I couldn't see you. I asked. I even went to the county hospital."

My heart dropped. "You did?"

Rider nodded as the tension eased around his mouth. "You weren't there. Or at least they didn't tell me. One of the nurses called the police. I ended up..." He shook his head. "It doesn't matter."

"You ended up...what?" I asked, because it did matter. Everything that had happened to Rider mattered, even when it had felt like the world couldn't have cared less.

His thick lashes swept down for a moment. "The police and CPS thought I'd run away, which was dumb as shit. Why would I have run away to a hospital?"

Probably because Child Protective Services had a file on us the width of the Honda. And also probably because Rider and I had run away before. More than once. I'd been eight and he'd just turned nine when we'd decided that we would do better on our own.

We'd made it to the McDonald's two blocks down the street before Mr. Henry found us.

Then there were the other times, too many to count.

Rider laughed then, and there was a tug in my chest, because when I looked up at him, there wasn't a smile on his striking face. "That night..." He swallowed. "I'm sorry, Mouse."

Flinching, I stepped back, but he kept ahold of my arm.

"I would've stopped him, but I didn't." His eyes were darker. "I shouldn't have tried—"

"It wasn't your fault," I whispered, sickened by what he was saying. I stared up at him. He seriously believed what had happened was because of him?

His head tilted to the side. "Yeah, I made you a promise. I didn't keep that promise, not when it counted."

"No," I stated, and when he started to reply, I pulled my arm free. Surprise scuttled across his face. "That...wasn't a promise you should've ever had to make. Not to anyone." He'd promised to be there for me forever, and he'd done everything possible not to break his word. There were things that couldn't be controlled, especially by a kid.

His brows flew up and then his lips did a slow curl. "I don't think you've ever told me no before."

I opened my mouth to point out that I'd never had a reason to, but the thump of music intruded. It was a weird wake-up call, reminding us that we weren't in our own little bubble. There was a world around us. As the music drew closer, the low bass rattling the windows of the truck beside us, Rider's gaze flicked behind me. Then he stepped closer, so close that his worn sneakers brushed my sandals.

He dipped his chin as he reached around, pulling a cell phone out of his back pocket. "What's your number, Mouse?"

It was obvious that he was leaving, and I didn't want him to. I had so many questions, a million of them, but I gave him my number as I smoothed my damp palms down my jeans.

"Yo, Rider, you ready?" came the voice from the thumping car. I recognized it from speech class. Hector. "We've got to roll."

Rider looked past me again and he sighed. Stepping back, he picked up his notebook and then grabbed my bag off the pavement. Moving forward, he draped it over my shoulder, his fingers agile as he scooped the strands of my hair out from under the strap.

A half grin appeared as his gaze moved over my face. "Mouse."

"Someone is gonna kick your ass," Hector called, and my heart jumped in my chest. But I relaxed when I realized his tone was light. He was teasing him.

Rider dropped his hand and stepped around me. As though he had some kind of gravitational pull, I turned. The car was idling behind mine, an older Ford Escort with blue racing stripes. Hector was in the driver's seat, grinning widely with one arm out the window, dark hand tapping along the side of the door.

"Hey, *mami*," Hector called out, his grin spreading as he bit down on his lower lip. *"Que cuerpo tan brutal."*

I had no idea what he'd just said, but it seemed to be directed at me.

"Shut up," Rider replied, planting his large hand in Hector's face and shoving him back into the driver's side of the car. *"No la mires."*

I still had no idea what any of that meant, but there was something about the words he and Hector spoke that didn't sound like the typical Spanish I heard from Rosa and Carl at home. Then again, it could've been Spanish and I wouldn't know, since they had given up trying to teach me the language a long time ago.

A rumble of deep male laughter rose from inside the car, with Hector kicking his head back against the seat. A second later I saw a younger face I recognized.

Jayden.

He was leaning from the passenger seat, across Hector. "Hey," he yelled. "I think I know you."

"You don't know her," Rider replied as he yanked open the back door. Twisting into the seat, he looked at me one last time. Our gazes locked for a brief moment and then the door closed, tinted windows shielding him.

The Escort peeled off.

I stood there, vaguely aware of someone climbing into the truck parked beside my car. In a daze, I climbed in behind the wheel and placed my bag in the passenger seat.

"Holy crap," I whispered as I stared out the windshield. *"Holy crap."*

CHAPTER 4

I couldn't recall exactly how I made it home, which was probably not a good thing. The drive had been spent in a daze. By the time I walked into the house, seeing Rider no longer felt real. As if I'd dreamed him up.

I drew in a deep, calming breath.

Four years. Four years of peeling back the frayed and damaged layers. Four years of undoing ten years of *crap*, of doing what I could to forget everything. Everything except for Rider, because he'd deserved not to be forgotten. But he was the past—the good part of my past, but still a past I didn't want to remember.

I barreled through the house, skidding into the kitchen. Rosa was there, wearing pale blue scrubs decorated with kitten paws and her hair pulled up in a ponytail. She had made it a point to be home early today. She raised her brows as she turned to me.

"Whoa, Speed Racer, where are you heading to?" she asked, setting her bowl on the counter. From where I stood, I could smell the Italian dressing.

So many words bubbled up in me, and the urge to tell her about Rider hit me hard, because I needed to make it feel real again, but my throat sealed off. If I told her about Rider, there was a ninety-nine-percent chance she would flip out.

Because Rosa had been there when every frayed and damaged layer had been peeled off me. Even though Dr. Taft had been Team Accept Your Past and they typically agreed with everything Dr. Taft said, she and Carl were Team The Past Is Your Past. They firmly believed that all facets of said past should stay where they belonged. And Rider was definitely the past.

So all I did was shrug as I veered over to the fridge, grabbing a Coke.

"How was your first day?" she asked, even as she frowned at my choice of beverage.

Turning to her, I smiled, even though it felt like there were tiny snakes wiggling around in my stomach. They'd been there since I'd gotten in the car.

Rosa tilted her head to the side and waited.

I sighed as I rolled the can between my hands. "It was okay."

Her lips curved into a smile, and tiny lines formed around her eyes. "That's good. Terrific, actually. So, no problems?"

I shook my head.

"Meet anyone?"

Seconds away from shaking my head again, I caught myself. "I... There is a girl in my English class."

Astonishment flickered over her face. "Did you talk to her?"

That got a shrug from me. "Kind of."

She looked like I'd sprouted a third arm and was currently waving it at her. "What does *kind of* mean, Mallory?"

I opened my Coke. "She's in my class and she introduced herself to me. I said like maybe...seven words to her."

The look of surprise gave way to a broad smile, and I stood a little straighter, momentarily forgetting about Rider's unexpected appearance. The smile on her face was full of pride and I basked in the warmth of it.

Show us. That was what Carl had said this morning, and that smile told me I was showing them. Rosa knew, firsthand, how far I'd come and how big a deal it was for me to be comfortable enough to talk to a stranger, even if it was only seven words.

"That is so good." Walking to me, she wrapped her arms around me and squeezed tight. I inhaled deeply, welcoming the weird scent of antibacterial soap and the faint trace of apples from the lotion she used. She brushed her lips over my forehead and then pulled back, clasping my arms. "What did I tell you?"

"That...that it wouldn't be hard," I said.

"And why?"

I fiddled with the tab on my soda. "Because I've already... done the hard work."

She winked. "That's my girl." She gave me another squeeze. "I'm sorry that I couldn't be there this morning. I really wanted to be."

"I...understand." My smile grew, stretching my face so much it nearly ached. Rosa might not have been my mother by blood, but she was everything a mother should be, and I was so damn lucky.

Her mouth opened, but her cell went off. Holding up her hand, she grabbed it off the counter, answering it quickly. Her posture grew rigid as she turned sideways. "Dammit," she said. "Can you hold for one sec?" She hit the mute button. "I've got to head into the hospital. There are some complications from the surgery this morning."

"Oh no," I whispered, hoping she didn't lose the patient. If you Googled the word *strong*, I swear Rosa Rivas appeared beside it, but she felt every patient's loss like it was a family member. It was the only time I saw her drink. She'd take a bottle of wine and disappear into the study, doors closed until Carl coaxed her out.

I always wondered if it was because of Marquette or if every doctor was that way. Marquette had passed away five years before the night I entered their lives, so they were coming up on a decade since her death, but I knew that couldn't have made their loss any easier to bear.

"These things happen," Rosa said with a sigh. "Carl is going to be late. There're leftovers in the fridge."

I nodded. Both of them worked at Johns Hopkins, where cardiac surgery was actually created—something I'd learned from them. Hopkins was one of the best hospitals in the world, and when they weren't in surgery, they were heavily involved in the teaching programs.

She hesitated, glancing down at the still-muted call. "We'll talk in the morning, okay?" Her dark eyes held mine for a moment and then she sent me a quick, fleeting smile and started to turn.

"Wait," I said, surprising the crap out of myself as she faced me, eyes wide. My cheeks heated. "What...does *no la mires* mean?" I'd totally butchered the words like a typical white girl who couldn't speak any form of Spanish would.

Her brows shot up again. "Why are you asking that?"

I raised my shoulders.

"Did someone say that to you?" When I didn't answer, because I was no longer sure I wanted to know what it meant, she sighed. "It basically translates to *don't look at her.*"

Oh.

Double *oh.*

She narrowed her eyes at me, and I had a feeling that was what we'd be talking about tomorrow morning. Giving her a wave, I hurried out of the kitchen and hit the stairs two at a time.

My bedroom was at the end of the hall, overlooking the street, and next door to the hall bathroom I used. Rosa had once called it a decent-sized space. I considered it a palace. It fit a full-size bed, a wide dresser and desk. The window seat in the bay window was my favorite. Great for people-watching.

The best thing about this room—and I always felt terrible for feeling this way—was that it hadn't belonged to Marquette.

It was hard enough driving her car and contemplating the college major that had once been her dream. Sleeping in her old bed would've been too much.

Dropping my bag on the bed, I grabbed my laptop off the desk and wiggled into the corner of the window seat, placing the soda on the ledge. As soon as the computer popped out of hibernation mode, my instant messenger dinged.

Ainsley.

Her profile icon was from the summer—her blond hair streaked by the sun and oversize sunglasses covering half her face. She was giving the camera some pretty hardcore duck face. Her message read:

You make it out alive?

I grinned as I shot her a short yes.

How was it?

Biting down on my lip, I closed my eyes briefly and then I typed out what I'd been dying to scream from the top of my lungs.

Rider is at my school.

My laptop immediately blew up with a long strand and different variations of *OMG* that flowed into an endless stream of *geeeeeeee*. Ainsley knew about Rider. She knew about how I grew up. Not everything, because some things weren't any easier to type out than they were to speak about, and she also understood that I sometimes wasn't the most talkative person. But she got what a big deal this was.

You haven't seen him in 4 years. I'm about to pee my pants, Mal!!! This is so epic. Tell me everything!

Still nibbling on my lip, I typed out a recap and was periodically interrupted by her *OMGs* and *squees*. When I was finished, Ainsley shot back:

Tell me you got his #?

Uh. I didn't get his number, I typed back. He took mine.

That appeared to be acceptable to her and we chatted until she had to go. Ainsley's online activity in the evenings had been limited after her mom discovered the pictures she'd been sending her boyfriend, Todd, back in July. They weren't even that bad, just her in her bikini, but her mom had freaked out with a capital F and had, much to my amusement and horror, made Ainsley watch videos on childbirth as a form of sex ed.

Needless to say, Ainsley was positive she would never have children but that hadn't stopped her and she was still super interested in sex.

She signed off after making me promise we would see each other this weekend. I spent the rest of the night puttering around the house aimlessly, too riled up to eat much of Rosa's leftover chicken even though it had been baked in slices of orange and lime. I tried not to think about school or Rider or stare at my cell phone because it had been silent all afternoon and evening, but it was nearly impossible to keep my mind off those things because, holy crap, today had not gone the way I'd expected.

I mean, I didn't end the day in tears, rocking in the corner somewhere, and even though I'd failed at lunch, I'd managed to speak to Keira. Seven words were better than none. I'd passed my first day without any major breakdowns. That was something to feel good about, and I did, but...

I didn't know what to think when it came to Rider.

Pacing in front of my bed, I idly ran my hand over the slightly raised skin of my inner arm. That overwhelming mix of desperation and anticipation swirled inside me. I was excited to see him, to talk to him again, but I... God, it was hard to even really think about, because when I thought about Rider, another emotion festered inside me.

Guilt.

Stopping in front of the window seat, I squeezed my eyes shut. Rider had taken... He had taken *beatings* because of me. Time after time, he'd gotten in between meaty fists and me, and the one time he couldn't stop it, I ended up escaping that life. I got a second chance, had been given a home with *doctors* for crying out loud, and practically had anything I want within my grasp. And Rider? I had no idea.

In my bones, I knew he didn't have *this* kind of life, though, and how was that fair? The acidic burn in the pit of my belly increased. How could he even look at me like he had today and not think of all he'd sacrificed for me?

Ugh.

I shook my hands out as I started pacing again. Okay. I needed to chill out and look at the positive side of all of this. Rider was alive. He was in school, might even be in a relationship with the pretty girl in speech class, and even though I knew worse injuries could be hidden, there weren't any fresh bruises that I could see. He didn't appear to hate me. I would count all of that as a win—and ultimately, the most important thing to focus on was the fact that I'd successfully completed my first day of school.

That was what was most important.

Speaking of which, I had to read the chapter assigned in history. I ended up reading ahead, until I heard the garage door open below. Closing the textbook, I rolled over and turned off my light, knowing that Carl or Rosa wouldn't come in if they thought I was asleep. Too many months of me not sleeping had made them wary of ever risking the chance of waking me up.

Just as I started to doze off, my cell dinged from where it rested on the nightstand. My arm shot out like a bullet and I snatched it up, my heart leaping into my throat.

There were two words texted from an unknown, local number.

Night, Mouse.

CHAPTER 5

The following morning I could practically see the wheels of doom churning behind Rosa's eyes as she quizzed me on why I'd asked her what I had the day before.

I should've kept my mouth shut.

Rosa was brilliant and she was as observant as a high-strung cat, and the fact I was asking her to translate what she informed me that morning sounded like Puerto Rican had her little ears twitching.

I'd stared at that text message—those two words—for a ridiculous amount of time. Absolutely paralyzed by...by the infinite amount of things I could've texted back that by the time I settled on a similar response, it was past one in the morning, and I was too worried about waking him up to respond.

I was such a dork. Seriously.

Now I was sleepy and I learned pretty quickly that trying to navigate the crowded halls of the high school while half-asleep could've been a plot straight out of one of the dystopian novels I'd read.

Dumping my speech textbook into the steel-gray tomb of my

locker, I grabbed my first two classes' texts, knowing I'd have time to swing by to switch out books later. I closed the door, doing everything in my power not to think about seeing Rider while telling myself that if Keira talked to me today, I would totally respond like a normal person. The door got stuck. Sighing, I pulled it out and put a little more effort into slamming it shut. It latched this time. Satisfied, I hitched up my bag and started to turn.

"You?"

Twisting at the waist, I searched out the sound of the voice and then I saw her. The girl from speech class. The girl who had touched Rider in a way that said that happened a lot and Rider was okay with it.

"It's you." Her brown eyes narrowed. "I want to live a life of denial right now, but it's really you."

Out of the corner of my eye, I saw the girl with the tiny braids who'd said hi to me yesterday stop a few feet from us, eyeing the locker this girl stood in front of. She backpedaled and spun in the opposite direction.

Oh, man, that wasn't a good sign.

The girl in front of me pursed glossy pink lips. "You have no idea who I am, do you?"

Slowly, I shook my head.

"I know who you are, and not because you're in my speech class. I just can't believe it's *you*," she continued. "I figured you'd be dead or something by now."

My heart dropped to my feet. Second day of school, and I was already getting death threats?

The strap of her beat-up, olive-green messenger bag slipped an inch on her shoulder. "I'm Rider's girlfriend," she said flatly.

Oh.

Oh.

Well, that did explain the touching.

There was a weird sensation in my chest. Wasn't quite disappointment. More like acceptance. Of course, I figured as much yesterday when I saw them walking into class. And he was gorgeous. This girl was stunning. It made sense, even to someone like me who had no experience with the whole boyfriend-girlfriend thing. But I *did* watch TV. I read books. I had Ainsley. I knew Rider's relationship with this girl made sense.

She eyed me speculatively, like she was trying to figure something out. "He's talked about—"

"What's goin' on?" Jayden appeared at the girl's side. Like out of thin air.

Up close this time, I realized he was probably younger than this girl and me. Maybe a freshman or sophomore? His eyes, the same light green color as Hector's, weren't as red as they'd been yesterday when I'd seen him in the hall.

The girl glanced down at him, as surprised as I was to see him. "What do you want?"

"Don't be a *puta*, Paige." Those green eyes rolled, but his lips twitched into a grin as he reached over and tugged on her thick braid. "What are you today? The ghetto Katniss?"

She snatched her braid free. "You don't even know who Katniss is, you little punk. You probably think *The Hunger Games* is what happens after you get high."

Um.

"Sounds about right." Jayden winked at me, his smile sly. "I know you. We ran into each other in the hall yesterday." He paused. "And I saw you talkin' to Rider after class—out in the parking lot."

My gaze darted to the girl—to Paige. Her stare was glacial. "Are you mute or something? You haven't said one word to me," she said.

I was *so* not mute.

Jayden's brows knitted together as he eyed her. "That's a stupid question, Paige. I just said I saw her talkin' to Rider."

"You know what?" Her face scrunched up and somehow she

managed to still look good. She twisted toward him, planting her hands on her hips. "Boy, you have enough shit going on, you don't need to be all up in my business."

He cocked his head to the side. "Brave words from the chick who's always all up in mine."

They were obviously distracted with one another, and as the two bickered in a way that said this wasn't the first or the last time they would, I pivoted around and eased into the mass of students heading to class.

Are you mute?

My cheeks were burning by the time I reached my class, and the embarrassment quickly festered into anger—mostly at myself. I could've said something to her, anything, instead of standing there like I didn't have a functioning tongue.

And God. She was Rider's girlfriend. For real. The girl that asked me if I was mute, the girl I'd just stood in front of like a loser, was his girlfriend.

I resisted the urge to bang my head on my desk.

Mute.

I hated that word with a passion.

Everyone had believed I was mute—Miss Becky and Mr. Henry, group home workers, CPS. Even Carl had thought that when he and Rosa first met me. Only Rider had known that it wasn't true. That I could talk just fine.

But I didn't speak today.

Dr. Taft had this fancy phrase for why I hadn't spoken for so long—post-traumatic stress syndrome, he called it, because of… of everything I'd experienced as a small child. Half of our therapy sessions had been dedicated to working on coping mechanisms and ways to combat it.

It had taken so much to get to where I was today, to a point where I no longer felt like I needed the therapy sessions, and a handful of minutes made me feel like I'd taken twenty steps backward. Like I was the Mallory I'd been at five years old, and then at ten, and at thirteen—the Mallory who did and said nothing. The Mallory who just stood there in silence because that seemed like the safest route.

I hated that feeling.

I clenched the pen tight in my hand, ignoring the way my knuckles ached. Tears of frustration burned the back of my throat, and it was hard to focus in my chemistry class, even harder not to cave to the messy ball of emotion, especially when it struck me that I was sitting in the back of the class again.

Not drawing any attention to myself.

★ ★ ★

Keira immediately swiveled toward me the moment she sat down in English class. "Okay. I have a really weird question for you."

Caught off guard, I blinked as my stomach dipped a little. Was she going to ask if I was mute?

She smiled as she tucked a stray curl back behind her ear. It popped right back out. Bright blue earrings dangled from tiny lobes. "Have you ever thought about trying out for cheerleading?"

I stared at her. This was totally a joke, right? Then I glanced around the classroom. No one was looking at us or holding their phones up, recording this moment for posterity.

"I mean, you look like you're pretty sturdy. You could be the base or a back spot," she said, shrugging like she hadn't just said I looked *sturdy*. "Look, we're kind of desperate. Not a lot of girls around here are into it and one of my teammates broke her wrist yesterday in practice, so I thought about you." She ran her hand down her slim arm, twisting the blue bangle at her wrist. "So what do you think?"

Uh.

"You're really cute and the blue-and-red uniform would go great with your hair," she suggested, glancing at the door.

My tongue felt thick and my throat swollen as I reached

deep down inside my head and forced myself to live up to all the work I'd done to get to this point. "Um, I'm...I'm not really the rah-rah type."

One dark brow arched elegantly. "Do I look like a rah-rah type?"

I shook my head, unsure if that was the right answer or not. I had nothing in common with cheerleaders. They were loud and talkative and popular and pretty and about a thousand things I had absolutely no experience with. Then again, I really wasn't sure if all cheerleaders were loud and talkative and popular and pretty. Keira was the first one I'd ever met, so I was basing my assumptions off movies and books, and Lord knew, the movies and books kind of sucked when it came to stereotyping things.

Wincing, I realized just how offensive my statement could've seemed to her. The rah-rah type? Sometimes it was better not to talk.

She laughed softly. "It's really fun. At least think about it, okay?"

The pen I was squeezing in my hand was seconds away from imploding blue ink all over my fingers. "Okay."

Her smile spread across her cheeks. "Cool. You have B lunch, right? Next period? Thought I saw you yesterday, but I think you left the cafeteria. And I saw you in speech class, right? Then again, it's hard to see anything other than Hot Hector."

Nodding, I wasn't sure where this conversation was heading.

"Well, if you get bored or anything at lunch, find me." Flipping her gaze to her notebook, she wrote out the date at the top of the right-hand corner. "I'm usually up front—at the loud table. Hard to miss us."

Was she inviting me to lunch? Oh my God, Paige and her Katniss braid could suck it. This was major. Like a huge step in the right direction, and as Ainsley would say, if I didn't speak up, I might as well sew my mouth shut.

"Okay," I breathed, feeling kind of stupid, but this was equivalent to four Christmas mornings rolled into one.

Keira shot me a quick grin. When the bell rang after forty long minutes of listening to Mr. Newberry wax poetic about dead male writers, she wiggled her fingers at me and then disappeared into the hall.

I made a pit stop at my locker, switched out books and was relieved that Paige didn't pop out of one of the doors. I wasn't going to think about her or who she was to Rider.

With a slightly stupid pep talk playing over and over in my head, I headed down to the first floor and past the stacked trophy case. *I can do this. I can do this.* As I stepped into the busy, crowded cafeteria, my throat tightened, and I decided I should probably get my lunch first.

But I couldn't help but look at the table I'd seen Keira at before. She was sitting next to a girl but the seat on her other side was empty. My breath caught. *I can do this.* I started toward the lunch line.

"You're breaking my heart."

At the sound of Rider's voice, I wheeled around, clutching my bag to my side. First thing I noticed was the faded Ravens emblem stretched over his broad chest, and then I forced my eyes up. The slight scruff along his jaw was gone. Nothing but smooth skin today.

No notebook. Hands shoved into the pockets of his jeans, a familiar, crooked grin pulled at Rider's lips, causing the dimple in his right cheek to pop. He stepped forward, and my heart did a backflip as he dipped his chin. I felt his warm breath on the side of my cheek as he spoke.

"You didn't respond to my text last night," he said, and there was a light, teasing tone I didn't remember from before. "I thought maybe you didn't realize it was me, but that would mean someone else would be texting you good-night and calling you Mouse. I'm not sure how I feel about that."

I shook my head so fast I was surprised the ends of my hair didn't smack him in the face.

He laughed under his breath. "I'm just kidding. You getting something to eat or…?"

My gaze drifted to the table, and I saw Keira. She was staring at us. So was the blonde beside her. Keira raised her brows at me as her dark eyes moved between Rider and me.

Rider reached down and took my hand in his. The contact sent a jolt through me, and my gaze flew back to his. "Come with me?" he asked.

Thrown by his appearance and by his touch, I let him lead me through the shorter lunch line for pizza. My gaze was wild, bouncing all over the faces of those in line and sitting at the tables. Then I realized why Keira and half of her table were staring at us.

Muscles in my stomach clenched.

I was holding hands with Rider—and he had a girlfriend.

Mouth dry, I tugged my hand free from Rider's. Even though he'd held my hand a thousand times in the past, it didn't feel right after what I'd learned about him and Paige. Everything was… It was different now.

Rider glanced down at me, expression curious. I looked away. He loaded up a single plate with two slices. My hand tingled as he grabbed a bottle of water and a milk.

"You still drink milk with everything?" he asked, scanning the drinks with his head tilted slightly to the side, and then he looked down at me. Our gazes met. "Like you need it to survive?"

I nodded as my heart turned into a gooey mess. He actually remembered that I drank milk every chance I got—that and Cokes, when Rosa and Carl let me get away with it.

He held my stare for a moment and then, before I could get to my wallet, he pulled out a series of crumpled ones and paid the cashier. I started to protest, but he sent me that look—the lowered-brows look he'd sent me a million times over when we were younger. The Don't Argue Look. It was strange seeing the eighteen-year-old version, and I mulled that over as he balanced the plate and drinks in his hands. He nodded toward the entrance of the cafeteria, and I glanced in Keira's direction. Her head was bent toward the blonde, her tight curls going in every direction. It seemed like she was in a deep conversation, and she didn't look up.

Tomorrow, I promised myself.

I followed Rider out of the cafeteria, curious about where he was leading us. We passed the gym. Doors were open, and I thought I caught a glimpse of Hector jogging, a basketball in his hands as he shouted something in what sounded like Spanish but was slightly different. Rosa had said it was Puerto Rican, and I was going to have to take her word for it.

"I have A lunch, but I heard you had B," Rider said, slowing down his walk so I fell in step beside him. "Remember the guy who was sitting in front of us in speech class yesterday? The ass in the car? That's Hector, and he has a younger brother that you apparently ran into yesterday, Jayden. He was in the car, too. Anyway, Jayden said he saw you in the hallway yesterday during B lunch."

Even though I already knew that, I didn't say anything. The whole time he spoke as we walked down the hall, I kept stealing quick glances at him. To the point I was surprised I didn't walk into anything.

"So in case you're wondering—" he paused, opening the doors to the outside pavilion "—yeah, I'm skipping class right now."

My jaw unhinged. "Rider."

He held the door open, head cocked to the side as I walked through. I stopped, because...well, because he was just standing there, with our plate and drinks. His eyes searched mine. "You know, hearing you say my name isn't something I ever expected to hear again. I don't give a shit about missing one class if that means we get to catch up a little."

When he started walking toward an empty stone picnic set, my tongue finally came unglued from the roof of my mouth. "You…you won't get in trouble?"

Glancing over his shoulder, he shrugged. "Worth it."

That didn't reassure me, but I'd be lying if I said my heart didn't do a happy set of jumping jacks this time. He placed our stuff on the table and then sat, straddling the bench. Patting the spot next to him, he grinned.

I dropped my bag on the tan pavers and as I swung a leg over the bench, I stopped to look at him. He was watching me through thick lashes, head still tilted, grinning so that lone dimple was begging to be touched. I realized that this was the first moment Rider and I had been alone. No prying eyes. No adults watching over us. No one walking past us as there had been in the parking lot yesterday. We were alone, just him and me, like it had been so many times in the past.

I don't know why I did what I did next, but a decade of emotion swirled up inside me. Maybe it had to do with everything he'd done for me in the past. Maybe it was just because he was sitting right there and we were in the present.

And I never felt more *present* than I did in that moment.

Bending over, I wrapped my arms around his wide shoulders and I squeezed him. Probably the lamest hug in history, but it felt good. It felt magnificent when he rose up a little and circled his arms around my waist. His hug was better.

When I pulled back, his hands slid off my waist, to my hips, and lingered for a moment. A strange sensation curled low in my stomach. He let go, but the heated awareness remained. "What was that for?"

Shrugging, I sat, tucking both legs under the table. My face was hot. "I…I just wanted to."

"Well, you can do that whenever you want to. I don't mind."

I grinned at him, and when he chuckled, another strange thing happened. I shivered. I wasn't cold, actually quite the opposite.

"Mouse…"

Our gazes collided, and dammit, it was like suddenly being thirteen again, sneaking food in a world that was just Rider and me, except we were older now, and it wasn't just him and me against the world. I wasn't a little girl. He wasn't a boy. And back then he'd been… Well, he had been *mine*. It wasn't like that now. He had a girlfriend who thought I was mute, for starters.

That realization really was like a kick to the stomach.

So I probably needed to stop with the hugs. The weird curling-stomach feelings. And most definitely the shivers. All of that needed to stop. The way my lips curved up at the corners wasn't going anywhere, though.

"You have to tell me what you've been doing all this time." He pushed one of the slices toward me and then handed over a napkin I hadn't even seen him grab.

The grin I was wearing like a dork spread as he did what I'd known he was going to. Picked up the pepperoni, eating the slices before he ate the pizza.

He cast me a sidelong glance, voice patient as it had ever been while he finished off the pepperoni. "Mouse."

My gaze flickered up to the scar above his eyebrow and my smile faded a little. I focused on the slice of pizza and took a deep breath. "That night… Um, the last night, I met someone in the hospital. Carlos Rivas—Carl. He was…is a burn specialist."

Grabbing the milk, he peeled it open with long fingers. I noticed what looked like red ink on the inside of his pointer finger. He handed the carton over to me, and I continued. "He's married to Rosa. She's a heart surgeon. They…both worked at the hospital, and I think CPS told them I was…mute or that something was wrong with me."

He frowned as he picked up his pizza. "You're not mute. And

nothing is wrong with you. You're freaking brilliant. Screw that shit."

I shrugged a shoulder. "They visited me a lot after I...I spoke to them." Pressing my lips together, I peeled off a huge slice of pepperoni. "When I woke up after surgery, I...I asked for you. I asked Carl."

It had been the first time I'd spoken to anyone outside that house in years.

His head swung toward me sharply, eyes more gold in the sunlight than brown. "I really did look for you, Mallory. Like I told you, I went to the county hospital. No one would tell me where you were. Just that..." He exhaled roughly. "Just that you weren't coming back."

"I wish...I'd had a way to see you. I kept asking, but..." But everything had been scary and overwhelming. "What happened to you?"

His brows lowered. "I was shipped out to a group home." Folding what remained of the slice, he eyed it. "So, there's more to this story. Tell me."

Pressure settled in my chest as I offered him the piece of pepperoni. His lips twitched into a small smile. "I spent a little time in the hospital and then...I was also placed in a group home."

"Where?"

Talking...talking with him was a release I'd missed. It got easier with every passing second. "The one near the Harbor... not far from the hospital. Carl and Rosa... They visited me, and they eventually were able to foster me."

His eyes widened as he stopped with the pizza halfway to his mouth. "You were taken in by doctors?"

I tensed, wondering if this was when he was going to demand how in the hell that was fair. I didn't know anything about what had happened to him. What if he was still in a group home... or worse, because there were worse things. I couldn't stop the churn of guilt. I nodded.

He dropped the pizza on the tray and his shoulders eased. His mouth relaxed. "Shit, Mallory, I'm so... Yeah, doctors? That's good." When he looked at me, I saw the relief in his gaze and wondered where he thought I'd been this entire time. "They've really taken care of you, haven't they?"

I nodded as I plucked off another piece of pepperoni, and he reached over, his fingers brushing mine as he took it. There was another zap to my nerves. I didn't remember his touch eliciting that kind of response before, but it sure was pleasant now.

"That car you were standing near yesterday? The Honda is yours?"

"It was their daughter's."

An eyebrow rose. "Was?"

"She died before I met them. Almost ten years ago. I think that's why they took me in," I explained, chewing slowly.

His brows flew up.

"I mean, they never...had any other kids." A moment passed. "They have been really good, Rider. I was very lucky."

"I wish you never had to meet them." Finishing off the slice, he wiped his hands on the napkin and then angled his body toward me. "I mean, I'm glad you did, because, Mouse, you deserve that kind of life, but..."

"I know...what you mean." Relief poured into me. There wasn't an ounce of envy in his tone or in the way he looked at me. I took a sip of the milk. "When they got custody of me, I was homeschooled," I explained. "And then I...I decided I wanted to go to public school."

His brows rose. "What made you decide that?"

"I want to go to college," I told him as I glanced up at the cloudless sky. College was ambitious considering talking to a teacher made me want to hurl, but it was a big deal to me. College meant, at least hopefully, that I would eventually get a job and would have a life where I didn't have to worry about my next meal or have to rely on someone to take care of me. College was freedom. "And Rosa and Carl… They want that, too. I mean, I could still be homeschooled and go to college, but…"

Rider waited.

"But you know how I am—how I was." My cheeks heated as I lowered my gaze to the milk carton. "I'm not…good with people…and they thought I should try high school first."

He was silent for a moment, but I could feel his eyes on me. "Well, I'm glad you decided to do this. If not…"

If not, our paths probably never would've crossed. My stomach dipped at the thought. I looked at him, and my breath caught. He was staring at me in a way I wasn't exactly accustomed to, but that I'd seen before. It was the way Ainsley's boyfriend stared at her. Maybe not as familiar, but definitely as intense.

I squirmed, not uncomfortable, just suddenly overly aware of him. "What about you?"

Dropping his elbow on the table, he propped his chin against his palm. "I'm not in a group home anymore." When I started to turn to him, he glanced pointedly at my pizza. "You're gonna eat. Right now."

My eyes narrowed.

He flashed a quick grin. "I'm with a foster family." He shifted closer as I took a huge bite of the pizza. "It's actually Hector's family. His grandmother has fostered kids for years. Helps with the bills and stuff."

I thought about the worn notebook and the frayed edges of his jeans.

"Not that she does it only for that reason, you know? She's really great. A damn good woman. Anyway, that's how I met Hector and Jayden. Been living with them for a couple of years." Extending his arm, he placed just the very tip of his finger against my cheek, causing me to suck in a soft breath. "Where did your freckles go?"

"I don't know," I said, my voice a strange whisper. "They ran away."

The deep chuckle came again, coasting over my skin. "You used to have three right here." He tapped my cheekbone lightly. "And then two over here." His finger grazed the bridge of my nose and then he lowered his hand. "Can I tell you something?"

"Yeah." I wished I could tell him it was okay to keep touching my face, but that would probably be weird. Totally sounded weird in my head. And would be really inappropriate. Totally inappropriate.

His lashes lowered and the lopsided grin appeared. "I always knew you'd be beautiful one day."

My breath hitched as I sat straighter. What was left of the pizza, just the crust, was totally forgotten. My ears had to be smoking crack or something.

A flush swept across his cheeks as one side of his lips kicked up. "I just never thought I'd get to see how beautiful you'd become."

Wow. He really had said that. Beautiful. Rider said I was beautiful. The statement floored me, left me staring at him. I knew I didn't look like the worst thing out there. Ainsley loved my hair and eye combination, a product of what everyone guessed was an Irish background, but I figured I was pretty average. Average face. Average body, neither big nor small. Beautiful wasn't an option that crossed my mind.

"You're beautiful, too. I mean, you're hot," I blurted out. "But I always knew you would be." My eyes widened as I realized what just streamed out of my mouth, and his grin turned into a smile. "Oh my God, I did not just say…any of that out loud."

"You did."

"Ugh."

Tipping his head back, he laughed deeply. And he laughed like he had in those rare instances when something truly amused him. He did so with a freedom I'd envied.

I started to place my hands over my flaming face, but he caught my wrists, holding them between us. His eyes were lighter, dancing. "I can pretend you didn't say that if that makes you feel better," he suggested.

Oh yes, that would be fabulous. I nodded.

"I won't forget it, though."

Embarrassment flooded me, but Rider was grinning as he scooted closer and tugged me over. Before I knew what he was doing, he'd tucked my hips between his thighs and circled his arms around me, holding me tight to his chest.

His really hard chest.

The contact jolted me, like touching a live wire. It took a couple of seconds for me to relax.

He was silent as he rested his chin on the top of my head, and I didn't say anything as I squeezed my eyes shut against the rising tide of emotion. Being this close to him again was something so powerful the connection was tangible, a third entity.

One hand drifted up my back, a slow slide under the weight of my hair. He curled his fingers around the nape of my neck. His chin moved, grazing my forehead, and the intimacy of the act was so different than any of the other times he'd been this close. An odd warmth settled in my muscles. Like stepping out into the sun for the first time after a long winter. There was a moment when I wasn't sure if he breathed, because I didn't feel his chest move under my hands.

In the back of my head, I wondered how...how okay this was. I didn't want to pull away and break the connection, but I thought that maybe I should. This was innocent. It had to be, but it was also different.

"Do you have someone to eat lunch with normally?" he asked, and his voice seemed off to me. Deeper.

Keeping my eyes closed, I wasn't sure how to answer that and I also didn't pull away. I wasn't sure what that said about me or if it said anything at all.

"Mouse?"

"There's a girl in my English class. She...invited me to sit with her."

The arm around my waist seemed to have tightened. "Who?"

"Keira... I don't remember her last name."

A heartbeat passed. "I know her. She's in our speech class. Pretty cool girl. You going to take her up on the offer? If not, I can meet you for lunch."

But he had a class right now that he was supposed to be in.

Then it hit me. Rider... Wow, he really hadn't changed. Even after four years, even if he was supposed to be in class and even though he had a girlfriend, he would be there for me if I told him I needed him. Stupid tears pricked at my eyes. "You don't need to do that. I'm going to sit with her."

His fingers moved along my neck, searching out the muscles. "You sure?"

My heart was a puddle of mush. "Yes. She invited me... She asked if I wanted to try out for cheerleading."

Rider's hand stilled. "Mouse..."

I grinned.

"You're not considering that, are you?" he asked after a moment. Then he trailed off and suddenly pulled back, arms and everything.

The sudden loss of the closeness forced my eyes open. His profile was to me, jaw taut, and he was staring out over the pavilion, toward the parking lot. There was a car idling in the rows of parked vehicles, some sort of sedan. From what I could tell, the windows were tinted to the point you couldn't see who or what was inside.

A door shut, and my attention swung toward the exit we'd come out of earlier. I saw Jayden walking out, hitching up his pants as he walked across the pavilion, toward the steel gate.

"Shit," Rider muttered under his breath.

I stiffened as a sense of wariness slipped over him. "Is everything okay?"

"Yeah." He watched Jayden slip out the gate and make his way to the car. The younger boy bent at the waist as the driver's window rolled down. Rider patted my leg, drawing my gaze. "The bell's about to ring. Why don't you go ahead in?"

Something cold and hard was etched into the lines of his face. I didn't like it. "Rider..."

"Everything is okay. I promise," he said, tapping my leg again, and then he stood as the double doors opened again. This time it was Hector who was coming outside, and the look on his face said he was not happy. Rider took my hand, pulling me up. "I'll see you in class."

Nodding, I gathered up my stuff and stepped over the bench. Hector didn't look at me as he joined Rider, and neither of them spoke as they pivoted, heading toward the gate. I watched them, knowing deep down that something was up and whatever it was, it wasn't okay.

CHAPTER 6

I didn't see Rider in speech class.

His seat was empty, and I couldn't help but think it had something to do with that car that had shown up. Although we got to spend some time catching up, I knew nothing about what Rider had been doing these four years beyond living with Hector's grandmother.

Some would probably disagree, but I wasn't completely naive or sheltered. I'd grown up in a house where I saw a lot of stuff. The month I'd spent in the group home was also pretty educational. Guys would hang around outside the building, recruiting younger kids to run drugs. I'd seen older kids in that house pass out mid-conversation. In a matter of a month, I knew kids who simply vanished, lost to the streets. I also had a good idea why Jayden's eyes were bloodshot yesterday, and a tinted-out vehicle rolling up into the parking lot probably wasn't full of people selling Girl Scout cookies.

A niggle of worry formed in my belly as I wondered what kind of stuff Rider could be up to. But under the worry was something else, something I wasn't sure I should acknowledge.

Because Paige wasn't in class, either, and I wasn't stupid. Rider had left school. So had Paige. Whatever was going on, they were probably together. A burning sensation hit the center of my chest, and I told myself it was indigestion, that it had nothing to do with Rider holding my hand, telling me I was beautiful when I knew he had to be telling Paige the same and meaning it in a totally different way.

It took effort to focus on Mr. Santos's lecture about different types of speeches. Santos paced, moving his hands wildly as he spoke. Excitement practically poured from the man. I glanced down at my binder, seeing only a half a page of notes. Not good. I focused, scribbling as much as I could.

When the bell rang, I felt a little better about my notes. I headed out into the hall, busy shoving my notebook in the bag, and I didn't realize that Keira had been waiting for me until she sidled up beside me.

"So, did you get a chance to think about cheerleading?" she asked.

Closing the flap on my bag, I winced. I seriously hadn't thought twice about her offer. I shook my head.

She sighed as she wrapped her fingers around the strap of her bag. "Yeah, I figured it was probably a stretch, but hey, doesn't hurt to try."

No, it definitely didn't hurt to try. That whole theory pretty much summed up my life right now.

"Anyway," she said, catching the door to the stairwell and holding it open. "I saw you at lunch today." There was a beat as we were crammed onto the steps. "You were with Rider Stark."

Warning bells went off as I looked at her sharply.

Her smile remained, completely open and friendly. "Do you know him?"

I nodded as I crossed the landing to the second floor, guessing she was going to follow me to my locker.

"Since you're new," she said, raising a shoulder as she glanced at me, "how do you know him?"

Part of me felt like it wasn't anyone's business, but then again, she was curious, and I probably would be, too, if I were in her shoes. Talking to her made me nervous, but I pushed past it. "We...we knew each other when we were younger."

"Really? That's cool." Keira leaned against the locker next to me as she pulled out her phone, glancing at the screen. "I figured you two had to know each other. He was really...uh, hands-on with you, which is strange."

Shoving my history text inside, I grabbed my English book since I had homework. I looked at her as I closed the door. "Why is that strange?"

"We've been in the same school since we were freshmen, and I don't think I've ever seen him hold another chick's hand, including Paige's," she said, grinning. "And they're together."

And why did that make me all kinds of warm and happy inside?

"Or something like that," she added.

What did that mean? And come to think of it, why hadn't I asked him about Paige during lunch? That would've been a normal question. But he had kept me busy answering all of his questions.

She laughed, because what I was thinking must've been plastered across my face. "I mean, I don't get the impression that whatever he and Paige have is really serious."

The warm and happy started to grow, and I stomped it down. It had no place here in this conversation.

"Anyway, he was in one of my classes last year, and you know, he kind of showed up whenever he wanted to. Me and Maggie—you don't know her—but anyway, we used to say he was gracing us with his hotness. He wouldn't take notes or really participate in class. Sometimes I swear he actually slept," she continued. "But anytime he was called on, he knew the answer. No one could figure it out, especially the teacher. Used to drive her crazy and it entertained the rest of us. One of my other friends, Benny, was in his class last year when we were taking the MSA exams, and he overheard the teacher saying that Rider totally blew the rest of the class away in terms of scores. One of the highest in the entire junior class supposedly."

That sounded like Rider.

"It's strange, considering he's a foster kid and—"

"I'm a foster kid." Those words burst right out of me.

Her eyes widened as she held up a hand. "Whoa. I didn't mean anything bad about that. I'm the last person to be judgey. Duh. It's just that..." She looked around before she continued. "He's hung out with some shady people and I know shady people. My brother, Trevor? He's in jail right now, because of the shady people in this broke-ass city. My cousin? Dead because he hung out with people like that." She paused, wrinkling her nose. "Well, my cousin was also shady, so..."

I thought about that car in the parking lot, and I wondered if Hector and Jayden were included in that shady people definition.

"Anyway, I've got to go to practice." She paused, looking hopeful. "I couldn't convince you to swing by and see what you think?"

Shaking my head, I bit back a grin at Keira's dramatic sigh. She wiggled her fingers and started to turn as I forced my tongue and lips to work. "See you...at lunch tomorrow?"

Okay. That was stupid, because I'd see her in English before lunch, but she nodded. "Yep. Bring Rider with you if you want. We could always use some hotness at the table."

Hopefully, Rider would be in class tomorrow during lunch, but after what Keira said, that sounded doubtful. Part of me wasn't surprised by the fact that he did what he wanted whenever he wanted. That was so him, but just like when we were younger, that willful side of him always got him in a load of trouble.

★ ★ ★

After I got off the computer with Ainsley, dinner was just hitting the table. Four years ago? I hadn't eaten at a dinner table. Not even once. This table, with its polished wood surface, was the first I ever ate at outside school.

I sat down, smoothing my hands over the surface. When I first came home with the Rivases, I had felt like…like an animal. Wild. Uncomfortable. Caged. Unsure. They had expectations and schedules. They complimented and praised—both me and each other. There hadn't been a specified dinnertime at Mr. Henry's house nor had there been a plate of food waiting for Rider and me. We ate whatever was leftover. That was if anything was leftover. More often than not, there hadn't been.

Sitting down at a table in the evening and listening to Carl and Rosa actually speak to each other instead of yell and curse had been a new experience for me. The kitchen table in my last home had been covered with cigarette burn marks and unread newspapers. Mr. Henry brought one with him every evening after completing his shift at a local packaging and receiving warehouse, but I'd never seen him read one.

But this table was almost always clear and had a centerpiece that changed with the seasons. Now the plastic blue-and-white flowers, along with the glass-encased pillar candle, sat on the counter.

It was rare that during the week both Rosa and Carl would be home for supper, and I knew they'd both be out of the house again in no time. As long as there were no emergency surgeries over the weekend, they always had Saturday and Sunday off.

"I was thinking we could go down to the Harbor on Saturday." Carl prodded his pork chop apart, almost like he was dissecting it. He loved heading to the Harbor in downtown Baltimore. "I believe there's some kind of fair being held there this weekend."

Rosa sipped her glass of water. "Or we could go to Catoctin.

It's supposed to be really nice, a little cooler." She grinned at her husband. "And we'd spend less money going to a park where people aren't going to be selling something."

She was really into the outdoorsy stuff—hiking, mountain biking, sweating. In other words, experiencing some form of pain. I was really into reading, sitting and not collecting sweat in places where sweat should not pool. Carl glanced at me, placing his fingers over his mouth to hide his grin.

"What do you think, Mallory?" Rosa asked.

I shrugged as I speared a piece of broccoli with my fork. If we went to Catoctin, I'd probably end the day with muscles I didn't even know existed hurting. "Ainsley wanted to get together this weekend."

"Then definitely the Harbor." Carl lowered his hand, not even trying to hide his smile. "The last time we took her to a park, I'm sure it was the first and last time she'd been to one."

My lips curved into a smile as Rosa rolled her eyes. Plans were made to spend the afternoon on the Harbor, which would definitely make Ainsley happy.

"Have you been carving?" Rosa asked, toying with the glass. "You haven't asked me to pick up any soap."

My gaze flew to her. I hadn't done any carvings since July, roughly around the time I mentally began preparing for—aka stressing over—school.

Carl eyed me. "You really should practice. You don't want to lose that talent."

I almost laughed. Carving things out of bars of soap with pencils or Popsicle sticks really wasn't something I'd consider a talent. It was just something I'd done...well, for as long as I could remember, whenever I was alone. Rider didn't even know I used to do it. Once I finished carving something, I used to destroy it.

Now Carl and Rosa kept most of my creations, over three dozen, in the dining room, stashed away in the glass china cabinet that smelled like Irish Spring.

The funny thing is that the whole odd soap-carving hobby was what really had caught Carl's attention while I'd been at Johns Hopkins. He'd seen so many burn victims, so many kids, so it wasn't my winning personality that had drawn him. Even with toasted and sore, bandaged fingers, I'd snuck the soap bar out of the bathroom and, using a tongue depressor I'd snagged from one of the nurses, I'd carved a sleeping cat over the course of a few days.

I don't know what it was about carving something, but it was always a source of...of peace. I thought the talent was kind of lame, and Rosa and Carl had been trying for eons to get me to move on to wood with no luck.

"Speaking of big accomplishments, you've survived your first two days at school," Carl said, clearly sensing they were getting nowhere on the soap front. "Want to tell us how it's going?"

Heart turning over heavily, I stared at my plate. Rider suddenly entered my thoughts. Now would be a good time to bring him up. I wanted to. I didn't like the idea of not telling them and I wanted... I wanted to talk about him. I wanted to share my excitement over reconnecting with him.

This could be a huge mistake. A big one, but I wanted them to know. Lying to them after everything they'd done for me would be so wrong. I folded my hands in my lap. "So...at school, I ran into someone..." I trailed off, because when I looked up, both of them were staring at me. They'd stopped eating and everything. Too much attention. My tongue stopped working. My brain screamed *Abort! Abort!*

Carl spoke first. "You ran into who?"

I probably should've kept my mouth shut.

Rosa leaned forward, placing her glass of water on the table. "Who did you run into, honey?"

When I didn't answer, they waited and I knew they would wait forever. "I ran...into Rider."

Silence.

The only thing making noise was the oval clock on the wall, ticking away.

Carl placed his fork on the table. "Rider? The boy you lived with?"

I nodded.

"He's at your school?" Rosa stiffened.

All I could do was nod.

"That is…unexpected," Carl stated, and then glanced at Rosa before continuing. "Did you two talk?"

There was no point in lying. I nodded. "He's in…a better foster home now."

This time they exchanged long looks with one another, and I could only imagine what they were thinking. "I'm sort of shocked," Carl said finally. "It never crossed my mind that Rider would be at Lands High."

The way he said Rider's name raised the tiny hairs along my arms. Not that his tone held any spite, but the word was spoken with heavy meaning.

A moment passed and then Rosa asked, "How do you feel about that? Relieved, I imagine?" She looked at Carl again. Some of the stiffness faded from her posture. "He meant so much to you."

I focused on her. "I am. I'm glad to see that…he's okay. We talked a little at lunch today." I smoothed my hands along my legs. "It was nice to…catch up."

Carl nodded slowly and as he took a drink of his water, I still had no idea what he was thinking. "It's good to know he's doing okay."

I forced a smile, and my eyes shot to Rosa. She was watching me closely. After another brief silence, Carl changed the subject, but I felt strangely trapped. I knew they weren't happy, and I hated that they felt that way. Disappointing them was the last thing I wanted. I tried to think of some way to make up for it, so I ended up cleaning up after dinner. It wasn't much, but it was something. When I left the kitchen, they were in the study, the door closed, and I had a sinking feeling I knew what they were discussing.

I headed upstairs and opened my laptop. I wanted to tell Ainsley how Rosa and Carl reacted to the Rider news, but she wasn't online. She was probably with Todd. As I closed my laptop and started to open my bag, there was a knock against my open door. I looked up and saw Rosa.

"Can we chat?" she asked.

My shoulders tensed. "Sure."

She walked in as I sat on the bed, crossing my legs. "Rider."

That was all she said, so I nodded.

Rosa perched on the edge of the bed, her body angled toward me. "How are you really feeling about this, Mallory? Rider was a big deal to you. For months when you first came to live here, you asked about the boy. It was, for the longest time, the only thing you would say. So I know this is big."

I nibbled on the inside of my cheek, wondering if I should shrug the whole thing off, but one quick peek at Rosa told me that wasn't going to work. She knew better. "I'm...excited," I admitted. "I'm happy. Mainly because I know he's okay, and I can see him."

She nodded. "I get that. I understand feeling that way."

Exhaling slowly, I grabbed the thick bobby pin off the nightstand and twisted my hair up. I knew there was more coming. I was right.

"Carl and I were caught a little off guard at dinner," she continued, tone gentle. "Why didn't you mention him yesterday?"

Ah, good question. "I didn't... I don't know. I thought you two might be...worried."

Her dark gaze searched my face. "Worried about what?"

I shrugged.

Rosa glanced down at where my hands rested between my crossed legs. "Is there something we should be worried about?"

Well, that felt like a loaded question.

She reached over and tapped my leg. "I'm going to be honest with you, like we've always been, okay?"

I nodded. Here it comes, I thought.

"We are worried. A little. Your ending up at the same school as Rider never crossed our minds. Starting school is a big enough change, but adding him into the equation? We don't want you to be overwhelmed."

"I'm not," I replied, curling my hands together.

She smiled faintly. "School is a lot to deal with. Rider is a lot to deal with. It may not feel that way right this instant, but honey, he's from a time in your life we don't want you focusing on anymore."

"I'm...not focused on my past."

Rosa said nothing.

My pulse started to pick up. "Rider is from my past, but seeing him doesn't make me... I don't know. It doesn't make me feel bad."

"I wouldn't think it did." She paused, seeming to choose her next words carefully. "We just worry about how this is going to affect all the progress you've made. Nobody's denying that your past is an important part of who you are. And I'm the first to admit that I'm grateful to Rider for all he did to protect you back then, especially since he was just a kid himself. But you've come such a long way from the terrified girl we first met. You've worked so hard to become the poised young woman you are now. We don't want Rider's presence to...interfere with any of that."

I opened my mouth, but I really had no idea what to say.

"Maybe it won't be too much," she added. "Maybe we're just worrying about nothing." There was a pause and then she smiled. "Either way, we're glad that you told us about him."

I wasn't.

"And we want you to keep telling us about him," she added.

Rosa patted my leg and then rose, moving toward the door. "How about some ice cream? I think there's some caramel left from when Carl picked it up. Sound good?"

Caramel ice cream topping always sounded good, so I nodded.

As Rosa quietly closed the door behind her, I squeezed my eyes shut and flopped onto my back. Staring up at the ceiling, I thought about the tiny bedroom I'd stayed in with Rider. The ceiling here was smooth as snow. In the other house, it had been cracked and splintered, reminding me of a spiderweb.

I bit down on my lip.

Telling them about Rider had been the right thing to do. I made them proud. My lip escaped my teeth. But telling them also wasn't the brightest idea I'd ever had, because even if Rosa was okay with Rider being back, I knew Carl wasn't.

Carl wasn't going to be okay with Rider at all.

CHAPTER 7

Paige wasn't lurking by my locker Thursday morning. Jayden was as I switched out my books. An act of God held up his baggy jeans. That faint earthy smell clung to his Ravens T-shirt.

His eyes were sleepy as he leaned against the locker next to mine. "Hey."

Surprised by his presence, I smiled in response.

"I just wanted to stop by and tell you that I know what *The Hunger Games* is," he announced, a grin creeping along his boyish face. "I'm not *estúpido*, even though Paige likes to make it seem that way." Shoving his hands into the pockets of his jeans, he wrinkled his nose. "So I hear you and Rider got an...interesting past."

I looked at him, brows rising as I closed the locker door. I was unsure of how to respond to that or how much Jayden really knew. Since his grandmother fostered Rider, I imagined both Jayden and Hector knew a lot, but had Rider told them everything?

"I think it's pretty cool that you got out of that shit. Got adopted. My *abuelita*—my grandmother—would adopt him, but the state don't pay for that, you know?" He stared up at the ceiling as he rocked back on his feet. "But yeah, I've heard and seen some horror stories. I don't know how Rider turned out the way he did."

I stiffened, knowing all about those horror stories, having experienced quite a few of them myself.

"I mean, Rider... He's cool." Jayden shrugged as he lowered his gaze. "A lot better than the ones my *abuelita* had in the house before. Rider got stayin' power and he never took advantage or anything. Kind of like another older brother I never asked for." A grin flashed across his face.

"He can be..." Heat started to flow across my cheeks. "He can be very...protective."

Jayden's eyes widened as his mouth opened slightly. The flush in my cheeks deepened as I pressed my lips together.

"Huh. That's the first time I've heard you talk." He pushed off the locker, falling in step beside me. Shorter than his brother and Rider, he was still a couple of inches taller than me, so my neck appreciated not having to look up to see him. "Cool. I'm quiet, too."

I arched a brow.

He laughed. "Okay. I'm not quiet. I'm sure if you Wikipedia'd my ass, I would show up as the opposite of quiet. But that's okay. You and I would get along like lime and tequila. You can make up for my nonstop talkin' and I can make up for your lack of talkin'." He nudged my arm with his. "We're a perfect team!"

The smile returned to my face. I didn't really know him, but I liked him. He was cute in a charming way and the fact that he was nice added about a thousand bonus points. He chatted on about some football game this weekend, and then we parted ways as we hit the stairwell, and I didn't see him again the rest of the morning. Not even before I hit the cafeteria, but Jayden was the furthest thing from my thoughts as I passed through its open doors.

Keira was at her table, the space empty beside her as it had been yesterday. She'd been late to English class, sliding into her seat just as the tardy bell rang and she rushed out of the room after class ended, so we didn't have a chance to talk or anything. I hadn't seen Rider or heard from him, and I wasn't sure if he was going to pop out of thin air and whisk me away again.

What if Keira changed her mind?

What if I walked over to her table and she laughed at me?

Sounded totally crazy, but also possible, because I felt like anything was possible.

As I headed toward the lunch line, trying to determine what the hell was on the menu, because what I saw a guy carrying did *not* look like roasted chicken, Keira glanced up and waved.

Relief nearly took my legs out from underneath me. If she waved, she most likely wouldn't laugh at me when I walked up to her table. My smile was probably really creepy, so I hurried to the lunch line, no longer concerned by the fact that what was being slopped on my plate actually smelled like fish instead of chicken. Still, my hands shook as I clutched the tray.

I faced the cafeteria, wishing Rider would show up and cart me away.

Hope sparked in my chest the moment that thought completed itself. I caught my breath. That was wrong—all of it wrong, the hope and then need that filled me. Relying on him to swoop in instead of doing this myself wasn't what I wanted or needed. My grip tightened on the tray as I squared my shoulders. Knots took over my stomach, leaving no room for an appetite.

I can do this.

Drawing in a deep breath, I forced my feet to carry me over to the table. I took two steps. I had to walk around it to make it to Keira's side, and that had to be one of the hardest things I'd ever had to do. Eyes lifted from cell phones, landing on me. The stares were curious and confused, and the weight dragged down each of my steps. My chest felt tight with unfurling panic as I heard a girl at the table whisper, and Keira looked up at me.

Time seemed to have stopped.

And then a wide smile broke out across Keira's face. "Hey, girl, I saved you a seat." She patted the space beside her.

There was a buzz in my head, like an army of bees had burst from a hive within me. It took every ounce of concentration and effort to place the tray on the table without spilling anything and to sit without falling over. When my butt finally hit the hard plastic of the chair, I felt like I'd just climbed a rock wall.

"This is Mallory Dodge—your last name is Dodge, right?" she asked, dark eyes glimmering in the bright overhead lights.

I nodded, trying to get my lips to form a smile that didn't make people want to run and hide their kids or something.

"Mallory's in my English and speech classes. This is her first year here," Keira continued, leaning back in the seat. She gestured at the girl with green eyes next to her. "This is Rachel."

The pretty blonde wiggled her fingers in my direction.

"And that is Jo." Keira nodded across the table at a dark-skinned girl with curly hair like hers. "And this is Anna. She's the one who broke her wrist. She's normally a base, but she was showing off. We all know how that ended."

The brunette next to Jo raised her left arm, showing off a hot pink cast that circled her forearm and half of her hand. "I probably should've just let my face break my fall."

Ouch.

"Yeah, if you broke your nose, you could still cheer." Jo grinned at her.

Anna flipped her off with her good hand.

Keira laughed.

I rubbed my damp palms along my thighs. I really hoped no one shook my hand. Did people shake hands anymore? I didn't think so. At least not at school, because that would be weird.

"You think?" Anna replied drily, raising brown eyebrows.

"Anyway." Keira drew the word out, and then continued to introduce the other people at the table.

Everyone smiled or waved, and I liked to think the grimace on my face was more of a grin. My hands were folded so tight in my lap that my fingers were bloodless. During the flash round of introductions, two guys ended up at the table. One of them, who I recognized from one of my classes and thought was named Peter, draped an arm over Anna's shoulder. The other sat next to Jo.

"You're in my history class, right?" Possibly Peter asked, eyes narrowing thoughtfully on me.

My tongue was a lead pipe in my mouth so all I could do was nod.

"Cool," he replied as he swiped a grape off Anna's plate. Leaning to the side, he pulled out his phone. "I thought I saw you in there before I fell asleep."

The other guy snorted.

Anna giggled. "I have no idea how you pass your classes. Seriously."

He winked at her. "It's my charm."

"That's doubtful," Keira replied wryly as she looked at Peter. "I saw your picture this morning on Instagram. Did your shirt happen to conveniently fall off?"

Peter looked up from his phone. "This body?" He waved his free hand over his chest. "Needs to be shared with the world. See. Two hundred likes already."

Jo rolled her eyes. "Two hundred likes isn't something to brag about."

I didn't have an Instagram account. Mainly because I had no idea what I'd take pictures of. Soap carvings? That would be lame, but now I felt like I really needed to get on that.

The group fell into an easy conversation that I was ridiculously envious of. The comradeship and joking, the genuine affection for each other, was something I had such limited experience with. I watched them as if I were a scientist studying an unknown species. I mean, I was close to Ainsley, but we didn't go to school together like this.

I coasted through lunch, picking at my so-called chicken and what I think might have been scalloped potatoes. Chatter surrounded me. Every so often someone would ask a question or make a comment, and I would nod or shake my head in response. If anyone thought it was weird, no one said anything or acted different, but they had to have noticed that I hadn't spoken a word.

Frustration bloomed inside me, because I knew I could talk, but every time there was the perfect moment for me to speak up, I got too caught up in overthinking what I could say. I remained silent, as if there was a cap plugging my throat closed, allowing only the minimal amount of air through.

Words were not the enemy or the monster under my bed, but they held such power over me. They were like the ghost of a loved one, forever haunting me.

Lunch ended without me talking but also without a major disaster, and I wanted to bound out of the cafeteria total *Sound of Music* style, with my arms spread wide. I was a complete dork, but as Keira and I parted ways, there was a happy buzz in my veins.

Today was a first.

I might not have spoken, but never had I ever sat at a lunch table with girls before. Years ago, when I attended school with Rider, I'd eaten lunch with him and sometimes with the other kids that came and went from our table, but never like this. Never on my own.

Never without someone there to speak for me.

It was major. There was probably a lame bounce in my step as I headed to class, and a small, almost triumphant smile was plastered across my face. Today was a freaking success. Go me. As speech class rolled around and I walked inside, I saw Paige in her seat, and some of the bounce went out of my step. She didn't say anything as I took my seat, but I could feel her stare as I busied myself with pulling out my textbook. Once that was on my desk, I took a deep breath and looked up. A moment passed.

"He's not coming. Neither is Hector."

I blinked at the sound of Paige's voice, and my gaze shot to her.

Paige was leaning back in her chair, her long legs stretched out underneath the desk and crossed at the ankles. Her dark eyes were fixed on me. "So, you know, you can stop staring at the door anytime now."

Sucking in a sharp breath, I opened my mouth to tell her that I wasn't watching for Rider, but that...that would be a lie. Heat invaded my cheeks.

One side of her lips curled up as she drew her legs in under the desk and leaned over, placing her hand on Rider's empty seat. Her voice was low when she spoke. "I'm not sure if you realize this or not, but Rider is not available."

Air caught in my throat as I stilled.

"Like I told you the other day, I'm his girlfriend," she continued. "And I've got to say, sitting here and watching you wait for him to come in here is not cool."

She was right.

It wasn't cool.

"And watching you two have the reunion of the century on the first day of class also isn't going to make the list of top one hundred things I want to repeat in my life," Paige added, and I could also understand that. This conversation wouldn't make my own list. "So I'm going to repeat myself just to make sure there's no confusion. He's my boyfriend. Stop acting like he's yours."

The tardy bell rang.

Paige straightened and flipped open her notebook as Mr. Santos started the class. My gaze crawled over the seats in front of us. No one appeared to have heard what she said to me, but I'd heard it loud and clear.

Message received.

★ ★ ★

Thursday evenings meant I fended for myself when it came to dinner since Rosa and Carl typically didn't get home until nine on Tuesdays and Thursdays, sometimes later, depending on what came in through the hospital. I didn't have much of an appetite, though.

Neither Rosa nor Carl had brought up the issue of Rider during breakfast, but he wasn't far from my mind. What Paige had said in class lingered, and every time her words popped into my head, I cringed, but it didn't stop me from worrying about him. Where had he disappeared to? And was he hurt or in trouble? Of course, my mind went to the worst possible scenario, even though I figured Paige would know if something bad had happened and wouldn't have spent the time virtually warning me away from her boyfriend.

I barely touched the bowl of microwaveable rice, even though I'd loaded it with so much sodium that Rosa would've snatched the bottle of soy sauce right out of my hands.

Giving up on eating, I stowed the bowl in the fridge and headed upstairs. I pulled my phone out of my bag and tapped on the screen. No messages. I opened up the last and only text from Rider. Should I message him? Would it be weird if I did?

Ugh.

I tossed my phone on the bed and then pulled my hair up in a loose knot. Too restless to do my homework, I walked to the linen closet out in the hall and grabbed a bar of soap. I snagged the bag of tongue depressors Rosa had stashed away for me in the closet and carried the little bundle back to the bedroom.

I would need to soften the soap with warm water. I also needed to get a grocery bag or something to trap the shavings, so I didn't leave a huge mess behind.

Staring at the wrapped bar of soap, I tried to think of something to carve. I'd already done trees, stars, footballs, ducks, boats, and Lord knows what else. Some were pretty simple, taking only an hour or so. Others had taken days if they were more intricate.

I started to peel the wrapping off the soap, but stopped. I didn't want to get the shavings all over my school clothes, which inevitably would happen. I sat the soap and depressors on the desk then changed into a pair of sleep shorts and a tank top. Grabbing an old shirt out of the dresser, I tugged it on over my head. Too big, it kept slipping off my shoulder.

Turning to my desk, I caught sight of my reflection in the mirror hanging on the interior of the closet door. I looked like a hot mess. Stepping closer to the mirror, I exhaled as I turned to the side. Pressing my hand on my lower stomach, I frowned. My belly was soft. My gaze dropped, and I winced.

The shorts were probably not a good idea. They were loose, but my legs were definitely...*sturdy*. Thighs were thick. Plucking at the hem of my shirt, I lifted it up. The tank top had a built-in bra, but the material was thin, just like the shirt. It didn't hide any lumps. I was definitely not little. I was *sturdy*.

The bar of soap sat untouched on the desk.

How many people my age carved soap? Right now Keira was probably just getting home from cheerleading practice, and if Ainsley wasn't with Todd, she was writing—she was always scribbling down short stories. Or shopping. For someone who didn't have a job, she did that a lot, too, thanks to a hefty allowance. If she was with Todd, then she was probably making out. Something else she did a lot.

Something I was also kind of jealous of.

Embarrassing factoid I didn't like to think about was that I'd never been kissed. Hell, I'd never talked to a guy on the phone, and definitely never gone out on a date. Ainsley had tried to fix me up with a friend of Todd's, but I had totally bailed on that. The idea of meeting him made me want to hurl.

Months shy of turning eighteen, and I didn't know what it felt like to be kissed or what it was like to be…to be wanted—to be loved in that kind of way.

Was I lacking in something?

I glanced down at myself and wiggled my toes as I narrowed my eyes. Sturdy. My body shape was sturdy, but Rider had said I was beautiful. Without any warning, an image of him formed in my thoughts. Brown eyes with golden flecks, broad cheekbones and incredible lips—lips I bet gave really great kisses.

Oh my God.

I could not, *should* not, be thinking that.

Shaking those thoughts out of my mind, I opened my eyes. What I was lacking wasn't thinner thighs or a flatter stomach. It was courage. The fact was, I was a giant scaredy-cat. How could I be thinking about a guy's lips when I couldn't even get mine to work to form words?

My gaze drifted back to the soap. I guessed soap carving was a hobby, but it was a silent one and it required no words to complete, no thoughts. How appropriate. I didn't have to put myself out there. Not like Keira did with the cheerleading. Shopping really wasn't a hobby and writing didn't involve getting out there, but Ainsley was outspoken, friendly and talkative. She didn't just step out of the box, she played happily outside it. Me? I carved soap. Maybe I should've—

From my nightstand, my cell phone dinged. Figuring it was Ainsley since I wasn't online, I headed over to pick it up.

It was not Ainsley.

R u home?

It was from Rider.

My breath caught.

Another text came through before I could get my brain to respond.

Alone?

My eyes felt as big as planets as I stared at my cell. This time I was not going to be crippled by indecision. I sent back a quick yes.

A couple of seconds passed. A minute turned into five, and I began to wonder if I was totally imagining things, but then a new text appeared and my heart stopped.

Two words.

I'm outside.

CHAPTER 8

Holy crap.

For a second I was completely frozen as I stared at the text. He was outside? No, he couldn't mean he was actually outside the—

The doorbell rang, echoing from downstairs, and I whirled around, my lungs expanding rapidly.

Holy crap balls.

My brain sort of clicked off as I darted out of the room and down the hall, my bare feet flying down the steps. I almost barreled right through the foyer, stopping just shy of throwing the door open.

I wasn't stupid.

Stretching up onto the tips of my toes, I peered through the peephole as I bit down on my lip. All I could see was the back of his head and the breadth of his shoulders.

It was Rider. He was really here.

Still clutching the phone and having no idea how this was happening, I swallowed hard as I unlocked the door and pulled it open.

Rider turned at the waist, and I ended up eye level with his chest. "I was beginning to think you weren't going to answer."

My gaze flicked up, and a strangled sound escaped me. I reached out, gripping his arm and all but dragged him inside. He caught the door with his other hand, closing it behind us.

"Your face." My grip tightened on his forearm. "What happened?"

His brows furrowed as he reached up, touching the skin around the inch-long gash above his left eyebrow. Blood had dried around the cut and a bluish-purple shade had already begun to spread out around it. "This? Oh, it's nothing."

I stared at him. "It doesn't…look like nothing."

"It's not a big deal." Looking around the foyer, he peeled my white-knuckled grip off his arm. Instead of dropping my hand, he threaded his fingers through mine. "I thought you'd ask how I figured out which one was your house. I'm pretty impressed with my craftiness."

Yeah, I was curious about that, but he was going to end up with a matching scar above his left eyebrow now. "Rider, your forehead…"

He glanced down at me as he squeezed my hand, grinning. "You told me you lived in the Pointe, so I took the metro to the Center and walked the rest of the way. Wasn't too hard to figure out." With his other hand, he ran the tips of his fingers over the fake daisies in the vase placed on the entry table. "I just looked for your car. Lucky me, it was in the driveway. So maybe I'm not that crafty."

Crafty or not, he was hurt and that made me feel sick. I started tugging him toward the living room.

"What are you wearing?" he asked, letting me pull him along.

My eyes widened. I'd totally forgotten I was dressed for bed and that the sleepwear showcased my *sturdy* body. "I was getting…ready for bed."

He arched his brow and then winced. "What time is it? Seven?"

"Seven-thirty," I murmured, guiding him out of the hall and into the living room.

Taking in the spacious room, his attention lingered on all the potted plants in front of the bay window, then moved over the entertainment center and the built-in bookshelves. Then he turned to me. His gaze dipped, taking a slow slide down the length of my body, and I felt my toes curl against the hardwood floors. A rush of heady warmth followed his gaze and the answering tight shiver did strange things to certain parts of me.

Our eyes locked.

The stare held that same level of intensity from the day before. The temperature in the room zipped up several degrees and my breath suddenly felt short. He shifted closer.

He was still holding my hand. "I probably shouldn't have come here."

"You shouldn't?"

His head cocked to the side, and I saw then that the collar of his shirt was torn. My heart dropped, and he shook his head as he let go of my hand. I thought he might leave, so I stepped forward, practically closing the distance between us. "Sit."

Rider looked down at me, his expression indecisive.

"Sit," I repeated. "Please?"

He looked behind me, seemed to have shuddered, and then he moved a pillow to the side before he sat. "Now what?" he asked, staring up at me with familiar yet strange eyes.

"Stay here." When he leaned back on the couch, shifting his attention back to the bookshelf, I hurried out of the living room.

In the downstairs bathroom, I grabbed the peroxide and a few cotton balls and didn't let myself think too much about this or worry about Carl and Rosa. I knew if they came home early, I'd be in so much trouble it wouldn't even be funny, especially after the conversation yesterday. And though Rider's presence might be a match to kindling, I honestly didn't know how they'd react if they came home and found any boy in the house. I'm sure that was another thing that never crossed their minds.

Or mine.

Rider was where I'd left him, and I exhaled softly as I skirted the coffee table. He looked at what I carried, and a half grin appeared. "I'm fine, Mouse. Seriously."

I shrugged as I came toward him, getting between his knees and the coffee table. "What happened?"

"Just some...some trouble," he said, rubbing his palm along his jaw. "It's nothing I want you to worry about."

Unscrewing the peroxide cap, I soaked a cotton ball and then placed the bottle on the table. The sharp scent went straight to my nose. "You...you always made everything sound like it's not a big deal. You're doing that now."

His lips continued to curve on the right and the dimple appeared. Then he sighed and scooted forward, spreading his legs. His hands suddenly landed on my hips, and I almost dropped the cotton ball at the unexpected contact. My breath caught as he lowered me so I was sitting on the edge of the coffee table and he kept moving forward, the inside of his legs sliding against the outside of mine. The rough material of his jeans touching my bare skin sent a raw, drenching rush of sensation through my veins.

"That better?" he asked, peering at me through lowered lashes.

I blinked, having no idea what he was talking about, and then I realized that seated like this, it was easier to reach him. His hands dropped from my hips to rest on his thighs, and they were oh so close to mine.

Stretching toward him, I gently swiped along the gash, and when he sucked in a breath, I pulled my hand back.

"It's okay," he said.

I tried again, and this time he didn't move or make a sound. "Are you going to tell me...what happened?"

A moment passed, and I glanced down at him. "This reminds me of old times," he said, and his lashes lifted. As his gaze drifted over me, it was focused but all too brief, because he looked away, a muscle working along his jaw. "Kind of."

A flush raced across my cheeks as I switched out the ball for a new one. He was right—this was like all the other times I'd cleaned him up. Well, when I was younger, I tried to clean him up, but had no idea what I was doing, but as we grew older, and he got into fights defending me or for some other reason, this was our routine.

Except I was pretty sure that when his gaze roamed over me just now, he'd checked out my breasts, and that was definitely something that hadn't happened before. Back then I doubted he even realized that I had them.

Probably because they didn't appear until about two years ago.

My thoughts whirled to the car in the parking lot and to what Keira had said the day before as I cleaned up the cut. Was this a result of the shady people he was hanging out with? Would he now have matching scars above both eyebrows? I didn't like the idea of that. "Why haven't you been in class?"

"I had some stuff to take care of."

"That's not an answer." When he said nothing, I tried again. "Are you… Are you safe, Rider?"

He turned his cheek toward me, and I almost dabbed him in the eyeball. "That would've stung," he murmured, catching my wrist. He plucked the ball out of my hand and tossed it on the coffee table. "I'm safe. I'm always safe."

I shook my head. "All those times you put yourself—"

"Mouse…"

"You put yourself in danger for me. You did, over and over again." Anger snapped at the heels of the concern welling in my chest. "You never really stopped to think about…what could happen to you."

He tilted his head back, meeting my gaze. "I knew what I was doing."

"You..." My throat thickened as memories rose like a vile, tainted wave. "You took *beatings* for me. You—"

"Mouse," he said gently. "I knew what I was doing then and I know what I'm doing now."

Was he basically telling me that he was now taking a beating for someone else? Without him saying any more, I knew it. I knew the bloody gash on his forehead wasn't because of something he'd done, but something someone smaller, weaker had done. "Are you a masochist?"

He stared at me a moment and then he laughed—that deep laugh that made me shiver. "That's a good question."

"It's not funny." I started to pull my arm away, but he held on to my wrist. Our gazes held again, and words bubbled up my throat like champagne. "I don't like seeing you hurt now any better than I did back then."

"But I'm not hurt." His voice was low. "See? You took care of me."

There was a swelling feeling in my chest again, but this one was different. Sort of like a balloon being filled. "Is that why you came here?"

He didn't respond immediately. "I don't know. I think I just missed you. Like not seeing you all this time after...after being around you every day for, hell, for a *decade*, and then...then I lost you. But now you're back." He smoothed his other hand over the top of mine. "It doesn't seem real. The odds of us ever crossing each other's path again had to be stacked against us, but here we are."

Here we are.

"So how long do I have before—what were their names? Carl and Rosa? Yeah, that's them. How long do I have before they come back?"

"I don't know. Maybe…maybe an hour or so?" My hands felt incredibly small in his.

That lopsided grin was back. "I doubt they'd be happy to find me here."

"Why?"

His brows rose. "Maybe I'm wrong. They used to coming home to find some strange guy sitting on their couch?"

I rolled my eyes.

"That's it, isn't it?" Rider tugged on my hands, and I rose, letting him pull me down to the couch beside him. He leaned back, sliding one arm around my shoulders and tucking me against his side. "Just par for the course with you, huh?"

I didn't know what to do with my hands since he'd let go of them, so I folded them in my lap. "I've never had a…guy here."

Rider stiffened and then he twisted his neck so he was looking at me.

Did I seriously admit that out loud? Squeezing my eyes shut, I sighed. "I'm just…going to shut up now."

He chuckled. "Don't do that. I like listening to you talk."

With our sides pressed together and his arm around my shoulders, it was like having one foot in the past and one in the present. Being this close now felt totally different than before. If only the TV had been on, I imagined we'd be following in the footsteps of couples all over the world, cuddled up as we were.

Except we weren't a couple.

I really needed to get that thought out of my head. "You didn't, um, miss much in class. We have to read examples of… informative speeches."

"Sounds fun."

Our gazes met briefly, and I looked away. "Where have you been, Rider?"

Rider was silent as he slid his hand up my arm. His fingers brushed over the bare skin of my shoulder as he curved his hand there. It seemed like such an unconscious move, but tiny bumps formed on my skin, chasing the caress. "Hector and I needed to talk to some people."

My gaze shifted up to his again. "Does talking involve fists?"

A wry grin formed. "Sometimes." He reached up, wiggling the knot of hair piled atop my head. "Hector's brother... he's young. Jayden's just fifteen, but sometimes he seems even younger than that. You know, mentally, and he gets himself into some trouble."

Staring up at him, I was struck again by the fact that some things didn't change. Or maybe it was some traits in people. "So you're helping him out of trouble?"

"Trying," he murmured, resting his head against the back of the cushion. His eyes took on a hooded, lazy quality as he continued to mess with my hair. I had no idea what he was doing. "Anyway, we talked yesterday. Made sure Jayden got his ass to class today. The talking didn't go as smoothly this evening."

Oh my God, I wanted to hug him and punch him. "Rider—"

"Did you ever think we'd be sitting here?" he asked.

"You're changing the subject," I pointed out.

"I am." He flashed a quick, impish grin. "But did you?"

"No," I admitted, swallowing against the sudden lump in my throat. "I never thought...I'd see you again. I hoped that I would."

"Hoping never really got us anywhere, did it?"

I shook my head. Growing up as we did, we learned real quick to get on a first-name basis with reality. Things like hope and aspirations had seemed like dreams and fantasies.

Rider's fingers kept moving along the knot and before I knew it, he'd worked the bun loose. My hair fell past my shoulders, a tangled mess of waves. "I like it down," he said, and the hollows of his cheeks pinked as he dropped his hand. His fingers grazed my upper arm. "Though I kind of miss the orange. Made it easy to pick you out in a crowd."

"Thanks."

He laughed. "Ah, I'm lying. Still easy to pick you out. A mile away," he added, almost as an afterthought.

"Because I'm shorter...than everyone in a crowd," I replied drily.

His gaze flickered over my face in that strange, concentrated way. "No, not that at all." Casting his gaze to my hands, his brows lowered. "So how have your first three days at school been?"

Only three days? Felt longer than that. I raised a shoulder. "Okay."

"That's not very convincing."

Lifting my gaze to his, I suddenly thought of Paige. I pulled away, putting space between us. How had I forgotten about her? I'd been caught off guard by Rider's sudden appearance and the condition he'd been in, but that wasn't a good enough excuse.

I glanced over at him, a hundred questions rising to the surface. One of them being why he'd come to me instead of Paige in the first place.

My heart started pounding. Part of me didn't want to bring her up, because if he didn't, then I could still... What? What could I still do? Even if we never talked about Paige, it didn't change reality. And his having a girlfriend didn't change what we were. Which was friends.

I drew in a deep breath. "You...you have a...girlfriend, right?"

"What?" Rider stared at me a moment and then he shook his head. "That kind of came out of nowhere."

True. I didn't let that deter me. "It's...it's the girl in our speech class."

Rider stared at me a moment. "You're talking about Paige. Yeah, we've been seeing each other."

Folding my hands in my lap, I smiled nervously. "That's... that's good."

He looked away, lips pursed. "We've known each other for

a while. She's known Hector since elementary school, so she's always been around, you know?"

I really didn't know, but I could imagine.

"And she's pretty cool. Not uptight," he said, and I wondered if he thought I was uptight. "I can...just chill with her, not really worry about anything. Anyway, we started dating last spring." He stopped and looked over at me. "How did you know? Did she talk to you?"

Oh, man. I didn't want him to know about the conversation from today. I closed my hands and told myself that none of this was any of my business. "No. I just... I saw the way you two were...um, together the first day of class."

His brows rose. "What way was that?"

Looking away, I sort of wished I'd kept my mouth shut. "She was very...touchy with you."

"Huh." There was a pause. "I'm touchy with you and that doesn't mean we're seeing each other."

Icy air hit the center of my chest as his words slammed into my consciousness. Whoa. He had a point, a very good point, and while I didn't think he meant anything when he'd said that, that icy air burned nonetheless.

"I mean," he said, knocking his shoulder into mine, "you and I have always been like that."

"True," I murmured, smiling again as I looked up at him.

Our eyes held for a few seconds and his narrowed. "She didn't say anything to upset you, did she?"

"Why...why would you think that?"

One side of his lips kicked up. "She's— Let's just say Paige is a tough girl."

The burn radiated out from my chest. Of course Rider would be into a tough girl. He was tough, and Paige had no problem putting me in my much deserved place today. If I'd been in her shoes, I would've sat there and said nothing.

"So she can be a little rough on people," he finished.

I shrugged.

His gaze turned sharp as he focused on me. "Did she say something to you? I can talk to her. Make sure she knows how—"

"No." I jerked, startled by myself. The word came out a little louder than I intended. I practically shouted it. "You don't need to talk with her."

A look of doubt crossed his features. "Mallory—"

"It's okay." Wiggling to the edge of the couch, I flicked one of the unused cotton balls across the table. "I mean…she didn't say anything to me. You don't have to say anything to her."

I looked over my shoulder at him, meaning what I was saying. As much as I…as I loved that he retained that fierce protective streak, I couldn't rely on him always being there to have my back. For the last four years, he hadn't been there, and we couldn't go back. I couldn't allow it, no matter how easy it would be. "I don't…I don't want it like that."

"How do you want it?" he asked and then raised his fingers to his brow, rubbing around the cut. His lips twisted in a harsh facade of a smile. "Don't answer that."

I wasn't sure what that even meant. Confused, I stared at him, feeling like I'd missed something really important.

"I should get going. I don't want to get you in trouble." He scooted to the edge of the couch.

Before I could protest, which wouldn't be wise even though I did want him to hang out longer, he placed his hands on my cheeks. My breath stalled out somewhere between my throat and chest. Leaning in, he pressed his lips against my forehead, dropping a kiss that squeezed my heart into slush. My eyes drifted shut as his lips lingered against my skin. Knocked off-kilter, I didn't move when he pulled back and stood.

An eternity might have passed before I dragged my eyes open and found him staring down at me, his golden-brown eyes bright, his lips parted. I cleared my throat. "I can…give you a ride."

His gaze dipped, and then he arched a brow. "No need. I got it taken care of."

Pushing to my feet, I followed him out to the foyer. He reached for the door and then turned back to me. "I'm glad you opened the door."

My smile felt wobbly. "I'm glad…you texted."

Rider tilted his head to the side. "Yeah?"

I nodded, probably a little too eagerly, but as the dimple in his right cheek took shape, it was like being rewarded. Our eyes met for a moment, and I didn't want him to leave. An urge took me like it had during lunch, and I all but bounced forward. Gripping his arms, I stretched up and kissed his cheek. It was pretty much just a peck, so I figured it wasn't crossing any lines, but the feel of his skin under my lips was still unnerving and unexpected.

"Be careful," I whispered, backing off.

Rider's grin faded from his handsome face. A moment passed before he spoke. "Always, Mouse."

CHAPTER 9

I tiptoed up the creaky stairs, wincing every time the boards groaned under my steps. I had to be quiet or Mr. Henry would catch me. That would be bad. Very bad.

I crept down the dark hallway. Miss Becky was sick again, in bed, but if I could get her up, she would help Rider. Inching the door open slowly, so that it didn't make a sound, I glanced around the bedroom. The lamp on the nightstand was on, flooding the room with muted yellow light. Empty brown bottles littered the top of the dresser. The room smelled funny. Stagnant. I moved toward the bed, squeezing my hands closed. Miss Becky was lying atop it, but she didn't look right. She looked like one of those mannequins in the stores, pale and still.

"Miss Becky," I whispered, breaking a rule. I was never to wake her up, but Rider needed help. There was no movement on the bed. I crept closer. "Miss Becky?"

Frightened, I hesitated near the bed. The room blurred. Burning tears filled my eyes as I shifted my weight from my left foot to the right. I tried to say her name again, but there was no sound. The strap of her tank top was halfway down her arm and her chest didn't seem to move.

I started to turn away, to go hide, because something was very wrong, but Rider was outside, and it was cold enough that my gloveless fingers had ached on the playground at school earlier. I lifted bony shoulders and rushed back to the bed. I reached out, grabbing Miss Becky's arm. Her skin felt cold and…and plastic. I yanked my hands back and spun, running out of the room. Miss Becky… She wasn't going to be able to help. It was up to me, and I wouldn't let Rider down. I crept back down the steps and quietly edged past the moldy-smelling bathroom.

Mr. Henry shouted a bad word from the living room, causing my heart to jump, but I pressed on, reaching the back door. Stretching up, I unlocked the door, the sound cracking like thunder throughout the kitchen. I turned the doorknob.

"What in the hell are you doing, girl?"

I flinched, shrinking back as my body locked up. I prepared myself for fists as I opened my mouth. Screams ripped through the air, through the house and—

"Mallory! Wake up!" Hands clutched my shoulders, shaking me. "Wake up."

Jerking upright, I yanked myself free as I scuttled across the bed. My right hand hit air. Balance thrown off, I teetered on the edge of the bed. The hand on my left arm tightened. Another scream built in my throat. My wild gaze darted around the brightly lit bedroom. The past slowly peeled back, like the stain of tar and smoke being washed away. No beer bottles. No newspaper-covered kitchen table. I stared into Carl's dark eyes. Concern was etched on his weary face. His hair stuck up in every direction and his gray shirt was rumpled.

"Are you okay?" he demanded as I dragged in deep, uneven breaths. "God, Mallory, I haven't heard you scream like that…"

In years.

He didn't need to finish the sentence. Hand shaking, I brushed hair back from my face as I swallowed. My throat was raw. I realized then that Rosa stood in the doorway, cinching the belt on her robe around her waist. She said something, but I couldn't follow. In my chest, my heart was pounding fast.

"It's okay." Carl patted my arm as he looked over his shoulder, at the door. "It was just a nightmare, *cariño*. Go back to bed."

How could it be just a nightmare? Nightmares weren't real. This…this was.

★ ★ ★

Morning came too soon, and it was all I could do to drag myself through the day. When speech class rolled around, I headed into class and immediately made eye contact with Paige. Today her hair was smoothed back into one of those ballerina buns and she was wearing large gold hoop earrings. She looked amazing. However, the pinched set to her face when she spotted me was not amazing.

Dragging my left foot, I stumbled and the crack of my flip-flop sounded like thunder. I didn't fall, but my hip bumped into an empty desk.

Paige's lips twisted up at the corners as she raised a brow.

Horrified, I froze for half a second and then I snapped out of it. Hurrying to my seat, I sat down. My cheeks were scalding. The way she had been staring at me before I tripped like an idiot made me think that Rider might've said something to her like he'd offered to the night before.

He wouldn't, I told myself as I opened my notebook and saw the notes I'd scribbled down the day before. Eyes narrowing, I couldn't figure out what the one sentence I wrote actually meant and—

"Mouse."

Air caught in my throat as I looked up. Rider had to be part ghost, because I hadn't heard him take his seat beside me or say anything to Paige, but there he was. Wearing an old shirt with a faded emblem and with his arms crossed against his broad chest, he was the picture of lazy arrogance.

Seeing him after last night had me feeling weird in the pit of my stomach. I hadn't told Carl and Rosa about Rider coming by the house. Worse, I didn't plan to.

Mouse.

Part of me hated that nickname, because of what it symbolized. The other half sort of loved it, because it was *his* nickname. I wasn't sure which feeling outweighed the other.

My heart decided to do something funny in my chest. "Rider."

His full lips curved up in a half grin, drawing my attention to his mouth. How could a guy have such perfect lips? It wasn't fair. And why was I staring at his mouth? The blush turned my face into a breathing strawberry, and his grin spread, showing off the dimple. "Miss me?"

My hands flattened across my open notebook as my gaze darted toward Paige. She was looking at something Hector was showing her on his phone, but I couldn't believe he asked that in front of her. Or maybe that wasn't a big deal and I was making a big deal out of it?

I forced myself to shrug as I glanced up and saw that the gash above his left eye wasn't as ugly as before. "How is your head?" I asked, voice low.

"Totally forgot about it." His gaze briefly dipped. "How was your day?"

Something warm shifted inside me as I heard the distant clang of the warning bell. "I ate lunch with Keira today. Second day in a row," I told him, then winced at how stupid that sounded.

Rider's grin turned into a full smile, transforming his handsome face into the kind of masculine beauty that was like a punch to the chest. "That's really good, Mallory." His voice dropped as he reached over, curving his hand over my arm. There was a near electric rush from his touch. "I'm proud of you. For real."

Giddiness surrounded my heart as I stared at his large hand, darker than my own. He knew how big that was, and I didn't feel so idiotic. He got it. He got me. And that meant the entire universe to me.

A shadow fell between our desks. Hector was in the process of sitting down, and had stopped halfway, his head cocked to the side. His eyes were on Rider's hand, and he looked like a chupacabra had just walked in front of him.

Rider drew back, folding his arms. "You okay, bro?"

Hector's green eyes flicked to him. "Are you?"

There was no response, and I had no idea what the heck that was all about, but as Hector sat, I realized Keira was also watching us from her seat a few rows up. I forced a smile, praying she hadn't heard me blurt out the thing about lunch. That would be awkward.

"Hey, babe," Paige said, gaining Rider's attention. "We still on for tonight?"

I bit down on the inside of my cheek as Rider turned toward her. "Tonight?"

"Yeah." Her smile was bright and big, like it had been the first time I saw her with him. "We talked about going to Ramon's party."

I had no idea who Ramon was, but envy unfurled in my stomach. I had never been to a party outside of something organized by adults. I had no idea what that kind of party would be like and I hadn't really thought about it until now. My gaze shifted between them, and it occurred to me then that even though Rider got me like no one else did, our worlds didn't orbit each other anymore.

Now Rider missed school whenever he wanted.

Now Rider had a girlfriend.

Rider was invited to parties.

Me? I was the way I'd been before and would be forever.

I would never miss school.

I didn't have a boyfriend.

I didn't go to parties, and with the exception of Ainsley's sweet sixteen last year, I wasn't invited to them.

"Not sure," Rider responded. "I have to head in to the garage. Might be there most of the night."

The garage? I wanted to ask about that, but figured this was not the time to step out of my shell and speak up.

Paige's smile froze. "I was really looking forward to going."

"Go," he urged, and he smiled at her. I couldn't see it, but I knew the right dimple was there. "If I can get out in time, I'll meet you there. Okay?"

Paige was still for a moment and then nodded. "Okay." Reaching over, she folded a hand around the nape of his neck. "I'm going to miss you, though."

I really needed to look away.

"Are you?" Warm amusement colored Rider's tone.

I didn't look away.

Paige's fingers tightened and... Was he leaning toward her? I looked away...for about five seconds before my gaze shot back to them. He was sitting straight, and all of Paige's body parts were in her chair.

A second passed and Rider looked over, catching me watching them and totally up in their conversation. His smile went deeper, and now I saw the dimple. Lowering my gaze, I refocused on my own desk...and my own business.

Mr. Santos appeared at the front of the class like there had been a trapdoor in the ceiling he'd fallen out of. That took talent. "All right, kiddos. We're going to start class off with a little exercise." He clapped his hands together, startling the boy in the front of the room that had already drifted off to sleep. "When it comes to public speaking, practice is key. The more you do it, the easier it gets. Trust me."

A tingling started in my fingers as I straightened.

"When I was your age—"

"A century ago," someone muttered.

Santos shot the kid a droll look. "Cute. Anyway, when I was

your age a *few* decades ago, the thought of talking in front of a bunch of people made me want to vomit."

"Yikes," murmured a girl.

There was a good chance I was going to hurl, myself.

"So it was something I had to work at. We all do. That means we're going to kick off with a quick introduction."

"Oh, shit," Rider muttered under his breath.

Santos continued, oblivious to the fact that I was staring at him with my eyes peeled so wide it was like I no longer had eyelids. "Each of you will stand up, face the class, give us your name and tell us one thing you like—keep it classy, folks—and one thing you don't like. Again, PG rated."

Laughter followed, but the blood was draining from my head so fast I felt dizzy. No. I had weeks to prepare for this. Talking in front of the class was not supposed to happen today or tomorrow *or* next week.

"Mallory." Rider called my name in a whisper.

My hands gripped the edge of the desk as my pulse did its own version of house music. My throat was tightening up as my eyes swung in his direction. Hector's and Paige's faces were a blur. A chair scratched across the floor and my gaze followed the sound.

A guy was standing, hitching up his pants. As instructed, he faced the class. "My name is Leon Washington." A big grin covered his face. "I don't like cheese. And I like the chicks in the vids."

Chuckles and giggles rose while Santos shot him a look. Leon plopped down, and up went a girl. My breath was coming out in fast gasps. Paige sat at the end of the first row, Rider at the second, and me at the end of the third. There were seventeen chairs in front of me, two empty.

Oh, God.

My wide gaze darted to Rider. Understanding was etched into his expression, in the hard set of his jaw. His gaze darted to the girl who was now standing.

"I'm Laura Kaye." She brushed shoulder-length brown hair back from her face as she turned to the class. "I...um, I like driving with loud music on. And I don't like..." Her cheeks flushed pink. "And I don't like gossiping bitches."

Mr. Santos sighed.

The class erupted into laughter.

Laura sat down with a satisfied smile on her face.

There was a good chance I was going to have a heart attack as another guy stood, his face already the color of a tomato.

"Mallory," Rider whispered, and my panicked stare drifted to him. Over his shoulder, I was aware of Paige watching us. "You can do this," he said in a hushed voice. "You can."

His eyes held mine, and he stared at me like his words alone held the power to convince me, but he was wrong. I couldn't do this. The plug at the top of my throat turned into a seal. Oh, God, there was no way I could get any words out. A viselike pressure clamped down on my chest, seeming to completely cut off my airway. An all-too-familiar icy burn splashed across the base of my neck.

I couldn't do this.

CHAPTER 10

I don't remember gathering up my textbook or shoving it into my bag. I also didn't remember picking up my bag or standing. I was in a tunnel that was dark around the edges and the only light was the doorway.

Another girl was standing and introducing herself, but I couldn't hear anything she said as my legs moved. In a daze, I was out of the classroom and into the silent hall. My chest burned as I kept walking, half running, and I didn't stop until I was outside, dashing toward my car as the thick, overcast skies threatened to let loose with the rain.

Oh my God, I couldn't believe it.

Stopping at the side of my car, I dropped my bag and bent over, clasping my knees.

I'd just run out of class.

Breathing heavily, I squeezed my eyes shut, clenched them so tightly, I saw tiny pinpricks of light. I was so damn weak and so *stupid*. All I had to do was stand up and say my name. Say one thing I liked and one thing I didn't. That wasn't hard, but my brain… It just didn't work right. It shut down, gave up on me in a moment of panic.

"Mallory?"

I jerked upright and spun around, nearly losing my balance as my gaze locked with hazel eyes. Rider stood in front of me, the fragile notebook clutched in his hand. Of course, he'd left class to come after me.

Nothing had changed.

A new rush of mortification burned my cheeks as I turned away from him, staring out over the empty football field. Tears of frustration leaped to my eyes.

"I said you got sick," he said after a moment. "No one thinks anything weird. Hell, you ate school lunch, so it's believable. Santos let me leave class to check on you. I'm supposed to go back, but…"

But he wasn't going to.

Closing my eyes, I shook my head. My skin prickled like a thousand angry fire ants had started marching across my arms and back. Four days at school, and I'd run. I'd done just what Rosa and Carl most likely feared. I'd done exactly—

"Mouse, are you okay?" There was a pause and I felt his hand on my arm.

Mouse.

I wasn't *her* anymore.

I pulled away as I faced him just in time to catch the flicker of surprise flashing across his face. He lowered his hand, his gaze searching mine intently, and all I wanted… All I wanted was to be normal.

God, normalcy *wasn't* overrated when you had a brain like mine.

"You…you shouldn't have followed me," I said after a moment.

"Why not?" he asked as if he genuinely had no idea.

"Paige, for one."

"She understands."

I seriously doubted that, because if I were in her shoes, I wouldn't understand. Not in a million years. "Then...you shouldn't have followed me because...I'm not your problem anymore."

He lifted his chin, his shoulders heaving on a lengthy sigh. "I want to show you something."

I frowned.

He extended his hand and wiggled his fingers. "Can I see your car keys?"

My frown increased. Was he going to leave the school? There was still at least thirty minutes left, and...and wait a second. I so doubted he cared about leaving early and it wasn't like I was going to head back inside.

"I have a license," he continued when I didn't respond. "I swear. I know how to drive. I'm not going to steal your car or anything."

My brows flew up. "I...I didn't think you'd do that."

Rider cocked his head to the side. Did he really think I believed that about him? Swooping down, I picked up my bag and dug my keys out then handed them over. His long fingers closed around them. Without saying a word, I walked around to the passenger side and got into the car, tossing my bag into the backseat.

He followed, his long body cramped behind the wheel. With a sheepish grin, he reached down and hit the lever on the seat, adjusting it. He turned the key in the ignition and then backed out. He glanced at me as he eased the Honda between the rows of cars, but didn't say anything.

My hands were curled into tight balls and my thoughts were rushing through my head with the speed of hurricane-force winds. Leaving school like this was crazy for a whole multitude of reasons. Just like when he showed up at my house last night, if Carl and Rosa found out about this, they'd flip out.

But right now none of that mattered.

How could I even show my face Monday? I leaned back against the seat, knuckles aching. I slowly forced my hands open.

Staring out the window, I had no idea where Rider was heading at first, but quickly, traffic clogged the roads and I recognized that we were heading out of the city, using one of the older roads that was still congested.

"Will you get in trouble if you don't come home immediately after school?" he asked.

Well, if Rosa and Carl knew what I was doing and where I was, that would be a big *hell yes*, but they wouldn't know. "They won't be home for a while."

"Cool." When I peeked at him, I found him focused on the road. "I don't want to get you in trouble."

Reaching back, I scooped up my hair and started twisting it into a thick rope. "Why would you get me in trouble?"

He shot me a bland look I didn't understand. A moment passed. His gaze flipped back to the road. "Do they know— the people who took you in—that we've run into each other?"

I nodded. "I told them."

His brows rose, and I thought he looked surprised again. "And they know about me? From before?"

I started to nod, but forced myself to talk. "They know."

"Everything?" he asked.

"Most of everything," I whispered.

He nodded slowly. "What did they think of me and you being together?" Pink swept across his cheeks. "I mean, that we're at the same school?"

Part of me thought that was a strange question for him to ask, but then I figured out where he was heading with it. He thought that the reason why Rosa and Carl wouldn't be happy to know he was back had to do with who he was, but he would be wrong. It was what he represented.

At least, I hoped that was it.

"They...are just worried about me...fitting in," I told him, and that was true. "About whether I can handle it, which...obviously I can't."

A muscle flexed in his jaw, but before I could say anything, he announced, "My name is Rider Stark."

Um.

"I like working with my hands," he continued as he slowed down, hitting the brakes at a stoplight. "And I don't like classrooms." He glanced at me, lashes lowered. "Maybe saying I didn't like classrooms would be a bad choice, but I could say something like I don't like bananas."

"Bananas?"

He nodded with a small grin. "I discovered about three years ago that I absolutely hate those damn things."

"But they're just bananas."

"They're the fruit of the devil."

A surprised laugh burst out of me. "That's ridiculous."

The half grin spread and the dimple appeared. "It's the truth. Now it's your turn."

I knew what he was doing. Trying to prove that what had been asked in speech class was something that I could do, but obviously that wasn't the case. What was the point in doing this now? It wasn't the same.

"Mouse?" he said softly, but I shook my head. He didn't respond immediately. "Okay."

Letting go of my hair, I looked out the window as the interior of the car darkened. We were driving through an underpass. A few moments later Rider turned right and pulled off into a small parking lot in front of a long, rectangular building that had more busted-out windows than it did glassed ones. "Where are we?"

Rider turned off the car and unbuckled his seat belt. "It's an old factory. Looks bad but it's safe. Promise you."

I glanced at the ominous building that seemed straight out of one of the ghost-hunting shows I liked to watch on TV. See?

Ghost shows. I could've said I liked those in class. If anyone else said this place was safe I would've kept my butt in the car, but even with the four-year gap between us, I trusted Rider. I took off my seat belt and climbed out.

He joined me on the other side, slipping my keys into his pocket. The pavement we walked across was cracked, and weeds poked through the fissures. Large chunks were missing. I glanced up at the sky. The scent of rain was heavy in the air as we neared double doors with faded red paint.

"We're not heading inside. Not today."

There was going to be a later? An odd flutter took root in my chest. I ignored it, thinking it was a good thing that we weren't going in. Mainly because I really didn't need to add breaking and entering to skipping school on the fourth day.

Also, I was sure the place was haunted.

Reaching down, his warm fingers found mine. Startled, I tried not to trip as he took my hand and led me around the side of the building. A musty scent clung to the old brick walls. He didn't talk as he led me around the side of the building, beyond long-forgotten Dumpsters. He headed to the left, and I saw several old stone picnic tables, and then the back of the building came into view.

I ground to a halt.

My lips parted in shock. I didn't know where to look; there was so much color. Someone had transformed a decrepit gray wall into a living kaleidoscope of reds. Yellows. Greens. Purples. Blues. Blacks. Whites. Letting my eyes rove everywhere, I saw giant letters—random initials and words that didn't look English. Then there were the murals. I could make out people and cars. Buildings and trains. All of it was spray-painted. Most of it put my soap figurines to shame. The talent implied by the intricacy of the letters and the detail in the faces was amazing. And to be able to do this with spray paint? I couldn't even do it with a paintbrush and Diego Rivera guiding my hand.

I thought about the red smudges I'd seen on Rider's fingers and I twisted toward him. Smiling a little, he let go of my hand and walked toward the decorated wall, his long legs carrying him halfway down the length of the building. He stopped in front of a painted young boy. I inched closer, folding my arms around my waist as he ran a hand over the shoulder of the dark-haired child. The detail was astonishing, down to the hands shoved into the pockets of worn jeans. The shirt was white and looked so real, so flimsy, that I expected it to blow right off the frail body. The boy was looking up at the graffiti above him, but it was the expression on the face that gutted me.

Hopelessness.

It was in his light brownish-green eyes. Devastation was caught in the line of the child's mouth. It was in the way his brows were furrowed together and lifted up. The bleakness was so strong it was tangible. It clouded the air. I knew that look. I'd seen it. I'd felt it.

It said, would my life be like this forever? Was there no future any different than today?

"I got busted for tagging a couple of times," Rider said, stepping back from the wall. He stuck his hands into the pockets of his frayed jeans, just like the child on the wall. "But this is one of the places where we're allowed to do this without getting in trouble. Helps me clear my head. Don't really think when I'm doing it."

"This… You did this?"

"Yeah."

Stunned, I stared at the boy. He had done this with a few cans of spray paint? Blown away, I slowly shook my head. Rider had always been talented. He'd doodled on any spare piece of paper growing up, but this was incredible. I couldn't stop staring.

And I couldn't stop the pressure squeezing my chest or the burn of tears clogging the back of my throat. I knew the tears wouldn't fall. They never did. Not anymore, but I wanted to cry as I watched him, because I knew deep down, even if I didn't want to admit it, that the sad, wrecked boy on the wall was Rider.

"Have you seen Graffiti Alley or the other warehouse?" Rider asked, referencing the locations where Baltimore's graffiti artists could do their work without prosecution by the city.

I nodded. "I saw the Alley once." I dragged my gaze away from him and scanned the wall. "It's beautiful...like this place. That's amazing. That you've done this."

Rider lifted one shoulder. "It's nothing."

"It's unbelievable." I thought again about my soap carvings and almost laughed. "I can't...do anything like this."

He tilted his head to the side. "I could show you."

I choked on a laugh. I was pretty sure that would be like handing a crayon to a toddler in the middle of a tantrum and telling them to color within the lines.

Facing me, he glanced up at the fat, rain-heavy clouds. "I mean, if you want me to. There're other places where you can do it without getting in trouble."

I looked back at the wall and tried to picture creating something so awe-inspiring. I would end up with a spray-painted stick figure. "I wouldn't want to mess anything up."

A lopsided grin appeared. "You wouldn't. Promise."

Unsure of that fact, I didn't respond as my gaze trekked back to the painted child. I wondered if Rider had brought Paige here before. Immediately, I knew that was a stupid thought. Of course he had. They probably did this—the tagging—together.

"Is...is Paige into this?" I asked, and my cheeks warmed.

"This kind of stuff? Tagging?" Rider's grin evened out as he shook his head. "In the beginning, maybe? I mean, she used to come and watch me, but I honestly don't think it was ever her thing."

I looked back at the wall. "Would she be okay with...you showing me how to do this?"

"Yeah." His response was immediate. "Why wouldn't she be?"

I really had no idea how to answer that.

"She knows you're important to me, Mouse." He stepped closer. "And like I told you, she's a tough girl. Doesn't warm up to people easy, but she will with you. Eventually." He paused. "She's not going to have a problem with me spending time with you."

Slowly, I looked over at him. I thought that I should explain that his girlfriend just might have a problem with that, and I couldn't blame her if she did, but I had to take what he said at face value. He knew her far better than I did, and Paige hadn't been mean yesterday in class. She was just stating her place in things. I could respect that. And Rider and I could be friends— we'd always been friends. Maybe she would warm up to me.

At least this part of my life, my life with this new version of Rider, could work.

I turned back to the painted wall. There was no way I'd be good at this, but what could it hurt? A mini cyclone formed in my belly. "Okay."

The dimple appeared, and the cyclone in my stomach grew. Our gazes collided, and I hastily looked away, suddenly feeling hot. I wanted to tug at the collar of my shirt, but that seemed too awkward to seriously consider.

"Do you want to head back?" he asked, and when I looked up, he was closer and I hadn't even heard him move. "Mouse?"

Class was over at this point, and I should really head home, but I...I didn't want to leave. Not yet. There was something peaceful about this place despite the distant hum of traffic and bleating horns. I shook my head.

He stared at me a moment and then walked over to the old stone picnic table and sat. I joined him after a minute. Neither of us spoke for a long moment, and it was like falling down a rabbit hole. How many times had we sat side by side in the past?

My tongue came unglued from the roof of my mouth. "Do you think it's weird?"

"What?" he asked, propping his elbows on the table behind him. He leaned back, his lashes lowered.

"This. Being here like…like no time has passed." Warmth crept into my cheeks. "It's just weird."

He was quiet again. "Yeah, it's weird, but in a good way. Right?"

"Right," I murmured.

Rider knocked his knee off mine. "I'm glad we're here, though, to experience this weirdness."

The warmth increased as the corners of my lips twitched into a small grin. "Me, too." He held my gaze for a heartbeat and then flipped his attention to the graffiti-covered wall. I drew in a shallow breath. This was the perfect chance to ask him about how the last four years had been. There were so many questions. "How long…have you been with Hector's grandmother?"

His brows furrowed. "About three years."

"And the…group home before then?"

"It wasn't that bad," he replied, stretching out his legs. "Not many kids." He laughed softly, under his breath. "I was actually surprised when I was sent to live with Mrs. Luna. I was almost fifteen. Like what's the point?"

I got what he was saying, but he was lucky, because not many people wanted to take on a teenager who'd been in the system their entire life. It was surprising that he found one that did. "You're happy with…Mrs. Luna?"

"Yeah…" He squinted as he moved his fingers, opening and closing them. A raindrop hit the table. "She's good people."

I waited for him to say more, to elaborate, but he went quiet in the way that made me question what he said. I opened my mouth, but he looked over at me. Words scorched the tip of my tongue.

His voice was so low it was barely above a whisper when he spoke. "Do you ever... Do you ever think about that night?"

Muscles in my stomach knotted, and I shook my head, which wasn't a lie. I did everything in my power not to think about that night. Except last night my brain had decided to give me a play-by-play recap.

"Do you?" I whispered, unable to look at him.

"Sometimes." There was a pause as he slid his hands along his jeans. "Sometimes I think about other nights, you know, when that asshole would get drunk and his friends would be over."

Every part of my body tensed, and I didn't dare make a sound then, because I knew what other nights he was referencing.

"And sometimes I hope that every one of them, including Henry, is dead." He laughed without humor. "That makes me a horrible person, doesn't it?"

"No," I said immediately. "That doesn't make you a horrible person." My mouth dried as my thoughts raced back to those nights when Henry's friends would be in the house. Some would look at me in ways no man should look at a little girl. Then there were some who looked at Rider in the same way—some that had *gone* for him. The others would've gotten me if it hadn't been for Rider. "Did they ever...?"

Rider shook his head. "No. I was always too fast and they were always too drunk. I was lucky."

I wasn't sure that made him lucky.

"We should head back," he said, pushing to his feet as another drop of rain fell to the cracked asphalt. "It's about to start pouring."

Standing, I followed him to the Honda. My movements were stiff. As Rider got into the car and closed the door, I turned and stared at the painted brick wall. The graffiti might just have been letters, a bright flower, a woman's face or a little boy staring up at the sky with no hope of a different tomorrow, but each piece of art had a story to tell. Each of them spoke without words.

And while I'd tried for years to do the same, I wasn't a painting on a wall.

"My name is Mallory…Dodge." I drew in a deep breath, speaking to no one. "And I like…I like reading. And I don't like…I don't like who I am."

CHAPTER 11

We didn't make it to the Harbor to meet Ainsley until noon on Saturday since Carl wanted to make breakfast and do the whole caring-is-sharing routine, which was a Saturday staple unless he or Rosa got called into work.

Carl had made his famous waffles—famous in his own head—but they were special to me. Special because I'd never had this before them. Waffles with blueberries and strawberries every Saturday morning. Special because I knew there were too many kids to count that weren't experiencing this and never had.

Halfway through breakfast, the idle chatter between them turned serious and it was directed at me. It was Rosa who spoke first, after her second full cup of coffee. "So, the school called us yesterday."

With a forkful of waffle and strawberry halfway to my gaping mouth, I froze. So much for my promise to Rider about not getting in trouble.

She placed her fork on her plate, next to the waffle crumbs. Her plate was otherwise clear. Mine looked like a syrup lake. "Actually, a Mr. Santos contacted us."

I closed my eyes.

"We both spoke to him," Carl added, and the waffle I'd so recently shoved down my throat turned sour. "He explained you had an issue yesterday in class during an exercise in public speaking."

Opening my eyes, I lowered my fork. I was so no longer hungry. And I was so... I shifted in my chair, uncomfortable.

"He said that another classmate spoke up for you, said you were feeling ill and that's why you left," Carl continued. "Now, he also told us it was Rider who covered for you."

Oh, God.

I wanted to crawl under the table.

"We'll talk about that in a moment." Rosa held up a hand, silencing Carl. "You weren't feeling ill yesterday, were you?"

Lying would probably be better than throwing my failure onto the table in front of us, but I shook my head. Silence stretched out, and I pressed my lips together as I shifted my gaze to my plate. They had to be so disappointed. One week into school and they'd already gotten a call concerning me.

"It's okay." Rosa reached over, placing her hand on my arm. I looked up. "Carl and I expected there were going to be some bumps in the road. We knew speech class wasn't going to be easy. You knew that, too."

She was right. That didn't make admitting my failure any easier.

"The school knows," Carl said, drawing my attention.

"Knows...knows what?"

Folding his arms on the table, he leaned forward. "We spoke to the administration back when you were registered, letting them know you might have some difficulties."

My jaw nearly hit the table. "You...did what?"

"We didn't go into detail, Mallory, and we only met with your teachers, the principal and Mrs. Dehaven, one of the counselors," Rosa explained. "It's just so they could keep an eye on you, just in case anything happened that we needed to know about."

Only everyone! Oh my God. Skin tingling and itchy, I sat back in the chair. I stared at them without really seeing them. All I could see was all these people knowing about my *difficulties* the whole week when this was supposed to be a fresh start.

"They needed to know," Carl said.

That was stated like it was a fact, and I begged to differ. My tongue untangled.

"We worked out a deal with Mr. Santos during yesterday's call," he continued, and my tongue went right back to the roof of my mouth. "He completely understands, Mallory. I want you to know that. He understands how difficult it will be for you to get in front of that class and speak."

I might've stopped breathing.

"Speech is a requirement for graduation, but they've made concessions for students before," Rosa said, her voice soft. "And Mr. Santos was more than willing to do so in this case."

I stiffened. "But—"

"He agreed that instead of you having to give your speeches in front of the class with the rest of the students, you'll have a set time to give them only to him," Carl explained, and I might've been having an out-of-body experience. "That way you'll be able to keep up with the assignments, but on your terms."

Rosa patted my arm. "This is good news."

"This…" I shook my head, at a loss. "Everyone…will know."

Carl frowned.

"The kids in my class will know…that I can't do it and that I'm getting something…they aren't. They all…have to stand up there and I don't? I need to…do it."

He tilted his head to the side. "Honey, what you need to do is pass the class."

"What I need more is to…be normal, and giving the speech

just to Mr. Santos isn't the same thing," I protested as I glanced between them. "I can do this."

"We know you can. Eventually," Rosa said, and I jerked back in my seat. *Eventually.* As in they didn't believe I could do it now. "But right now it's baby steps. You've already made tremendous strides the past four years. It's okay to proceed with caution after so much change. Okay?"

I wasn't okay with any of it, but the burn of the fight was reduced to nothing more than a simmer as I lowered my hands to my lap. "You never had to...intervene like this for Marquette, did you?"

Rosa and Carl stared back at me.

I didn't know why those words flowed out of my mouth. No idea. I wanted to take them back.

Carl drew in a deep breath. "We didn't."

My fingers twisted together in my lap.

Rosa stood, picking up her plate and Carl's. "You done?" she asked me, and when I nodded, mine was swiped off the table.

"That was nice of that boy to cover for you," Carl stated, and my gaze flew to his.

"That boy?" I asked.

"Rider," he corrected, and my shoulders tensed. "Mr. Santos said he left class to check on you. He didn't come back."

Oh jeez, could I just start today over and never get out of bed? I wished I was upstairs, finishing the owl I'd started to carve last night. Nothing numbed me out quicker than working with soap. It had helped after everything with speech class and Rider. I'd carved out the tiny body, etching in tiny feathers and small, flat ears.

I drew my attention back to the topic at hand. "He...he made sure I was okay."

Carl studied me. "Have you been spending a lot of time with him?"

"Just...in speech," I said, feeling a little guilty about not telling the actual truth. I smoothed it over with something that was true. "But I've been…sitting with a girl at lunch who is in my English and speech class. Her name is Keira."

"That's really good to hear." Rosa's back was to us as she dumped the crumbs into the trash. "Does Rider not share the same lunch schedule?"

"No." I doubted they'd appreciate knowing Rider had skipped class to spend lunch with me earlier in the week.

Carl was still staring at me like he was trying to read my thoughts. "Is he interested in you, Mallory?"

"What?" I blinked once and then twice.

Rosa spun around, her gaze fixed on him.

"Is he interested in you as more than just a friend?" he repeated.

Oh, my…

Oh my Lord…

My face was going to melt off. "He has a girlfriend!"

It was Rosa's turn to blink.

"He does?" Relief colored Carl's tone. "Well, then…" He trailed off as he sat back, smiling. "I think it's time we got cleaned up and hit the road."

I stared at him.

Rosa stared at him.

Then we got up and we cleaned up, followed by hitting the road. They didn't bring up Rider or school after that, but the moment I saw Ainsley once we arrived at the Harbor and they were out of earshot, that was the topic of discussion.

We were sitting on one of the many benches facing the Harbor while Rosa and Carl were checking out a fund-raising fair several yards away. A cool wind blew off the bay, tossing Ainsley's long blond hair across her face.

Ainsley was gorgeous. Like one of the universally pretty girls that no one would describe otherwise. With blue eyes and a perfect set of cheekbones to match a pert nose, the only thing more beautiful than her looks was her personality. Seriously. Ainsley could be feisty and mouthy, but she was sweet to the core. Unless provoked. Then it was a different story. In the beginning, when we first met in homeschooling class, she had been incredibly patient with me, drawing me into conversations that most had given up on a long time ago, but each week all of us kids were brought to learn together, she made the effort.

At first it had been strange to have a friend. For so long it had just been Rider and then it had been... It had been no one. Talking was still difficult sometimes since I only got to see her about once a week, sometimes twice, but she was possibly the best thing to happen to me after the Rivases.

Plus, she could wear a romper without looking like an overgrown toddler. Today she wore a light blue one with a darker blue cardigan and she looked adorable. If I ever put on one of those things, I would willingly lock myself in my own room.

"I'm glad you told them about Rider," she was saying, but I really wasn't following why she was relieved, because I wasn't. Angled toward me with one leg dangling off the bench and the other curled in, she kept her voice low just in case we had company. "Because what would you have done if they showed up at school and saw him?"

I seriously doubted they'd randomly show up at Lands High, but since they'd already called the school to make sure people were keeping an eye on me, there was a chance one of their spies could've told them about Rider. When I'd told Ainsley about that and the deal Carl had made with Mr. Santos, she totally understood my mortification.

"I kind of...wish I didn't...tell them," I admitted.

Ainsley didn't get uncomfortable once during my long pause. "Telling them is better!" she whisper-yelled, and I grinned. "Look, you know I'm not the paradigm of honesty over here, but I'm just saying I think it's smart of you to be up-front with them."

It was smart for a ton of obvious reasons, but there was being smart and then there was being *smart*, and the latter meant I should've kept Rider a secret for now.

She paused. "Though I wouldn't tell them about him being at the house."

I rolled my eyes and grinned.

"But the whole point of telling them is so you can, you know, invite him over without having to lie about it," she reasoned, her blue eyes hidden behind oversize sunglasses. It wasn't that bright out, but she'd been complaining lately about how sensitive her eyes were getting to light. We'd joked about her turning into a vampire. "And I know you want to spend more time with him."

Biting down on my lip, I cast my gaze out to the bay. The water rippled slightly. Farther out, boats drifted. I did want to see more of Rider, especially outside school. There was so much we hadn't talked about, and I... Well, I just wanted to be around him.

"Mallory?" She nudged my arm with hers.

I looked over at her, unsure of how to put all of that into words. It would require effort, and right now the sound of my own voice was as shrill as the squawking mallards in the water.

A moment passed. "Do you not want to get to know him again?"

Know him again. Such a strange phrase. I squinted. "I do."

She caught a strand of her hair and tossed it off her face. "But?"

"But it's...weird." I smoothed my hands over my thighs. "I mean, things are...the same between us but different. Like he's... he's moved on and I..."

"You've moved on, too," Ainsley said softly.

Had I? Some days I felt like I had come a long way since that life of fear and hopelessness, but there were other days when it felt like I was still cowering in the back of the closet, listening to the sound of fists slamming into flesh.

I thought briefly of the boy spray-painted on the warehouse wall and the things Rider had talked about. Maybe I wasn't the only one who still fought that battle.

I shook my head, clearing my thoughts. "He has...a girl-friend."

Her brows climbed up over her sunglasses. "Okay." There was a pause. "Please don't take this the wrong way, but what does that have to do with anything? I mean, you guys just re-connected and all."

"I know, and I'm not saying that him having...a girlfriend is the issue," I explained, and it wasn't. Well, obviously I was no-ticing Rider in a way that was more than just friendly, because who wouldn't, but I knew he didn't see me that way. Never had, never would, girlfriend or not. I couldn't even entertain the idea of him reciprocating so much as a fraction of those more-than-friendly feelings. "It's that I don't think she's too happy with Rider and me...reconnecting."

"How so?"

I told Ainsley about the way Paige had talked to me at the locker and what she'd said to me in class when Rider hadn't shown the second time.

"Yikes." Her brows knitted. "Part of me can understand why she wouldn't be a fan of yours. You come out of nowhere and he's thrilled to see you. That's got to be hard to deal with."

"I know."

"But you guys are old friends, so she needs to deal with it. And it sounds like Rider wants you in his life. The first thing he did the moment he got a chance was to hug you?" When I nodded, she continued. "And then he showed up to your house one day, followed you out of class when you freaked."

Ainsley didn't mince words.

"Then he took you to this awesome place and showed you his artwork—super-cool artwork, might I just add. So he re-ally wants you involved in his life. She's going to need to cope."

I nodded slowly.

A moment passed and then she asked gently, "How are you handling things with him being around? I know he was a big part of your past."

She sounded so much like Rosa. "I'm okay."

"You sure?"

I nodded again. She stared at me for a moment and then she dropped it. We'd been friends long enough for her to know when I wasn't going to talk about something.

Ainsley respected that.

I looked over toward the fair, seeing the Rivases checking out a stand of used books. Carl held Rosa's hand in one of his and in the other, he held a book. I smiled and then looked back at Ainsley. "How...how are you and Todd?"

They were pretty serious. Well, at least I thought so since they'd had sex. I'd figured sex officially made things serious. She had told me that it had been pretty awkward but not bad. Not exactly a ringing endorsement, but now that I was thinking about sex, I thought of Rider.

And whoa, that came out of freaking nowhere.

But while I didn't have an ounce of experience, Ainsley had told me everything and I had a vivid imagination. And also an internet connection, so...

I was now picturing those broad shoulders, but with no shirt, and from his hugs, I could tell that he was fit. Electricity invaded my veins, and I suddenly wished I was wearing a tank top and shorts. I was hot and I wondered if he—

Oh my gosh, I really needed to *stop*. My cheeks were burning, and thank God, Ainsley was watching a guy jog by. A shirtless guy. Who was also fit.

"It's good. I haven't seen him much since school is back on." She shrugged, not sounding all that disappointed. "He's obsessing over colleges right now. It's all he talks about."

I knew Ainsley planned to go to University of Maryland,

same as me. I had already gotten early acceptance to the college, and her parents had gone there, but I wasn't sure about Todd. "What...college?"

"Oh, about a million of them." Even though I couldn't see her eyes, I knew she rolled them. "I think he wants to go someplace up north. He thinks he's going to get into an Ivy League School. I know this sounds mean, but he's not that smart."

I'd met Todd once, and while I wasn't sure about his intellectual status, I thought he was a pretty okay guy. I also thought he probably thought I was on the lower end of the cool scale.

"Ugh," she muttered, stretching out her legs. "He wants me to go to the movies tomorrow with his friends."

Yikes. I'd heard enough of Ainsley's rants to know that wasn't good.

"And I cannot come up with a good excuse to back out, because he knows I'll take any chance to get out of the house." She paused, looking at me. "Can we pretend you have chicken pox and I need to take care of you?"

I laughed.

Ainsley sighed. "Guess not. I just... I hate his friends. They all think they're better and smarter than me, because I'm homeschooled. They constantly make these comments suggesting how hard it must be for me to socialize with 'normal' people. You know what?"

I raised my brows.

"It is hard for me to socialize with them, because I'm pretty sure most of them sincerely believe that the First Amendment actually means they can say anything they want without consequences. Like no, that does not protect your butt when you say something ignorant on Facebook and end up getting kicked off the football team or whatever!"

My lips twitched.

She threw up her hands, and I hid a smile. "That's not how that works, you know? It is not a free pass. Do you know, one of his friends last week actually argued with me about that? He was all like, *let me wannabe mansplain this to you* while incorrectly explaining the First Amendment. He was trying to tell me that it meant he could say whatever he wanted to say, because it was his opinion and it was protected. Free speech, he yelled. Um, maybe from the government, but not from anything else when it comes down to it. I was like, is he for real?"

At least I wasn't thinking about sex anymore.

"Besides the fact that not all speech is protected in the first place, I'm pretty sure our founding fathers stated it pretty damn clearly." She drew in a sharp breath. "Oh my God, I'm like that insurance commercial. I want to scream, 'This is not how this works! This is not how any of this works!' Look, shout your opinions from the rooftops, but please, dear Lord, stop thinking the First Amendment is going to protect you from losing your job or from getting kicked out of a frat house. Or—or! From other people having a difference in opinion."

Ainsley was entertaining a future in law.

"And yeah, I can speak three languages *fluently*," she continued. "But they want to treat me like I'm some kind of simpleton, just because I'm homeschooled." Her shoulders slumped. "I hate saying this, but I...I don't like them."

"I'm sorry," I said.

She shook her head, and long straight strands of hair flew in the wind. "It's whatever. I'll deal."

Ainsley would. She always did.

After a few moments, she said, "Oh, man, I have such a headache." Lifting her hand, she rubbed her brow, above her left eye. "I don't know if it's stress over tomorrow or sinuses or my eyeballs or what."

My brows furrowed. "Your...eyes have been...bothering you a lot lately."

"Have they?" Her lips pursed. "I guess so. I just have crap eyesight. You know that."

Did I ever. Ainsley probably should wear her glasses more often, since I had no idea how she saw anything without them. I'd tried them on once, and it was like seeing the world through funhouse mirrors. Once I had asked her why she didn't wear them, but she swore that she could see, as she put it, what she needed to see.

Throwing an arm around my shoulders, Ainsley snuggled close, resting her head on my shoulder. "Don't hate me, 'cause I'm about to bring the conversation back to Rider, but it's for purely selfish reasons. I hope you guys end up hanging out a lot and then we can double-date. Not that it'd be a *date*-date, but close enough. Do you know why I want to double-date with you?"

My lips kicked up at the corners.

"Because you're awesome," she said, giggling. "And I could use some extra awesome when it comes to Todd."

Something occurred to me. "Do you...really like Todd?"

Ainsley sighed. "Good question. I don't know. I guess I like him for now, but not for forever."

I could've told Ainsley that *for now* was pretty darn good. That none of us knew what the future held. That forever could be yanked out of reach. Instead, I smiled and tried not to picture all the *dates* she was planning for Rider and me, *dates* that were never going to happen.

I was going to give *for now* a try, myself.

CHAPTER 12

I white-knuckled the drive to school Monday morning, my stomach twisting and churning the entire time. A huge part of me didn't even want to show up, because what was the point? The deal Carl had made with Mr. Santos meant I wasn't really pushing myself.

But I had to go to class. Even if I would only be giving my speeches in front of one person, I had to show my face. If I didn't, I would be that same girl who could barely look at herself in the mirror, let alone hold a conversation with anyone.

I thought of Ainsley, of how hard it still was to talk in person to even my closest friend. I loathed that I took shyness to a whole new, crippling level. *Shyness* wasn't even the right word, according to Dr. Taft. But it was still what people had always labeled me.

Mallory was just shy.

Mallory needed to come out of her shell.

If I really was in a shell, it was titanium-laced and wrecking ball–proof.

When I turned the corner leading to my locker, my step stumbled as I saw Paige leaning against it.

Oh no.

I had a feeling that her waiting for me wasn't the same thing as Jayden waiting for me.

Instinct flared to life, demanding that I turn around and go to class. I didn't have my morning books, but I could stop by afterward, maybe, and grab them. Or maybe this wasn't going to end badly. I wanted it not to. I wanted things to be okay between Paige and me. She was important to Rider.

Paige turned her head, spying me. Too late to run. Or not. I could still run. Her red lips curved into a smirk. "Hey, *Mouse.*" Rider's nickname dripped with derision as she pushed off the locker, remaining a few feet in front of it. "I'm kind of surprised you're here after your little incident in class on Friday."

My steps slowed like I was walking through cement. My initial suspicion was correct. This was not going to end well.

She folded her arms as she eyed me, oblivious to the students stopping around us, watching. Maybe she wasn't oblivious. Maybe she knew she was drawing the attention of others. My mouth dried.

"I'm not going to even ask why you freaked out," she said, raising a honey-colored eyebrow. "I know why. Poor little Mouse doesn't like to talk."

Someone, a girl, laughed. There was a chuckle from a guy. My stomach kept dropping. I could feel my throat closing up.

Run, that tiny voice in the back of my head screamed. *Run away.*

My jaw clamped down with such force a sharp bite of pain lanced across my cheek. Heart pounding like a steel drum, I started to walk around her. Maybe she'd let me get to my locker. If she just wanted to say crap to me, whatever. I'd been on the receiving end of worse. I edged past her and started toward my locker from behind. She couldn't say anything I hadn't heard before.

"I know what you're up to," she said, turning to follow me. "You're after Rider. And that's pathetic. Really pathetic."

I flinched as I reached for my locker. I was not after Rider. Not the way she meant. If she would just leave me alone, she would eventually see that.

Couldn't she just go away? Was that seriously too much to ask?

Paige wasn't going anywhere.

Her cool fingers wrapped around my forearm, her grip firm but not painful. My chin jerked up and our eyes met. She lowered her head. "The last thing Rider needs right now is your shit. What? You think I don't know about you and him? You think I don't know that to Rider you're still the poor little mouse he needs to protect?"

My fingers curled around empty air as the muscles along my back tensed.

The cruel twist of her lips faded and then she was no longer staring at me like I was barely worth the air she was breathing. Her gaze was steady and serious. "He spoke about you—about this girl who never talked and how bad he felt for her. He talked about you a lot." She exhaled roughly. "He talked about you more than he did about himself in the beginning—when he came to stay with Hector. He told me what happened."

My stomach hollowed as I stared at her. Distaste dripped from her tone. My chest grew tight. I'd told Ainsley a lot about my past, but Ainsley would never use that knowledge against me. But this girl could. She could tell everyone. How could Rider tell her these things about me? A ripe sense of betrayal rose, clogging already scattered thoughts. I didn't know this girl and she knew things about me that had taken me months to share with Ainsley.

"I'm not trying to be a bitch," she said, and I thought she was doing a good imitation for someone who wasn't trying. "But

Rider has been living with a guilt trip since I've known him, and it wasn't until this past year that he seems to have moved on. And now you're back. That kind of crap is the last thing he needs right now."

Guilt trip? I blinked slowly as the empty sensation spread across my chest. Numbness followed as what Paige was saying began to really sink in. Rider had shared heavy stuff with her. Unspeakable things about both of us, and he felt guilty—he felt bad for what had happened to me. His pity cloaked me in a stickiness that couldn't be washed off.

Her eyes narrowed and then she shook her head, letting go of my arm. In that moment I realized we had an audience. I didn't think they could hear us, but they were definitely watching. In a rare moment, I was too startled to feel humiliation.

"God, you're so stupid," Paige bit out. "You're looking at me like you have no idea what I'm talking about. Why else do you—"

The words erupted from me, bursting through the seal that had plugged the top of my throat. "I'm not stupid."

Paige's jaw gaped. A moment passed, and the sound of the students around us faded away. "Did you just speak to me?"

A voice intruded. "Don't be a *cabrona*. I know it's hard and it's like all you have in this world, but Jesus, knock it off."

My gaze darted to where Jayden stood. I dragged in a deep breath, welcoming the earthy scent that seemed to always cling to the younger boy.

Paige's cheeks flushed pink as she turned to Jayden. "What did you just call me?"

He tilted his head, eyeing her. "You know what I said. And you know it's true, unless you're the *estúpido* one."

Her eyes narrowed, but Jayden edged her out of the way, allowing me to gain full access to my locker. Without looking at the small crowd that had gathered around us, I tugged open the door and quickly switched out my books, barely aware of what

I was doing. My head was thousands of hours in the past, and when I turned around, Paige was gone and Jayden was standing with his signature sleepy smile on his face.

"Walk you to class, *muñeca*?"

I'd heard *muñeca* used before. Carl called Rosa that every once in a while, and she smiled when she heard it. Hands shaking, I nodded as I hefted the strap of my bag.

"My locker is actually down the hall," he added. "I have a reason to be in this hallway. Paige doesn't."

The twisting motion in my stomach increased since that meant Paige was seeking me out.

Jayden fell in step next to me, and I kept my chin down, eyes on the floor as we navigated the congested hall. I wondered if this would mean he'd be late to homeroom, but doubted he cared.

"Can I ask you something?"

I nodded again.

He scrubbed a hand over the close-cropped curls. "Why don't you talk? I mean, you can. I've heard you. So why not talk, like, you know, all the time?"

Don't make a sound.

Those four words echoed in my thoughts as I struggled now to get my tongue to work. Would "conditioning" make sense if I gave Jayden that explanation, or would he think I was weird? Probably weird. Dr. Taft had explained to Rosa and Carl that my lack of…speaking came from PTSD and that I had been conditioned to be as quiet as possible. I'd done research on the whole conditioning thing and learned all about Pavlov's dog. At least I didn't drool when a bell was rung. I'd just been trained through negative reinforcement to not make a sound, to not be seen or heard.

"You know, it's all right. No worries. Like I said the other day, I'll do the talking. It's kind of like my thing. You know what they say about me, *muñeca*? That I can sell ice to an Eskimo.

I'm just that cool and charmin'." With his grin, I couldn't tell if he was being serious or not. "I think that's what I'll do once I get out of this damn place. Go into sales. I'd rock that shit." He paused. "Unlike Paige. If she was tryin' to sell somethin', she'd just piss that person off."

I drew in a shaky breath. "How can...Rider like her?"

He stopped and looked up at me. "Paige?"

"I'm sorry," I immediately said, thinking of how Rider explained that Paige had known Hector and Jayden since they were young. "She's your friend and..."

"Yeah, she's my friend, but she ain't actin' right with you, so you don't need to apologize. She's not like that with Rider. And I doubt she'd act that way when he's around. She wouldn't pull any crap with him."

Jayden pulled out a phone from his pocket—a new, shiny and large cell phone. He hit the screen, quickly scanning a text message. His brows knitted. "Anyway, just ignore Paige. You probably already..."

Jayden trailed off, and when I looked up, we were near my homeroom class, but that wasn't what he was staring at. Up ahead, a really big dude was coming down the hall. Had to be a senior—a senior that might've repeated the final grade a year or three. He was staring at Jayden in the way that other guy was eyeballing him the first time I'd seen Jayden.

"Mierda," Jayden muttered, and then started backing up. He glanced at me. "Check you later, *muñeca.*"

There was no chance to respond. He wheeled around and started power-walking down the hall, hitching up the back of his pants with one hand.

"Yo! Jayden," the older boy shouted, picking up his pace. "Where you going, bro?"

Glancing back, I saw Jayden round the corner, and when I looked up, his older brother appeared out of freaking nowhere, coming up behind the guy. Hector's jaw was clenched as he clapped a hand down on the guy's shoulder.

"What's going on, Braden?" Hector demanded.

Braden wheeled around, shrugging Hector's hand off his shoulder. Anger colored his tone. "You know exactly what is going on. Jerome is pissed, because of your stupid brother, and that shit rolls down. It ain't gonna roll on me. He needs to get right—"

I ducked into my class just as my homeroom teacher ambled out into the hall, calling both of the boys' names. I worried my lower lip as I hurried to the open seat in the back. Nearly every time I saw Jayden, trouble hovered. That couldn't be good.

Then it hit me with the power of a speeding truck as I took my seat and the tardy bell rang, and thoughts of Jayden floated away. I realized I'd done something I'd never, ever done before.

I stood up to Paige.

It had only been three words.

But I'd done it. I'd stood up for myself.

CHAPTER 13

My sense of accomplishment was strong, a bright spot in the day that glowed throughout lunch and into my afternoon classes. I sat with Keira again. I also didn't talk, but no one seemed to be bothered by the lack of communication on my part.

Standing up to Paige was huge. Like climbing-Mount-Everest-and-not-dying level of huge. It had been Jayden who'd intervened twice now, but this time, it had been me. Might not have been much, but it had been all me.

Only when I was heading out of my next-to-last class did my stomach start doing somersaults again. Speech was next. The morning and my small victory felt like forever ago. Not only was I going to have to show my face again, but I was also going to have to see Paige once more.

Gathering up my textbook, I shoved it into my bag and stood. If I'd thought walking this morning had been like pushing through wet cement, this was like trudging through quicksand laced *with* cement.

But as I looked across the hall, my heart skipped in my chest. Wrong reaction, so wrong, but there was no stopping it.

Rider was waiting outside the classroom, leaning against the lockers across from the class, hands shoved in the pockets of the worn jeans with frayed edges.

There was an odd hitch in my throat, and my stomach cartwheeled for a whole different reason than it had before. Warmth zinged through my veins as he lifted his lashes and those soft gold-brown eyes collided with mine.

Rider looked... Goodness, he looked *good*.

Good in the way I didn't know a teenage boy could look. Like they did on TV, when played by twenty-five-year-olds.

His brownish-black hair was messy, as if he'd woken up, washed it and then let it dry whichever way it fell. Bright yellow light glanced off his high cheekbones. The full lips were slightly tipped up in one corner, the dimple in his right cheek absent. Stretched across his broad shoulders, the emblem on his blue shirt was so faded I couldn't make out what it was.

As he straightened, he lifted a hand and brushed the hair off his forehead. The new cut above his brow was faded, barely noticeable. That made me happy. I walked up to him, trying to keep a goofy smile off my lips.

"Hey, Mouse," he said, and the way he said *Mouse* was so different from how Paige hurled the nickname. It was soft and deep and infinite. "What's the plan?"

It hit me then, as I shuffled out of the way of the sea of students, that he was outside my class waiting because he knew what was coming next for me. He wanted to know the plan. Was I going or bailing, and deep down, I knew he would be right beside me no matter what I picked.

My insides turned gooey, and I told myself that anyone would feel this way, but a wisp of guilt curled around the warmth. My insides were not allowed to turn gooey for Rider. He was a goo-free zone.

A second thing occurred to me. Paige had said that Rider had always protected me and that I was somehow influencing him to do the same again. She believed I was after Rider. I hadn't knowingly done anything, but she was right in a way. Rider had taken up for me when I left the class, followed me out, and he was here now, willing to do whatever I needed him to do.

He was still protecting me.

And that made me pathetic.

"You in or out?" he asked, glancing up as someone lightly bumped my shoulder. His eyes narrowed.

I cleared my throat. The urge to run was there, because it would be the easiest thing to do, but it was short-term. I knew that, and if I didn't go back to class, I would never forgive myself. Squaring my shoulders, I nodded. "I'm in."

His expression was impassive with the exception of the corner of his lips tipping up more. The dimple made an appearance, blessing the hallway. "Let's do this, then."

"Wait." I grabbed his arm.

Astonishment scuttled over his face. He wasn't used to me grabbing him. I opened my mouth, prepared to ask him about what he had told Paige. I wanted to know what he told her. I wanted to know if pity was what drove his actions. I started to speak, but people crowded us. We weren't alone, and this seemed like a private conversation. One that really couldn't be carried out in the minute or so between classes.

"Mouse?"

I forced a smile as I dropped his arm. He lifted his hand, rubbing it along his jaw.

Blue smudges on his fingers this time.

"Did you... Did you paint more?" I asked, touching on safe ground.

He shifted his ratty notebook to his other hand. "Kind of."

I waited for more of a detailed response as we headed down the staircase. Rider walked beside me, taking up most of the space. Students had to squeeze past him, turning sideways, but he didn't seem to notice.

Or care.

He didn't elaborate, so as I ran my hand down the cool metal railing, I got my tongue working. "What does...*kind of* mean?"

We rounded the landing. "I work in the evenings. Sometimes."

Surprise flickered through my system. "You work?"

"After school, a couple of times a week." He glanced at me and then let out a low laugh. "You look like I just told you I'm thinking about joining a crab-fishing boat."

I blinked as we went down the final steps. "I just didn't... know. Where do you work?"

"Not too far from where I'm staying," he explained.

"Staying?" I repeated, thinking that was an odd way of referring to where he was living with Hector and Jayden's grandmother.

He nodded. "At a body garage down the street from Mrs. Luna's house. I do some detailing for the owner. Custom paint jobs, that kind of thing."

"Wow," I murmured, remembering him mentioning a garage to Paige on Friday. He pushed open the door, holding it as I passed through, under his arm. "That's pretty amazing. I mean, they must really...trust you to do that."

Rider shrugged one shoulder like it wasn't a big deal, but a slight flush crawled across his cheeks. I didn't know a lot about custom paint jobs on cars, but I knew that had to be hard work with little room for error. The fact that someone trusted a teenager with that was astonishing, and I wanted to ask how he got the job, but before I knew it, we were walking into class.

He stayed by my side, and as I headed for the back of the class, Keira raised her hand and wiggled her fingers. I returned the gesture. During lunch, Keira and Jo had spent the bulk of the period talking about a new routine they were learning, much to Anna's dismay.

I took my seat and immediately opened my textbook. The

words were blurring when Hector dropped into the seat in front of Rider and asked, "How you feeling, *bebita*?"

At first, I didn't get why he was asking and I thought about him chasing down the guy called Braden, but then I recalled the mad dash out of class Friday and Rider's excuse. I nodded and then glanced over at Rider. He was leaning back in his chair with his arms crossed over his chest, and legs stretched out under the desk, his heavy-lidded gaze centered in my direction.

The dryness in my throat increased, the response twofold. I wanted to ask a question, but the way Rider was staring at me made me hyper self-aware. Keeping my focus on him, I got my mouth moving. "What does...*bebita* mean?"

Rider blinked and his lips slowly parted. Surprise splashed across his face. Yeah, I'd spoken in front of Hector. I felt sort of giddy. Might've only been a handful of words, but it was the first time I spoke to him. It was the first time I'd spoken to anyone in front of Rider since we crossed paths again. He'd never been around when Jayden had.

Biting down on my lip to stop from grinning, I dared a peek at Hector.

His light green eyes were wide, then he smiled broadly. "Means, uh, baby girl."

"Oh," I whispered, feeling my cheeks heat. That was kind of nice.

"It also means something he doesn't need to be calling you," Rider added, and my gaze darted back to him.

Hector chuckled, and when I glanced at him, he was grinning. One arm was flung over the back of his seat. "My bad," he murmured, but nothing about the way he looked suggested he felt any guilt.

My lips twitched into a small grin.

Rider cocked his head to the side. "Uh-huh."

I saw Paige enter the class just then, her long legs eating up the distance. She smiled at Hector as she rounded her desk. Paige didn't sit immediately. She placed a hand on Rider's shoulder and bent down, her face heading for his.

"Hey, babe," she said.

I cut my focus to the front of the classroom. I didn't need to see them kiss to know that they did. I still didn't look when I heard a chair scratch across the floor, signaling that she was seated. A weird, burning sensation lit up my insides. It tasted bitter in the back of my mouth.

Hector was watching me.

I smiled.

The side of his lips kicked up.

A few seconds later Mr. Santos kicked off class with a clap of his hands. I tensed, my gaze swinging to the front of the classroom. Part of me expected him to make eye contact with me, nod or something that showed he was on board for Carl's plan.

But he didn't.

Santos cracked open his manual and passed in front of the chalkboard, going over our first speech, which we were to present in three weeks. An informative speech. The length would be three minutes. My stomach dropped to the scuffed floor. Three minutes? The first speech would be three minutes long? That was *forever*. Even though I only had to give mine in front of Mr. Santos, my heart started slamming against my ribs, but I slowed my thoughts down. I had three weeks to freak out, so I needed to chill out and I needed to pay attention right now.

I managed to get my head under control so I could hastily scribble down notes. Whenever I glanced over at Rider, he looked half-asleep. Definitely not taking notes. Paige was actually jotting things down. Hector was, well, he was looking at the cell phone he had perched on his thigh. I thought I saw exploding candies on the screen at one point.

When the bell rang, signaling the end of class, I wanted to jump and thrust my fist into the air, *Breakfast Club* style. I managed not to do that, thank God, and instead sedately packed up my stuff.

By the time I stood, Hector was already out of the class. Keira was in the front of the room, talking to Mr. Santos. Rider was wrapping his long fingers over the ridge of his notebook, waiting.

For me.

As I swung the strap over my shoulder, the flip-flop feeling hit my tummy again, and then I realized Paige was also waiting.

For Rider.

"Hey." Paige stepped over, curling her hand around his free one. She leaned into him.

Just like I'd done earlier, I smiled and then hightailed my butt out of there before anyone could say anything. Or at least I tried to.

"Mallory." Mr. Santos was by the door. "Can we speak for a moment?"

Tension seeped into my shoulders as I followed him over to the podium. I watched him close a notebook.

"I won't keep you long. I'm sure you're ready to get out of here," he said. The dark skin crinkled around his eyes as he smiled. "I just wanted to let you know that I'm a hundred percent behind you delivering your speeches to me."

This was the time to speak up, to tell him that I wanted to give my speech like everyone else. I said nothing.

Mr. Santos kept talking. "I wanted you to also know that I understand. Public speaking is hard for anyone and for some, it's nearly impossible. I'm not going to force any of my students to get up and do something that would potentially be detrimental to them."

That was actually…kind of him.

But I could tell Mr. Santos that I could give the speech, that it wouldn't damage me. I could find the courage and strength inside myself to do it.

I still said nothing.

"Okay?" he said.

I nodded.

Mr. Santos's smile spread and then he nodded. "Have a good night, Mallory."

Pivoting, I walked out of the classroom and before I could process my conversation with Mr. Santos, I saw Rider sans his girlfriend.

I looked around. "Where's…Paige?"

"She headed out. Couldn't wait with me," he said, as if it was something totally cool with her, leaving him to wait for me.

My mouth opened and I started to tell him about what happened this morning, but I snapped my lips shut.

"You've got to go to your locker?" he asked. Thinking about what homework I had, I shook my head. He jerked his chin toward the end of the hall. "Walk you to your car?"

And that was what he did.

We filed out among the thinning stream of students heading outside, their excited voices surrounding us. It wasn't until I saw the roof of my car glistening in the afternoon sunlight that Rider spoke. "I'm glad today was uneventful."

There was no stopping my smile. It spread from ear to ear. "Me…me, too." Lifting my chin, I sucked in a soft breath. Rider stared down at me, a lopsided grin tilting his lips. In a split second, I was thrown back a decade.

I'd been smaller, perched on the edge of a lumpy, narrow mattress. My stomach had been empty, twisting and churning from the hunger pains. In the middle of summer without any air-conditioning, my hair had clung to my cheeks, and sweat pooled in areas it shouldn't have when you were sitting still.

Rider had been gone all day.

Miss Becky, during one of her rare moments of sobriety, had taken Rider to the mall with her—the nice, air-conditioned mall. Rider had been Miss Becky's favorite. I remembered crying, because I'd wanted to go, but she had scolded me, telling me to stop acting like a baby. I'd stayed in the airless room all day, because Mr. Henry had also been home, and I hadn't wanted to draw his attention. It was when Rider came home that night that he'd brought the doll with him.

"I felt bad," he'd said, handing it over. He'd worn the same grin then as he did now, an odd and charming mixture of uncertainty and confidence.

What Paige had said earlier resurfaced with a vengeance.

I felt bad.

She had said that Rider had been on a guilt trip for the last four years, and now I could totally see that so clearly. It made sense. Rider had suffered in that home, but in some ways, he had been treated better than me. His guilt spurred the crazy and sometimes fatalistic need to put himself in front of Mr. Henry's fists and me. My reappearance in his life had caused him to immediately step, once again, into the role of the protector. I felt... Suddenly, I felt gross. Like I'd been outside all day when it was muggy. I wanted to go home, strip off my clothes, burn them and then shower for days. The weight of the pity he must have felt for me and the level of guilt he'd carried was suffocating. Stupid tears burned the back of my throat.

God, this was humiliating.

I stepped back, tightening my grip on the strap of my book bag. Now was the time to have this conversation. "Do you feel guilty?"

Rider blinked. "What?"

"Have you been...on a guilt trip, because of...because of me?" I asked, forcing the words out even though it sort of hurt to do so.

His mouth moved for a moment, forming words that weren't spoken, and then he stiffened as if someone dropped steel down his spine. "Why are you asking that?"

"Why won't you answer it?" I returned.

"I don't even know what kind of question that is, Mouse. Or why you would even think that."

My brows rose. "You...really don't?"

A moment passed and his hand tightened around his notebook. He didn't answer, and I drew in a deep breath. "You... you told Paige about me."

"Jesus." Looking sideways, he hung his head. A muscle thrummed along his jaw. "Did she say this stuff to you, Mouse? For real?"

I raised a shoulder. One he didn't see, because he wasn't looking at me. He was watching a bright yellow Volkswagen Bug back out of a nearby parking spot. "No," I lied. "Not really, but it... It got me thinking about things."

"When? I haven't seen you two talk at all."

"I ran into her this morning." Which was sort of true and better-sounding than saying that she was lying in wait for me.

"Mouse..."

I waited.

"I told her some of the stuff about what went down. Looking back, I probably shouldn't have done that. Shit. I never expected you to come back or that there'd even be a chance that she would talk to you."

I wasn't sure how to feel about that since I didn't ever expect to see him again, either, but the sense of betrayal was still there, brimming low in my stomach. Even in that moment I realized it was irrational. Talking to Paige didn't make Rider disloyal to me, because there was nothing to be loyal to, but that didn't change the festering hurt.

"I didn't tell her everything."

I sucked in a sharp breath. "She knew...I didn't talk a lot."

"That wasn't me. I never told her that." He turned harder eyes on me. "Last Tuesday she was over at Hector's place and he was asking about you. I was talking to him, letting him know that you were quiet and not very talkative. She must've overheard me, because I never told her that directly." There was a pause. "Did Paige say I did?"

Although it wasn't true, I shook my head.

His shoulders rose with a deep breath and then he used his fingers to brush a strand of hair that had fallen loose throughout the day back behind my ear. A sweet tingle radiated across my cheek and then spread down my spine as he clasped his hand around the nape of my neck.

I didn't know what to say as we stared at each other. Conflicted, I was sure that even if I didn't have a problem using my voice, I'd still have no idea what to say in this situation.

Rider held my gaze for a moment and then, using his hand along the back of my neck, he guided me toward him. His other arm swept around my back as he pulled me in for a tight hug that was warm and solid.

He stepped back, his hand lingering. "Talk later?"

I smiled and nodded, but even though his touch had been nice and the hug even better, I couldn't help but notice that Rider hadn't answered my question.

CHAPTER 14

The second week of school was pretty much like the first one.

Well, kind of. I didn't flee any classes. Score. Rider had texted me Monday night. Just a small text that said good-night and he'd called me *Mouse*. Unlike the last time, I managed not to be an utter dork and responded with my very own good-night. After Monday, Paige didn't make any surprise visits at my locker. Score number two. Talking back to her Monday seemed to have done the trick. Score number three. She pretty much ignored me in speech class while busying herself with flirting with Rider. Monday through Thursday I'd eaten lunch at Keira's table, and yesterday I'd actually managed to respond to a question asked of me. Not one but two! That was a score implosion.

It had come from Anna, who had held up her broken wrist and asked, "Have you ever broken a bone, Mallory?"

The spaghetti I'd been chasing around my plate had settled in my stomach as if each noodle was weighed down with lead. I'd gotten out a hoarse, "Yes."

"Which one?" Keira asked, her dark eyes sharp.

The next two words were a little easier. "My nose."

Luckily, no one asked how, probably because Jo's boyfriend told us how his younger brother had broken his nose with a wiffle bat and ball, and I figured that took some talent. What I'd said during Thursday's lunch wasn't much, an accumulation of three words, but it was three words spoken in front of an entire tableful of people. As corny as it was, I was so…well, proud of myself that I told Carl and Rosa the moment I saw them late that night, after they got home from work.

They were proud, too.

And relieved.

There was no mistaking the quick, wordless exchange between them. I tried to not let it bother me. It wasn't like they didn't believe I could handle high school, but I knew they worried. I knew they were concerned that it would be too much, but I was doing it and I'd lasted longer than I had in middle school.

On Friday, Rider was hanging out by the entrance to the cafeteria, hands shoved in his pockets. Apparently, he'd decided to skip class again, and while I shouldn't promote that behavior, I was happy to see him there. We didn't get to chat much before speech or after, and he hadn't made any impromptu visits. We went through the lunch line, and he grabbed what he had the first time—pizza and milk.

"Do you want to sit in here or outside?" I asked.

Rider's lips curved up at the corner as he glanced over at Keira's table. "Wherever you want. The world is your oyster."

I grinned at that. I felt like if we went to the table, we wouldn't have a chance to really talk. Plus, it had cooled down, as if summer had decided to make an early and hasty exit well before it was over. "Outside?"

No one stopped us as we headed out to the old picnic tables. Several of them were occupied, but we found an empty one. Rider sat beside me. Not across from me like some of the other students were sitting. He was close, his thigh nearly touching mine. I…I liked that.

It made me super aware of him as he sat my tray in front of me. I caught each breath he took as he peeled open the milk carton and placed it on my tray, and I felt every shift on the bench as he rested his left elbow on the table.

I took a drink of my milk. "Do you get in trouble for skipping this class?"

He shrugged, causing his arm to brush against mine. I liked that, too, but I didn't like the noncommittal answer. "Rider?"

Picking up his slice of pizza, he glanced over at me. "It doesn't matter."

I frowned. "Why not?"

He took a bite and once he'd chewed, he said, "I'll pass the class in the end. So it doesn't matter."

Rider was smart. Even Keira had recognized that about him. As a kid, he picked up things faster than anyone else, but going to class did matter. I knew I sounded like a dork thinking that, but how did he not get in trouble? So I asked as I peeled off a piece of pepperoni.

He didn't answer immediately. "Honestly? They don't care."

"Who?" I went to drop the slice of pepperoni on his plate, but he snagged it and popped it in his mouth. "The teachers?"

"Yep. I think what they expect from me is the bare minimum." Taking a drink from his bottle of water, he grinned at me. "Like, showing up to class is enough."

I shook my head slowly. "I don't think that's true."

"The school doesn't even call Mrs. Luna anymore. Stopped that back when…hell, when they realized I was a foster kid." He snorted, and I couldn't believe it. "Same with Paige and she's not even in the system. It's just because of where she lives. Hell, same with a lot of others. They see an address and they check out."

Confused, I shook my head. "Your address?"

He shook his head. "Your address is the type that impresses them. Half this damn school? Hell no." Stopping, he glanced at my plate. "You eating?"

I rolled my eyes. "I'm not a child. I can...eat on my own."

Rider raised a brow and there was no mistaking the slow slide that started at the top of my head and traveled downward. My cheeks pinked. "Trust me," he said, his voice gruffer. Deeper. "I know that. Trying to wrap my head around it, but I know that."

I gaped. Now I had no idea what to say.

He eyed my pizza.

Okay, then. I picked it up and took a bite. Better than sitting there staring at him like a fool.

"Anyway, I'm not in trouble," he said, picking up a napkin and wiping his fingers off.

I thought about that as I took another bite and then dropped the pizza on the plate once more. "You don't get in trouble, because they..." I peeled off another pepperoni and handed it over. His fingers brushed mine this time, warming my skin. "They don't expect anything from you? Is that what you're saying?"

Rider lifted a shoulder again, not responding.

Holy crap, that was what he was saying. Unsettled, I glanced at my half-eaten pizza. "Is that true?"

He glanced at me and his lashes lowered, shielding his eyes. "I think it's kind of...kind of good that you even have to ask that."

I folded my hands in my lap. "What do...you mean?"

Finishing off his pizza, he twisted at the waist and faced me. I straightened, but there was little room between us. As close as we were, I could see the golden flecks in his eyes when his lashes lifted. A small grin was on his lips, but it seemed lacking. "You're in a good place," he said. "Have been the last four years. You were taken in by great people. Doctors. You're not living that other kind of life anymore."

"But...but you said Mrs. Luna was good?" Worry rose. Had he lied?

He reached into the small space between us and tapped his forefinger off my hand. There were no paint smudges on it today. "She is. She's great, but...look, it doesn't matter." His finger traced the line of the bone, skating across my palm, toward my wrist. "I'm not in trouble. I'm not going to get into trouble."

It did matter, though, because it made me think the school didn't think Rider was worth the trouble. Or worse yet, he didn't think that he was. And he was. I started to tell him just that, but he turned over my hand and threaded his fingers through mine. My thoughts briefly scattered.

Rider was holding my hand.

He'd done that a lot when we were little, but it felt so very different now. So much so that I couldn't help but stare at his hand, at how much larger it was than mine, rougher and harder.

You're not living that other kind of life anymore.

But he was, even though I had a feeling he didn't have to.

Knowing that I should pull my hand away, I mentally lectured myself when I didn't. His holding my hand seemed innocent, but I doubted that Paige would see it that way. Wouldn't blame her if she didn't.

Rider squeezed my hand. "What do you think about the speech we've got to do?" he asked, changing the subject. "Your topic is the three branches of the government, right?"

I nodded. I'd told him about the deal Carl had made with Santos, and he had thought it was a great idea. Everyone probably thought it was a great idea, because no one thought I could do it anyway.

Santos wouldn't let us pick our own topics for our first speech, which wasn't surprising. Rider got different art styles in painting. I stared at our joined hands. "The topic...should be easy."

"It will be." He let go of my hand, his fingers trailing across my palm and leaving behind a wake of shivers. "You got this."

Seeing that I had two weeks to prepare for the speech, plus a few days until I had to give mine, since I didn't have to give it in front of the class, I thought I had this handled, too.

"You wanna practice?" he asked, picking up his water.

"Seriously?" I asked. I was planning to ask Ainsley to help me, because even giving my speech in front of Santos alone would be super difficult for me. Just thinking about it right now had my stomach churning. There had been no way I could ask Keira. I would be way too embarrassed.

Rider nodded. "Yeah. Whenever you want to get together, we can."

My heart flip-flopped. "What about work?"

"It's flexible." He glanced at the plate, and I knew what he was going to say before he asked it.

"Yes," I intervened. "I'm going to finish that."

A grin appeared and the dimple winked. "That's my girl."

My breath caught, and I felt silly, but it did. I finished my slice of pizza and then downed my milk. "Will...Paige practice with us?" I asked, thinking it was a smart question considering she had to practice, too.

He nudged me with my arm, and I almost dropped the milk. "Yeah, I don't think so."

I looked at him sharply. "Why?"

Rider shrugged.

"I haven't talked...to her," I said slowly, unsure of what to say since I hadn't told Rider everything Paige had said.

"I know," he replied.

"You..." Then it dawned on me. My eyes narrowed. Disbelief and irritation flooded me. "You...you said something to her."

Rider raised his brows.

"I... You can't do that," I said, leaning back as a soft breeze caught a strand of my hair and tossed it across my face. Rider's eyes met mine. I'd stood up to her when she called me stupid, and I'd believed that was why she hadn't bothered me since. I'd been wrong. "What did you say to her?"

His eyes searched mine. "I just told her that you are impor-tant to me and since I never thought I'd have you back in my life, I didn't want anything or anyone messing with that. She understands."

"Understands what?" I whispered.

Rider's gaze held mine again. "She understands that if I have to pick between you two, it's not going to be her."

A flutter started deep in my stomach and spread into my chest, because, well, that was sort of, really sweet and nice and a little crazy, but still, I didn't want him doing this—fighting my battles. And I didn't want him having to pick between us. "That... I don't even know what to say. You shouldn't have to pick between us and I...don't need you sticking up for me anymore."

"Really?" he murmured.

"Yes!" I all but yelled, earning a glance from the nearby table. I was surprised that I even raised my voice, but I was mad. Really mad. Here I was thinking that I, all by myself, had driven Paige off, and it hadn't been me. "I don't need...someone's protection," I said in a much lower voice.

He smiled, wide and bright, but I didn't care.

I punched him on the arm. "It's not something to smile about." I cocked my arm back and went to punch his arm again, when he caught my hand.

"Mouse!" Rider laughed deeply. "Did you just hit me?"

I ignored the question. "I don't need you...standing up for me. I need..." I trailed off, because he'd drawn my closed hand to his chest. I could feel his heart beating strongly under my hand.

His eyes took on a hooded quality. "You need what, Mallory?"

Talking was hard for a whole different reason. "I need...I need to handle things by myself."

Rider's brows knitted as he stared at me like I spoke an unfamiliar language. "Why?"

"Why?" I sputtered. "Because I need to do that for myself. You can't...step in every time you think something happens. You can't always...protect me."

"But I want to," he said, his voice low again. Smooth.

My heart was jumping around in my chest. "You can't."

One side of his lips curled up. He kept my hand against his chest. "It's kind of an old habit to break."

Those lashes lifted again and his stare pierced me. "You... you need to try."

"Okay." He lowered our hands to his knee. With his other hand, he brushed back a strand of my hair, tucking it behind my ear. "I can try."

I didn't know what to say as we stared at each other and I had no idea what anyone must think if they were looking at us. I was still irked at him. Not that I didn't appreciate his concern, but I wasn't a damsel he needed to rush in and save.

Or I was trying not to be.

Because the Mallory I wanted to be wasn't weak or pathetic. She wasn't the kind of girl Paige's *boyfriend* needed to stand up for.

I drew in a shallow breath. "If I need your help, I...I'll ask for it. Okay?"

He tilted his head to the side, and good Lord, it lined up our...mouths almost perfectly. "Okay."

"Good," I whispered.

Rider slowly lowered his hand, but he still held mine in his other for a few seconds longer. His eyes didn't leave mine even as he let go. "You're different now, Mallory."

I straightened. "I am."

"Good," he whispered.

CHAPTER 15

Paige prowled the hallway like it was her own personal runway. Confidence bled from every step. Envy surfaced. I'd never had that kind of self-assurance, didn't even know what it felt like on my skin. Her hair was pulled up in a tight ponytail, and she was with a dark-skinned girl I hadn't seen before.

Gripping the strap of my bag, I walked forward, keeping my eye on her. Part of me wanted to dart to the left and edge close to the lockers, but so many of the doors were slamming shut. It would be too crowded.

And it would make me a coward.

I couldn't do that, especially after I'd told Rider on Friday that I didn't need him sticking up for me. Now it was Monday, and time to prove I meant what I said.

My heart went from tap-dancing to doing leaps straight out of Riverdance as I walked past her. Paige didn't say anything, but she lifted a pale, slender arm and extended a middle finger.

Right in my direction.

The girl with her laughed.

And then from somewhere on my other side, I heard it—a word I loathed with every fiber of my being.

"What a retard."

A burn splashed across my cheeks. I knew the girl wasn't talking about Paige, but I didn't blink an eye. I didn't look in her direction, and I didn't give anyone the satisfaction of my attention. I kept walking, my chin tipped up, and went to my locker.

Blindly, I grabbed my books and hoped they were the right ones. The last thing I wanted to do was come between Paige and Rider, but if the middle finger was any indication, I already had. And whatever he'd said to her had *not* made her happy.

But that wasn't even what got to me.

That word, that horrible word, had burned a fist-sized hole through me by the time I joined Keira at her lunch table. In the group home and in middle school, I'd heard that word a lot. So much that it felt like a label had been stapled on my forehead, and maybe a part of me started to believe in it. Maybe that was why I didn't talk. Even then I knew that wasn't the right or kind word to use. It had been the first thing I'd ever said to Dr. Taft. I'd asked him if it were true, while Carl sat in on the session with me.

Later that night Carl and Rosa had sat me down and told me that it wasn't true, but even if I had developmental challenges, it wouldn't matter. I was still me. And they still loved me.

It had been years since someone had called me that.

Obviously, someone had been saying things. Why else would this random girl I barely recognized in the hall say that? I didn't want to think that it was Paige, because she was tied so intricately with Rider, but who else could it be?

Swallowing a sigh, I picked at the Salisbury steak as I watched Anna and Keira check out each other's bracelets. Gold and silver bangles with charms.

Maybe it was what I heard this morning. I had no idea, but

I forced my tongue off the roof of my mouth. "They are so... pretty."

Anna glanced at Jo quickly and then grinned at me, covering her surprise. "They're Alex and Ani bracelets. I have a few at home," she said. "They're the best."

Jo extended her arm and shook her wrist. She had three on. "Vilma got us addicted."

I concentrated on cutting a piece of steak. "Vilma?"

"She graduated last year," Keira explained. "Used to be the captain of the squad. She's actually cheering for WVU now."

Anna nodded as she picked a crinkle fry off my plate. "I swear, she would hand-sell those bracelets."

I inched my plate closer to her, and she snatched up a couple of the fries. The conversation quickly changed, and I started to think about speech class. I couldn't remember what Keira was doing her informative speech on, but I wondered if she planned to practice.

My lips parted and my tongue started to wrap itself around some vowels and syllables, but could I even practice my speech in front of her? It would take forever for me to work up the nerve. Would she think I was weird? Probably. I'd end up having to eat lunch in the library or something. I chickened out before I even got one word out.

Sigh.

I was almost done with what I was hoping wasn't kangaroo meat, when I felt someone drop into the empty seat beside me. I recognized the earthy scent as I glanced up.

Keira grinned. "Hey, Jayden."

"Yo," he said, sitting sideways in the chair with his arm propped on the table. "You beautiful ladies looked lonely. Thought I'd come over and bless you with my presence."

Jo snorted. "Looks like you just woke up and got to school."

"Maybe I did." Jayden went for my fries, ignoring Anna's narrowed gaze. "Thanks, babe."

"You two know each other?" Jo gestured between Jayden and me with her fork.

Before I could nod, he dropped an arm over my shoulders. "She's my bae."

I grinned.

"*Bae?*" Keira sighed. "I hate that word. Do you know what it really means?"

"Poop," I answered without thinking. "In Danish."

My eyes widened. Holy crap. I'd spoken without hesitation at lunch! Holy crap! No one recognized my internal freak-out over it, but I couldn't believe it. I sat there and spoke with no problem.

I needed to give myself a cookie.

Anna giggled. "Oh, man. I know. I know. Still think it's a cute word."

Across from her, Keira rolled her eyes. "It literally means shit."

"Mallory *is* the shit, though," Jayden reasoned as he dropped his arm.

I raised a brow.

"Where's your brother at?" Jo asked. "I'll be his bae."

Jayden snorted. "Why? He's a loser. Me? I'm baby-faced fresh. He's old, crusty news."

Laughing, I brushed my hair over my shoulder as Jo wrinkled her nose. "*Crusty?*" she said. "That's not a word I normally associate with Hector."

"You should."

Jayden went back and forth with the girls for the rest of the lunch period, and he was... He was something else. Hilarious. Oddly charming. In a few years, I bet he was going to be as much a handful as I imagined Hector was. I smiled so much listening to him that I wondered if I'd have premature wrinkles from it.

The smile didn't go away when I ran into Rider in the stairwell as I was making my way to speech. It was the first time I'd seen him today. Wearing another faded shirt and worn jeans, his hair a little disheveled, he looked like he might've slept through his last class.

A lazy grin pulled at his lips. "I was just coming for you."

My smile, unbelievably, kicked up a notch as I joined him on the landing. He wheeled around and walked beside me.

"I was thinking about the whole speech-practice thing," he said. "You still want me to help you with that, right?"

A nervous flutter started deep in my belly. I wanted to practice with Rider, but after what happened this morning, that would not be wise. I took a deep breath. "You don't have to do that. I mean, I'm sure...you have better things to do."

"But I want to help you." He caught the swinging door and held it open as he frowned. "If I didn't, I wouldn't have offered."

I stepped through, forcing the words out. "I know, but..."

"I want to help you practice," he repeated without a moment of hesitation, and that flutter in my stomach spread to my chest as we started down the stairs. "Why wouldn't you want to practice?" He paused. "With me?"

Glancing up at him as we rounded the landing, I saw the confusion in his hazel gaze. I bit the inside of my lip. Dammit. "I just wanted to make sure...you didn't feel like you had to."

He grinned. "I'm free Thursday."

Thursday? This week? My eyes widened. I'd drafted the speech over the weekend, so I could do it, but Thursday was not so far away.

"At least you'll have a practice run in before you have to give your speech to Mr. Santos next week." He nudged my arm with his. "I can come over after school."

Thursday worked out perfectly, because Carl and Rosa were both at the hospital, and the likelihood of either of them stopping by the house was slim. Or I could just ask them if it were okay if Rider came over to help. I found myself nodding.

Class kicked off with us breaking into small groups of fours for practice runs of the speech, and I felt like hurling all over the place. Luckily I was paired up with Hector and Rider. Unluckily, I was also paired with Paige. There wasn't a lot of relief...

Or a lot of practice.

Neither boy had their speech ready. I had a rough draft that I really did not need to read out loud. Paige had a speech, I guess, but she also had her cell phone in one hand, hidden in her lap, and her hand was on Rider's leg. Anytime she looked in my direction, she smiled, which was a vast difference from this morning.

As Hector scribbled down something to practice, I watched Rider and Paige, but mostly Rider, because I...I kind of couldn't help myself.

He'd sucked his lower lip between his teeth as he...*sketched*. No speech-writing going on there. I leaned over. His brows were lowered in concentration. His wrist flicked in varying degrees of motions, creating short strokes with his pen. Within seconds he had an entire strand of flowers drawn, complete with the beginnings of what appeared to be baby's breath.

"You should be working on your speech instead of staring," Rider said, never taking his eyes off his notebook.

Paige's dark eyes flew to me and then narrowed.

Heat exploded across my cheeks.

"And you should actually be working on, I don't know, your speech?" Hector grinned as he gestured to his paper, which appeared to have actual words on it. "And please don't stare at him, Mallory. Because of Paige, his ego is already big enough. He doesn't need any help."

"*Pendejo,*" Rider murmured under his breath.

Hector stretched an arm back and extended his middle finger. "You wish."

I had no idea what was said.

Paige lifted her hand from Rider's leg and jabbed her elbow

onto the table. Her chin plopped into the palm of her hand. "So, Mallory, are you excited about giving your speech next week?"

I stiffened. Assuming that the class had no idea that I didn't have to give my speech like they did, I dreaded them figuring it out.

"Who would be excited about that?" Hector asked.

Paige lifted a slender shoulder as she watched me. "So, are you?"

Beside her, Rider lifted his head. He opened his mouth, and I knew he was either going to say something to distract Paige or he was going to answer the question for me. I couldn't allow that after the conversation we'd had.

I forced my tongue to move. "I won't...be giving my speech... in class." Warmth seeped into my cheeks as I continued to force the words out. "I have to...give mine during lunch."

"What?" She laughed.

Rider stared at me, surprise shining through his gaze.

Tension straightened my shoulders. "I don't...have to do it... like everyone else."

"Really?" Her eyes widened as she glanced between the guys. "That doesn't seem fair."

My heart dropped.

"Who cares if it is?" Hector responded, shrugging. "Doesn't affect me."

Paige leaned back in her chair. "But it's so not cool. The rest of us have to do it and she doesn't? Why?"

"The why doesn't matter," Rider said, his gaze still on me. "And Hector is right about this not affecting him or any of us."

I started to respond.

Slowly, Paige turned her head to him. "And if it were, say, Laura or Leon who didn't have to give their speech, would you think it was okay?"

Rider broke eye contact with me. "Yeah. Because it wouldn't affect me and I wouldn't care."

"But you do care," she shot back, and I wanted to slink under the desk, because there was no way anyone missed her tone.

"Paige," sighed Rider as he shook his head. "Let's not do this."

She leaned to the side and stretched her neck out. "Let's not do what, *Rider*?"

"Oh, man," Hector muttered under his breath.

Mr. Santos was suddenly there, silencing us as he eyed Rider's work. I tensed, expecting him to get upset since Rider wasn't working on his speech.

His absentminded smile didn't fade as he leaned in, eyes squinting behind wire-rimmed glasses. "The detail and the shading are amazing. It's like the strand of flowers is going to just come right off the page."

My jaw might've hit the floor.

Pink spread across Rider's cheeks as he lowered the pen he still held.

"Not surprised, though." Mr. Santos clamped a hand on Rider's shoulder. "Your work has always been on point."

My brows rose. Santos had seen Rider's work before? And why in the heck wasn't he reprimanding him?

Rider said nothing as Santos squeezed his shoulder. "But try working on your speech now and the sketch later? All right?"

"Sure," Rider muttered, dropping his pen onto his desk.

Mr. Santos turned his attention to my paper and he scanned the page. "Interesting," he murmured, and I cringed. His smile didn't falter as he stepped closer to my desk.

I wetted my lower lip nervously and forced the words floating in my head to reach my tongue. "I...I am not...very good at writing speeches." I paused, taking a deep breath. "Or at... giving them."

There! I spoke to Mr. Santos all on my own, without anyone speaking on my behalf. I sat a little straighter.

"Public speaking is much like art. Being good at it is very subjective, Mallory."

Pressing my lips together, I lifted my gaze to him, having no idea where he was going with this.

"But it's all about trying." Santos nodded at my paper, and suddenly I wondered if he was talking about my mad dash out of the classroom the first week of school and the subsequent call with Carl and Rosa. I hadn't tried then. "It's not about getting it right the first time and it's most definitely not about perfection, but if you try, you succeed. Just like you would in art. Or in life, for that matter." He then patted my shoulder. "And by the looks of it, you're trying."

I blinked slowly.

Santos roamed off, back to the front of the class.

"What in the actual hell," murmured Paige.

I looked over at Rider, and his grin was slow, but the dimple in his right cheek appeared. "Deep thoughts," he murmured.

My nod was just as slow. "How…did you not just get in trouble?"

"I'm gifted."

I narrowed my eyes on him. "And how…does he know about your artwork?"

Hector snorted as he looked up from his paper, responding before Rider could. "Because when Rider was a sophomore, he decided to do some exterior decorating on the outside of Lands High."

Rider rolled his eyes.

"He tagged the entrance and got busted the next day, because the dumbass wore the same shirt he'd done the tagging in," Paige jumped in, her lips curled up in a smirk as her gaze met mine. Something in her stare told me she was happy to point out that she knew all about this, and I didn't. "Mr. Santos was probably the only staff member that appreciated it."

My gaze swung back to Rider. His cheeks were a deeper pink again. "I didn't get in too much trouble," he said, not looking at me. "It was a misdemeanor. Had to help clean it off, which sucked."

"A misdemeanor?" I stared at him. "How is that not trouble?"

Hector laughed, turning back to his notebook. "Misdemeanor isn't a charge you catch that you really got to worry about."

I did not understand that at all.

A moment passed and Rider's gaze slid toward me. His grin was sheepish. "Okay. I was in trouble, but no big deal. Santos actually went to bat for me, so I didn't have to actually find a way to pay for the damages. That's why I had to clean it up."

"I bet you don't know that Santos had one of Rider's sketches placed in a gallery in the city, do you?" Hector asked. "That was the part about Santos going to bat for him. Told him he needed to produce something that could be on display. You know, not on the side of a wall."

My mouth dropped open for the second time. "What?"

"*Cállate*, bro." Rider leaned forward, glaring at Hector. "Seriously."

Hector tipped his head back and laughed.

"Where?" I asked.

A sigh rattled out of Paige. "It's not a big deal. It was just graffiti on a canvas."

"That is still a big deal," I stated. No pauses there.

She rolled her eyes.

Rider shook his head as he focused on his sketch. "It doesn't matter."

I thought it did. "That sounds amazing."

Something in my tone drew his gaze to mine, and another long moment passed before he responded. "It's down at City Arts. Or it was. No idea if it's still up."

I wanted to see it if it was, because that was... That was extraordinary.

So much of Rider was the same from before. The kindness,

that unshakable protective instinct. But there was so much I didn't know about this older, newer Rider.

Shaking my head, I looked back at my speech without seeing the words. I thought about what Santos said. It made sense. Life was like doing this speech. It wasn't necessarily about the end result, but more about trying.

I could...I could get behind that.

★ ★ ★

As class ended, Hector announced, "I'm hungry."

"Okay," Rider responded as I shoved my notebook into my bag. "What exactly do you want me to do about it?"

Hector grinned as he glanced over at me and winked. "I want you to take me out and feed me."

Rider snorted.

"We can hit up Firehouse. I'm in the mood for their fries and fried hamburgers."

Standing, Rider lifted his arms and stretched. His shirt rode up, baring a sliver of his stomach. My gaze dropped and focused in. His lower stomach was unbelievably taut. Defined.

Nice.

Very nice.

Cheeks flushing, I looked away and caught Hector's knowing gaze. Crap. I needed to be better about checking out guys. Like incognito style. I didn't even look in Paige's direction to see if she caught me.

"You should come with us," Hector suggested.

I blinked. Was he talking to me?

He was. Because Rider lowered his arms and glanced over to where I was, which was still sitting in my chair. "You want to grab something to eat?"

"Of course she does," Hector replied. "She wouldn't turn down our company. Who would?"

Goodness, he and Jayden were very much alike.

Rider's grin was lazy. "So, what do you think?"

My mind raced over the possibilities. Besides Ainsley and my family, I'd never gone out and grabbed food with anyone else. I most definitely had never gone out to eat with one guy, let alone two. Carl and Rosa would probably flip.

Okay. They would absolutely flip.

But I wanted to.

Heart thumping in my chest, I felt myself nod.

Rider's grin spread and the dimple in his right cheek blessed the world once more. "Perfect. You want to ride with us?" he asked. "Since we know where we're going?"

"Works for me," Hector replied. "I can drop you back off at the school later."

That made sense, so I nodded again.

"Good." Rider paused, his smile reaching his eyes. "But there's just one thing you're going to have to do first."

My brows rose.

"You're going to have to get up."

I got up.

Paige spoke as she rose from her own seat. "I can't go with you. You know I have to watch Penny on Mondays."

"Hell." Rider scrubbed his fingers through his hair as I wondered who Penny was. "Want me to pick you and your sister up something to eat? I can swing it by afterward?"

Her head cocked to the side. "Are you serious? You're going anyway?"

Oh no.

I stepped back, slinging my bag over my shoulder. This was not going to end well. Not at all.

Rider faced his girlfriend as he spoke to us. "I'll meet you guys outside, okay?"

"Sure," murmured Hector, and when I didn't move, he gently cupped my elbow. "Let's go."

I let Hector guide me out of the classroom. We didn't speak, not the whole way outside. I wanted to talk about what had just happened, but as usual, I said nothing as we neared the parking lot. It wasn't hard. I could talk. I'd talked in front of him before. I could do it now. It was easy.

Clenching my hands, I focused on the backs of the people in front of us—and pretended I was talking to Carl or Rosa. Or even Rider. The words came unstuck, slowly. Sort of painfully. "Maybe...I shouldn't go."

There.

I said it.

Thank Jesus.

And baby animals everywhere.

If my speaking surprised him, he didn't show it. "There is no reason for you not to."

Stopping by his Escort, I looked up at him. Tiny balls of nervous energy filled my stomach. Standing out here talking to him was not easy, no matter what lies I'd just told myself. "I...can think...of one big reason...why."

A small grin appeared as he walked to the rear of the car and tossed his book bag into the back. "Paige?"

I nodded.

He chuckled, and I didn't think it was very funny. Coming back to where I stood, he leaned against the driver's door. A moment passed. "I don't think Rider knows what he's doing. I don't think he ever knows what he's doing."

I frowned. "What...does that mean?"

Hector studied me for a moment, and this time he laughed under his breath. "Just thinking out loud." He paused as he scratched at his chin. "You know, by this point in any other school year, Rider would've been in in-school suspension at least twice. Hasn't gotten it once so far this year."

I didn't like the sound of that, but I was glad it appeared to be in the past.

"He also used to be out tagging every night he didn't work," he continued, eyeing the pathway Rider would be coming up.

"He didn't really spend that much free time with Paige, you get me?"

I totally did not get him.

"He's respectful of my *abuelita*, don't get me wrong, but Rider always has been..."

"Has been...what?" I asked, brushing a strand of wind-blown hair out of my face.

His moss-green gaze drifted to where I stood. "He's always been *here* but not."

I knew what that meant.

My chest clenched as I looked down at the oil-stained asphalt. Here but not. Existing but not living. I knew that feeling. Lived it for several years. Some days it felt like I was still wearing that feeling like a heavy jacket buttoned up too tightly. I didn't know Rider felt the same, or that others had noticed that about him.

And that... Well, that made me sad.

"Here he comes." Hector pushed away from the car.

Looking up, I saw Rider jogging along the pathway. He slowed as he reached our car. Paige wasn't with him. I searched his face for some clue of what happened as Hector got into the car. His jaw was a firm line.

My throat dried. "Is...is everything okay?"

Rider's brow furrowed. "Yeah."

"Maybe I—"

"Don't." He stepped toward me, chin lowered. "I know what you're going to say. Don't. What happened back there doesn't have anything to do with you."

I stood still. "That...had everything to do with me."

Rider looked away, a muscle flickering along his jaw. A moment passed. "You're right. In a way, you're right. But that doesn't change that Hector invited you or that I want you to come with us."

The window rolled down and Hector stuck his head out. "You guys coming?"

I looked at Rider, still unsure.

Please.

He didn't speak it. He mouthed it.

I was going.

★ ★ ★

Twenty minutes later I found myself at a small diner that was only a couple of miles from the school. From the looks of it, the diner at one time had been a legit firehouse, which obviously explained the name. The place was old—from the vintage photos hanging on the wall to the red vinyl booths. It had a homey feel to it, as if at any given moment you'd hear the older woman behind the register yelling at her son, who was cooking the food. I had no idea if that was the case, if it was family owned or whether the kind of unhappy-looking woman perched on a stool had any kids, but that was the feel of the place.

I liked it.

All of us ordered virtually the same—hamburgers and fries. Rider and I added cheese. Hector added every condiment under the sun. The food was delicious, so much better after forcing myself to eat the mystery meat at lunch.

I was glad I'd decided to go.

It was almost like there hadn't been a reason for me to not have gone. I was having a good time listening to the guys give each other a hard time. Sometimes, Hector would slip into Puerto Rican and Rider would respond in kind. I got the impression they were insulting each other. I learned that *cállate* meant shut up, which was something they said to each other often.

I kept my phone in my bag. On the way here, I'd sent Rosa a message that I was grabbing a bite to eat with friends and then I'd be home. The text—a text that millions of normal teens probably sent every day, but that was all new to me—left me feeling a little giddy and I turned my phone to silent so I wouldn't stress out if Rosa tried to get in touch with me. My phone had vibrated in my bag about fifteen minutes into the drive. I didn't need to look to know it was either her or Carl. When I got home, I would tell them that I was driving and couldn't answer.

I did feel bad—for the lying part.

Admittedly, it did not stop me from enjoying this.

Hector leaned back in the booth and patted his flat stomach. "Aw, man, that hit the spot. I could live off their burgers."

Beside me, Rider snorted. "As much as you eat here, you already do live off them."

"Whatever," he replied, grinning as he shifted forward, dropping his arms onto the table. "I eat different stuff here."

"Like what?"

He rolled his eyes. "Let's see. I get their hamburger sub."

I grinned.

"That's practically the same thing as a regular hamburger," Rider said as he sat back and dropped his arm along the back of our booth. "Try again."

His eyes narrowed. "I get their onion rings."

"That doesn't count." Rider tapped my shoulder with his fingers. "Does it?"

I shook my head.

"You're not helping," Hector replied as he snatched a fry off my plate.

So. Much. Like. His. Brother.

Rider chuckled as he shifted in the booth next to me. "You got to work tonight?"

Hector shook his head. "Nah. Tomorrow, though."

"Where…do you work?" I asked.

"At someplace really cool," he replied without missing a beat. I peeked up at him. He smiled. "At McDonald's."

"Which is why you'd think he'd eat something other than hamburgers," Rider added.

"Firehouse hamburgers are not the same as McDonald's. I can't even believe we are having this conversation." Hector looked at me. "Anyway, I started there about a year ago. It was the quickest and easiest place to get hired. My *abuelita's* social security isn't cutting it."

I felt Rider's fingers brush my hair as he said, "Mrs. Luna also works. Full-time."

"I'm trying to get Jayden to get an app in." Hector lifted a hand, scrubbing his fingers through his hair. "He can work there at fifteen, as long as he gets a permit." Pausing, he glanced over at Rider. "That ain't going over too well. He wants everything easy and fast, except easy shit isn't no way easy."

Rider was quiet, but I felt like there was a wealth of words unsaid. They were planning to meet up with some guys to play basketball, so we left shortly after that, and Hector drove me back to my car. There were a few still left in the parking lot. Football and cheerleading practice was going on, their shouts heard from off in the distance.

Rider followed me out of the car, walking around the back to join me. He waited as I opened my door. "Thanks for coming out. It was…it was good."

Looking up, I was startled to see that his cheeks were…deeper. He was blushing again, but I didn't quite follow why. I'd started to learn that happened when he was complimented or when attention was drawn to his artwork. He wasn't comfortable with it, but I didn't get what was making him uncomfortable now.

He wrapped his fingers around the edge of the car door as I tossed my bag onto the front seat. "So, yeah, thanks."

I grinned at him while Hector tapped the side of his car. "Thanks…for letting me tag along."

He tipped his chin down. "You weren't tagging along. You were right there with us."

My grin skipped into a smile. I liked the sound of that, but then I remembered what Hector had said earlier. "So were you."

Rider blinked and then he said softly, "Yeah, I was."

I glanced over his shoulder. "I'm…sorry about Paige."

"I..." Our gazes met and held for a long moment before he looked away. "I am, too."

Having no idea how to respond, I settled in behind the wheel.

"Yo," Hector shouted and then smacked the side of his door from the driver's seat. "They're gonna start without us."

Rider started to close my door, but bent down instead. Our gazes connected again. An eternity stretched out and then he leaned in. My heart stuttered when his lips brushed my forehead, lingering for several seconds.

"I probably shouldn't have done that," he whispered so quietly I wondered if he'd said it or if it was my imagination. But then he spoke louder. "See you tomorrow, Mouse."

CHAPTER 16

"Mallory, can you come down here?"

My stomach tumbled at the sound of Carl's voice. He'd beaten Rosa home from the hospital, and didn't waste any time calling my name the second he was through the front door. I glanced over at the nightstand and saw it was close to nine. Part of me wanted to pretend I was asleep, and I knew if he came up here and thought I was, he wouldn't wake me. But that was such a chicken way out of things, especially when I'd made the choice to go out with Rider and Hector.

Scooting off the bed, I made my way down the stairs, my fingers twisting my hair. In my chest, my heart was pounding wicked fast. I wouldn't lie, I told myself. If Carl asked who I was with, I would tell the truth. Because as corny as it sounded, they deserved the truth.

But I was petrified.

Carl was in the kitchen, pulling a bottle of juice out of the fridge. He was in his scrubs. "Not going to beat around the bush with you, Mallory. I was surprised when Rosa texted that you were grabbing food with friends after school."

Folding my arms over my chest, I watched him grab a glass out of the cabinets. "Is it so strange…to think I'd do that?"

He looked over his shoulder at me, dark eyebrow raised. "With Ainsley? No. But in the four years you've been with us, Ainsley has been the only one you've been comfortable enough around to spend time with." He paused as he poured ruby red juice into the glass. "And you didn't answer the phone when I called."

"I…I was driving." I was such a liar. "Then I just forgot about it. When I got home, I started on my homework." Not such a lie, and while he screwed the lid back on the juice, he didn't seem like the statement was suspicious.

"Who were you with?" he asked.

I wanted to lie, but I also didn't want to. Strange. Biting the inside of my cheek, I prepared myself. "I was…with Rider."

Carl's head whipped in my direction so fast I was reminded of *The Exorcist*. "Rider?" he echoed.

I stiffened all over and could barely nod as I struggled to get a breath through what felt like my throat sealing shut. "Rider and his friend…Hector. We went to Firehouse—"

"The Firehouse Grill?" he asked, brows slamming down. "That isn't in the greatest part of town, Mallory."

I didn't think the part of town was *that* bad. "We just ate burgers and…then I came home. It was…fun."

Carl took a drink of his juice as he eyed me over the rim of the glass. "Who is Hector?"

Explaining who Hector was, I grew more and more aware of Carl's displeasure. "He's really nice. Works at McDonald's and has a younger brother named Jayden, who is really funny. Their grandmother, Mrs. Luna, fosters Rider," I rambled on, shifting my weight from one foot to the next. "And we all have speech class. Rider is going to help me—"

"He's helping with your speech?" He sounded doubtful.

I nodded and then added, "Yes. He…he knows I struggle

with these kinds of things and even though I don't have to deliver my speech in class, I...still have to practice. We're going to practice after school on Thursday."

The man seemed to stop breathing. "You made plans with him without talking to us?"

Uh-oh. I shifted on my feet again. "I...I didn't think it was a big deal. I need the help."

"And Ainsley can't help you?"

Double uh-oh. "Rider is in my class, so it...it makes sense to practice with him."

"And what about this Keira girl?" he rapid-fired back at me. "Isn't she in your speech class?"

Dammit.

He remembered me saying that. Of course he did, but I had a valid reason why I hadn't asked Keira. "That's... That would be too embarrassing to practice in front of her, and Rider knows how...how I am."

Carl opened his mouth and then closed it as he set the glass on the counter. He got that. "I'm not exactly thrilled about this. You haven't seen this boy in years, but you're going out to eat with him and now he's helping you study."

I swallowed hard. "But...but he's my friend...and that's normal."

"Not for you."

I flinched as I took a step back. Not for me. Never for me. That giddiness I'd felt after sending them such a normal text vanished. The feeling wasn't lasting, because normal was never for me.

"I don't mean it like that," he quickly added, reaching out and putting his hand on my shoulder. "And I'm sorry if it came across that way, but you don't know him, Mallory. Not anymore."

"I know him," I insisted, looking up and meeting his gaze as I pushed the momentary hurt away. "He's a good...person."

"I'm not saying he isn't." Carl dropped his hand and sighed

as he turned sideways, unclipping the pager from his waistband. "At least, I hope he is. You never really know someone, not even family sometimes. People show you what they want you to see. You have to remember that."

I didn't understand what he meant by that. I mean, I did get it. After all, it wasn't like the caseworkers knew how Mr. Henry and Miss Becky really were. They'd hid it well, but what did Carl *really* know?

He continued, "I want you to be careful, Mallory."

The corners of my lips started to turn up. "I will."

Carl studied me for a moment and then he nodded. "Where will you be studying on Thursday?"

I shrugged a shoulder. "I guess here?"

Those brows rose again. "I'm not sure I'm comfortable with you being here alone with him," he said, and I thanked myself for not telling him that Rider had already been here when they hadn't been home. "Then again, I'm not exactly comfortable with you being anywhere."

"With him?" I stilled.

He shook his head and smiled faintly. "With any boy, Mallory."

My cheeks heated. "We're…just going to study and he has a girlfriend, remember?" A burn hit my chest as I spoke the words, because I thought about the way Rider had kissed my forehead earlier and then said he shouldn't have done that.

And he really shouldn't have. Even if a kiss to the forehead was as chaste as they came, it still hadn't been right.

"I know." He pinched the bridge of his nose.

Several moments passed, and I grew antsy. "I have homework," I told him.

Carl lowered his hand. "Don't stay up too late." When I started to turn, he stopped me. "Thank you for telling me the truth about who you were with."

My brain actually cringed, because I had been lying about

the whole not-answering-the-phone thing, but I forced a smile. And then I all but ran up to my bedroom. Carl had thanked me, but it was obvious he wasn't happy about me hanging out with Rider. Or maybe it was just because Rider was a guy.

I hoped it was just because he was a guy and not because Carl had something against Rider. I couldn't even fathom why he would, but the truth was, I really didn't know *this* Rider very well. Carl was right about that, but this Rider couldn't be that different from the Rider I loved as I child.

I was sure of it.

★ ★ ★

Rider walked me to my car after speech the following day. He was quiet, though, not saying much as I opened the back door of my car and tossed my bag on the backseat. I worried it had to do with what happened between him and Paige and the chaste kiss on my forehead that I knew he had to have regretted. Or maybe it had to do with the fact that Paige had been a no-show in class today.

Keys in hand, I closed the door and faced him. He stepped to the side and opened the driver's-side door for me. I murmured my thanks and started to slide in.

"Hey," he said, staring at the stained asphalt. "I was thinking about Thursday." His lashes lifted, and air slowly leaked out of my lungs. "We're still on, Mouse?"

My response was immediate even though my stomach flipped over. I nodded. "Yes."

His lips kicked up. "Really?" He sounded surprised, and I didn't understand why and I wasn't going to let myself think about Carl's conversation last night. "Cool. Looking forward to it."

So was I, but those three words were frozen among the swell of anticipation and excitement. Rider wanted to hang out. Holy crap, this was like a red alert. I so needed to talk to Ainsley immediately.

Rider grinned as he shoved one hand in the pocket of his jeans. "Okay, then."

"Okay," I managed to whisper.

He dipped his chin and started to turn away, but then stopped. Like yesterday, he then lowered his head and pressed his lips against my forehead, and also like the day before, I felt that brief sweep of his lips all the way to my toes. My heart joined my stomach, flip-flopping all over the place.

Rider straightened and took a step back, tapping his notebook off his jeans. "See you tomorrow."

And unlike yesterday, he didn't say he shouldn't have done that.

★ ★ ★

When I got home, a spicy scent lured me into the kitchen. My stomach grumbled and I might've started drooling the moment I spotted the cheesy enchiladas cooling on the counter.

They were drenched in homemade queso.

My favorite.

Dropping my bag on the floor, I skipped over to where Rosa was placing the plates on the table. I wrapped my arms around her from behind and squeezed.

Rosa laughed as she turned. "It's the queso, isn't it?"

Nodding, I dropped my arms and stepped back. My tummy growled again as Carl carried the baking pan over to the center of the kitchen table. I wanted to plant my face in it and slurp it down.

"Hey there," Carl said, tossing the oven mitt into an open drawer as he looked up. "How was school?"

"Good." I washed my hands and then grabbed a soda out of the fridge. Carl narrowed his eyes at my choice of drink but said nothing. Good thing, because he'd have to pry the Coke out of my cold, lifeless fingers.

Rosa grinned as she tucked an errant strand back behind her ear. "There's also salad. Make sure you're eating that, too."

Salad? Who wanted salad when I had beefy enchiladas smoth-ered in cheese? Come on, now. The look on my face must've given away what I was thinking, because the salad bowl magi-cally ended up closer to where I sat.

As I plopped down at the table, a horrible thought occurred to me. Did Rider have warm dinners ready for him when he got home from school or the garage? Hector had said his grand-mother still worked. Did the boys have to fend for themselves?

Rosa cut out two enchiladas and placed them on my plate. Did he get meals like this? Someone scooping out his food and placing it on his plate for him? I didn't enjoy the enchiladas as much I normally would and the chitchat between Rosa and Carl, the ease and the warmth, felt amplified by the knowledge that I was so incredibly lucky. Not like I hadn't realized that every single day since Carl walked into my hospital room, but tonight I felt like I…like I needed to really acknowledge it more often.

I was lucky.

"Did you look at the papers I left in your room this morn-ing?" Carl asked.

Papers? My thoughts raced until I realized he was talking about the pamphlets on the bioengineering and biology depart-ments at University of Maryland. I hadn't looked at them, so I shook my head.

Carl squinted as he lifted his glass. "You have early accep-tance at UM, so there is time, but declaring a major is impor-tant. You really need to be taking that seriously."

Considering I had several years before I really needed to do that, I thought I was taking it seriously.

"Need to make sure you're still focusing on the ultimate plan," he continued. "Picking the right major will decide your entire future."

My eyes widened. That sounded intense.

"The first two years of college are so important to gaining an early assurance into George Washington's medicine and research programs." Rosa smiled like she always did whenever she spoke of George Washington. She was an alumni, as was Carl. And that had been Marquette's plan. Go to UM and then gain early assurance into George Washington. "Getting into any med- or science-related graduate program will not be easy. Planning starts way before you start your freshman year."

I shifted uncomfortably as I focused on my plate. Trying to picture myself studying bioengineering or chemistry sort of made me want to break out in hives. Not that I couldn't do it. I liked to think I was smart enough, but I... It didn't excite me.

There was a pause and Rosa said, "Can I ask you something, honey?"

I nodded once more.

She placed an arm onto the table and leaned toward me. "Is this what you want to do?"

My heart turned over heavily. This was the first time that question had been asked of me. I sat back in my chair, unsure of how to answer, because I didn't know. If I didn't follow this plan, what plan would I have? What did I want to do? I knew I wanted to do something that helped others. A job that meant something at the end of the day. I knew I wanted that because I was given a huge second chance. I wanted that to *mean* something. But spending a life in a lab wasn't the only thing that helped people. There were police officers, psychologists, social workers and teachers and—

Social work.

A twisting motion in the pit of my stomach felt like excitement. Social work? I blinked once and then twice. Something about that felt right. Like it totally made sense for me, who had grown up in the system, to want to give back. That kind of job would be super hard, to see the kinds of things social workers had to deal with, but what if I could stop what happened to Rider and me from happening to another child, to help them know that they were real, they were wanted and loved? That would mean something at the end of the day. That would mean something for a lifetime.

Taking a deep breath, I opened my mouth.

"Of course that's what she wants to do." Carl laughed. "It's all we've ever talked about."

Rosa arched a brow. "If that's what she wants, then I think she would've looked at the pamphlets."

Carl squinted again.

I squirmed some more. "I…I am interested in that, but there are a few…other things I want to check out."

The squint increased. "Like what, Mallory?"

My fingers tightened around my fork. "Maybe social work?"

"Social work?" Carl laughed again. "You'll never be able to pay back the student loans required to get that degree."

My lips pursed as Rosa shot him a look.

"What?" He shook his head. "That wasn't even a serious answer from her. Anyway, there's something else we need to talk about."

I cut off a huge chunk of enchilada as the conversation veered away from college studies to another topic I would just as soon avoid.

"Carl told me about tomorrow," Rosa announced as I was about to shove a huge forkful of enchilada into my mouth. I froze, eyes wide. Round two was about to begin. "I think it's a…good idea."

Huh.

My gaze darted to Carl. He was cutting his enchilada with his fork in short, stabby motions.

"But I do have a favor to ask," she continued, sitting back in her chair, and I went still, fork halfway to my mouth. "Try setting up a study date when we're actually home."

Holy balls.

Rosa smiled at me. Carl kept murdering his food. And I finally put the fork in my mouth. Okay. Round two was not happening.

After dinner I cleaned up and stored the leftovers in the fridge. They'd be perfect for tomorrow, for when I—*oh my God*—hung out with Rider, and then grabbed my bag and headed upstairs. Carl and Rosa were settled in the living room, and I could hear the *Jeopardy!* music playing. Once upstairs, I opened up my laptop and clicked on the messenger app. Ainsley was online.

Clicking on her icon, I sent her a message.

You there?

A bubble appeared below and then her response:

Always.

I carried my laptop over to my bed and sat down, resting it in my lap.

I need your advice.

I am your sensei.

Rider is going to come over after school tomorrow and help me with my speech, and I'm not sure if I should have extra soda and food. I paused. And stuff.

The bubble immediately popped up.

Wait a sec. Back up. Rider is coming over to your house tomorrow?

I grinned, because I could practically see her face in my mind.

Yes.

Do Carl and Rosa know?

That grin faded and my stomach knotted.

Yes.

I paused.

Carl wasn't too happy about it, but Rosa was okay.

Mallory Dodge!!! I'm so proud of you! You're no longer a rebel. LOL.

My fingers flew over the keyboard.

Should I have soda or some food?

You normally have that stuff at the house anyway. So yes? I guess.

Ainsley was right. I already had those things and I was being stupid, but as I stared at her message, I wondered if it was smart to bring him here. Maybe studying at my house was too...too intimate and also not the coolest idea.

As much as Paige was a complete jerk to me, she had valid reasons. Rider coming over to my house would just be another reason for her to dislike me.

My mind raced over the possibilities. We could just go to the library. They had private study rooms. Going there would fix the problem about what snacks to serve. There would be no makeup retouching. That was probably another good thing. I wasn't that great at putting makeup on and my face couldn't handle a lot. Ainsley, on the other hand, could teach the beauty vloggers a thing or two.

Satisfied with my decision, I relaxed.

I think I'll just ask if we can go to the library.

A couple of moments passed before she responded.

Um. Why?

I think it's just smarter, I sent back after a few seconds. His girlfriend wouldn't be happy with him being at my house.

Who cares about his girlfriend?

Ainsley!!!

I'm just kidding, she typed back. Though you'd think if it was a problem, he wouldn't have agreed to come over to your house in the first place.

Good point.

It's just easier to go to the library.

The bubble reappeared.

You're weird, but I still love you and I have a question for you. A serious question. Totes serious.

My brows rose.

Okay.

Do you like Rider, like really like him?

The knots were making another appearance, but for a totally different reason. Did I like him, *like him*? The knots were
pretty telling, but saying it made it real and something I couldn't
take back.

And I couldn't make it real.

I liked Rider, *really* liked him, in a way that was so different
than when we were kids. It was like being twelve all over again,
but the crush this time around was much more powerful. And I
knew it wasn't right to have those feelings. He had a girlfriend
and no matter how much I liked him, that wouldn't change. I
was okay with that. I had to be. What I was beginning to realize I felt for him belonged only to me.

It was all mine and no one else needed to know about it.

I exhaled slowly.

I didn't respond, but Ainsley did with:

That's what I thought.

I waited for her to say more, but when she didn't, I typed:

Are you still there?

A minute or two passed and then her bubble popped up.

Sorry. Mom was in here making sure I wasn't setting up meet-
ings with random thirty-year-olds on Facebook.

Knowing she wasn't joking, I laughed.

Another message from Ainsley popped up.

Text me and let me know how tomorrow goes. I'll need some entertainment while waiting at the doc's office.

I frowned and quickly typed back.

What doctor?

Mom is taking me to the eye doctor to get new glasses.

Didn't you get new glasses last year?

Yeah, but I don't think the prescription is good anymore. I have crap eyes. Plus, I think I need to get prescription sunglasses. The sun is sooooo bright. Anyway, I'm going to be bored waiting, so I expect updates.

I stretched out my legs.

I'm not sure if there's going to be any exciting updates.

Oh, there should be.

She added a smiley face.

There better be.

Setting my laptop aside when the conversation ended, I threw my legs off the bed and walked over to where I left my bag on the desk. I fished out my phone and went to messages. I bit down on my lip as I sent Rider a quick message about practicing in the library.

Once done, I placed the phone on my bedside table and then picked up my history text and got down to studying. It wasn't until it was close to nine o'clock that my phone dinged. I picked it up, seeing that it was a text from Rider.

That's cool, he'd responded.

For some reason, I wondered if it really was.

CHAPTER 17

Thursday officially became the day that would never end. The hours ticked by slowly and I turned into a nervous little freak when I left the class before speech and Rider wasn't waiting for me. Immediately, my brain went into worst-possible-scenario mode.

What if Rider wasn't in school? What if he really didn't want to help me with my speech? What if he bailed? What if he didn't want to jeopardize his relationship with Paige? All of these things felt like very real possibilities.

I hurried to class and took my seat in the back, my eyes glued to the door.

Paige came into class and I almost didn't recognize her. She was wearing loose, black sweats and an oversize shirt. Her hair was pulled back at the crown in a ponytail, one not as sleek as before. As she drew closer, I could see that her eyes were slightly swollen.

She took her seat and as she dropped her bag onto the floor, she turned her head toward me. "What the hell are you staring at?"

Flushing, I cast my gaze back to the front of the classroom.

"Stupid bitch," she muttered, and I flinched.

Retorts formed and then fizzled out on my tongue. I pressed my lips together, inhaling through my nose.

Next into class was Hector. He strode in, smiling at something Keira was saying. My chest squeezed at the ease in which she spoke and laughed with him. God, I wanted that.

My throat thickened, and I told myself that if Rider didn't show, it wasn't personal even though I knew I was going to take it personally. Just when I was about to face-plant the top of my desk, Rider moseyed on into class, notebook in hand and sleepy grin on his lips. Of course. He hadn't bailed.

Tension eked out of my shoulders, and I told myself that I needed to get a grip.

"Yo." Hector nodded at him as he passed his desk.

Rider murmured a response and then took his seat. He leaned over toward Paige, speaking too low for me to hear. I saw her shake her head. He put his hand on her arm. Surprise flickered through me when she jerked away. She slammed her textbook down on the desk, and I thought I heard him sigh.

He glanced over at me. "Hey, Mouse."

"Hey," I replied softly.

And that was the extent of what I said to him the entire class, which probably didn't bode well. I was suddenly so incredibly nervous as we packed up our stuff at the end of the class and Rider waited for me.

"We heading straight over?" he asked.

I nodded, noticing that Paige had already exited the classroom. He arched a brow and said nothing as we filed out of the room, waving goodbye to Hector and Keira. It was a good thing that I was driving, because I could focus on that instead of the internal freak-out that was occurring.

We were heading to the library that was about a twenty-minute drive from the school, and I was white-knuckling it the moment we pulled out of the parking lot.

Rider noticed. Of course. "You doing okay over there?" he asked.

I nodded and then cleared my throat. I wanted to ask him about Paige, but the plug was filling up my throat. So stupid. I never had that problem with him, but I was just too stuck in my head. I needed to get my mouth to work.

"Is...is everything okay with...you and Paige?" It was painful but I managed to get the words out.

A moment passed. "Not really."

"Do...you want to talk about it?" I asked.

"No."

"Okay," I breathed.

"I want to talk about anything other than that right now," he added. "Okay?"

I tightened my grip on the steering wheel as I glanced up at the red stoplight. I could do that even though I was more than curious about the whole Paige situation now. But there was so much I wanted to know about him.

"How...did you...?" I glanced up at the red stoplight, mentally stringing together a litany of curse words until my tongue untied. I was so nervous it was like it was two years ago. "How did you start working at...the garage?"

He didn't answer immediately, because I probably caught him off guard with the pure randomness of my question.

I flushed and squeezed down on the steering wheel. "I... I was just wondering about it. So I thought I'd ask. Sorry."

"No. No, it's cool." When I peeked at him, he was staring out the windshield. "Razorback Garage is about a block or so from where I live. So I saw the owner—Drew—often. We talked whenever we crossed paths, you know? Sometimes I would hang out at the garage, because they had this detailer who did amazing work. Anyway, about a year ago or so, I got busted for tagging—unrelated to the school thing."

"You get…caught a lot," I said, turning right.

"Ha. Yeah. Apparently. Anyway. Drew ended up hearing about it. So when I saw him again, he asked me to show him some of my stuff. And I did. He liked it. Thought it was pretty cool. The rest is history."

I slowed for another stoplight. "That's really…amazing."

"I'm lucky," he replied, grinning then. "Drew pays me pretty good."

"Because you're really good at what you do," I told him.

The dimple appeared. "I could, um, show you some of my work at the garage if you want? I mean, it's not that exciting and you'd probably like to do something else, but—"

"I'd love to." My heart was tripping over itself.

His dimple hung around for that.

"Do you…save the money from working?" I asked.

"Nah. I spend it all on liquor and girls."

I shot him a look.

Rider chuckled. "Yeah, I save the money. I'm eighteen, going to graduate in May. Need to be looking toward the future. Got to get a place. The checks will stop coming in and even though I know Mrs. Luna wouldn't kick me out, it isn't right. She'll have to bring in another kid."

At the library, I pulled into the parking lot and searched for a space. "What about college?"

"Ah, I don't see that in my future to-do list."

"Why?" I didn't understand. "You're…really smart. College will probably be a breeze for you."

He shifted in the seat. "I don't know. That costs money, Mouse, and I'm not saving up that kind of money."

"But there are scholarships and grants." Finding a parking spot near the back, I eased in and turned off the car. I looked over at him. "What about that?"

A muscle flexed along his jaw. "Yeah, I know, but...I just don't see it in my future. I mean, hell, people would probably fall over dead from shock if my ass ended up in college."

I frowned. "I wouldn't."

He glanced over at me as he unlocked his seat belt and his grin tipped up a notch. "You've changed. A lot. But there are still things about you that are the same."

I wasn't sure if that was a good or bad thing.

Rider reached over and unhooked my seat belt. "You've never seen what everyone else sees when it comes to me," he explained.

Now I was just confused. "What is that supposed to mean?"

"You think— I don't know. That I'm something that I'm not." Stretching behind him, he grabbed my bag off the backseat. "You see me as a white knight."

What in the hell?

I watched him open the car door and climb out with my bag in hand. Frozen for a moment, I snatched my keys out of the ignition and hurried after him. "I don't think you're a white knight."

Rider cast me a long side look. "You're pretty much the only person who thinks my name and college go together in the same sentence."

I had to pick up my pace to keep up with his long legs. "That's stupid."

He eyed me warily as he opened the door. "It's whatever."

"No, it's not." I stopped inside the set of doors and stared up at him. He was suspended in motion, reaching for the main entrance. "You could do college if that's what you wanted. Your name and college...make total sense together."

His gaze lifted to the ceiling as his lips pressed together. What felt like an eternity passed before he said, "Huh."

That was it?

Rider walked into the library, and after a moment I followed him. He went right up to the circulation desk and we lucked out

since there was only one room available. As we walked through
the tall, stocked stacks, I breathed in deeply, loving the scent of
books. A memory wiggled loose.

*I curled onto my side, knees tucked to my chest. Tears had dried on
my cheeks. Tonight had been bad. Mr. Henry's friends were over and I
knew they wouldn't be leaving for a while. The room was cold and dark
and the ratty blanket was so thin. I huddled down, shoving my hands
between my legs to keep them warm.*

*The door cracked open and a slight form slipped inside. I let out the
breath I was holding. Rider crept toward the bed. I scooted over, against
the wall. The mattress shook as he settled in beside me. A second later
a soft yellow light flipped open. The small flashlight wouldn't draw attention.*

*Rider brought his knees up, pressing his against mine as he took a
deep breath. "There was once a Velveteen Rabbit, and in the beginning
he was really splendid."*

Drawing in a sharp breath, I looked up at Rider and for a moment I saw him in the past. "Do you remember reading to me?"

He nodded as his lips curled up. "Of course."

I didn't say anything else as we walked into the room. It was
cool inside, and at once, I was grateful for the long-sleeved shirt.

Rider flipped on the light and then dropped my bag on the
table. "So why did you change it to the library?" he asked before I could start harping on the college thing again.

Ainsley's question from last night resurfaced and I shoved
it away. I could tell him it was because of Paige, but I figured
he didn't want to hear that right now. "I thought…it would be
easier."

He nodded in response.

I watched him for a moment and then walked over to my bag
and unzipped it. The tinny sound echoed in the cool, white-
walled room. There was nothing in here except a round table
and four chairs. A lone black Sharpie rested in the center of the
table.

Rider sat and leaned back, tossing his arm along the back of the chair next to him. He looked over at me, a small grin teasing his lips. Our gazes collided and held. A flutter took flight deep in my chest. His grin spread and the flutter increased.

"Why are you looking…at me like that?" The moment the question left my lips I sort of wanted to shove it back in. It was a stupid question.

The dimple appeared. "I like staring at you."

My brows rose.

He chuckled. "That kind of sounded creepy, didn't it? What I meant is that… Well, yeah, I like staring at you. So it is as creepy as it sounds."

Smiling, I shook my head. "It's not…creepy. I just…"

"What?" he asked when I didn't continue.

What could I say to him? That I didn't get why he would enjoy staring at me? That there were much better options out there for him? That would sound terrible. It wasn't like I thought I was the ugliest person in the world. I was…I guess, passably pretty. But I was realistic about the way I looked, and I didn't look like Paige or Keira or Ainsley.

I shook my head, focusing on something else. "You want…to go first?" I offered, pulling out my notebook. I flipped it open, and pulled out the speech I had folded.

"Would love to." Rider leaned forward with a grin. "But I haven't written mine yet."

My mouth dropped open. "What?"

"I'll get to it." He waved his hand dismissively. "Go ahead."

"But you've seriously only been drawing in class? Not working—"

"I'll have it down, Mouse. Promise." He lifted his hand, wiggling his pinky at me. "I'll pinky promise."

I sighed. "I don't…need a pinky promise."

Rider just grinned as he leaned back and crossed his arms. Taking a deep breath, I stared down at my speech. The words blurred a bit, as if there was something wrong with my vision. My heart rate kicked up. I drew in a deep breath that got caught.

"You can do this," he said quietly.

I closed my eyes briefly. I could do this. "The United States of America…has th-three branches of the…"

I did it.

Well, I struggled through it, and I was pretty sure my first run did not come in under three minutes. More like ten as I got hung up on a word and then I started stuttering, because my eyes kept wanting to read ahead, so that didn't help. At Rider's suggestion, I tried it sitting down. Then standing again. I did it so many times there was a good chance I might be able to re-member it by heart.

Rider was patient through the whole thing, which pretty much raised him to saint status, because who seriously wanted to listen to me pause and stutter through an informative speech about a dozen times. Someone could record it and Satan could play it over and over, on an endless loop, to torture people in hell.

"I…I hate that I have to think about every single word." I sat down and dropped the paper on the table, my arms falling into my lap. "It's embarrassing. People are going to make fun… of me."

"People are assholes, Mouse. You already know that." He paused as he scooped some of my hair back, gently tossing the strands over my shoulder. "And there's nothing to be embar-rassed about."

I glanced over at him. Everything about his steady gaze and the serious press of his lips screamed earnest. But he was wrong. "It *is*…embarrassing."

"Not if you don't let it be." His leg brushed mine as he turned in his seat, facing me. Our eyes met. "You have the power over that. People can say crap. They can think whatever they want, but you control how you feel about it."

Damn.

That was deep and mature.

"You sound like Dr. Taft," I blurted out.

His brows lifted. "Who's that?"

"He was..." Oh. Hold up. Rider didn't know I'd been seeing a therapist.

He tilted his head to the side and waited. "He was what?"

Oh no. I should've kept my mouth shut. Deep down, I knew that having received therapy wasn't something to feel bad about. With my background—our background—it was, frankly, expected. But just like with not talking, there was an ugly and oftentimes brutal stigma attached to therapy.

And Rider? He appeared to come out of our childhood relatively unscathed. Hadn't he? He wasn't seeing a therapist. He talked normally. Was he really unscathed, though? I thought about all the classes he skipped and how he said no one really cared. Rider believed that, so did he expect nothing for himself?

"Mouse?" He tugged on a strand of my hair. "Who's Dr. Taft?"

I looked away, focusing on the printed speech. What did it matter anyway? I knew Rider wasn't going to disown me as a friend. I drew in a shallow breath. "Dr. Taft was my...therapist. I saw him for about three years. I stopped a little bit ago, because I...I felt like I was ready."

"Oh. Cool."

Cool? Okay. How often did he hear seventeen-year-old chicks admit to seeing a therapist, that his only response was *cool*? I peeked at him, and he was just looking at me, expression open. "Really?"

Rider raised a shoulder. "Makes sense. You saw some—yeah, some rough shit. Dealt with some crazy stuff. I'm actually kind of relieved you saw someone."

I studied him for a moment. "You...really believe that?"

He nodded.

"What about you?" I asked, and when he blinked, he looked confused. "You grew up...with me. You've seen some bad shit."

"I'm fine," he replied, shifting his gaze to the books.

I stared at his profile. "I was there, Rider. I remember some—"

"And I'm fine," he interrupted, lifting his gaze to mine. "I promise. I swear."

Pressing my lips together, I slowly shook my head. "You said you thought...about that night."

Rider stiffened and then exhaled slowly. "Sometimes," he repeated quietly and then louder, "When I do, I'm thinking about what happened to you."

My stomach churned, and I was for once grateful that I hadn't eaten anything since lunch. "Rider—"

"I should've been there," he stated, his eyes darkening. "I should've found a way to get back into that house. I knew that son of a bitch would do something with that doll eventually."

I opened my mouth, but dammit, I had loved Velvet. Besides the fact that Rider had gotten her for me the day Miss Becky had taken him to the mall, she was the only thing for *years* that had been simply mine. The doll was not a hand-me-down. She belonged to no one before me and I hadn't had to share her. The doll was all mine and she was beautiful.

Had been.

At twelve years old, I didn't carry Velvet with me everywhere. I was too old for that, but Mr. Henry and Miss Becky knew how much I treasured that doll. Mr. Henry had gotten ahold of her and... Yeah, that hadn't ended well.

Rider thrust his hand through his hair, clasping the back of his neck. "If I hadn't talked back to him that night, that wouldn't have happened. You wouldn't have been left alone in there. You wouldn't have seen what you did." Dropping his hand, he tipped his head back. "It's one of the biggest things I regret."

"That?" I croaked. "It wasn't...your fault."

What happened *wasn't* Rider's fault.

"He threw the doll in the damn fireplace," he said gruffly.

And in an ultimate act of desperation and stupidity, I'd tried to save the doll. If I hadn't already seen what I'd seen that night, I might not have done what I had. The act with Velvet broke me. I panicked as I saw the only thing I'd ever owned, a gift from Rider, on the brink of being destroyed. I rushed past Mr. Henry and reached into the fire. I vaguely remembered Mr. Henry laughing and then there was this horrific screaming and this terrible smell.

The screams had been mine.

Rider didn't say anything as he reached between us and picked up my left arm. His fingers were cool against mine as he pushed the sleeve of my shirt up to my elbow. He turned my arm over, like he had done the first day, in the parking lot.

"I still can't believe there's hardly any scar." He smoothed his thumb just below my wrist, causing me to suck in a soft breath. The caress zinged all the way to my spine. "Just a little more pink than the rest of the arm. Amazing."

My mouth dried. His thumb kept moving, traveling over my skin, making its way to my elbow.

"I wish this had never happened." He swallowed. "I wouldn't have lost..." Trailing off, he peered up through his lashes and grinned. "It worked out, though. Weird how something good can come out of such a big screw-up."

"It wasn't your fault," I insisted, meaning it. "You couldn't watch over me twenty-four hours a day. I wasn't your responsibility."

His gaze held mine and a moment passed where he seemed to be considering what he wanted to say. "Anyway," he drew the word out. "None of that really matters, right? You don't have anything to be embarrassed about. The way you talk isn't a big deal. And if people are asses, they're not important. Only you can let yourself make them important."

"And what if none of that works?" I asked.

Rider's lips tipped up at one corner. "I'll just start beating people up."

My brows flew up.

"Seriously."

Tipping back my head, I laughed—laughed long and hard—and when I looked at him, he was staring at me in his intense way. "What?" I asked, my smile starting to fade slowly.

He gave a little shake of his head. "Nothing." He paused. "It's just that I haven't heard you laugh like that in...yeah, a long time. It's nice."

I was smiling again.

"Really nice," he repeated, and our gazes locked again. He was still holding my arm and his thumb was still moving in slow, smooth circles. "I hope you do it more often."

CHAPTER 18

I knew this wasn't happening.

In the furthest corners of my mind, I knew what I was seeing, what I was hearing, wasn't occurring right now. I knew that, but I couldn't pull myself out of it. Not when it started with the voices. Loud. Sharp. Explosive. Detonating a bomb loaded with terror.

Clapping my hands over my ears, I inched backward, pressing against the wall. I wanted to close my eyes, but I couldn't. They felt like they were peeled wide open, held by tiny pins. The pain radiating from the center of my face was forgotten.

Cheeks flushed a bright red and eyes bloodshot, Mr. Henry dragged Rider across the dirtied, ripped linoleum floor by the arm. Rider was almost as tall as Mr. Henry now, but the man had a good hundred pounds on Rider. He was yelling so loudly I couldn't make out what he was saying, but Rider wasn't struggling. He covered his nose with one hand. Blood ran between his fingers. My tummy twisted.

Mr. Henry threw open the back door. Cold air rushed in as tiny snowflakes fell across the yellowish-white floor. The storm door, broken, swayed unsteadily in the wind. "I'm done with your shit, boy. You think you have it bad? Maybe you'll realize just how lucky you have it after a couple of hours out there."

In a stuttered heartbeat, Mr. Henry shoved Rider outside, onto the snow-covered porch. I cried out, peeling myself off the wall. Rider couldn't be outside. He was just in a shirt and jeans. It was too cold.

The door slammed shut. It was too late.

Mr. Henry whirled on me, and trepidation seized my heart.

Fists pounded on the door, from the outside, and I started to back up. Nothing was between Mr. Henry's unfocused gaze and me.

"Get out of my face, girl," he shouted, spraying spittle into the air. "Or you're gonna regret it real quick!"

Spinning around, I ran out of the kitchen and into the den. I pressed myself against the wall as I lifted my arm, dragging my fingers against my nose. Pain spiked, but there wasn't a lot of blood on my hand when I lowered it.

Please wake up. Please wake up. Please wake up.

Heart pounding fast, I listened to Mr. Henry stomp into the living room. A second later, sound blared out of the TV. He was seriously going to leave Rider outside. Oh my God, he wouldn't last out there in the cold and the snow. I had to do something.

Waiting a few minutes, I turned and slipped around the wall. I crept up the stairs, careful to not be heard, and I walked down the hallway.

Don't go inside the room. Don't go in that room.

I pushed open the door. Soft yellow light flickered. Miss Becky was on the bed. Calling out her name, I walked up to the bed and I touched her. Her skin felt wrong, and I knew. I knew deep down, something was very wrong. A scream bubbled up in my throat.

Don't make a sound.

Screams—there were screams, and I couldn't keep quiet, because they were mine. I backed out of the room. Mr. Henry shouted from downstairs as I ran down the steps. I had to get to Rider and we had to get out of here. My heart was pumping so fast, and I knew what was coming, and I didn't want to see it, but I'd already seen it.

Please wake up. Please wake up. Please wake up.

I reached the kitchen door and then Mr. Henry was there, yelling and spitting. I couldn't get any words out. He grabbed my arm, hauling me toward the living room. Flames crackled from the fireplace as he stopped in front of his recliner. Still holding on to my arm, he bent over, reaching behind it.

This is just a dream. Just a dream. Wake up.

Straightening, he clutched Velvet in his fist. I'd known that the doll was there. He'd taken her from my room three months ago because I hadn't put the cap back on the milk tight, like he wanted. I'd known exactly where the stuffed doll was, but I also knew not to touch her.

He shoved Velvet in my face as he let go of my arm. I stumbled, the back of my legs digging into the edge of the coffee table.

Wake up. Wake up.

Mr. Henry cursed. "Fucking sick of this shit. Got a little smart aleck and a damn retard I got to take care of." Squeezing the doll in his fist, he stormed toward the fireplace.

My eyes widened and—

"Mallory!"

I came awake, jackknifing up as I gulped in air. I wasn't alone. Hands were on my arms. I screamed again, voice hoarse as I tore myself free.

"It's okay," the voice came again, and I was slow to recognize that it was Carl. "It's okay, Mallory. You were having a nightmare…again."

"Dark," I managed, pushing back against the headboard. "It's—" The bedside light flipped on, flooding the room in soft light, and there was Carl, sitting back down on the edge of the bed. His hair a disheveled mess, sleep clinging to his eyes and his white shirt wrinkled as he placed his hand on my forehead.

My chest hurt.

"It's okay, Mallory." Carl smoothed his hand over my damp hair. "It's just a nightmare. Everything is okay. You are safe now."

Safe.

I squeezed my eyes shut. I was safe now, but the past…the past wasn't. It never would be, and it would be haunting me forever.

Carl left the bed and returned a few moments later with a chilled bottle of water. He handed it over. "I want you to drink it slowly."

With shaky fingers, I unscrewed the lid and raised the bottle to my lips. I took a small sip and then another, cooling the back of my parched throat.

He waited until I lowered the bottle and said, "We're worried, Mallory."

My breath caught. He didn't mince words. Carl never had.

"You haven't had nightmares in almost two years, but you've been getting them quite regularly since you started school," he said, eyeing me intently. "We're worried."

"About?"

He tilted his head to the side. "About you and school, about Rider being back in your life, and maybe it's too much, Mallory. You—"

"It's not too much," I interrupted. "It was just—"

"You're having nightmares again," he continued as if I didn't know this about myself. "We're just concerned. We don't want you overwhelmed."

Overwhelmed. Like I was this frail creature that would shatter under the stress. Anger sparked deep in my chest, and it was strange to feel that toward Carl. "I'm fine." I forced the two words out. "I'm not overwhelmed. It was just a…nightmare. No big deal. And it has nothing to do with school or Rider."

"I'm going to have to disagree on the Rider part." He held up his hand when I opened my mouth. "Only because it would make sense that his being back in your life would cause…" He drew in a deep breath. "Would cause a resurgence of old feelings, many of them scary."

What he said *did* make sense, but I shook my head. "I'm fine."

Carl stared at me a moment and then he nodded with a sigh.

"Okay." He started to rise. "Don't forget that if you ever need to talk, you come to us."

Talk about what? I had no idea, but I nodded. He studied me for a few more moments and then he stepped out of the room, quietly closing the door behind him. I'd told him I wasn't over-whelmed and I was fine, but I knew Carl didn't believe me.

I wasn't even sure if I was telling the truth.

★ ★ ★

Rider was a no-show Friday.

Paige didn't show up for class, either, and while I figured the two were together, little knots of unease still formed in my belly. With the exception of the start of the school year, he hadn't missed school.

When class ended, I gathered up my stuff as I eyed Hector's back. Asking him about Rider would be the smartest, simplest thing to do. He would obviously know. The edges of my bag's straps bit into my palm as I forced the words out. "Hector?"

He turned in my direction, lips tipping up. "Yo."

I stepped around my desk. "Is Rider...okay? I mean, he's not in class," I said, stating the obvious. "I figure...he's with Paige, but I just wanted to make...sure he's okay."

The smile dropped a notch as his gaze flickered to the empty seat. "He's not with Paige. Not today." Those light green eyes landed on me. "At least, I don't think he is."

"Oh." I bit the inside of my lip.

He looked over his shoulder and then sighed. "They got into it pretty hard-core last night, so I'm not surprised she's out, too, but..."

Over his shoulder, I saw Mr. Santos turn in our direction. "But what?"

"But he got tore up last night." Hector slung his bag over his shoulder. "There was no way he was getting up this morning."

"Tore up?" I repeated dumbly, and then it hit me. Tore up as in drunk.

"I've got to get going. Have to head to work," Hector said. "See you later, *bebé*?"

Dazed, I nodded and didn't move for a long moment as Hector walked off. Rider had fought with Paige last night and then gotten drunk. Stomach churning, I started toward the front of the class.

"Mallory, can I talk to you for a second?" Mr. Santos called out. I stopped as he met me by the door. "How does Wednesday sound to give your speech?"

Mind a million miles away, I nodded.

"Great." He patted my arm. "Looking forward to it."

Dismissed, I left the class and made a stop by my locker so I could grab books needed for the weekend. I wasn't really focused on the walk to my car. That burn in my stomach felt a lot like guilt.

Friday night I spent an indecent amount of time staring at my cell phone, my fingers hesitating over the screen. I'd chatted with Ainsley earlier and she'd told me to just text Rider before she made me promise that I'd see her tomorrow.

Just text Rider.

As if it were simple.

It was simple. Who was I kidding?

But it also seemed like a big step, because I'd never initiated contact with him or any guy before. And I was overthinking it as usual, because Rider was my friend and checking in on him was normal.

Frustration washed over my skin, making me hot and uncomfortable. My eyes narrowed on the phone and I tapped on Rider's name, opening up the texts.

Are you okay?

I paused and then deleted that. Then I typed out:

Is everything okay?

That sounded less dramatic, so I clicked Send. Then I threw my phone to the foot of the bed.

It was close to ten when Rider responded.

Yes. I'll see you Monday.

Relief hit me hard, but my head was in a thousand places and it had been tough to fall asleep. At least I didn't have another nightmare, because the last thing I needed was Carl and Rosa freaking out and yanking me from school.

If they thought it was the right thing to do, they would do it.

★ ★ ★

Homecoming banners appeared over the weekend in the halls of Lands High. They were everywhere. Posters on the walls. Covering the lockers. As I walked to second period, I eyed the dates. Homecoming would be held during the last weekend of October, two weeks from now.

I couldn't believe that I'd been at school for almost two months. Time moved fast even when it felt like it was taking forever.

Rider returned to school on Monday, as did Paige. He'd met me outside class and had walked with me to speech. I hadn't asked about what happened between him and Paige or about what Hector had told me. He hadn't brought it up. I did notice that Paige came to class seconds shy from the tardy bell ringing. She'd looked in Rider's direction, but he didn't look in hers. I didn't know what was going on there.

It was then, in speech class, my thoughts switched to something far more important. It was when the first speech was given that it hit me that this was really happening. Everyone in class was going to give their speech and come Wednesday, I'd give mine during lunch.

Panic grew like a noxious weed, surging in my veins. Everyone was going to know that I...I couldn't do it like them. Listening to the other students stand up and give their speeches, I focused on what I could control and remembered what Rider had said in the library.

People were going to be jerks and that wasn't on me.

All I could do was make sure I gave my speech to Mr. Santos, so I threw myself into practicing the speech every chance I got, using Carl and Rosa when I wasn't going over it by myself. I realized that Rider still hadn't written his speech. He didn't seem at all fazed by his lack of progress, and whenever I brought it up, he flipped the conversation and said, "Once you ace the speech, I'll take you to the garage."

I'd eyed him wryly, but I was curious about the garage thing. I wanted to see some of his work. Despite how wrong it was, I wanted to see *him*. But I wasn't a gerbil that needed a reward.

Unless the reward was homemade queso dip. Then yes, reward me.

Homecoming was the topic of conversation at lunch on Tuesday. Seemed like half of the school was interested in attending. The other half couldn't care less. The table I sat with fell into the first group. To be honest, I hadn't even thought of Homecoming until I saw the banners and stuff this morning. It hadn't even come on my radar. Not because I was too cool or that high school dances weren't my thing. It just wasn't something I had the chance to consider, and now that I did, there was a part of me that thought it would be fun. It would be an *experience*.

But I didn't have a dress.

Or a date.

"When do you have to do your speech?" Keira asked at lunch. She was scheduled to go on Wednesday, during class, like a normal person.

It was the first time I was asked that question. I didn't want to answer, but that would be weird and I was weird enough without adding to it. "Tomorrow," I said, staring at my plate. "Tomorrow...during lunch."

Keira didn't immediately respond, and I dared a quick peek at her. Her dark brows knitted. "So you just have to give your speech to Mr. Santos, then?"

I nodded, hoping she wouldn't think what Paige had.

"Cool," she said, picking up her napkin as Jo and Anna sat across from us. "I get super nervous when I have to do the public speaking thing."

"Really?" My brows rose.

"Yep."

"God, I hope you don't hurl," Jo said, plopping her chin in her hand. "Have you seen *Pitch Perfect*?"

I nodded.

"She totally pulled an Aubrey two years ago, when she had to give her first presentation in science class," Jo continued.

Keira scowled. "I made it to the bathroom."

"It was still aca-gross," Jo quipped as she stabbed her sauce-smothered noodles.

I didn't get it. "But you're...a cheerleader."

Looking around the table, Keira's gaze finally settled on me. "So?"

My cheeks warmed. "You...you get up in front of people all the time and...cheer."

"Yeah, but I'm with a group of people doing it with me," she said as she brushed tight curls over her shoulder. "It's easier when you're not alone and it's totally not the same thing as getting up in front of the class and talking out of your butt about something you barely understand."

"True," murmured Anna, who was staring at her cast.

I couldn't believe it as I stared at Keira. She was nervous. Her food was untouched, like mine, but she talked all the time and she didn't stutter. She was still nervous.

"Did you really h-hurl?" I asked.

Jo burst into deep, infectious laughter that drew the attention of those around us. "Hurling would be an understatement."

"It wasn't *that* bad," Keira insisted, shooting Jo a dark look. "Anyway," she continued, looking at me. "I get nervous, too, so let's both make a pact."

"A pact?" I whispered. At once, I was so very grateful for Keira and her friends—my friends. I'd been so incredibly wrong about them. Not like I hadn't realized that during the last couple of weeks, but I *should* feel embarrassed at how easily I believed the cheerleader stereotype.

She nodded. "If I start to look like I'm gonna hurl, you'll grab the basket for me, and if you get sick while doing your speech with Mr. Santos, you can tell me and I promise not to laugh."

My lips parted.

"Deal?" she asked.

I laughed without meaning to, but I couldn't stop it. It was probably the most bizarre deal I'd ever made. "Deal."

★ ★ ★

I woke up Wednesday morning, the day of my speech, with my stomach in knots, a burning lump in my throat and a headache.

Rosa was waiting in the kitchen, a bowl of cereal I couldn't even begin to touch sitting on the counter. She didn't say anything as I grabbed a glass of milk from the fridge. She didn't push it when I was unable to touch the cereal. All she did, before I left for school, was hug me close and say, "You are going to do an amazing job, Mallory."

I held those words close to my heart all day.

Clutching my notebook, I made my way down the hall toward speech, ignoring the way my heart pounded. I rounded the corner and drew up short.

Rider pushed away from the wall when he spotted me. A half grin formed as he shoved his hands into the pockets of his jeans. "Hey, Mouse."

"What…are you doing here?" I asked. "You have class."

That lopsided grin spread and the dimple appeared. "And that matters because…?"

I stopped in front of him, raising a brow.

He tipped his head to the side. "I had to be here. I had to let you know that you got this."

My heart swelled in my chest so fast and quickly that I thought I'd float right to the ceiling. He had to be here for me. That wasn't out of some need to protect. It was because he was my friend and he cared. I wanted to hug him.

My gaze dropped to those full lips.

How would they feel— I cut those thoughts off. I needed to focus. Those three words were a reminder that dropped steel down my spine. He was right. I got this.

I smiled at him and then turned, opening the door. Mr. Santos was at his desk. A paper bag was open. The scent of tomato soup was strong. Brushing his hands, he rose as I closed the door behind me.

"Excuse me, I was sneaking in some lunch." He smiled as he pushed his chair back. "I'm sure you're hungry yourself, so get started whenever you're ready."

Placing my bag on the seat of an empty chair, I walked to the podium with my notebook. My stomach churned. There would be no lunch for me.

Mr. Santos sat in one of the seats, folding his hands on the desk. "Take as much time as you like."

Could I take forever?

Hands shaking, I opened my notebook to where I'd shoved the printed-out speech. The paper was crisp and pristine. All the words blurred. My knees shook. It was just one person I was standing in front of. Not an entire class. Should've been an entire class, but it wasn't.

You got this.

My shoulders tensed as I drew in a breath that got stuck. This wasn't hard. I could do this. I had to do this. The paper was rattling softly, like dry bones.

I can do this. I can do this.

The words blurred again, as if I was experiencing yet another weird lapse in vision. My heart started pounding in my chest so fast that my knees felt weak. My hands trembled.

I can do this. I can do this.

"The United States of America…has three branches of government. The first being…the…" I stopped, realizing I'd gone too far and skipped a line. Panicked, I looked up and saw Mr. Santos waiting.

He nodded at me, expression patient.

I started again. "The U-United States of America has three branches of government—the legislative, executive and judicial," I forced out and then forced myself to keep going. "The l-legislative branch oversees…"

It sucked.

God, the speech sucked so badly.

Like there were thousands of professional speakers turning over in their graves, it sucked that bad, but I did it. I finished my speech a few seconds before Mr. Santos would've called time. I finished the speech, my first ever speech.

I did it.

And I didn't throw up.

Keira would be happy to hear that.

Mr. Santos smiled as he rose from his seat. "You did good, Mallory. You got a little hung up in the beginning, but you started over and then moved on. The speech sounds very well researched."

Hands still shaking, I turned in my paper to him. "Thank… you."

"You'll get your grade along with everyone else," he explained, and I nodded. "Congratulations. You've completed your first speech."

I walked to my bag, shoving my notebook into it. My first speech. I'd done it. Granted, it had only been in front of Mr. Santos, but I'd still done it.

Rider was waiting outside the class. He was looking down at his phone, but he put it in his pocket and angled his body toward mine. "So?"

My lips tipped up at the corners. "I did it."

His answering smile brightened the entire hallway. "I knew you could."

"You did."

Our gazes connected and the look on his face was soft. The swelling motion was back, and this time I let it lift me to the ceiling.

I'd done something I never thought I could do.

CHAPTER 19

"Want to grab something real quick to eat?" Rider offered as we walked down the hall, away from speech. "You have time."

My stomach was still in knots, but since the speech was done, I knew I could eat a slice of pizza. I nodded.

"Awesome."

We headed toward the cafeteria and the closer we got, the more I realized that the hum of conversation and laughter wasn't as harsh to my ears as it had been the first week. Today there was something welcoming about the noise and the scent of un-identifiable food. My steps felt lighter. I was—

"Mr. Stark," said a deep voice. "Why am I not surprised to see you in the hallway when I am ninety-nine percent confi-dent you're supposed to be in class right now?"

I stopped and turned. Rider did the same. Principal Wash-ington stood by an open door with his arms across his chest. Light glinted off his smooth, bald head.

Uh-oh.

"You're not a hundred percent sure?" Rider replied, much

to my surprise. "Don't you think you should always be a hundred percent sure?"

Principal Washington smiled. "Clever, Mr. Stark. It's a shame you don't take that quick wit and apply it to your studies, but that would be expecting too much, wouldn't it?"

A muscle thrummed along Rider's jaw. "I guess so."

The forced smile faded. "Get to your class, Mr. Stark."

For a moment I didn't think Rider was going to leave. He eyed the principal, a challenging smirk on his lips. Then, after a stuttered heartbeat, he stepped back and to the side. "I'll see you later, Mouse."

"Hopefully not in the hall when you're supposed to be in class," Principal Washington interjected.

Rider laughed under his breath as he pivoted around. "I don't know, man. That might be expecting too much."

The principal's large chest rose with a deep, patience-seeking breath and then he looked at me. He squinted. "That's not the kind of boy you want to be spending your time with," he advised, and I flinched at the wild assumption. I didn't even think he knew who I was, even if Carl and Rosa had spoken to him. "The path that boy's heading down is not one you want to be along for the ride on. You'd better be on the way to wherever you're supposed to be."

Before I could respond, Principal Washington was off, stalking down the hall and toward the offices. The happy buzz from completing my speech faded as I replayed the principal's words and tone, the way he'd treated Rider, in my head.

No expectation.

No respect.

★ ★ ★

Keira gave her speech in class without any projectile body fluid, so the good feels returned and the run-in at lunch felt like forever ago. I was even happy for Paige when she strutted up to the front of the class and delivered her speech on the first five presidents of the United States.

She was back to herself. Sort of. Gone were the baggy sweats and messy ponytail. She was back in skintight blue jeans and sweater, and her hair was sleek and straight. She'd been ignoring me the last couple of days, so I wasn't surprised when she didn't look in my direction when she took her seat.

There hadn't been a lot of brain space lately to think about where Paige and Rider were, but I did notice that there wasn't any touching or kissing. They spoke. They smiled at one another. Well, Paige smiled at him and I couldn't see his response, but that was the extent of it.

When the bell rang, I heard Paige ask Rider to call her and then she left the class as Keira walked up to my desk. "How did you do at lunch? No hurling?"

"Good…I guess. No hurling." I paused as my right hand squeezed tight against my thigh. "You did awesome."

"I know!" she exclaimed. "God, I am so glad to be done with it."

Rider stood and reached over to my desk, picking up my notebook and paper as he rose a brow. "One speech down. Only a billion more to go."

Well, realizing that sucked.

Keira laughed. "Yeah, but neither of us threw up!" She clapped her hands together. "Yay, us!"

A smile broke out across my face.

"There were a couple of rough seconds where I thought it was going to happen," she said, watching Rider as he swooped down and picked up my bag. "But I managed not to do it."

"We all appreciated that," Rider teased. He put my notebook in my bag.

"I bet," she replied. "So what about your speech? I'm sure you're just going to be awesome."

"Something like that," he said.

Standing, I reached for my bag. Our fingers brushed, the brief touch a strange jolt to my system, and I jerked my hand back. My gaze flew up to his and our eyes met. Pink infused his cheeks as he looked away, focusing on what appeared to be the monumental task of finding the perfect spot in my bag for my notebook to occupy. The skipping in my pulse turned into a hopping in my chest.

"So, yeah…" Keira murmured as she glanced at Rider. Grinning, she started to back away. "I'll see you guys tomorrow."

Rider gave a curt nod as he zipped up my bag.

I wiggled my fingers in her direction.

"You ready?" he asked.

Nodding again, I followed him toward the front of the classroom, but before we could walk out, Mr. Santos appeared.

"Rider," he said, taking off his glasses. "You got a moment?"

He glanced at me and back to the teacher. "Yeah."

Mr. Santos smiled in my direction as he placed his hand on Rider's shoulder and led him to the center of the chalkboard. Even though I was by the door and there was a lot going on out in the hallway, I could still hear them.

"You ready for your speech?" Mr. Santos asked.

"Of course," he replied.

A look of doubt crossed the teacher's face. "Are you sure about that?"

One side of Rider's lips curled up, but he didn't say anything.

"I've given you a lot of passes in class. I know you get bored and you'd rather be using your hands, creating something, but I need you to take this class seriously."

Rider didn't respond, and I shifted where I stood, uncomfortable.

"You know I'm here if you need to talk," Mr. Santos said, and the smirk slipped off Rider's face. He stiffened. "Don't throw your talent away. Okay?"

Rider didn't reply and then he was dismissed. My gaze was

glued to him. A muscle along his jaw worked as he walked over to me. Why would Rider need to talk to Santos? What did Mr. Santos know about Rider that I didn't?

I knew the answer to that question without asking.

Everything.

We walked out into the crowded hall. "Is…is everything okay?"

"Yeah. Yes." He glanced down at me, features slightly relaxed. "Look at you."

"Look at me?"

Rider reached down and folded his hand around mine, causing a jolt to travel up my arm. He started walking, still holding my hand. "You had this huge smile on your face the whole class. I want to see that smile again."

"I'm…just happy I did it even though I sucked."

"I'm sure you didn't suck."

I begged to differ on that. Mr. Santos probably would, too, but he was too nice and patient to do so. My gaze dropped to our joined hands. This…this was new, and deep down, in my heart of hearts, I liked the feel and weight of his hand, but it was wrong. Some friends might hold hands, but I knew enough to know that wasn't how people would perceive it.

Avoiding his gaze, I slipped my hand free and folded my arms across my chest.

"You need to stop at your locker?" he asked after a moment.

Thinking about it, I shook my head. We walked out into the overcast afternoon skies.

Only when we stopped by my car did I allow myself to look at him.

His expression was unreadable as he leaned against the back passenger door. "There was something I wanted to ask you earlier. I want to show you the garage—Razorback." Lifting a hand, he knocked the hair back from his forehead. "I thought you might want to see what I've been working on. What are you doing Saturday?"

My heart started pounding like I was being chased by a chain-wielding serial killer. "Um…" I trailed off a second before screaming *nothing* from the top of my lungs, but that wasn't true. Ainsley wanted to get together Saturday and even if she didn't, there was the whole Paige thing.

Rider arched a brow.

I could feel my cheeks heat. Who knew what he was thinking while I was standing there staring at him. "I'm supposed to meet Ainsley for lunch and then…we're hanging out."

He was silent for a moment and then shoved his hands into his pockets. "Cool." His gaze flipped up and over me. I turned slightly, spying Hector's car coming down the center aisle. "I'd like to meet her."

Wait.

What?

He wanted to meet Ainsley?

Rider bit down on his lower lip. "So, you know, I'm sort of inviting myself along."

He really wanted to meet my best friend?

His head tilted to the side. "And if you think that's not cool, this is about to get real awkward."

I blinked, realizing I needed to say something. Anything. Hector's car stopped a few feet back from mine. Should we do this? I searched my head for rules I wasn't really familiar with. This really wouldn't be the first time we were together outside school. We grabbed food together and we'd gone to the library. He'd been to my house, but I wasn't counting that. Friends did hang out together.

But I didn't look at Rider, think about him, like someone who was just a friend. Though he didn't know that. Yet I did know that.

I was so confused.

"Will it...be cool for us to hang out?" I asked.

His brows lowered. "Yeah, it would be cool."

Unsure if he got what I was asking, I inhaled deeply. I wanted him to meet Ainsley. She was super important to me. I made my decision. "I...I would like that."

Rider's reaction was immediate. He smiled and the dimple appeared. My breath caught. I'd actually invited Rider along to meet Ainsley. I wanted that. Really wanted that, but I had no idea what to do with *that*.

Regardless, excitement hummed through me. Hanging out with Rider and Ainsley was normal. Something a million people probably did every day, because they were actually living life, but it was a first for me—a huge first. It was my best friend and it was the guy...the guy who'd been my best friend and who now, despite everything, felt like something deeper, richer and more intricate, hanging out together.

It felt important.

"Perfect," he said, pushing off the side of my car. "Glad it's not going to get really awkward now."

"Yo," Hector called out as he extended an arm out the window. "You ready, man? I've got to head out."

"Yeah. Be right there." Rider handed my bag over as he lowered his head toward mine. I stilled as the air rushed out of my lungs. His lips brushed over the curve of my cheek, sending a rush of tight shivers down my spine. "I'll text you later and we'll talk about Saturday."

I thought I said okay. I wasn't entirely sure. I might've just stood there and stared at him. But Rider smiled that smile that reached deep into my chest and wrapped around my heart. I watched him hop into Hector's car, waved at Hector as he peeled out of the lot, and then I climbed into my Honda and sat behind the wheel.

I didn't turn the car on.

What was I thinking? Feeling?

It didn't matter.

Staring out across the rapidly emptying parking lot, I realized something extremely important. Almost earth-shattering in its simplicity. Caught up in excitement for Saturday, I'd forgotten all about Mr. Henry and Miss Becky, about Carl and Rosa calling the school, about speech and me not talking. I forgot about *everything*.

Because it wasn't that important.

Something else was.

Living life was.

★ ★ ★

It was an ice-cream kind of night, or so Rosa told me when she came into my bedroom later that evening, carrying two bowls of the stuff.

Chocolate.

With tons of chocolate syrup.

Celebration for my successful speech was on.

Carl had to work late so it was just the two of us. Seeing her in sweatpants and a cotton shirt seemed so odd, because I almost always saw her in green surgical scrubs.

Rosa sat beside me and handed over the bowl. "I hope you still have some room in your stomach for dessert."

I grinned. "I always...have room for dessert."

She smiled. "Are you sure we're not connected by blood?"

I laughed as I scooped up some of the cool, soft, syrup-covered goodness. Rosa glanced around the room, her gaze landing on the dresser. "Is that the latest carving?"

I nodded. "It's an...owl."

She stood, balancing her bowl in one hand as she walked over to it. Picking it up, she looked over her shoulder at me, her dark eyes glimmering. "Mallory, this is really good."

"Thank you."

"All of the carvings are good, but the details on this?" She carefully placed it back on the dresser. "It's amazing." She returned to the bed and sat. "I really wish you'd reconsider trying it out on wood. Carl still has the tools in the garage."

I wasn't really a fan of power tools.

She swallowed a spoonful. "Carl wants to take us out to dinner Saturday night, for a more official celebration."

Suddenly, the ice cream turned sour in my stomach. "I've made plans with...Ainsley for Saturday."

Excited didn't even capture how Ainsley felt about finally meeting Rider. My IM had started blowing up when I'd told her the good news after school, and she was probably still sending me *OMGs* even as I sat there stuffing my face.

"Oh! That's right." In went another spoonful. "How about Sunday, then?"

I nodded, but my stomach was still twisting. "Um, Rider..." My mouth dried as Rosa lifted her chin. "Rider wants to meet Ainsley on Saturday."

Her spoon clanged off the bowl. "He does?"

I nodded. "I would...I would like them to meet." The skin around her mouth tightened. When she didn't respond, I grew concerned. "Is that okay?"

Her shoulders rose. "Yes. I think so."

Think?

"So, what are you guys going to do on Saturday?" she asked.

"Ainsley and I are going to lunch, and that's where Rider will...meet her. Then Ainsley and I were planning to see a... movie in the evening."

"Sounds like a long, busy day." She swiped the spoon around the inside of her bowl. "You don't think you'll have homework this weekend?"

I shook my head as I placed my bowl on the nightstand. My stomach was a pretzel now.

"Carl isn't exactly going to be okay with you spending your free time with Rider," she said, and I might've stopped breathing. "He was the same way with Marquette," she added with a sad smile. "Now, I think it's a good idea for your two friends to meet, because both of them are important to you, but it's also important that we meet him."

Oh no.

"So I think we should meet him before Saturday. That will probably go a long way to alleviate Carl's concerns, and, well, mine, too." Her gaze met mine. "So that's the deal we're going to make. You want to see Ainsley and Rider this weekend, then he needs to come over for dinner on Friday. Both of us will make sure we're home."

Oh, my.

Oh, my, my, my.

"Okay?" she urged.

I nodded and said, "Okay," because what else was there to say? I had no idea if Rider would even be okay with that, and now I was thinking I really shouldn't have told her about my Saturday plans.

A beep radiated from the pocket of her sweats. Leaning to the side, she pulled out her pager. I'd only seen Carl and Rosa use them. It was weird, seeing doctors use what seemed like an obsolete piece of technology. She grabbed her cell out of her back pocket and called in.

"*Dios,*" she murmured, rising immediately after she finished the quick call. "Can we hit Pause on our conversation?" she asked, frowning. "I hate to ask this, but I've got to. I have a gunshot victim coming in. Looks like a young kid."

I nodded. "It's...okay."

Rosa leaned over and kissed my forehead. She was out of the bedroom and out of the house in under two minutes. I hoped she had a successful surgery. Losing patients wasn't easy on her, and in this city, it happened far too often.

I picked up my phone as I heard the front door close. I typed out the text that made me feel like I did right before I gave my speech earlier.

Carl and Rosa would like to meet you Friday for dinner.

There. There was no other way I could say it, so I hit Send.

Taking my bowl downstairs, I found hers on the kitchen counter. I washed both out and then placed them in the dishwasher. By the time I went back upstairs, there was a text from Rider.

Sounds cool. Let me know the time.

Holy crap.

Sounds cool? A smile raced across my face as I texted back a quick okay. He disappeared from the convo while I washed my face and when I returned, the text he'd sent created a flutter deep in my chest.

Looking forward to it.

I wasn't quite sure about it.

In the middle of the night, I heard Rosa come home. I crept to the top of the stairs and listened to Rosa and Carl talk about her patient. The kid was thirteen. Shot twice. Once in the chest and the other in the back. Rosa had been able to repair the damage to the chest, but the spine was done. She disappeared into the library, and I knew she'd stay there until morning with a bottle of wine. She didn't take losing patients well, and even though this one hadn't died, the outcome still affected her.

Thirteen. And this kid wasn't ever going to walk again.

CHAPTER 20

Watching Rider give his speech on Friday was like tuning in to my favorite TV show. I had no idea what to expect, but I knew I was going to enjoy the view. He showed up to speech class at the last possible moment and then delivered his informative speech on different types of art like it was no big deal. He was smooth and almost a little careless, grinning on and off throughout it, but he appeared happy as he spoke. Rider knew his art and he was good at doing this—at standing in front of the class and effortlessly keeping everyone's attention.

Well, almost everyone's.

The whole time he spoke, Paige's fingers were flying across the screen of the cell phone she had hidden in her lap. They didn't speak in class that day, and I wondered if Paige knew he was coming over tonight.

Tomorrow I was going to find out.

We just had to get past tonight.

Rider also wasn't bothered by the dinner he'd be having with Carl and Rosa. I, on the other hand, barely made it through the day, and I showered after returning from school just to burn off excess energy.

I had no idea how tonight was going to go.

But the house smelled wonderful.

Rosa had put a pot roast in the slow cooker and even though I was incredibly nervous, I wanted to shove the entire thing in my mouth.

That would probably be a bad idea.

Hair dried, I didn't put what I'd worn to school back on. I wasn't sure if that was weird or not, but I thought tonight… Tonight was special. Three out of four of the most important people in my life were finally meeting. I pulled on a pair of jeans and the soft cream cap-sleeved sweater Ainsley had given me for my birthday last year. It was fitted at the chest and waist, flaring out slightly around the hips. I twisted to the side while I checked myself out in the mirror.

Pressing my lips together, I smoothed my hands down my sides and over my hips. An unexpected thought hit me, flushing my cheeks. It wasn't necessarily a thought. More of a…an image, a feeling—of Rider doing the same. His hands. A shiver curled lower in my stomach.

So wrong—so very wrong.

Rider was just a friend. That was his place in my life.

I turned from the mirror and dropped my hands. Taking a couple of deep breaths, I left the bedroom and went downstairs. I checked out the wall clock in the foyer and my heart skipped. Rider would be here soon.

Rosa was in the kitchen, setting the table for four. For Rider. Oh, gosh. She glanced up, smiling. Her dark hair was pulled back in a low ponytail. A timer went off. "Can you grab the pot off the stove? Be careful. It's hot."

Happy to have something to do, I grabbed an oven mitt out of the drawer and walked over to the stove to retrieve the pot of steaming veggies.

"Are you nervous?" she asked, moving back to the cabinets. Smiling, I nodded.

"Don't be." She started pulling down cups. "This is a very exciting moment for us all."

It was.

Once the glasses were on the table, it struck me that Rider and I...we had never shared a dinner like this together. Not once. We'd eaten together. But it was usually on a floor or...

"I want to ask you something before Carl comes down here." She placed her hands on my shoulders. She smiled, but her dark eyes were serious. "How do you feel about Rider?"

My eyes widened. There were so many ways I could answer that. So many things I could say or think, but the first thing that popped in my mind was what I had felt when I stood in front of the mirror.

"Ah, that's what I thought."

I looked up at her. "I..."

"You don't have to say anything." She placed a hand on my warm cheek. "It's all right here."

"He has a girlfriend," I told her.

"Honey, that doesn't mean you don't end up feeling something for someone when you shouldn't."

Oh.

"You're growing up." Her gaze lifted to the ceiling. "And I am so not ready for this again."

Um.

"But I'm going to have to be, aren't I?"

Uh.

Rosa's gaze searched mine. "I'm going—"

"What are you two doing?" Carl crossed the living room toward us. "Having a special meeting without me?"

"Just a little girl talk." She dropped her hand and curled her arm around my shoulders. I'd totally just dodged a bullet that had *awkward* written all over it. "Don't you dare lift that lid—"

Carl had stopped at the counter, where the pot roast was cooling on a platter. He feigned innocence. "I wouldn't dare."

"Uh-huh. We both know better, don't we, Mallory?"

I nodded. We totally knew better.

The doorbell rang suddenly, and I jumped. My gaze searched out the time. It was five till the time Rider was supposed to be here.

Carl turned toward the entryway.

"I'll get it." I took off, squeezing past him.

Sliding to a stop in front of the door, I all but threw it open without even looking to see who it was. But it was him.

Rider stood on our porch, and he... He had changed his clothes, too.

Relief washed over me, immediately followed by a keen sense of awareness, because he looked—he looked *hot*. I shouldn't notice that about him, but I did. He was wearing a button-down gray dress shirt and dark jeans. My gaze got hung up on his hands.

His full lips curved into a half grin. "Can I come in?"

I blinked.

The grin spread into a smile. "Mouse?"

"Oh. Yeah." I moved to the side. "Yes."

Rider stepped in, his gaze drifting over me. I inhaled, catching the scent of cologne. Our gazes caught for a moment and then he looked toward the living room. The centers of his cheeks were flushed a darker shade. "Dinner smells amazing."

"It's...it's pot roast." I was no longer hungry. I glanced at his mouth and quickly looked away. "Um, Rosa is... She's a great cook."

Hyperaware of his presence, I started to lead him toward the kitchen. We walked through the living room, and Rider stopped suddenly in front of the china cabinet. "What are these?" he asked.

I turned, following his gaze. My eyes widened. He was staring at the soap carvings he must not have noticed the day he'd stopped over after school. "Um..."

He leaned in, tilting his head to the side as he studied a sleeping cat. "Were they bars of soap?"

"Yeah," I whispered.

"Wow," he murmured, his gaze crawling over the heart and the sun I'd done a few years ago. "Did Carl or Rosa do this?"

I shook my head. "No. Um. I...did them."

"What?" He straightened and looked at me, surprise filling his expression. "You did this? Why haven't you said anything?"

My cheeks were burning. "No...one but Carl and Rosa know about it."

He stared at me then looked back into the cabinet. "Mallory, that's pretty amazing."

I lifted a shoulder. "It's just...soap."

"It's soap you carved into very recognizable things," he said. "I can't do that."

"But you can spray-paint and draw and—"

"And I can't do this," Rider repeated. "Those carvings take just the same amount of skill as spray-painting does."

I was going to have to disagree with that. Uncomfortable with the attention, I gestured toward the kitchen. "You ready?"

He watched me a moment longer then nodded.

Carl and Rosa waited at the kitchen table.

"This...this is Rider," I said, twisting my hands together. "And this...this is Carl and Rosa."

Rosa's brows lifted and there was a slight widening of her eyes.

Carl eyed Rider from the scuffed toes of his boots to the top of his messy blackish-brown hair, and his brows slammed down.

And that was the moment I knew this dinner was going to be all kinds of awkward.

★ ★ ★

It started with the food.

And then the questions.

Both things were related. The moment we sat down, Carl

began grilling Rider. Caught off guard by the tactic, I only managed to cut into my slice of roast and eat a chunk of potato.

Rider also hadn't touched most of his food, probably because Carl was apparently interviewing him. When there was a break in the Spanish Inquisition, Rider turned to me. "Are you going to eat?"

I nodded as I speared a potato. Rider watched until I actually ate the vegetable, and I resisted the urge to roll my eyes only because I knew what drove him. Like the times at lunch, he always made sure I ate. It was hard to break the habit after years of sharing scraps and leftovers. I ate another potato and Rider spooned up chickpeas.

Cutting into the pot roast, I glanced up and across the table. Carl and Rosa were staring at us. Knowing they probably didn't understand the exchange, I flushed.

"So you work at some kind of body shop?" Carl cleared his throat. A piece of perfectly cooked pot roast dangled from his fork. "Part-time?"

I closed my eyes.

"Yes, sir. At Razorback Garage. The owner calls me in to do custom paint jobs," Rider answered patiently. He'd been patient throughout the whole—the whole *ordeal*.

He answered every question Carl posed. How long was he in a group home? What neighborhood did he live in? What subject in school was he most interested in? Which, not surprisingly, turned out to be art class. The questions kept coming and coming, so much so that Rosa didn't get a word in edgewise.

I was so embarrassed.

And so incredibly disappointed.

"What do your foster parents do for a living?" Carl asked.

My fingers tightened around my fork as I breathed through my nose. This…this was getting out of hand.

Rider was unfazed. "I only have one foster parent. Mrs. Luna's husband passed away before I came into the picture. She works at the phone company."

"And what do you plan to do when you graduate high school?" Carl kept on firing. "You'll age out of the system and I assume you don't plan on staying with Mrs. Luna. Are you heading to college?"

"I currently don't have any plans to go to college," Rider responded as he pushed his chickpeas across his plate. "That costs a lot of money, and Mrs. Luna has already done so much for me. I couldn't expect her to pay for my college."

"There are grants and scholarships," Carl reasoned as he cut into the slice of pot roast. "I'm under the impression that you're very bright."

"He is," I said. "And he's also very talented. He...he has artwork displayed at a place in the city."

Rider grinned at me.

"You do?" Rosa responded smoothly. "At an art gallery?"

As Rider answered her question, I prayed that Carl would stop with the third degree.

Rider looked over and asked for a second time, "You're not eating?"

Half of my mouthwatering pot roast sat untouched. I was too frustrated to chew my food without spitting it onto the table.

He nudged my arm and said in a low voice, "Eat."

Sighing, I picked up my fork and stabbed the meat. "Happy?"

His dimple appeared in his cheek. "Thoroughly."

Carl's perpetual frown faded a bit and he eased off at that point. Sort of. When he asked what we planned to do tomorrow, it was me who answered, but he kept directing the questions to Rider. Thirty minutes after dinner was finished, I kind of wanted to flip a table.

It had been a very, very long time since I'd felt that way.

"Mallory tells me you have a girlfriend," Carl said, and I

nearly choked as my eyes widened. "How does she feel about you coming to dinner tonight?"

Rosa looked over at her husband, her brows raised. I opened my mouth to point out that his girlfriend really, seriously wasn't any of his business when Rider shocked me.

"I don't have a girlfriend, sir."

I jerked back in my seat as my head swung toward him. "What?"

"I mean, I did." Rider's cheeks pinked as his gaze met mine. "Paige and I... Well, we broke up."

My stomach dropped to my feet as I stared at him. A thousand thoughts whirled. I couldn't have been more shocked. He hadn't mentioned anything. Then again, I hadn't asked about him and Paige since last week, but how could he not have mentioned that?

"Well, this appears to be a surprise to everyone." Carl's tone was flat.

He continued to speak and Rider continued to answer his questions, but I wasn't paying attention as I stared at Rider's profile. There had been signs recently that things weren't normal between them. They really hadn't been talking to each other. Paige hadn't sought me out. Hector had said that they'd gotten into it and that was why Rider wasn't in class Friday. He'd been *tore up*. Maybe he hadn't been drinking. Maybe he'd been torn up because they'd broken up?

Maybe Paige was done with his friendship with me. Rider had said before if he had to choose between us... Oh, God, I really hoped it had nothing to do with our friendship. I didn't want to be that person who showed up and just...screwed up other people's lives.

I was still stunned when the table was cleared and Rider was leaving. "Thank you for dinner," he said to the Rivases, polite as ever. "It was delicious."

Snapping out of my head, I rose with him. "Do...you need a ride?"

He shook his head as he pushed the seat in.

"It was lovely meeting you." Rosa rose, placing her napkin on the table. "Don't be a stranger," she said, leaning in to give Rider a quick hug.

Carl nodded in his direction as we walked around the table. Rider stopped, extending his hand while Carl stood. "Thank you again, sir."

He smiled tightly as he shook Rider's hand. No words were exchanged, and I walked Rider outside. Streetlamps were on, casting buttery light on the smooth cement of the sidewalks.

"You sure I...I can't give you a ride?" I asked.

Nodding, he stopped on the steps and faced me. Our gazes connected, and that heady warmth was back. "I had a good time."

I raised a brow. "Really?"

He laughed as he shoved his hands into the pockets of his jeans. "Yeah. They're pretty cool people."

"Carl wasn't... He wasn't very friendly. He asked you so many questions and he...he wasn't very kind about it." Anger surfaced, scratching at my skin. "I'm sorry about that."

"You don't need to apologize, Mouse."

I folded my arms across my waist, realizing the roles reversed a little tonight. Instead of him defending me, it was the other way around, and that was a strange feeling. "I feel...feel like I have to."

One shoulder rose. "He's just protective of you and I'm glad you've got people wanting to look out for you." He paused. "Don't worry about me. It's all good."

Nothing about how Carl acted screamed *all good* to me.

"I'm not scared off easily," he said after a moment.

Shoving aside my anger with Carl, I asked what I'd been dying to know. "You and Paige really broke up?"

Rider nodded. "Yeah. Last week. Thursday night."

I slowly shook my head. "You...never said anything."

"It's not really something I wanted to talk about," he said, his gaze steady. "Paige and I have been friends since I first moved in with Hector and Jayden. I'm not sure if I…I can still say that."

"I'm sorry." And I meant that. Despite the feelings I had for him, the way I responded whenever he was near, I was still sorry he was hurting.

He smiled slightly. "I am, too. But being with her… Well, it wasn't right. Not anymore."

Well, that answered who broke up with who. I glanced over my shoulder, wondering why it wasn't right anymore. I wanted to ask what had broken them up, but couldn't exactly find the courage to speak those words. "You missed school last week… because of it?"

His brows knitted. "The breakup sucked, Mouse. I didn't want to hurt her and I know I did. Hurting her was the last thing I wanted." His shoulders rose with a deep breath. "We'll talk more about it tomorrow, okay?"

Tomorrow.

"Okay," I breathed.

He stilled as he watched me. Then his gaze slipped over my shoulder, and he seemed to make up his mind about something, because the next second he was coming back up the steps. He stopped just below me. "The soap carvings are pretty cool, and I hope to see more of them," he said, and then he leaned in, kissing my cheek. My breath caught.

Rider pulled away, his gaze serious. "See you tomorrow, Mallory."

My cheek tingled as I watched him pivot on the step and walk down, out onto the sidewalk. He glanced over his shoulder, saw me and smiled before continuing to walk. I stood there until he disappeared from sight, allowed myself the moment to replay his parting words, and then I prepared myself.

The shock of Paige and Rider's breakup along with Rider's request to see more of the soap carvings faded a bit and I allowed the anger and frustration to resurface.

Carl was leaning against the counter as Rosa was placing the last of the dishes into the dishwasher when I walked back in. For once in my life, I wasn't thinking about the thousands of different words I could speak. I knew exactly what I wanted to say.

I stopped in front of the island. "You weren't very nice to Rider."

Carl faced me, his expression blank. "I'm sorry?"

"You weren't very nice to Rider," I repeated. "You treated him like he was...a suspect at a crime scene."

Rosa's lips parted.

He straightened as his eyes widened. "Mallory—"

"Rider doesn't live like we do," I said, eyes and throat burning. "His foster mom isn't a doctor and he doesn't think he can afford college. None of that makes him...a bad person."

"We didn't say he was a bad person." Rosa stepped around Carl, expression earnest. "And if we gave the impression—"

"You did." I spoke directly to Carl, my voice shaking. "You kept questioning him and no matter...how he answered, it wasn't enough."

Wrinkles formed around his eyes. "If you want to talk about Rider, let's talk about the fact that he doesn't have a girlfriend."

"He did have one. They broke up."

"Convenient," Carl murmured.

"See!" I all but threw up my hands. "You think...that's convenient. As if I've lied about it, or Rider has. I want him to be a part of my life...of our life. And I was so excited about tonight—about you all finally meeting him." My lower lip trembled. "He...he saved my life many times and I thought... I thought you would respect him for that."

"Mallory," Carl said.

Turning around, I did something I'd never done before. I ignored Carl as I climbed the steps. I was done with the conversation.

CHAPTER 21

The desk lamp in the library had been left on, casting the space in soft yellow light. It smelled faintly of peaches in the room. I drifted along the bookshelves, running my fingers over their spines. I stopped at the center bookcase and my hand fell to my side. Somehow I'd found myself in our home library that morning, after a crappy night's sleep following an even crappier dinner.

I'd woken early and roamed the house while Carl and Rosa slept, restless and unable to go back to bed. Some of that had to do with seeing Rider and Ainsley later. Some had to do with learning Rider and Paige weren't together.

Ainsley had offered up her usual brand of wisdom when I'd filled her in on the dinner disaster. She said Carl's reaction was normal, that when she first brought Todd home she was convinced her father was going to toss him out the front door.

I wasn't quite so sure that was the case.

Then she focused on the Paige and Rider drama, convinced the breakup meant something for me. I couldn't even allow my head to go there, because it didn't know what to do with all of that.

I thought about the book that Rider used to read to me when we were little—a story that always made me cry but also filled me with hope that one day we'd be real, too, that we'd be loved.

Because that was how it felt growing up. Like Rider and I weren't real. No one thought about us or worried. We were forgotten, left behind to virtually fend for ourselves.

Now I had two people who thought about me, who fended for me and who worried. I should be grateful for that, as Rider had reminded me last night, but right now I just felt mad.

Carl and Rosa knew all about Rider, all about everything he'd done for me growing up. I'd thought that would've put Rider in a good place with Carl, but he'd been skeptical and distrustful. Judging.

And I still couldn't believe I'd said what I said to Carl. Even now, my pulse kicked up and I sort of felt sick. I knew Carl was upset with me, most likely even mad for saying what I said. I wanted to…I wanted to be perfect for him—for them, and I wasn't perfect last night.

I'd avoided both of them last night and that was the game plan for today.

Sighing, I moved along the bookcases. The two center shelves were full of framed photos, starting with a happy-looking baby and moving all the way up to a beautiful, bright teenage girl with long dark hair and shining brown eyes.

I stared at the pictures of Marquette, and I couldn't help but think how unfair it was that she was no longer here. And it wasn't fair that the kid Rosa worked on would never walk again. All the terrible things that Rider witnessed, experienced, hadn't been fair. It wasn't fair that I'd—

Closing my eyes, I shut the path of thoughts off. If I went there now, in my head, I'd be a mess. There'd be things I didn't want to think about.

When I reopened my eyes, Marquette stared back at me in a picture taken a few months before her death. She was at the beach, wearing a pretty black two-piece bikini that I doubted I'd ever have the confidence to pull off. Hot pink sunglasses shielded her eyes, and her smile was huge. White sand glimmered under her feet, and the ocean sparkled behind her.

Marquette had a boyfriend, one she had started dating during her junior year. I didn't know his name, only that he'd existed from the bits and pieces of conversations I'd picked up over the years. She also had a lot of friends. Popular. Smart. In all of her pictures, she looked like someone who was nice. Someone like Keira.

I thought about the boy who would never walk again. What was his life like? It didn't matter, I quickly realized, if he was unkind and not well liked or if he was the most popular boy at school. It wasn't fair.

Stepping back from the pictures, I wondered something I'd thought about a million times. And it was wrong, such a horrible thing to consider, but I couldn't help it. If Marquette was still alive today, would I be where I was? Would Carl and Rosa still have fought to bring me into their home? Given me all the opportunities that so many others had missed out on?

I didn't know the answers to that and they nagged at me, but I did know two things.

Her life was cut short.

And I was given a second chance.

I continued to stare at her picture. I had a second chance when so many people only had one chance, and I couldn't let it be in vain.

What had Santos said in speech class about trying and living? It was all about trying, and that was what I would do.

I would try.

★ ★ ★

"Oh my God," Ainsley squealed as I neared the bench she was sitting at. She popped up, adjusting her sunglasses as they started to slip down her nose. "You look freaking adorable!"

Slowing, I glanced down at myself in relief. Picking out my outfit for this moment had been a pretty stressful endeavor. I'd ended up settling on black leggings, a white lacy cami and a pale blue cardigan. I'd left my hair down and smoothed it out with Rosa's flatiron. I'd been amazed by the fact I hadn't fried my hair in the process and I'd washed the makeup off my face about three times before settling on what was supposed to be a "fresh" look I'd learned from watching YouTube, which took about thirty minutes to pull off.

Ainsley grabbed my hand and started pulling me toward the door of the café she'd picked out. "Okay. So you're about five minutes early, and he's going to be here any minute, and I want to freak out."

I grinned. She wanted to freak out? I felt like I was seconds from hyperventilating.

She led us into the restaurant. The place wasn't that busy and we were seated immediately, at a table big enough for four. She sat across from me, leaving the seat next to me open, and my heart jumped.

Pushing the sunglasses onto her head, she winced when she looked to our left, at the all-glass front. Bright sunlight poured into the restaurant. She shifted her chair so she wasn't sitting directly in the light.

"Are your...eyes still...bothering you?" I asked.

Rolling said eyes, she sighed. "Yeah. I don't know what's going on with them. The eye doctor where I went to get new glasses told Mom I needed to see some kind of specialist."

Concern blossomed in the pit of my belly. "What...for?"

She raised a shoulder. "He saw something weird when he was looking at my eyes and thinks a retina specialist needs to take a look at them. He doesn't think it's a big deal."

A specialist sounded like a big deal. "Does he think something is wrong?"

She shook her head. "Not sure. He didn't really say much beyond that."

"When is...your appointment?" I asked, pausing when the waitress appeared and filled our three glasses with water.

"Two weeks from now. Anyway, enough about me. Are you nervous?" she asked, wrapping her fingers around the menu.

I nodded even though I wasn't sure if Ainsley was telling me the whole truth about whatever was going on with her eyes. "Yes."

"You know what this is like, right?" She tugged the menu to her chest. "This is like a date."

My stomach dropped all the way to the floor. I shook my head.

"Yes. Yes," she reiterated. "It's just like a date. Like a practice date."

Practice dates? Were there such things? I started to ask her, but she continued, "Okay. Let's look at the evidence here. From the moment you two saw each other, he has made every attempt to reach out to you, right? He's skipped class to have lunch with you. When you freaked out in class, he left to make sure you were okay and then showed you that graffiti stuff. He helped you with your speech, and he actually came over to meet Carl and Rosa. That means he's interested."

It also meant he could just want to be a part of my life, but before I could point that out, I saw him. Rider was here. He turned sideways and scanned the restaurant.

I stiffened. His gaze locked with mine and a slow grin appeared on his face. He didn't look like he had last night. More like he did every day at school. Worn jeans. A black henley instead of a T-shirt and beat-up sneakers, but goodness, I couldn't think.

Okay. Not true. I could think, but I was thinking things I really had no concept of. I was thinking about those full, slightly curved lips and how they must feel in places...other than my forehead or cheek. I was thinking about his hands and how strong they were and the oddly pleasant calluses on his palms. I was thinking about...about a lot of things—things that now didn't feel so wrong since he was actually single.

Noticing my near-prone position, Ainsley looked over her shoulder. "Oh, my good God almighty," she murmured. "That's him?"

"Yes," I whispered. That was so him.

She whipped back around, her blue eyes wide. "Mallory. Wow."

I couldn't respond, because I was focused on Rider. He walked through the center of the restaurant with a confidence that oozed from him. An older woman sitting with her husband looked up as he passed her table. She smiled, her gaze following him.

And then he was at the table. I might've stopped breathing as he stepped around and pulled out the chair beside mine and sat. "Sorry," he said, looking at me. "I'm a few minutes late."

He was?

"Hector gave me a ride in," he continued. "He's around here somewhere. Didn't want to crash our lunch, though."

Had Rider invited him? If so, did that change the fact that Ainsley thought it was a practice date? Did those really exist? Did any of this matter?

Ainsley jerked forward, smiling at Rider. "I'm Ainsley. Hi."

Rider cocked his head to the side, grinning at her. "I'm Rider."

"I know," she said. "You are definitely Rider."

I narrowed my eyes at her.

She ignored me. "I'm so glad to finally meet you. I've heard so much about you."

"Really?" He lifted his brows, glancing over at me. "What have you been telling her, Mouse?"

I opened my mouth, but there were no words. The right side of his lips kicked up. The dimple came out. Oh, Lord.

"Mallory has said you're an amazing guy," she said, and I wasn't quite sure I'd ever said that in those words. "And you two grew up together. Best friends?"

"Yeah," he murmured, still looking at me with that...that damn grin. "We were best friends." Pausing, he finally looked over at Ainsley. "But I think I've been replaced."

"You have," she quipped. "It's a good thing I like to share."

He chuckled. "I guess so."

My heart pounded fast and I knew I needed to say something. Anything. "Have...you eaten here before?"

That kind of sounded lame.

Rider shook his head, unfazed by my lameness. "No." He glanced down at the menu. "But the burgers look good."

Suddenly, I thought about the Firehouse. The small-time diner was more his style, laid back and well-worn. This place, with all the glass and shiny white tabletops... It was the kind of place Ainsley and I ate at all the time now, but I would've never set foot in before Carl and Rosa.

Did Rider feel out of place? Did he even care? Or was I just being stupid?

Probably stupid.

"Their hamburgers are awesome," Ainsley advised. "So is their hummus."

"Hummus?" Rider tipped his head back and laughed. "Not my style. Give me meat."

"Have you tried hummus?" she asked. "On meat?"

My nose wrinkled.

"No." He laughed again. "I've never tried that."

"You should," she replied.

"You shouldn't," I said.

When the waitress arrived, Rider ordered a hamburger without hummus. I got the same and added a Coke. Ainsley went for the hummus appetizer that she would consume all by herself.

Rider and Ainsley fell into an easy conversation. She asked him about school. He asked her about homeschooling, and by the time we'd finished our lunch, they were chatting like they'd known each other for years. I chimed in, but stayed quiet, which wasn't a surprise. I relaxed, but was hyperaware of every movement Rider made and every time he looked in my direction.

"Are you guys doing something after lunch?" he asked, dropping his arm along the back of my seat. "Movies or something?"

"Actually, I can't go to the movies. I have to... My parents have something for me to do this evening, so Mallory is completely free," Ainsley said in a rush.

I stilled. What? She never mentioned having to change the plans.

Rider's gaze flicked between us. "But I thought you two were hanging out all day?"

"Nope," Ainsley replied quickly. "Just for a few hours. She's all yours for the rest of the day, and word has it, her curfew is, like, eleven p.m."

My eyes widened. Oh my God. What was happening? I looked at her and she smiled innocently at me. A heads-up would've been nice.

One side of his lips kicked up as he picked up his drink. "Sounds good to me." He tapped his fingers off the back of my shoulder. "You want to head to the garage?"

The low rumble of his voice sent my heart racing into overdrive. Ainsley was staring at her empty plate. Before I could formulate a response, a cell phone rang at our table.

Rider shifted, pulling his phone out of his pocket. He glanced down at it and stood. "Be right back."

The moment Rider was out of earshot, Ainsley turned to me. "Mal, he is hot."

I flushed as I picked up my drink. Rider was hot with two

extra *T*s. There was no questioning that, but it went beyond the physical hotness. Underneath all of that good stuff was a really… really good guy. A shiny heart.

"You were not kidding when you described him." Ainsley grinned as she sat back in the chair. "Are you going to go with him? I mean, you kind of have to because I totally just threw you out there—but I threw you because you want to be thrown. You *need* to be thrown."

Blinking, I nearly dropped my glass as I looked at her. "But I'm…hanging out with you all day."

"We had our hang. Even if I couldn't convince you to try hummus. Now's your chance to hang with someone else. A very *hot* someone else."

My stomach twisted, the feeling not unpleasant and all too familiar. "But—"

"Rosa and Carl think you're with me. So as long as you get home by whenever, they'll never know. It's not like they're going to talk to my parents." Her grin was sly. "Especially considering they're doing their own thing tonight. Date night or something." Her nose wrinkled. "So, it's no problem."

I glanced up to where Rider stood and the twisting motion increased. My mind wheeled. I couldn't believe I was actually considering this. Yes, I'd left school without Rosa and Carl knowing and Rider had been over to the house without them knowing, but this…this would be different. It was like some kind of invisible line that I was stepping over. The Rivases thought I was with Ainsley, but I wouldn't be.

I would be with Rider.

On a Saturday afternoon and maybe evening. The practice date felt like a real date.

This did seem like a major step.

If I got caught, they would say it was Rider and that he was a bad influence, but in reality, he didn't know I wouldn't be allowed. Hell, I didn't even know if I wouldn't be allowed, but I sure as heck wasn't asking.

I wasn't even sure if I was doing something wrong and I wasn't going to ask, because that sounded like a really stupid question to ask.

Rider lowered his phone, slipping it into his pocket. Could I even do this? Go hang out with him? I hastily picked up my drink and took a huge gulp. Why was I freaking out about this? Rider and I grew up together. Sure, there were years when we didn't see each other, but we were friends and he'd just gotten out of a relationship. This wasn't a practice date.

And I could do this.

"You...you think I should go?"

Ainsley's blue eyes were wide with excitement. "Yes! Oh my God, yes!" She smacked my arm. "This is the perfect time for alone time."

I frowned. "But we...we have a lot of alone time."

She stared at me a moment and then rolled her eyes. "This is a different kind of alone time, Mallory. This is *Saturday* alone time."

My brows rose.

Shaking her head, she picked up her drink. "Trust me. It's different."

I was going to have to trust her with that.

"You're interested in him, so just a heads-up—I think he's interested in you, too. I mean, come on, why wouldn't he be? But guys are kind of dumb sometimes, so he's probably gonna play it cool and act like he's not interested."

I opened my mouth.

"That's what Todd did. He acted like he wasn't into me until we were alone and then he made his move."

Would Rider make a move? My heart started to swell with the possibilities of it and then my stomach twisted again.

Ainsley was practically rocking in her seat. "I know this is all new for you, but just take a couple of deep breaths and have fun. Maybe he'll do more than hold your hand."

Oh my God, this was too much. I should've never told her about Rider holding my hand. I so needed an adult.

"Look," she said, lowering her voice as she reached over, placing her hand over mine. "Only go if you're comfortable with it. If it's something you want to do. If you don't, it's not a big deal. I just know you like him as more than a friend. I can tell because of the way you look at—" she paused, glancing over her shoulder "—him. Holy hell, who is *that*?"

Brows knitting, I followed her gaze and saw that Rider wasn't alone anymore. Hector was standing with him at the entrance to the café. Concern rose. Their heads were low and the hard set to Rider's jaw said they weren't talking about something fun.

I glanced out the front windows, expecting to see Jayden, but he wasn't out there. Come to think of it, I hadn't seen Jayden at school the last couple of days.

"Do you know who that is?" Ainsley asked.

Swallowing as I placed the glass down, I nodded. "His name is…Hector. He's Rider's friend."

A slow smile curled her lips. "He's yummy."

Just at that moment Hector laughed at something Rider must've said. The sound was deep and it traveled, turning several heads in the café. Hector was yummy. No doubt about that, but my gaze strayed to Rider. He smiled slightly, the dimple in his right cheek playing peekaboo. His lips moved and Hector glanced over at our table.

Surprise flickered over his face and then his full lips kicked up when his gaze settled on Ainsley and stayed.

"Me likie," she whispered. "Does he have a girlfriend?"

I shrugged, wondering if she still had a boyfriend. I wasn't sure if Hector had someone serious. I'd seen him with a couple of girls at school, but I didn't think he was dating any of them.

Rider and Hector made their way to our table. Rider re-claimed his seat next to me while Hector sat beside Ainsley.

"Esa chica esta bien caliente." Hector laughed as Rider shook his head. Ainsley stiffened across from me. She was pretty fluent in Spanish and even though Hector was Puerto Rican, I had a feeling she was getting the general gist of whatever he was say-ing and she was not happy about it. *"Me gustaria a llevarla a mi casa y comermela."*

Ainsley cocked her head to the side as she brushed her long, blond hair over her shoulder. *"Gracias! Pero no hay ni una parte de mi que tu te vas a comer."*

Hector's eyes widened.

Rider threw his head back and burst into laughter. "Oh, shit. Priceless."

"What?" Ainsley blinked big eyes at the stunned Hector. "You think some white chick can't possibly understand another language so you're going to sit in front of me and talk about me like I'm not here?" Her smile was brittle and fake. "Bitch, please."

"Man..." Hector sat back, slowly shaking his head as he stared at her. "You're...brutal."

"Damn straight," she replied, her eyes like chips of blue ice. Whatever yumminess she'd seen in Hector was completely out the window now. "And you're a *mal criado.*"

Hector's eyes narrowed.

"I really like your friend, Mouse." Still chuckling, Rider winked at me. "She basically called him a classless ass, and I agree."

Oh dear.

Ainsley arched a brow as she eyed Hector's worn shirt. "If the shoe fits..."

"Que carajo..." Hector muttered. *"Nena,* you don't know me."

She raised a shoulder. "And I don't want to."

Oh. Oh, wow. This was going downhill fast even though Rider looked like he wanted a bucket of popcorn.

Ainsley twisted in her seat and faced me, her cheeks slightly flushed. "Are you going with Rider?" she asked, voice low but still audible.

"Where are you guys going?" Hector asked, gaze still fastened on her.

She ignored him, and my stomach was doing cartwheels again. "I was going to take her to the garage," Rider said.

Hector's lip curled. "Sounds legit." He smirked when Rider lifted his hand and extended a long middle finger. "You're not going to Ramon's tonight? Big party."

Rider's gaze met mine, and there was a hitch in my throat. "Not if Mallory's going to go with me to the garage."

"You can bring her," he said, and then looked at Ainsley with a smirk. "I would invite you, *mami*, but it's probably not classy enough for you."

"If you're involved, probably not," she replied drily. "But I'm not interested anyway, so whatever."

I barely recognized that Hector and Ainsley started arguing at that point, most of it in Spanish. A party? As lame as it sounded, I'd never been to a party before. Nowhere even near one. My pulse fluttered in my neck like an out of control hummingbird. Dropping my hands to my legs, I ran my palms over my thighs.

What would I do there? I'd be clinging to Rider like an octopus. I would be expected to talk—to mingle. To drink. The only time I'd ever tasted alcohol was when I was nine and I'd ended up spitting it out. I could barely speak in front of multiple people right now, let alone hang out at a party.

Rider's gaze met mine, and I knew I must've looked panicked. I could practically feel the blood draining from my face. "Nah, I'm not really feeling up to a party tonight," he said when there was a break in the two arguing. "You okay with that, Mallory?"

Part of me knew he was saying that just for my sake, because

I was sure a party had to be more fun than him trying to teach me how to spray-paint. But there was no denying the sugary-sweet relief buzzing through my veins.

I was taking steps—baby steps—but going to the party felt like a huge jump off a cliff with no rope. Swallowing, I nodded. "I'm okay with that."

"Good," he murmured, sitting back. "Then the garage it is."

Trying to play it cool, I lowered my gaze, but I couldn't stop the smile from tipping up the corners of my lips. It was definitely a goofy one, too big and out of control, but I was excited. Nervous. But so much more excited.

No matter what went down tonight—tonight would be a first.

CHAPTER 22

Rider was behind the wheel of my car for the drive to the Razorback Garage. Made sense since he knew where to go and I was a bundle of nerves. For the first couple of moments, as we made our way out of the parking garage, we didn't talk.

I took that time trying to come up with something to say. "Did...did you like the café?" I asked. "I know it was...different." Once those words were out of my mouth, I winced. Could I have come up with anything lamer? Like, how's the weather? Ugh.

He bit down on his lower lip as he glanced over at me. "It was cool. How was it different?"

"I was just...thinking that before, I...would've never set foot in a place like that." I paused, wondering where I was going with this. "We wouldn't have."

He slid his hand over the wheel, easily navigating the turns. "So, what you're really asking is if I was comfortable in a place like that?"

I opened my mouth, but the words got stuck again. As usual. Heat swept into my cheeks. That was what I was asking, wasn't it?

"Mouse?"

Shaking my head, I fiddled with the strap of my seat belt. "I didn't mean it like that."

He was quiet as he pulled out in traffic. "You didn't?"

I didn't know what to say.

"Seems like a pretty obvious question, though. I mean, we don't have the same lives anymore, do we?" he asked.

I peeked at him. He was staring straight ahead. One hand on the steering wheel and the other resting on his thigh. My natural reaction was just to stay quiet. If I did, I knew Rider would move on to something else, but I put that out there. I had to own it. I couldn't stay quiet forever.

Drawing in a shallow breath, I focused on the red truck in front of us. "We don't, but I...I really don't think about it. That's why I didn't think twice about...the café."

"I'm as comfortable in a place like that as I am anywhere else," he replied after a few moments, his voice level but devoid of any emotion.

Glancing over at him, I felt like a total tool. "I've probably... offended you. I'm sorry."

"You didn't," he responded, squinting. "Honestly."

I nodded as I pressed my lips together. There was so much that Rider and I shared in the past, but sometimes it felt like there was a gulf between us. I could sit here and think about it or I could try to forge a bridge over that gulf.

Forcing my fingers to relax around the seat belt, I dropped my hands to my lap. "In...class yesterday, it sounded like...you and Mr. Santos know each other."

"He helped me out when I got busted tagging the school," he replied. "Thought I told you that."

"It seemed like...more than that." I glanced at him. "He put... your artwork in a gallery."

Rider didn't respond immediately. "He's kind of kept an eye on me since the tagging incident. He's like that, you know. Pays attention." One shoulder rose. "He's always checked in. Doesn't see what others do."

"What...do you mean?"

His fingers tapped off the steering wheel. "He doesn't just see neighborhoods and addresses or any of that crap." Pausing, he looked over at me as we hit a stoplight. "He's been on my ass about pursuing a future in art. Talked to me about looking into MICA." He laughed, shaking his head. "He has lofty goals."

Maryland Institute College of Art was a well-known art school in the city. Like one of the best. "If Santos thinks you have...what it takes to go there, why wouldn't you?"

His brows flew up. "I'm pretty sure a semester there costs more than a brand-new car."

"What about financial aid?"

He didn't respond.

And I didn't drop it. Not for the same reasons Carl was hounding him the night before, but because Rider had real talent. "If not MICA, there are cheaper...colleges. Ones easier to get into."

"I know," he replied, and that was all he said.

I frowned as I studied him. "When we were younger, you talked about going to college. You did when I...didn't."

His hand tightened on the steering wheel. "I was a kid then, Mouse."

"So?"

"Things are different now."

"Things are better now," I replied. "Aren't they?"

He slowed down, turning onto a narrow side road. "Have you noticed that when you feel strongly about something, you don't take pauses?"

I had noticed that, and part of me was thrilled he'd paid close enough attention to recognize it. But seriously, that wasn't what we were talking about. "Things are better, aren't they?"

"Yes, Mouse," he said with a sigh.

My eyes narrowed. "When you say it like that, I'm not sure I believe you." I studied him, deciding I might as well ask more questions. "What happened…between you and Paige?"

"Why the third degree?" he returned as he pulled into a parking spot in front of the garage.

"Because I care," I blurted out. He was right about the third degree. I was kind of doing the same thing Carl had done the night before, but at least I was coming from a good place.

Rider's head swung toward me and our eyes met. I didn't regret spewing those words out, because it was the truth. I cared about him. I had *always* cared about him. Without looking away, he turned off the ignition and pulled the key out. His hands settled in his lap as he studied me.

"It wasn't fair to Paige," he said. "The relationship."

"How so?" I asked.

He stared at me a moment and then one side of his lips curled up. "I don't even think we should've gotten together. We were better off as friends, and it…" His gaze slid to the gray, squat building. "I mean, I really did care about her. I *do* care about her. And maybe there was a part of me in the beginning that thought that…that it ran deeper, you know? The thing is, it doesn't run deep." His shoulders rose with a deep breath. "I think I've known that for a while. And I think I convinced myself that it was the same for Paige. I don't regret the relationship, but I regret that I waited to end it. I hurt her because of that and, man, that sucked. She is important to me…"

He shook his head. "After you and I finished at the library, I went over to see her. I ended things like I should've done before. So I drank last Thursday—drank a little too much."

Pausing, he reached over and his fingers brushed my side as he unhooked my seat belt. "Being with her wasn't the right thing to do, you know?" He slipped the seat belt off my shoulder. "I felt like I was stringing her along. Especially now."

"Now?"

"Yeah." His gaze searched mine. "Especially now."

My lips parted on a soft inhale.

A long moment stretched out between us and he asked, "You ready to head in?"

Pressing my lips together, I nodded. I opened the door and waited for Rider to come around the side. A truck drove past us, the music a heavy thump echoing as it traveled down the block. I looked around as we crossed the street. The neighborhood wasn't bad. Lots of storefront businesses and farther down, I could see brick row homes.

"You live near here?" I asked.

Rider nodded as he stopped in front of a gray, windowless door. "Yeah. About three blocks down." He fished out a key and unlocked the door. "The shop is kind of a mess. Sorry."

"It's okay." It was a body shop. I expected it to be messy.

He opened the door and stepped inside, holding it for me. I followed him. A heavy scent immediately hit me, a combination of paint and oil mixed with gasoline. It smelled like hard work.

When he threw a switch along the wall, a low hum reverberated through the building. Hanging ceiling lights flickered on, spaced every couple of feet. The light was faint at first, but grew stronger.

Rider moved ahead, shoving his hands into his pockets. "Follow me?"

Wrapping my arms around my waist, I walked behind him as he made his way around a car that was jacked up into the air. Tires were missing, revealing exposed wheel wells.

Workbenches and tool chests were everywhere. Splotches of oil and grease covered the cement floor. The farther we walked in the long and wide building, the more cars we saw covered by thick canvas, and the heavier the scent of paint grew. It was darker back there.

Faint yellow light glanced off Rider's cheeks as he looked over his shoulder. He stopped by a covered car. "I don't have set hours here. Drew calls me when he has a job. Been lucky the last couple of months. Work's been steady."

Stretching up, he caught ahold of a chain. Muscles along his back tensed, and his shirt strained over his shoulders and biceps as he tugged it. That warm, heavy feeling infiltrated my veins.

Light flooded the space. The first thing I noticed was a large canvas draped across the wall. It was covered with paint. As if a hundred different colors had been tossed on the canvas in no particular pattern.

Rider followed my gaze. "That's where I test out the colors. Sometimes I have to mix them before I put them in the sprayer."

"Sprayer?"

Nodding, he turned toward a bench. Several silver canisters with nozzles were laid out across the top. He walked over, picking one up. "Paint goes in here." He ran his finger along the canister fitted to the top of the sprayer. "And the bottom hooks up to a hose that runs to the air compressor." He laughed, sounding a little off as he put the sprayer back on the workbench. "Not that you were asking for a lesson on a sprayer."

"It's okay." I stepped closer. "It's interesting."

Rider laughed again as he walked away from the bench. He went past me, stopping in front of a covered car. "I've been working on this car for the last week." He grabbed the canvas at the hood of the car and pulled it off. "Almost done."

My mouth dropped open.

I didn't know what kind of car it was. A white two-seater. Probably a coupe. It didn't matter. It was what was painted across the hood and front fender that caught my attention.

It was the American flag. Now, that didn't sound too special, but the detail of the flag took it to a whole new level. Not a single red line bled into the white lines. The stars were perfect bursts of white among deep navy blue. The flag wasn't a stagnant square. It rippled as if it were a real cloth placed over the hood, draping the fender, and wind was washing over it. It made it look like the car was actually moving.

How could he do that with paint sprayed onto the surface?

"The guy wanted something Americana." He stepped forward, brushing his hand along the fender, wiping away an imaginary speck of dirt. "We ended up settling on a flag."

In awe, I shook my head as I placed my hand over my chest. I couldn't believe it. I'd seen what he'd painted on the warehouse, and that had been awe-inspiring, but this was something else. "This is amazing."

"Really?"

"Yes." I looked at him, eyes wide. "How can you not see how amazing this is?"

Rider shrugged as he flipped his attention back to the car. "It's just a flag."

"It looks real!" My voice pitched, but I didn't care. Rider came from nothing. *Nothing.* Was raised in darkness and violence, but he'd had this ability the entire time. What he'd experienced hadn't snuffed out this talent. "Like I could walk over…and lift it up."

"Huh." There was a pause. "Thank you."

"Do you…keep track of your work?"

He shook his head. "Not really."

"You should have pictures of this," I insisted. "Of all that you do."

He lowered his chin. "I have some at the house. Not together or anything. Drew usually takes a picture. Puts it up on the website."

"A portfolio book!" Excited, I rocked back. "That's what you need."

The corner of his lips tipped up and then he bent down, picking up the tarp. I watched him drape it back over the car, straightening it as he walked around the sides.

I inhaled softly. "I…I would like to see more of your stuff."

"I can show you some later. Gather up the pics," he said, tugging the material over the trunk of the coupe.

Smiling, I unfolded my arms. An idea formed while I watched him fix the other side of the tarp as he made his way back to me. Rider wouldn't get a portfolio book. For some reason, he just couldn't recognize his talent, but that didn't mean I couldn't help him.

"Want to try it?" he asked.

My eyes widened. "Try painting a car?"

Rider's hazel eyes twinkled as he laughed. "No. Not painting a car, Mouse." Walking toward me, he gestured at the canvas tacked to the wall. "Paint there."

Turning, my gaze crawled across the canvas. There were spots untouched by paint. Mostly the lower half.

Rider walked to the bench and opened the drawer, pulling out two white masks. "Fumes can get a bit much." He walked back to me. "So what do you think?"

Smiling, I nodded.

The twist of his lips kicked up higher and he placed the mask over my head, letting it dangle below my chin. His eyes met mine as he scooped my hair out from under the band. He hesitated, staring down at me. His mouth opened as if he wished to say something but then changed his mind. He slipped his own mask on, letting it hang as he pivoted around, approaching a tall plastic cabinet near the bench. He opened it, and out came regular-looking spray cans.

"Figured we'd start with this before we moved on to that stuff," he explained, tone light as he handed over a can with a red top. "The color suits you."

I felt my cheeks heat as I wrapped my hands around the can. Rider led me over to the canvas, shaking his can as he went. I did the same, probably looking a little deranged.

"How about we start with just a letter—the letter *M*." He

tugged his mask up over his mouth and when he spoke, his voice was muffled. "Here."

Shoving the can under his arm, he turned to me and pulled the mask up, situating it over my mouth. His hands lingered along the band, sending a shiver dancing down my spine. "There you go."

He popped the lid off the can and it hit the floor with a soft clang. Eyes bright, he knelt down and with a series of flicks, he had a bold letter *R* in black paint. "Your turn."

At first I just stood there, frozen with indecision. I didn't know what I was doing. I mean, spray-painting a letter wasn't hard, but the idea of even trying to do it was frightening, because... because of what? Failing? How could I fail at spray-painting a letter? I mean, come on. And if I did somehow manage to be that ridiculous, Rider wouldn't care. I shouldn't care.

But I was scared of just *trying*.

A tremor curled down my arm, and I stopped thinking, stopped stressing. I popped the lid off and then walked forward. I knelt down and painted a giant, bubbly letter *M* in red.

There.

No big deal.

No one was injured or killed by my lame *M*. I looked up at Rider, and even though I couldn't see his mouth, I thought he was smiling.

"So..." He added an *I* beside his *R*. "You're looking at college, right?"

I started to nod as I drew an *A*, but forced myself to talk. "Yes. I want to...go to College Park, but I..."

"What?"

My brows knitted as I concentrated on what I was doing. "Carl and Rosa want me to go into...one of the health sciences, focus on research. Marquette—their daughter—was going to become a doctor like them."

Rider was quiet as he worked slightly above me, to my left. "Is that what *you* want to do?"

"I…" I stopped, lowering the can as I stared at the first three letters of my name. I already knew the answer, but I thought about how Carl had laughed and outright dismissed my idea of going into social work. I didn't want Rider to do the same. "I don't…know." I looked over at him. "Do you think that's not what I want?"

He paused, his gaze finding mine. "I don't know the answer to that, Mouse. You're not the same girl I knew four years ago."

Sometimes I felt like I was exactly the same girl.

He started spraying again and the heavy scent of paint puffed into the air. "As long as it's what you're passionate about, go for it."

I was so not passionate about research, but I had a feeling I would be when it came to social work. I just didn't want to disappoint Carl and Rosa, and I knew if I decided to do something like that, I would. But what else was I passionate about?

Rider talked about the different jobs he'd done, some of the shapes he had to paint. I'd laughed when he said he had to do a clown on a van once. That was about fifty levels of creepy. We filled in our letters. Rider got all fancy, zig-zagging designs throughout the letters. I tried it and it looked like blood splatter.

And I thought more about what I was passionate about. What screamed my name, and I realized as I finished filling in the *Y*, I had no answer. Everything about me was superficial, barely scratched the surface. I liked to read. I liked to carve soap. I liked to watch *Project Runway*. I didn't love any of those things.

I didn't want to write like Ainsley did. Carving soap was more of a weird hobby—my own version of meditation. And I couldn't design a white cotton T-shirt to save my life.

Man, I was…kind of blank. Like the spots on the canvas that had just the tiniest drops of paint on it. There were things

I liked, things that had caught my attention over the years, but for the most part, I was empty.

Over the past couple of years, I'd been slowly unpacking all the emotional baggage from the past, all the trauma and fear, but that mess had done more than just keep me silent, existing in the background. It had held me back from—from *living*. Wasn't that what being passionate really was? Living? Except that fear was still there and because of it, I was this blank thing.

Oddly, a pressure lifted from my shoulders. I didn't feel bad about this as I rose. I was basically a blank canvas and that wasn't a bad thing, I decided in that moment, because that meant I...I could be whatever.

I could become *anything*.

I just had to do it.

But my name looked like a bloody marshmallow.

I grinned behind the mask.

"I like it." Rider removed his mask as he walked over to the bench, dropping the can and mask there. "What do you think?"

Tugging the mask off over my head, I smiled at him. "I like it." I glanced back at our names. "Thank you for bringing me here. I'm sure the party...is probably more interesting—"

"Not true. I can't think of a place I'd rather be," he said, twisting his long and lean body toward mine. "Honestly."

My brows flew up. I wasn't sure if I should believe him or not.

He picked up a cloth. "Show me your hands."

I did. Two of my fingers had red smudges on them, much like his always seemed to. Taking my hand between his, he gently scrubbed at the paint. "I'm being serious, Mallory. I'm happy you're here. I don't care about a party."

Staring up at him as he diligently cleaned my hand, I decided to let myself believe what he was saying. To take his words at face value. Pulling the cloth away, he inspected my hand. "You don't see what I see."

"What?"

His brows furrowed together as he swiped the cloth over my pointer finger once more. Then he dropped the cloth behind him and picked up the red spray can.

"I want to back up to this whole caring about me thing," he said, surprising me as he made his way back to the canvas. "I know you care about me, Mallory."

My heart started beating fast as he shook the can.

"I care about you." He knelt halfway down. A second passed and he moved his arm, spraying on the canvas. "And I think this was missing something."

Having no idea what he was doing or where he was going with this, I waited until he rose and stepped back, to the side. My lips parted on a soft gasp. Rider had spray-painted a heart between our names. I saw it with my own eyes:

Angling toward me, his grin was sheepish. Boyish. "That was probably really corny, wasn't it?"

My heart was doing overtime, thumping so fast I thought I might have a heart attack.

"Or it was too much?" He tossed the can in a nearby trash can and slowly approached me. His cheeks were a vibrant pink. "It was definitely too much."

I didn't know what to say or do.

Rider wasn't doing any of those things Ainsley said he'd do. He wasn't playing it cool or hard to get. He was putting it out there, and I...I was...

"I like you, Mallory. And God knows you deserve a hell of a lot better than me." He dipped his chin, laughing as he thrust his hand through his hair. "God. I suck at this. Can we just forget—"

I snapped out of it. "You like me?"

His gaze flew to mine. "Yeah, I do. And I know I've been with Paige and I'm not going to pretend that meant nothing, but it's not how I feel for you. Not remotely like how I feel for you. And it's not because of our past—because of you and I knowing each other for so long," he said, and the words kept coming out in a rush. "At first, I thought that was why—this attraction I have to you. I thought it was because of everything we'd shared. And then the night I came to your place and you fixed me up, I thought it was just this physical thing." Pink raced across his cheeks. "And it is most definitely a physical thing, but it wasn't just that. I think part of me knew that from the very first time you said my name."

Now my pulse was pounding. He liked-*liked* me. Oh my God, this was unexpected. This was totally unplanned. It was an infinite, vast sea of unknown.

"I know you deserve better, but I want to be better. I want to be *that* for you." His voice dropped low as he stopped in front of me. "That's why I'm going to ask what I'm about to."

The fluttering was deep in my chest and in my stomach. I felt breathless as I stared into his eyes. "Ask me what?"

A muscle flickered along his jaw as his chest rose sharply. "Can I kiss you?"

CHAPTER 23

There wasn't a series of halted moments where my mind raced to analyze every little detail of what was happening before I made a decision.

I didn't think.

I acted.

"Yes," I whispered.

Rider made this sound in the back of his throat. It was deep and masculine, part groan and growl, and it made me shiver. He folded one hand along my cheek and lowered his head to mine, but he didn't kiss me.

No.

His warm breath glided over my forehead as his hand slid across my cheek, his fingers spreading into my hair at the base. His other hand landed low on my back, and the weight did insane things to my insides. He drew it up my back, leaving a trail of fire in its wake. My eyes fluttered shut as his lips brushed over the curve of my cheek. It was the craziest torture. My entire body tensed, prepared for the moment when his lips met mine.

And it was the sweetest pressure, a featherlight brush of his lips over mine. Once. Then twice. I felt the touch everywhere, a jolt to the system that zipped through my veins, and then the pressure increased.

Rider kissed me then.

It was a real one, soft and beautiful, and when the kiss deepened, it wasn't a shy one. He knew what he was doing, and even though I didn't, an innate knowledge told me it didn't matter. His lips mapped out mine, and my insides were in tight coils.

Kissing was awesome. Amazing. Astonishing. I could probably think of a couple of more words to describe it. Kissing blew me away, and when he lifted his mouth, both of us were breathing hard. He rested his forehead against mine. Neither of us spoke for several moments.

I still wasn't thinking. I had no idea how my hands had gotten to Rider's chest, but his heart pounded under my palm as fast as mine did. My mind was blissfully blank as I breathed in his scent, a mix of his citrusy cologne and the faint trace of paint.

"Did you like that?" he asked, dragging his fingers out of my hair and over the line of my jaw.

Screaming *yes, oh, God, yes*, would've probably been a little too excessive, so I managed a somewhat subdued, "Yes."

As Rider grinned, his lips brushed mine. "Good. Because I really liked it."

I turned my cheek into his hand. None of this felt real, like I was dreaming and would wake up at any moment and be thrust back into reality, a world where there was just the past and a present I was barely living in. Not this reality where I'd been kissed for the first time. Not a reality where I was actually experiencing each second as it happened instead of rushing forward and then having to look back on it.

"We should really talk about what we're doing, but I want…" Rider drew in a deep breath and his voice dropped again, became rougher. "I want to do it again."

The swelling was back in my chest, and I swore it would lift me right up to the ceiling. Talking would be smart, but I was tired of being smart. "I...I want...that, too."

Rider didn't hesitate.

He tilted his head ever so slightly and his lips were the softest of all pressures against mine. My second kiss was just as amazing as the first, but it was different after a few seconds. He lingered longer, as if following the path of my lips, learning it and committing them to memory. I wanted to do the same.

I leaned in, sliding one hand up his shoulder. The hand on my lower back moved, and then his arm was around my waist. He drew me closer, until we were chest to chest. A rush of sensations hit me, and even though our bodies touched, I wanted to be closer. Needed to be closer. I felt the tip of his tongue. Instinct guided me. My lips parted and—

We jerked apart as a loud, shattering bang came from the front of the garage. Rider looked up sharply, his brows furrowing. "What the hell?"

My lips were still tingling as he slipped his arm from around me. "Are we going to...get in trouble?"

"Nah. But no one should be here." He looked down at me, his jaw set hard. "I want you to stay here, okay?"

"But—"

"I'm sure it's nothing, but I want to check it out." He let go of my hand. "Just stay back here for now, okay?"

I folded my arms across my waist and nodded. He stared at me for a moment, like he wasn't sure he believed me, and then wheeled around. He walked over to the bench and picked up a long, slender piece of metal.

A tire iron did not signal *nothing*.

Rider started back down the covered cars, and there was no way I was going to stand here. Nothing about this situation felt good. I started forward just as a voice rang out from the front of the garage.

"Yo! Rider. You in here?"

"Jesus," muttered Rider, and then louder, "Jayden, is that you?"

There was a pause. "Yeah. Where you at?"

Rider glanced back at me, and I hurried toward him. "His... voice sounds weird," I said, and it did, like his letters were mushed together.

He nodded and then reached down with his free hand and found mine. He didn't drop the tire iron on the way to the front of the garage. "Where in the hell have you been, Jayden?" Rider called out as he led me around a car that appeared to be in pieces. "Hector and your grandma are going crazy looking for you. Why...?"

Gasping, I smacked my hand over my mouth.

At the front of the hall, Jayden stood with his back to us. He was shirtless. A bruise covered the side of his back, a horrible mesh of red and blue. Jayden turned around.

Rider stiffened, dropping my hand. "Damn."

Jayden lifted his chin, and it got worse. One eye was an ugly purple color, swollen shut. An angry red slash split his bottom lip as he stepped forward. "I'm in a lot of trouble, man."

CHAPTER 24

Rider escorted Jayden to a break room that was at the back of the garage. It was a small, harshly bright room with a scratched table and a refrigerator that hummed and clanged around like it was on its last leg. He'd gathered ice from the freezer and wrapped it in the cleanest rag he could find.

"Man, I'm sorry." Jayden mumbled the words as he pressed the ice to his eye. "I didn't know you had her here. I just thought you'd be here and I could clean up." Pausing, he slowly turned his head toward me, and I forced myself not to show a reaction to how messed up he looked. I called on the many years of experience with Rider after Mr. Henry got ahold of him. "Serious, *bebé.* I wouldn't bring this shit to you on purpose."

"I know," I whispered.

"But you did," Rider fired back, surprising me. "You brought this shit to me—to her. That's not cool, man."

My wide gaze shot to Rider.

The muscle in Rider's jaw was spasming as he lowered his phone. "Hector's on his way. Heads-up. He's pissed."

I sat beside Jayden, unsure of how to help other than sitting there and staying out of their way.

"You didn't need to call him." Jayden lowered the ice. "This has nothing to do with him. *No te preocupes*."

"No need to worry? Are you out of your fucking mind? Have you seen yourself? And put the damn ice back on your eye." Rider shook his head. "This was Braden, wasn't it?"

I recognized that name from the guy I'd seen in school.

Jayden said nothing.

"I told you to stay the hell away from him. So did Hector. You've disappeared the last couple of days, doing God knows what for that piece of shit and now look at you."

The younger boy lowered his chin as he placed the cloth back to his eye. "I thought I could recoup what I lost."

I lifted my gaze to Rider and he read the question in my stare. I expected him not to answer, but he did.

"Jayden here, being extraordinarily bright—"

"Man," Jayden muttered under his breath.

"Thought he could run shit for Braden. Front the stuff," Rider continued, and it didn't take a wild leap of logic to guess what *shit* meant. "Except he sold the junk and didn't exactly return the money in the amounts he was supposed to."

"People do it all the time," Jayden argued. "You've done it!"

You've done it.

I stilled and might've stopped breathing. My gaze swung to Rider. I knew what fronting was. Selling stuff that was given to you under the promise of whatever it was being sold and the money being paid back. I also knew they weren't talking about fronting sunglasses.

They were talking about fronting drugs.

Nausea rose.

His eyes remained on Jayden. "I used to. *Used* to, Jayden. Then I decided to rub two brain cells together and realized I didn't want to end up dead in a damn alley just to make a hundred bucks."

Rider used to deal drugs. Used to. I wasn't sure if I was supposed to feel relief or not as I stared at them. All I could feel was rising horror.

"I'm not going to end up dead."

Rider looked like he wanted to add to Jayden's bruises. "Really? What happened to your cousin? Last time I checked, he'd parted ways with his pulse."

"Man," Jayden said again, dropping his chin.

Rider folded his arms. "Why are you doing this? Hector said he can get you a job—"

"At McDonald's? Making minimum wage just to smell like yesterday's grease?" Jayden winced as he shook his head. "You know I help our *abuelita* with that money so she don't have to work so many damn hours." He held up the bag of ice. "She can't keep up. You know that, and the state's going to stop payin' for you."

"I know that, Jayden."

"I don't want her to have to keep takin' in kids just to pay the damn electric bill. Not all of them have been like you," he said.

Rider closed his eyes. "And I know that, too, but dammit, you're...going to get yourself killed."

The twisting increased as my breath caught. A cold rush of air swept down my spine as I listened to them. This...this was serious. Like way more serious than anything going on in my life.

"Nah, man. You stressing," Jayden replied as he started to lower the ice again, but one look from Rider stopped him. "I got this taken care of."

Rider snorted. "Looks like it."

Jayden looked away, focusing on the fridge.

A moment passed and then Rider spoke again, voice low. "You're like a brother to me, Jayden. You and Hector have been there for me. Opened your home to me. I don't want to see this happening to you."

"Nothin' happening," he muttered.

Rider kept going. "Do you think your grandma needs to see you like this? What do you think that'll do to her? Do you think she wants money you bled for?"

Things started to click into place as I listened to them, and I didn't like the pieces my mind was putting together. I thought about the day Rider and Hector had followed the older guys out of the school parking lot. The night he showed up with his forehead cut open. The hushed conversations between him and Hector. Rider was involved in whatever Jayden had going on.

"I'm cool," Jayden said, voice hard. "Ain't nothin' gonna happen to me. I'm cool."

★ ★ ★

When Hector showed up, for a moment I worried that this Braden wouldn't be the most immediate problem for Jayden. Hector looked like he wanted to murder Jayden. He yelled at his brother, alternating between Puerto Rican and English at a rapid clip. Hector didn't even look in my direction, not once, which I was okay with as he hauled his younger brother out of the garage, leaving Rider and me alone once more.

Rider closed the door behind them, and for a moment, he didn't turn around. His shoulders rose with a deep breath and then he slowly faced me. "Sorry about that."

"It's...not your fault," I told him.

Jaw clenched, he lowered his chin. "Yeah, but this..."

"This what?" I asked when he didn't finish.

He lifted his hand and scrubbed it along his jaw. "This kind of shit doesn't need to touch you. You shouldn't be around any of that."

"It's not like...you knew this was going to happen," I reasoned. Part of me wanted to approach him, to touch him, but I held back. "I hope...Jayden will be okay."

He didn't respond immediately. "He will be if he gets his head out of his ass."

"How...bad is it?"

There was another pause. "It's bad. It's always bad, Mouse. He's mixed up with some seriously bad people, and once you fall down that rabbit hole, it's not easy to get back out."

I folded my arms over my chest. "And you...used to do what he's doing?"

He stiffened as he lifted his head. "I didn't want you to know that."

Pressure clamped down on my chest. "I know it now," I said quietly.

"I was stupid. So stupid. Seemed easy, you know? Make a few runs. Make a few dollars." Rider leaned against the closed door and shut his eyes. Suddenly a vulnerability seeped into his expression, and he looked his age instead of someone who'd lived triple that. "I didn't get in too deep, not like Jayden. I got out."

I felt like I needed to sit down. "How...did you get out?"

"Their cousin ended up dead, shot in the back of the head," he said flatly, and I flinched. "When that happened, I was done. And I was lucky. I am lucky. I didn't get mixed up with anyone else who cared what I was doing or not doing. That's all."

"What about...Hector?"

"He's actually smarter. He never got messed up in any of that. That's why he works. Saves every damn penny, too. He wants to go to the technical college. Get a job that isn't him flipping burgers. Jayden's just a kid," he added as if he were ancient in years compared to him.

"It sounds like he wants to help Mrs. Luna."

"He does, and that's what makes it worse. Don't get me wrong. He spends some of the money on himself. That's how he got in trouble this time, but he buys groceries and sneaks money into Mrs. Luna's purse." Rider sighed again. "We all do."

In that moment, I knew I couldn't hold what he used to do

against him. Rider…Jayden…so many other people were a product of their environment. Some got out. Others didn't. Rider was right. A lot of it was luck. Sometimes it was determination. But mostly it was luck, and I was the luckiest of them all.

Forcing myself toward him, I unfolded my arms. "You're involved…in this, though." When he opened his mouth, I kept going. "The day you and Hector left school after Jayden did. You…showed up with your head busted open. Why?"

Rider pushed off the door and lifted his hand. He brushed the hair back from my face, tucking the strands behind my ear. "Jayden had a problem."

I waited.

His fingers traveled down the side of my face, over my jaw. He curved his hand around the nape of my neck. "He was going to meet Braden. We stopped him."

When his thumb smoothed over the space where my pulse fluttered, I felt the touch throughout. I wasn't going to be distracted, though. "You stopped him with your face?"

His lips twitched. "Braden's boys didn't appreciate us retrieving Jayden."

My heart flopped over heavily. "Who is Braden?"

"No one you ever have to worry about," he responded immediately, and I pinned him with a look. "Seriously. There is no reason why you'd ever come across him."

"But you will?"

He raised a brow. "Not if I can help it. Hopefully Jayden will learn from what happened tonight."

"And if not?" My stomach kept flipping around. "I want to know who he is."

For a moment I didn't think he was going to answer and then he sighed. "Braden is in school with us. He runs shit for Jerome, who is way older. When Jayden didn't have the money, Braden and his crew were going to have to answer to Jerome for that since Braden was the one to bring Jayden in. Of course, they were pissed at Jayden, and when they get pissed, they aren't about talking."

They were about fighting. "And you and Hector took Jayden's place or something? Is that how you got hurt?"

"No. We persuaded them to give Jayden more time," he explained. "It took a while to persuade them and some of the persuasion wasn't talking."

Oh, God. I couldn't even fathom what it would be like to be in *that* situation. "Are you going to get involved...again? These people sound scary. I don't..." I took a deep breath and said possibly the most selfish thing ever. "I don't want you involved in any of that."

"Because you care about me?"

"Of course." I narrowed my eyes. "I don't want to worry about you getting hurt."

He stepped in and his other hand settled just above my hip. "Because you want to be with me?"

"Yes." That word was easy to speak.

Rider smiled then and the right dimple appeared. "You want to be my girlfriend."

I opened my mouth and then I laughed. It sounded strange after the seriousness of our conversation, but the statement was sweet and silly.

His cheeks pinked. "Not sure how I feel about that laugh," he teased. "But I do love the sound of it."

My breath caught at the word. *Love.* Oh, gosh, was that what was happening here?

"So do you? Want to be my girlfriend?" he asked, and then chuckled. "Probably should've brought this up before I kissed you, but I want...I want to see where this goes, Mallory. I feel like we got a second chance, you know? I've been thinking that since I sat down in speech and saw you sitting there. We have a second chance. And who gets second chances?"

I searched his gaze, feeling a rightness deep in my chest. I had thought the same thing before, about second chances.

"I don't want to pass that up."

"I don't, either." Slowly, I placed my hand on his chest again. Carl and Rosa wouldn't be happy with it. Neither would Paige. And maybe this all was a little crazy, but I wanted this—wanted him. "Yes."

The smile broke out across his face and he started to speak, but seemed to change his mind. Without saying a word, he lowered his head and he kissed me—my *third* ever kiss—and it felt just as right and perfect and complete as the first and second one.

And when he lifted his mouth from mine, he pulled me to his chest, wrapping his arms around me, and I went, holding him just as tightly as he was holding me. I pressed my cheek to his heart, and pushed everything with Jayden aside for the moment. I focused on Rider and me, and what was happening here and what it meant.

Because this…this was a beginning.

CHAPTER 25

Ainsley clutched the bowl of popcorn to her chest as she stared at me from the foot of my bed. Only the kernels were left, but Ainsley liked to root around for the half-popped ones. I had no idea how she didn't crack her teeth gnawing on those things.

It was Sunday evening, less than twenty-four hours after Rider and I kissed, after Jayden showed up and after we went from friends reunited to definitely not just friends.

Boyfriend.

Girlfriend.

Even though I'd been present for all of that, I had no idea how it all happened. A hyena-like squeal built in my throat and I resisted the urge to bury my face in the pillow that lay in my lap.

"Back up," Ainsley said, blue eyes glimmering. "You told me a lot. Everything. But I have to go back to something. He drew a heart between your names?"

I nodded.

"For real? Oh my God, Mal. That's so corny, but so cute, so it strikes out the corniness and just makes me swoon."

It made me swoon, too.

"I told you it seemed like he really liked you. And he didn't even do what other guys do, like pretend that he wasn't into you. He put it all out there," she continued as she fished out a half-popped kernel and chomped down on it. "It's like a fairy tale."

My brows rose.

"It is!" she insisted, pausing to crack down on the kernel. "You guys grew up together, and he was like your white knight. Then you were separated and then brought back together. It doesn't even seem real."

"It doesn't." I pulled the pillow to my chest. "I almost don't know...what to think of it."

"Just think it's amazing. Because it is." She tucked her hair back behind her ear. "That's all you have to think about."

A little bit of reality seeped in. "But Paige..."

"They were broken up, apparently for a week, so it's not like you broke them up." She paused, scrunching her nose. "Actually, you kind of did break them up, but not on purpose. I doubt this Paige girl will see it that way, but whatever. Not your problem."

I so dreaded the moment Paige realized that Rider and I were, well, a thing. "I told Rosa this morning that Rider and I...that we were seeing each other. The whole boyfriend-girlfriend thing." I flushed. "I don't think she was upset about it or really happy about it. Carl hasn't said anything, but..."

"But he probably will and it will probably be super awkward. You've just got to give them time," she replied rather sagely. "It's your first real relationship."

"I just... I don't know. It just feels like there is more...to it," I said.

Ainsley studied me for a moment. "Don't stress over Carl and Rosa."

"I'm—"

"And don't say you aren't going to stress over it. You stress over everything." She smiled while I snapped my mouth shut.

"Sometimes you're so stuck in your own head that you're not—Well, you're not really living."

My brows rose.

She glanced down at the bowl of popcorn. "Please don't take that the wrong way. It's just that I think sometimes you miss what's going on around you, because you're so worried about what others are thinking about you and your choices."

I wanted to argue against that, but I couldn't. "You're right." She was so right, because I constantly worried about what Carl and Rosa thought, what even Ainsley thought, and then Rider and Keira, Jo, Mr. Santos... The list went on and on.

"I know," she chirped, and then she sobered. "It's really sad about the stuff with Jayden."

Typical Ainsley, moving from one conversation to the next. I fiddled with the hem of my pants. "He was so...beat up."

"It doesn't seem like Rider is heavily involved in whatever is going on." She set the bowl aside, next to her book bag. She'd come over Sunday afternoon under the guise of studying alongside me. We hadn't even opened a textbook. "Still, it was sad and scary."

I wasn't sure I agreed with Rider not being involved. Yes, it had nothing to do with me, but Rider had been involved and I doubted he would stay out of it if things continued to go bad for Jayden. It just wasn't in Rider's nature. He had a near suicidal hero complex.

My stomach tumbled.

And I also really liked Jayden. He had always been kind to me, even when he really had no idea who I was. I wasn't sure how I could help him or if it was even in my power to help.

"So tell me about Hector. I want to know everything about him."

I cocked my head to the side. "Thought you didn't like him?"

"I don't have to like him to be all up in his business from a distance." Ainsley grinned.

I smiled. "I don't know a lot about him. He...works at Mc-Donald's part-time, and he's...nice."

"Nice?" She laughed as she tossed her hair back. "You should've heard what he was saying about me, in *front* of me. He's a jerk—a dirty-minded, perverted jerk-face."

I stared at her.

"But he is hot," she added with a sly grin. "There is that."

I nodded in agreement. "How's Todd?"

Her eyes rolled. "Boring. Snobby. I don't want to talk about him, because there is something we do need to talk about." Ainsley glanced at my closed bedroom door. Carl and Rosa were somewhere downstairs. "You're dating Rider now, right? You're his girlfriend and don't you have Homecoming soon? Your first dance!"

I winced. "We...haven't even talked about that."

"You can talk about it now."

"I don't know," I responded.

She raised a brow. "You should at least ask if he wants to go. It's kind of like the normal thing to do," she said, lowering her voice.

I nodded, liking the sound of that. "I want to be normal."

Her mouth opened and then her nose scrunched. "Okay. Pause. Normal is subjective, and you are normal, Mal."

I wrinkled my nose.

"What? You don't talk a lot and sometimes you occasionally freak out. How does that make you abnormal? There are tons of people out there like that." She threw her hands up. "So what? And you came from foster care—a crappy foster home, but again, unfortunately that's also not unusual. That doesn't make you weird."

I started to explain that I was weird, but I stopped myself. Ainsley had a point. I didn't have a common childhood and I didn't talk, but that didn't make me some strange, unknown creature.

Ainsley knew a lot about my childhood. She knew it had been rough for me and Rider, and that I'd been burned, but there were things I hadn't told her. Stuff that I had only ever talked to Dr. Taft about. Things Carl and Rosa knew, because they'd seen the police reports and my case file.

My gaze swung around the room, settling on the owl soap carving before coasting over my neat desk and the thickly cushioned window seat. This bedroom was so different than the ones in that house. Clean, bright and airy. Welcoming.

The back of my throat dried as I looked at Ainsley. Never in the past had I wanted to tell her the things I never talked about, but the need blossomed, burning through my stomach and chest.

I forced my tongue to become unglued from the roof of my mouth. "I have...a problem with noise and talking." Heat flooded my cheeks as I lowered my gaze to the pillow I held. It was hard to explain why a dance might be too much. "I had to be quiet, because Mr. Henry didn't like...noise. He didn't like a lot of stuff, but staying quiet kept me out of...trouble for the most part."

Ainsley stilled, quiet.

Drawing in a deep breath, I continued. "Rider would always...tell me 'not to make a sound' so...I couldn't be found when Mr. Henry was drunk or when I...did something wrong. Sometimes, he would get mad if I ate cookies or...walked up the stairs too loudly. He never liked it if I spoke. And I...I guess— I *know* that's why I don't like to talk and I don't like noise. The therapist I saw used to say it was post-traumatic stress syndrome...and conditioning." The heat lessened as I continued. "Anyway, the night...I was burned, something else happened."

She didn't know how I was burned, so I told her. It was rough and painful to get out. The room was so quiet, even with the TV on low in the background, I could hear a cricket sneeze. I told her about Velvet and how much I treasured the doll Rider had stolen for me, no matter how old I got. I explained how a few weeks before, Mr. Henry had gotten mad over something insignificant and had taken the doll, stashing it in plain sight, really just to taunt me. I told her how Mr. Henry had tossed Rider outside after he'd asked if we were having dinner that night.

"He…threw the doll in the fireplace," I explained, smoothing my hands over the pillow. "I didn't think. I reached in…and tried to grab it. That was how I burned…my arms."

"Oh my God," she whispered.

"I know it sounds stupid, but Velvet was the…only thing that was mine. It never belonged to anyone but…me. I just panicked." I shook my head. "But before that, I…tried to get Miss Becky to wake up. She always…liked Rider. I thought she would step…in."

"She didn't?" Her voice was quiet.

I swallowed the sudden burn in my throat. "I went…into her bedroom even though I wasn't supposed to. Miss Becky drank a lot. When I was younger, I thought it was because she was sick. I…went into that room and she was lying on the bed…"

My breath caught as the image of the room formed. *Empty bottles. Messy floor. Miss Becky on the bed, her thin chest unmoving and her skin a weird, waxy color.* "I thought…she was sleeping. She slept a lot. I called her name and when she didn't wake up, I went to the bed. I tried to shake her." Wincing at the memory, I barely heard Ainsley's soft inhale. "She wasn't asleep. She'd… died sometime that day. Later I heard that it was an overdose. Pills and alcohol. Mr. Henry didn't even know. I guess her passing out…was so common, he…he didn't even check on her."

"Oh my God," Ainsley repeated.

"I've been dreaming about that night, about touching her. I don't know why. For a while I didn't think of her, but it… messed with me."

"It would mess with anyone, Mal. God, I would be traumatized if I saw a dead person from a distance, much less up close and personal." She tucked long blond strands behind her ears. "What happened after you were burned?"

"I...I was screaming. I guess. I don't...remember exactly. I just pieced it together from what I heard later, but Rider heard my screams and he...went to the neighbors. It took a couple houses...before anyone answered the door. They called the police." I forced myself to keep going. "When the police showed up, Mr. Henry answered the door like...nothing was wrong. So crazy. Mr. Henry ended up in jail for what he did to Rider and me. I...I doubt he's still in jail. I don't think about that," I said, and that part was true. "I don't know why, but I...I don't."

I lifted my gaze just in time to see Ainsley spring forward. She wrapped her arms around me, nearly tackling me. I froze, unused to this. I didn't hug a lot. For the most part, I didn't like to be touched, but I got over it quickly, because the hug was warm and good. Different than Carl's and Rosa's. Different than Rider's, but just as good.

Wrapping my arms around her, I hugged her back. I didn't even know why I'd told her, but I was glad I did. A weird rush of tears pricked the backs of my eyes. Not sad ones. More like relief. Confiding in Ainsley felt like I'd just stripped off a layer of bulky clothing.

Ainsley pulled back, her eyes shining. "Thank you for sharing that with me."

I didn't know what to say, but for once I didn't mind. Right now there was nothing to be said and that was okay with me.

★ ★ ★

My heart was racing so fast Monday morning I wondered if it would pop out of my chest and run circles around me. Today looked like every Monday that came before it, but it would be different. It was the first day in school since Rider and I had gotten together and I didn't know what to expect. I doubted things would change significantly. Wasn't like I was wearing a badge that said "Rider Stark's girlfriend," but going to my locker in the morning felt different, and it wasn't because Jayden wasn't there.

I worried about him during lunch. He'd been so bruised and bloodied, but I knew from previous experience that sometimes bones could be hard to break, as if they were laced with titanium. Other times, bones were like dry branches, easy to snap. Had Jayden suffered broken bones? That nose hadn't looked too good.

I'd picked at my salad until lunch was over. I didn't even like salads, but I wasn't sure what the heck the alternative was.

At the end of lunch, Keira stayed at my side while Jo and Anna walked ahead. "So." She drew the word out. "There's a party at Peter's house this week. It'll be really fun. It's an annual thing he does the weekend before the homecoming game. I just wanted to make sure you knew that you're invited, and I hope you come."

My step faltered as I dragged my right foot.

Anna looked over her shoulder. "Of course she's coming. Right, Mallory?"

I nodded, almost afraid if I did speak, I'd ruin the moment, and it was a big moment because I was invited to a party. A real party.

"Cool." Keira nudged me with her hip. "You can bring whoever you want with you. There's really no limit."

I felt myself nod. Normally that invite would have me stressing out, but my stomach had started doing cartwheels for a totally different reason, and the giddiness continued into calculus. I had no idea what was being covered in that class and when the bell rang, I bit down on my lip to stop myself from grinning like I was deranged. Shoving my textbook into my bag, I walked out of my class and there was no stopping my smile.

Rider was waiting for me.

He pushed off the lockers opposite the classroom, unfurling his long body. Parting the sea of students, he shoved the ratty notebook under his left arm and prowled up to me. I stopped, smile widening as I lifted my chin and looked up at him. His hair was wavy, as if he'd shoved his fingers through it a dozen or so times and it flopped onto his forehead in a careless way.

"Hey," I said, speaking first.

The dimple in his right cheek appeared, and he dropped his arm over my shoulders as he lowered his head. We were surrounded by people, but in that moment, as he lowered his mouth to my cheek and kissed me, it was like we were on our own island. There was something sweet and familiar about that feeling.

He squeezed my shoulders. "Hey."

My smile spread.

"Ready?" he murmured.

I was so ready.

Dropping his arm from my shoulders, he reached down and folded his hand around mine. It wasn't the first time he'd held my hand, but there was an intimacy there that hadn't been present before. A tight shiver curled its way down my spine as his thumb moved along my palm while we walked down to class.

He had *not* done that before.

Rider let go of my hand when we entered speech, and I stepped in front of him, walking toward my seat. I dropped my bag on the floor and started to sit when Rider swooped down, kissing my cheek once more.

I flushed as I glanced over at him.

He grinned as he sat. "Couldn't help myself. Your cheek looked like it was missing my kiss."

A wide smile raced across my face as I took my seat. I wanted to say thank you, but saying thank you seemed weird. I wanted to say something, but I couldn't grasp any of the words fluttering back and forth in my mind.

Rider's grin grew until the dimple appeared.

And I realized my wordlessness was… It was okay. In this moment, it was all right. More than that.

The warning bell rang, dragging my gaze to the front of the

room as Paige walked in. My smile slowly faded. Her long legs carried her to the back of the class.

"Hey," she said to Rider.

Rider nodded in her direction. "Hey there."

She didn't say anything to me, which was kind of normal, and as class started, I wondered if she knew that Rider and I were together. My stomach shifted. Even though I was not a fan of Paige, I felt bad for...for her, because I believed she really did like him and that had to hurt. People broke up all the time, but that didn't make it easy. I didn't know what to do with those feelings.

Mr. Santos announced our next speech would be a persuasive one. I waited for someone to point out that I hadn't given my speech yet. Either no one noticed that I hadn't or they didn't care. I hoped it would stay that way.

When class ended, I quickly gathered my stuff as Hector stood and faced us. He started to speak as Keira walked toward us, but Paige beat him to it. "Can we talk?"

I didn't have to look to know the question was directed at Rider. Pressing my lips together, I focused on zipping up my bag while my heart thumped in my chest. Would Rider talk to her? Was that okay? Should it be okay?

"What's up?" Rider replied after a moment, and I looked up. He was standing beside my desk.

Paige stepped closer as Hector turned away, but I caught sight of the wide-eyed look he shot in Keira's direction. She halted, seeming to know not to come any farther. "I was thinking we could talk somewhere a little more private. What about later tonight?" Paige asked.

"I've got to work," Rider replied, and I stood, swinging my bag over my shoulder.

Paige ran her tongue along the inside of her mouth. "What about after?"

Rider looked away, rubbing a hand across the center of his chest. "Paige…"

"What? You can't talk to me now? I thought we were still friends?" She folded her arms across her chest. "Friends talk."

He opened his mouth and then closed it. A moment passed. "We are friends, Paige. You know that."

"Hey," Hector spoke up, stepping toward her. "Walk with me?"

She snorted. "Uh. No."

"I think you should," Hector insisted. "Because you really don't want to do this right now."

"Do what?" she shot back. "I just want to talk to Rider."

"It's okay." The two words spilled out of me, and all of them looked in my direction. I swallowed hard. "I mean, it's…okay if you two need to talk. I'm going to head…out to the car."

"Don't." Rider reached out, catching my hand. His fingers threaded through mine.

Paige's gaze sharpened on me and then dropped to our joined hands. Her glossy pink lips parted as understanding flashed across her face. Her chin jerked up as her brows rose. "Seriously?" Her question was directed at Rider. "You…you did break up with me to get with her?"

Oh, God.

Keira pursed her lips and started backing up. Hector closed his eyes.

"I never said I wasn't," Rider said so quietly I almost didn't hear him. He squeezed my hand.

Paige unfolded her arms, and I tensed, because for a second I thought she might come across that desk and strangle one or both of us, but then her lips curled into a smirk and she barked out a harsh laugh. "Yeah. Whatever. Like I didn't see this coming the moment she showed up."

I wanted to hide, but that would make me a coward, the worst kind of coward, so I forced myself to stand there.

"I don't know what to say," Rider said, and his hand tight-ened around mine again. "I really don't."

"That's okay, because I do." Paige lifted her chin once more. "Don't come crawling back to me when she lets you down. Be-cause that will happen."

My eyes narrowed and the words burst from me. "That's not going to happen."

Paige looked at me and laughed again. "Whatever. You and I both know how this is going to play out." She wiggled her fingers as she pivoted. "Peace out."

Standing there, I watched Paige stalk out of the class while Hector twisted toward us. "Shit," he said. "That was awkward as hell to witness."

"True dat," Keira murmured.

"Try being in my shoes," Rider said, sighing. He pulled me into his side. "You okay?"

"Yeah." I blinked. "Why...wouldn't I be?"

Rider raised a shoulder in response. I started to ask if he was all right, but Paige's words had left me cold in the chest, because she'd said them with such certainty.

Like she knew Rider and I wouldn't last.

We wouldn't be forever.

CHAPTER 26

"Hey, *bebé*."

The words came from behind me as I rummaged through my locker Tuesday morning. Recognizing the voice, I looked over my shoulder.

Jayden stood there, his face bruised under his eye and swollen along his cheek. I shoved my history text into my bag, squeezing it in next to my binder. "How...are you feeling?"

"Like a million bucks." He laughed at my doubtful expression. "Okay. I'm feelin' like a quarter and maybe a nickel."

My lips curved up as I closed the locker door.

"I wanted to say again that I'm sorry about Saturday." Jayden's bloodshot gaze moved away from me, to the scuffed floor. "I didn't know you'd be with Rider."

"It's...all right." I turned away from my locker. "Are you okay?"

"Yeah. Yeah." He shoved his hands into the pockets of his baggy jeans. "So, you and Rider are a thing now, huh?"

Biting down on my lower lip, I nodded. Rider had worked

last night at the garage, finishing up the job on the car he'd shown me. "We're...hanging out today after school."

"That's real good." He smiled, lifting that swollen cheek, and it looked painful. "Rider is a good guy."

We walked down the hall side by side. "He worries about you."

"He always has." He paused. "I...uh, I looked up to them, you know? Hector and Rider. They don't think I care, but I do listen to them. And I am listening. Got new plans now." When we reached the doors, he looked up. His gaze was distant. Off. "I got to head down the hall. Just wanted to swing by. See you later, *cariño.*"

Jayden was off, dodging taller kids before I had a chance to say another word. I stared after him for a moment and then slipped through the open door, hoping that Jayden wasn't just listening to Hector and Rider, but that he was *hearing* them.

★ ★ ★

"Keys?" Rider asked as we walked to my car after school. Curious, I fished them out of my bag and handed them over.

I tossed my bag in the backseat, and Rider dropped his notebook next to it. "Where are we going?"

"It's a surprise." He opened the driver's door.

A giddy, probably dumb smile appeared as I walked to the other side. The whole relationship thing was brand-new and I didn't really have any idea of what to expect, but I knew enough to know that surprises were good.

Once inside, Rider turned the key in the ignition and looked over at me. His hair brushed his brows as he grinned. "What time are you expected home tonight?"

"Eight," I said since they both were at the hospital this evening.

"Perfect," he said, backing out. He stroked his fingers along the steering wheel as we left the parking lot. "I've been saving up money for a car. I like this one. Probably out of my price range, though."

Stretching out my legs, I looked over at him and for a moment I was struck silly by the fact that we were here and this was happening. Then I pulled it together. Barely. "What...are you looking at getting?"

One shoulder rose as he pulled out of the parking lot. "Not sure. I'm thinking about a truck. Not a big one, but Drew has been keeping an eye out for me, and the older ones definitely fall into my budget."

I thought about that for a moment. "I like that."

"What? Trucks?"

"Yes, but I like that you're planning ahead," I explained, watching him.

One brow rose and then he chuckled. "I'm not sure how to take that."

I smiled softly. It was hard to explain, but Rider didn't see much for himself. Literally had little to no expectations, but he was planning ahead. Buying a truck might not be a big deal, but it was something.

My gaze didn't stray from him often as he drove and we talked. Well, Rider talked mostly, and I listened. It was weird. Things were the way they'd been last week, but different all the same. Whenever he glanced in my direction, the intensity to his gaze, no matter how brief, was infinitely more. It was heavy and warm.

"Keira invited me...to a party this Saturday," I told him, remembering the conversation from yesterday. With everything that had happened in speech class with Paige, I'd temporarily forgotten.

"Peter's?"

I nodded. "Yeah. You've gone?"

He shook his head. "You thinking about going?"

"I don't know," I said honestly. I'd brought it up to Ainsley last night via IM, and she'd thought going would be an amazing idea. Then invited herself along. "Would you...go?"

"If you wanted me to." He flashed me a quick grin. "His parties are pretty big. A lot of people show up."

My stomach dipped. "I think...it might be fun."

"Probably will be." There was a pause. "How are Carl and Rosa going to deal with that?"

I almost laughed at the idea. "I...don't know. I don't think they'd be totally against it. I mean, they want me...to be more social."

"Uh-huh" was all he said, and I wasn't sure what that meant. But then he started speaking again. "Speaking of social, have you thought about Homecoming?"

"I..." My tongue twisted into a pretzel. Several seconds passed before I could get it to catch up to my brain. "Not until I saw the banner last week. I don't...know. Part of me wants to, but..."

But it was a lot and so much had changed. To some it was just a dance, but it was a dance with people crowded together and loud music. I frowned. A party would also probably be like that, but with slightly fewer people. My palms were suddenly damp and I wiped them across my thighs.

There was a part of me that was excited by the prospect of finding a pretty dress and seeing Rider dressed up, because that alone would be *wow*, but the school was new, the relationship was new and going to a party was one thing. A dance?

"I just...don't know. I've never been to a dance. Some... homeschooling programs have dances, but I never went to them."

He was patient while I forced the words out. "Then how about this? Why don't we skip Homecoming and plan for prom?"

Prom?

Holy crap, that was like forever from now, and that meant Rider was planning for forever from now with me, no matter what doubts Paige had planted in my head. There was no stopping the smile.

"I...I can do that," I said.

He reached over, found my hand and squeezed it. "Good."

Smiling like a maniac, I glanced out the window and blinked. I recognized the street from this weekend, the narrow one with the garage, but when he drove past it, my heart started thumping in my chest. "Are you...taking me to your house?"

His sidelong look was sly. "Well, it's not really a surprise anymore."

The pounding in my chest moved to my throat.

"Though, it probably isn't much of a surprise. I mean, it's just my... It's just a house. Nothing exciting," he added, flipping his gaze ahead as he came to a stoplight. The car idled. "No one's home. Hector's working and Mrs. Luna won't get in until around seven or so. I have no idea where Jayden is, but he's probably out, doing something that's going to make me want to punch him later."

Anticipation swirled. I was going to get to see his house, maybe even his bedroom, and besides that being incredibly intimate to me, I was going to finally be able to confirm that he did have a nice home. Deep down, I knew things were good with Hector and Jayden's grandmother, but knowing wasn't the same thing as seeing that when he left school, when he wasn't in front of me, he was somewhere safe.

These were the kinds of things a lot of people never had to worry about, but I did—*we did*—because we know that having walls and a roof over your head didn't equal safety.

Sometimes it was the most dangerous place of them all.

Parking on the block he lived on was reserved for residents so he found a space pretty quickly, and didn't even have to parallel park. When we climbed out into the cool afternoon air, I tugged the sleeves of my light sweater down. Soon, I'd have to break out a jacket.

Rider grabbed my book bag from the backseat, slinging it over his shoulder. "We're down here."

He reached down and wrapped his hand around mine, and my heart did a little dance. We walked down the street as the brisk wind played with my hair, tossing strands across my face. The street was nice, lined with bare trees. It didn't smell bad, like it had outside the group home and Mr. Henry's house. It was just normal. Not a mixture of urine and sewage and exhaust.

He led me up the cracked cement steps of an older, narrow brownstone. The red brick and green shutters were typical of the style, as was the stacked bay window. There was an autumn-themed wreath, burnt orange and red with little plastic pumpkins, on the door.

Hope swelled as he pulled out his keys. This was good, really good. Wreaths didn't equate to safety, but all the windows were intact and someone, I was guessing Mrs. Luna, cared enough to decorate for the season.

Rider let go of my hand and opened the door, holding it for me so I could step through. Inhaling, I immediately caught the scent of apples and cinnamon. My gaze was darting everywhere as he closed the door behind us.

The brick row home was very much like Carl and Rosa's, except older and smaller. Across from the front door were stairs that led to a second floor. The two bottom steps had an array of sneakers tucked against the wall. An old table was by the door, covered with unopened mail.

Rider stepped around me. "Want something to drink?"

I nodded and followed him through a rounded archway and into a living room. A coffee table was covered with magazines. A decent-sized TV sat on a stand, across from a comfy couch and recliner. Framed photos of Jayden and Hector covered every square inch of the wall behind the couch. There were several photos of an older man who reminded me so much of Hector. I guessed that was Mr. Luna.

The next room was a small dining area and then we walked into a surprisingly large kitchen that looked like it still had the same appliances it had when originally built. Cabinets were stained dark and the countertop a smooth tan surface.

"I think there's some Coke in here. That cool?" Rider asked, glancing over his shoulder. "I think the milk might be expired."

"Coke is fine." I watched him open the fridge, and hand to God, I could've cried. The fridge was full of food—Tupperware with leftovers, eggs, cases of soda, packs of lunchmeat and even a vegetable or two.

Looks could be deceiving. I was smart enough to realize that. Sometimes, clean floors and a stocked fridge were nothing more than a facade.

But the hopefulness was growing.

Rider grabbed two sodas out of the fridge. "Is going upstairs to my bedroom okay?" His cheeks flushed pink. "If not, the attic has been converted into a chill spot."

It was sweet that he asked and even sweeter that he blushed. I nodded, feeling my cheeks heat also. "Bedroom…is fine."

His lips twitched as he handed me the Coke.

Upstairs was just as homey and warm as the downstairs. We walked past two closed doors and a bathroom. Rider's room was next to the last, and when he opened the door, he flipped on the light.

Only a small window cast light in the room—a surprisingly neat room. Like crazy neat. My eyes were wide as I looked around. A narrow twin bed was made or never slept in. A clutter-free, small desk butted up to a dresser.

Walking around me, Rider placed his soda on the nightstand and my bag by the foot of the bed as I turned in a slow circle. Nothing was on the walls. No posters or pictures. In the corner of the room was a bookshelf. I roamed over to it, fingering the tab of my soda. I knelt down and started checking out the spines. There was a complete set of *Harry Potter*, all in hardcover, and a bunch of thrillers by authors I recognized.

"Yours?"

Rider sat on the bed. "Most of them. The *Harry Potter* books were here when I came." The half grin appeared. "But I read them."

Smiling, I turned back to the books. There were a few Stephen Kings, ones I hadn't read. Actually, I hadn't read any of his books. I wasn't a big horror fan. One of the titles, a thin book, snagged my attention. It was smaller, square-shaped. My hand jerked as recognition dawned.

Oh my God.

I pulled it out and stood, placing the Coke on the desk as I faced the bed.

He saw what I held and he started to smile, but it seemed to get stuck. His face blurred a little, and I blinked rapidly.

"Aw, shit," he said gruffly, starting to stand. "You still cry when you see that book."

I laughed, a wet and choked laugh. "No. Not really." I stared down at the cover. It was an old copy. Oh, God, it looked like the exact one from before. The yellow cover was dulled, and the illustration of a small boy clutching a stuffed rabbit was faded. The book smelled like a book—that old, musty scent that clung to faded pages. "Is this...?"

He took a deep breath. "It is."

Slowly, I lifted my gaze and our eyes met.

"It was your favorite book," he said after a moment. "I have no idea why since it always made you cry."

My lower lip started to tremble. "It was sad."

"The rabbit becomes real in the end." He laughed, but it was hoarse and thick. "I don't know how many times I explained that to you."

"But he was old and shabby and..." I swallowed the lump in my throat as I walked over to the bed and sat down beside him.

I stared at the old cover. "All the rabbit wanted…was to be real and loved." I said the last word as a whisper and then lifted my gaze to his again.

I'd empathized with that poor rabbit. I'd been too young to realize that, but I'd wanted to be loved and real, because I didn't feel like either of those two things growing up in that house.

"I took it with me when I was removed from that house and I've… Yeah, I've kept it with me."

My breath hitched. "That's… I don't know what to say."

"I never stopped thinking about you," he said in a low voice. "Not one day, Mallory. That book… I don't know, it was something that tied me to you."

Oh my gosh. My chest squeezed, and a tremor coursed down my arm again. The book slipped from my fingers, landing on the carpet. He reached for it at the same time I did, and we both froze, bent at the waist, our faces inches apart. He got to the book before I did. We straightened, our gazes locked.

He'd kept a book I was positive he hated reading because it reminded him of me. My heart practically exploded in my chest, into a puddle of goo. Spray-painting the heart between our names had been cheesy-sweet, but this? This meant the world to me.

"After you were gone," he said, swallowing hard as he placed the book aside, "it was all I had of you."

My lips parted, and I didn't even stop to think. I lurched at Rider, throwing my upper body toward him. It was awkward and possibly the most unattractive thing ever, but I didn't care. His arms swept around me the same second I clasped mine around his neck. I didn't say anything. There was no need. I buried my head in the space between his neck and shoulder, and he held me as I held him.

We'd been separated.

But we had never really been apart.

I don't know how long we stayed like that, but eventually

the embrace changed. We ended up lying down on that neatly made bed. Rider was on his back and I was on my side, my head resting on his shoulder. There was a space between our bodies, but lying like this had my pulse jumping all over the place.

Rider was right there. I could reach out and touch him. Anywhere. And I wanted to touch him. But I kept my hands folded in the space between us, and he kept one hand on my waist and the other planted on his stomach.

The old copy of *The Velveteen Rabbit* rested between us.

We talked and listened to each other. I told him how I confided in Ainsley Sunday night.

"That had to be hard to do." His thumb moved along my waist. "I'm proud of you."

Grinning, I wiggled closer as I talked to him about Jayden and how I believed that he was finally hearing Rider and Hector. Inch by inch, I moved closer to him, which left just the book between us. His hands stayed where they were even though I wanted him to touch me.

And I didn't want him to touch me.

That made no sense, but I had no idea what to do with…all of that. I wanted to learn, really wanted to, but I had no idea what I was doing. Lifting my chin, I watched his lips move as he spoke quietly about the time he'd gotten in trouble for tagging the school. He'd done it on a dare.

I was listening, but I was also fascinated by how his lips curled around each word. I remembered how they felt against mine. At night, when I lay in bed, it was all I thought about. Those memories made me feel hot.

I wanted to feel that again.

Was it too soon to kiss again? He hadn't kissed me that way since Saturday. Granted, he'd only seen me in school in the last two days and he'd kissed my cheek a handful of times, but I wanted more.

He'd stopped talking and his eyes were closed.

Taking a deep breath, I shifted up, putting my weight on my elbow. His eyes fluttered open as my hair slid over my shoulders, curtaining my face.

His gaze searched my face as he lifted his hand off his stomach. His fingers hesitated at my cheek and then he tucked the hair back behind my ear.

"Mouse?" he whispered.

There was a good chance I was going to start wheezing, and how unattractive would that be? "I want..." I wetted my lips, and I saw his gaze drop. "I want to..."

A long moment stretched between us. "Do you want to kiss me?" he asked, thick lashes lowered, shielding his eyes. "Is that what you want?"

Now I wanted to bury my face into a pit of nothing. I could *die*, but I pushed down the wave of embarrassment. Rider had to know I had no experience in this even though I bet he had tons.

"Yes," I gasped out in barely a whisper.

"You want that? You can have it. Whenever." His voice was deep, rougher. "You don't even have to ask. Ever."

Good to know. "Okay."

I didn't move. "I don't know what...to do."

His eyes met mine and then he moved his hand, curling his fingers around the nape of my neck. "I'll show you."

My heart jumped and I nodded.

With the slightest pressure, he guided me down. Our lips touched, and sparks ignited in my veins. He slowly moved his lips against mine, and I mimicked the act.

After a few moments I realized that if I tilted my head to the side, the pressure increased, and I liked that, really liked it. Rider seemed to like that, too, because his fingers tightened against my skin. Shifting my upper body closer to his, I reached out to steady myself, placing my hand on his chest.

His lips parted under mine and I felt the tip of his tongue. Blood pounded through me in a heady manner, and as our tongues touched, I was drenched in feeling, in sensation. The kiss changed, and he tasted like soda and something good, something I couldn't name, but knew I wanted more of.

I don't know how long we kissed like that. Seconds? Minutes? When we finally stopped, my skin felt flushed and muscles low in my stomach were clenched tight.

Goodness.

I blinked open my eyes. What I was feeling, the dizzying warmth in my muscles and the sweet pulsing in certain areas of my body? It was exhilarating and frightening. It was beautiful and messy.

Rider exhaled softly. I settled my cheek back on his shoulder. His chest rose and fell heavily, as if he'd exerted himself. My chest moved the same. We lay in silence again, our hands joined, resting on his stomach.

"Yeah." He cleared his throat. "You want to do that anytime? You just go right ahead."

Closing my eyes, I giggled. I might do just that, I thought.

We lay there for a while, and when it grew close to when it was time for me to head home, Rider tapped my hip. I grabbed my bag and before I left his bedroom, I took one last look at *The Velveteen Rabbit*.

My heart got all gooey.

"I can ride with you," he said once we were downstairs. "Catch the—"

"That's not necessary." Sweet of him to offer, but that was majorly going out of his way. I held out my hand for the keys. "I know my way back."

One side of his lips quirked. "I know."

I stared at him as he dropped my keys in my palm. Then he lowered his head, kissing me softly and far too quickly.

"Walk you to your car?" he offered.

I nodded, and we both headed into the living room just as the front door of the house opened. An older woman walked in, a blue lunch bag in one arm and a black tote dangling from her wrist. Her black hair was liberally sprinkled with gray and pulled back in a low ponytail. I guessed this was Mrs. Luna, but she didn't appear to be that old. I stilled as the door swung shut behind her and she turned in our direction.

She came to a complete stop, her dark eyes widening. A prickly sensation crawled over me as her gaze moved from me to Rider.

"Hey, Mrs. Luna." Rider stepped forward, slightly in front of me. "This is Mallory. She stopped over after school."

Mrs. Luna blinked once and then twice. "Mallory?" she repeated. The bright gaze zeroed in on me. "*This* is Mallory."

Oh my God.

"Yeah, this is her," he answered.

"Oh." The woman shook her head and then stepped into the living room. "It's a pleasure to meet you. I didn't know you were coming over. I would've made sure I got here earlier." The skin crinkled around her eyes as she narrowed them at Rider. "This young man should've told me. I could've made my—"

"You don't have to make anything," Rider replied. "Mallory has to head home anyway."

Mrs. Luna walked over to drop the tote onto the recliner. She glanced at Rider as I stared at her. Words darted around, and I grasped at them. They slipped through my fingers as the silence stretched out between us.

She shrugged off a light jacket, draping it over the back of the chair. "Well, I hope I see you again. For dinner next time. I am famous for my *arroz con gandules*." Her smile was warm. "You'll love it."

"It's basically ham, yellow rice and pigeon peas," Rider explained with a grin. "It's really good."

I nodded.

"And you'll see her again." Rider nudged my shoulder. "Right?"

I nodded once more.

Rider placed his hand on my lower back. "Well, Mallory needs to get going…"

My cheeks burned and irritation rose swiftly, swirling inside me. This time it had a different effect. It forced words out. "It's nice…to meet you." My face burned even hotter, because I tripped all over the words, but I spoke them.

Mrs. Luna nodded as she stepped to the side. The front door opened and a second later Jayden came in. A lazy grin tipped up the corners of his lips when he spotted us in the living room. The bruise around his eye had only faded a shade or two, and I wondered what Mrs. Luna had thought when she first saw it.

"Hey, you couldn't get enough of me? Followin' me home, now?" Jayden toed off his sneakers, placing them near the door as he smiled at me. "Stayin' for dinner?"

"Nah, Mallory's got to get home," Rider responded.

"Too bad." Jayden walked toward his grandmother. "Let me get that," he said, taking her lunch bag from her. "I'm gonna make you dinner tonight."

Rider raised his brows at that.

"Really?" Mrs. Luna smiled at Jayden. "You're so good to me," she said, letting Jayden usher her toward the kitchen. "What would I do without you, *mi nene hermoso?*"

"You'd be lost without me," he teased, wrapping an arm around her waist. "Just like Mallory."

I smiled as Rider guided me outside. Dusk was rapidly fading into night. Streetlamps shone dully on the sidewalk. Rider took ahold of my hand.

"Can I ask something kind of personal?" I asked.

"Sure," he replied.

"What happened to…Hector and Jayden's parents?"

"Their father was Mrs. Luna's son. He died of cancer when they were little." He squeezed my hand as we passed a tree. "And their mother kind of lost it, I guess. Or maybe she never had it? I don't know. She's on drugs pretty bad. Stops by once a year. Last I heard she was living in DC."

"That's...sad," I said, wishing there was more that I could say.

"Yeah," Rider murmured. We stopped by my car. "You sure you don't need me to ride back with you?"

I nodded as I stared up at him. My gaze searched his. "Can I...ask you something else?"

Rider grinned. "You can ask me whatever."

"Are you happy there?"

"There? You mean in Mrs. Luna's house?" When I nodded, he placed both his hands on my shoulders and then lowered his head so we were eye level. "I'm as happy as I can be. Got a roof over my head and four walls with food on the table. After school, it's my goal to keep those things."

"But...but home should be more than that," I told him. "Life...it should be more than that."

He brushed his lips across my cheek. "It should be, but it's not for everyone. You know that."

CHAPTER 27

Rosa and Carl sat at the dinner table Wednesday evening in stunned silence as they stared at me. The broccoli I'd forced down my throat started to sprout roots and dig into my stomach.

I tensed as Carl looked at Rosa. Their eyes met, and once again I marveled at how they had the whole silent communication thing down to a science.

Clearing his throat, Carl placed his fork onto the table. "You were invited to a party?"

I nodded slowly. "I've...told you about Keira. She invited me."

"And this party is at a boy's house?" he asked.

Perhaps I should've kept that part to myself. "He's a...friend." That part wasn't necessarily true and it wasn't a lie. In reality, we were acquaintances.

"A *friend*?" Rosa's normally level voice pitched. "Who isn't Rider?"

"I do have...guy friends," I replied drily, thinking of Hector and Jayden, and she blinked. "Ainsley will go with us." Which was true. Ainsley was going. I'd even told Keira at lunch today that I'd invited her, and she was excited to meet my friend. "I really...would like to go."

Silence.

The two resumed their mental telepathy.

I started to squirm in my chair as I stared at my half-eaten pork chop. If Rosa and Carl gave me the go-ahead for Saturday, I'd pick up Ainsley first and then Rider. The three of us would go to the party together.

A real, actual party.

My stomach twisted tighter.

Carl took a sip of his water and then said, "Are this guy's parents going to be there?"

I had no idea. Probably not, but that wasn't what I was going to say. "I think so."

More looks were exchanged. Maybe I should've sounded more certain.

"We would like to talk to his parents," Carl said.

My eyes widened. "What? That would be...embarrassing."

"Mallory—"

"No one's parents do that," I insisted, horrified by the prospect of them setting up a parental powwow just the way they had with my teachers behind my back. "If you have to...talk to them, then I shouldn't go. I just wanted—"

"I think it will be fine," Rosa injected, earning Carl's sharp look. "I do," she said, meeting his gaze. "And I think it's wonderful that you were invited and want to go. I also don't think we need to speak to anyone."

I about fell out of my chair.

Carl raised his brows.

She looked at me, long and hard. "I think you're ready for this."

I jumped out of my chair and hugged her.

"And I think this is good," she continued, her gaze never wavering, but she smiled, and I could tell that she really meant it. "You have a curfew, Mallory. It's eleven o'clock. We expect you home at that time and not five minutes past it."

Pressing my lips together, I nodded.

"There are probably going to be...things there I need you to handle with maturity," she said, and Carl squeezed his eyes tight. "Be responsible with Rider."

I blushed as I thought about all the ways I could be irresponsible with him.

"No drinking. No drugs," she added.

"Of course," I immediately responded, and that was also true. I had no plan to partake in illegal substances at my first party. Goodness, I was already a dork most of the times. I didn't need to be a drunk or high dork.

Carl opened his eyes, but he still looked like he was about to stroke out.

"We're going to trust you with this, Mallory." Rosa smiled, and I wanted to smile, too. "And trust is a big deal. Don't let us down."

"I won't," I promised, and then I did smile, glancing at Carl. He appeared to have aged about twenty years. "Thank you."

"Don't thank me," he replied. "This is all on Rosa."

"Hush it," she replied with a grin and then winked at me.

My smile grew and I could not wait to tell Ainsley and Rider the party was a go, but...but a little nugget of worry formed deep in my belly. Part of me hadn't expected them to agree, and now that they had, there was still a little part of me that wished they'd change their minds.

★ ★ ★

I was smiling as I zipped up my bag before lunch on Friday. Rider had taken a different route between classes just so he could catch me outside my locker to give me a kiss.

My lips still tingled minutes after he'd sauntered off to get to class. I might've still been a little embarrassed at the PDA, but it occurred to me as I swapped out my morning books that the things that stressed me out at the beginning of the school year—things like the prospect of being late to class, having nowhere to sit during lunch or not having anyone to talk to—weren't things I actually worried about anymore.

Now I worried about the exam in calculus next week and what I was going to wear Saturday night. I slung my now much-lighter bag over my shoulder and turned around. My step faltered as I saw Paige coming down the hall with another girl. Paige's smile slipped off her face when she spotted me.

Crap.

I started walking, pretending as if she wasn't there. Her steps slowed as she neared me. Then she stopped right in front of me.

Tension poured into my shoulders.

"I'll meet up with you later," she said to her friend while she stared at me. "You and I need to talk."

Pressing my lips together, I inhaled through my nose. This day had been coming. I knew it. And the longer it had gone without Paige saying something to me, the more I hoped she wouldn't. Hoping was stupid.

She crossed her arms over her chest as she eyed me. No book bag. I wondered if she was supposed to be in class. "I bet you're happy now, aren't you? You waltz right back into his life and become the center of his universe like before. Poor little *Mouse* needed him and he dropped my ass in a heartbeat."

I wasn't the center of his universe.

I wasn't poor little Mouse anymore.

And "dropping" her had been hard for him. Hadn't he told me how much he hated hurting her?

I didn't say any of those things, though, because the seal was in my throat, cutting off all words.

Paige laughed under her breath as she shook her head. "You know, this is unbelievable. He left me for this." She laughed again. "Whatever. Part of me wants to beat your ass down, right here."

My stomach dropped.

"And I could. What would happen? I'd get suspended. Big deal. Wouldn't be the first time. But I'm not going to. You know why?"

I didn't know why, but I was relieved to hear that.

"Rider would never speak to me again if I did something like that. He'd never—" Her voice cracked. A fine sheen covered her eyes. "He'd never forgive me. He might've dropped my ass, but I still care about him. I won't do that to him."

Those...those were tears in her eyes.

Oh my God.

"But you know what?" she said. "You're too good for him now."

The seal dropped and I wasn't thinking about her having tears in her eyes. "I am not too good for him."

Surprise flickered across Paige's face.

"Because I'm not better than him," I continued. "He's not... below me or anyone."

"No. You misunderstood me," she said, lowering her voice. "You knew Rider. *Knew* him. And that was a lifetime ago for both of you. Sooner or later, you're going to realize that, probably when you're sitting in your nice house in your perfect little neighborhood. Or maybe when you're in college and he's looking for a place to live. At some point you're going to realize all you two have in common is your past and when you do, you're going to break his heart."

I stepped forward. This was what she'd meant in speech, when she'd told me someday I'd let him down. "You're...wrong."

She blinked.

"I'd never do that...to him," I swore. "I'd never hurt Rider."

"Really?" Her brows flew up. "You're doing a bang-up job of not hurting him so far."

I had no idea what she meant by that. I distantly heard the

final bell ring, signaling the next period had started, but neither of us made a move to leave.

"He's lived for years with guilt because of you," she spat, anger flushing her cheeks. "He had no idea what happened to you and he blamed himself for it all."

"It—"

"And now you're back and still convincing him he needs to protect you from everything. Do you think you're the only one who's had a tough life?"

I didn't think that at all.

"Think again, *Mouse*. I've been taking care of my little sister since she was born because my dad is a worthless drunk and my mom is working two jobs just to put food on the table. And what do you think happens when my dad gets pissed?" she continued, cheeks flushing pink with anger. "I turn into a human punching bag so he doesn't go after Penny. But do you see me moping around about it? Expecting anyone to take care of me?"

Oh my God.

"But you could never take care of yourself and that sure as shit hasn't changed. Jesus, you can't even stand up in front of a class and give a damn speech!" Her voice grew dangerously calm as she delivered that well-aimed blow. "Why do you think no one in class has given you shit about that? Anyone else they'd eat alive, but not while Rider's there. Oh no, they see him with you and they know not to mess with you. But he can't always be there. So there's going to come another time when you can't handle anything, when you can't stand up for yourself, and he won't be there. You'll fall and he'll be left picking up the pieces, blaming himself. That's how it works. That's how it will always work for you two."

My mouth dropped open as I stepped back.

"Even now." Her voice dropped to a whisper. "You can't even stand up for yourself. You know what? You're right. You're not too good for him. He deserves better."

Paige stalked away, leaving me standing there in the middle of the empty hall, alone with the truth of her words.

★ ★ ★

I woke up early Saturday morning and gathered up my carving supplies. I went through several bars in several hours. My room smelled like Irish Spring. After lunch, and on my third pack of soap, wings took shape along the right side and then the left, held together by a center no wider than my thumb.

I hadn't slept well Friday night.

Nightmares had woken me up every couple of hours, and it had nothing to do with the party later today. My nerves had taken a backseat.

Paige's words were haunting me.

They were mean and spiteful, but they were also true. I'd come far, but I…I was still *Mouse*. I couldn't even stand up in class to give a speech. I stood there and let Paige drag me through the mud. I didn't stand up for myself.

Not yesterday.

Not when Carl had dismissed the whole social work thing.

Not when Rosa and Carl made the deal with Mr. Santos.

Paige and I had more in common than I ever would've thought we would. She came from a bad home, still lived in one, but she wasn't like me. She *dealt* with it. I hid from it.

I'd come so far, but I still…felt weak. Like glassware. If I fell, I would shatter, and Rider would… He would pick up the pieces and he would blame himself. I knew that. Paige was right. That was what we had.

But I couldn't let that be all that we were.

★ ★ ★

By the time I needed to stop to get ready for Peter's party, a butterfly had formed. I'd never done one of those before. It still needed detail, I thought as I carefully placed it on my desk and turned to my closet.

Going to this party was huge, but the excitement was tainted as I slipped on the dress I'd picked out the night Rosa and Carl had said I could go. It was quarter-sleeved and royal blue. I paired it with black tights and flats. It wasn't dressy, but I thought it was cute.

I stared at myself in the mirror for several seconds. That was all it took to hear Paige's words again. I thought about speech class and why none of the other students had said anything about me not giving the speech along with them. As soon as that thought finished, a memory formed.

"You can come out now," Rider said, crouched in front of the closet door. The room was softly lit behind him, but he was nothing more than a shadow.

Clutching Velvet to my chest, I shook my head. Tears had dried on my cheeks. I was never going to come out.

"It's okay, Mouse. I promise." Rider lifted his arms. "He's gone. It's just us and Miss Becky. You can come out."

I lowered the doll. If Mr. Henry was gone, then it was okay. Uncurling, I pushed onto my knees and crawled forward. The moment I reached the door, Rider grasped my free hand. He pulled me onto my feet. I looked up and saw his face. His lip was split and turning an angry red. Fresh cut. Mr. Henry's fists. I'd hidden while Rider distracted him.

"You're safe now," Rider said. "I'm here. You're safe, Mouse. And I know you might not believe it, but I'm going to keep you safe forever." He swallowed and swiped at his lip. "That's a promise."

Forever.

He'd promised he'd be there for me for forever.

But I was of the mind that there were two types of forever.

The good kind.

The bad kind.

I'd learned early on that the good kind of forever was, well, it was a lie. That kind of forever literally and figuratively ended in flames, because no matter how tightly you tried to hold on, that kind of forever slipped between the fingers.

The bad kind of forever lingered like a shadow or ghost. No matter what. It stayed, always in the background.

Closing my eyes, I focused on breathing past the burn. I couldn't think about that right now. Tears clogged my throat, but I knew I wouldn't cry. I hadn't cried since I left that house.

Holy crap, I seriously hadn't cried since that night. Realizing that just now left me feeling like there was a pit of snakes in my stomach. It wasn't like my tear ducts were defective. My head was stuck. Everything was stuck. And I had to get...unstuck.

Starting with tonight.

I took the time to do just that on the way over to Ainsley's. She lived in Otterbein, in one of the historic row homes pretty close to the Inner Harbor. I had no idea what houses went for in this area, but I knew they had to cost a pretty penny.

"You can sit...up front," I said when she climbed in the back. She looked amazing, as always, wearing tight black jeans and a loose blouse that slid off one shoulder.

"That seat is reserved for Mr. Hotness Incorporated," she replied, buckling herself in and then leaning forward to grab the back of my seat. "Plus, I kind of like being driven around while I sit in the backseat. You're like my chauffeur."

I snorted. "In...a decade-old Civic."

"Whatever." She smacked the seat. "I've gotta admit. I'm still surprised that Carl and Rosa were down for this."

"Me, too," I admitted. Before I left, they went over the ground rules once more. Carl still didn't look like he was a hundred percent behind this.

Traffic was a pain, so it took a bit to pick up Rider, and when he climbed into the passenger seat, he sent a grin in Ainsley's direction and then leaned over, kissing my cheek.

"Mouse." He pulled back, his gaze moving over me, and even though I was sitting, I had the feeling he was seeing everything. "You look beautiful."

I flushed.

"Do you know anyone like you that I can steal?" Ainsley asked, and I fought a grin. I was guessing things were not looking good for Todd.

Rider twisted in the seat as I pulled away from the curb. "Yeah, I do. His name is Hector."

My lips curved up.

"Hector? What? He's a jerk," she replied, sitting back. There was a pause. "Is he going to be at this party?"

This time I didn't fight the grin.

"Nah, he's got to work tonight." Rider flipped back around and reached over to me, running his finger along the curve of the arm closest to him. "You really do look beautiful."

My grin spread into a smile. "You look great, too."

"In other words, she says you look freaking hot," Ainsley added from the back.

And that was true. It was always true, but tonight Rider looked especially hot with the dark denim and worn white button-down shirt. I don't know what it was about the shirt that I liked so much. Maybe it was because the material was so thin that I imagined if he held me, I could feel his body heat. Or maybe it was the way he had the sleeves rolled up to his elbows, revealing dusky-skinned, powerful forearms.

Or maybe it was just him.

Probably just him.

Peter's party was being held at his grandparents' house since they'd left for Florida in September. The house was in the opposite direction of the Rivases', on the outskirts of the city, where there were larger homes with yards. Keira had explained that Peter's older brother would be there as unofficial chaperone, but he was twenty-one, so he wasn't an *adult*-adult.

"Wow," Ainsley murmured as the narrow, heavily tree-lined road cleared and the house came into view.

The house was really a farm—a big old farmhouse, and there were cars everywhere, parked in haphazard lines. My stomach twisted as I took in the sea of vehicles and the people milling around the side of the white-and-red farmhouse.

This...this was a lot of people.

"Probably smart to park back here," Rider advised. "Alongside the road and keep some distance behind this car. You know, in case someone pulls..."

Oh my gosh, this was seriously a lot of people here.

Sweat dotted my brow. Blood pounded in my ears. Hot, I blindly smacked against the door until I hit the button. The window rolled down and cool air poured into the car. That wasn't all. My mouth dried. Acid churned in my stomach. The scent of burning wood was choking me. Music pumped and the hum of conversation and laughter echoed in my ears.

I jumped when a hand landed on my arm. My head swung to Rider. His mouth moved, and for a second I couldn't make out what he was saying. All I could hear was all the noise—screeching laughter and loud voices. I struggled to focus on what was happening in the car.

"Mallory?" he said.

I swallowed. "What?"

His brows slammed down as he searched my face. "You zoned out."

"You okay?" Ainsley asked, clutching the back of my seat. "You're super pale."

"You are." Rider cupped my cheek. "Holy shit, your skin is clammy."

Our eyes met. "This is...so overwhelming."

Concern tightened the corners of his lips as he leaned over. "We don't have to do this."

"We don't," Ainsley agreed from the backseat. Her arm reached out and she squeezed my arm. "Actually, I'd rather do something else. This is just a stupid farmhouse party, and I bet they don't even have horses or cows. Now that would be cool."

Rider's gaze held mine as he nodded. "Ainsley's right. It's just a stupid party."

But it was...important.

It meant I was trying.

And leaving wasn't even trying.

"I don't want to...be like this," I whispered as I looked away, and once I said it, I didn't even want to take the words back. A weird sensation hit me, almost like...like relief. That didn't make sense. Or did it? "I don't like who I am."

My gaze returned to his, and the concern was still there, filling his hazel eyes and thinning out his mouth. Tears crawled up the back of my throat. Humiliating actually, to admit something so intimate like that, but now I wasn't the only one who knew this about myself. It wasn't my secret.

"It's okay. You're not going to feel that way forever." Rider smoothed his thumb along my jaw. I closed my eyes, wanting to believe him. Needing to. He kept his voice low as he spoke. "Nothing lasts forever, Mouse."

★ ★ ★

We didn't go to the party.

We ended up going to a movie.

I didn't even drive to the theater. Rider had. And then he dropped Ainsley off, and then once I convinced him that I was fine, I dropped him off. Tonight had been a first—the first time I'd gone to the movies with a boy, and I wasn't even there for it. My head was stuck on the fact that tonight had been an absolute failure.

I was pretty sure Carl and Rosa had waited up for me, but they were considerate enough not to jump on me when I entered the house and quietly climbed the stairs. My cell phone rang about five minutes after I closed the bedroom door. It was the first time Rider had ever called me on the phone for, well, obvious reasons.

"You there, Mouse?" he asked.

"Yes." I clutched the phone to my ear.

There was a pause. "There's something I need to say to you and I want you to listen, okay?"

My stomach dropped. I sat on the edge of the bed, my legs curled under me. I hadn't gotten changed yet, just stripped off the cardigan that smelled faintly of popcorn. I braced myself—tried to at least—for Rider to say this whole relationship thing was a bad idea. A million things raced in my head before he spoke again.

"You said something tonight that really bothered me," he said, and I heard a door close on his end. "You said you didn't like yourself."

I focused on the incomplete butterfly on my desk as I opened my mouth. No words.

"I hated hearing that, Mouse. I don't like knowing you think that way," he continued, and I closed my eyes. The burn was back, building in my throat. "There's so much about you that you should like. You're smart. You've always been smart. You're planning to go to college and maybe even do something med school–related."

I squeezed my eyes tight then, because I...I didn't think I really wanted to do that, and thinking that made me feel like I was floating with no anchor.

"You're kind," he went on as I covered my face with my hand. "You're a sweet person who has her entire future ahead of her. Not to mention you're a great kisser. You kind of suck at the whole graffiti thing, though. That's true."

A choked laugh escaped me.

"But we can work on that," Rider added. "And those soap carvings I saw? They were amazing, Mallory. You are talented. You just don't talk a lot, Mouse. That's it. You're shy. That's no reason to not like who you are, because who you are is wonderful. You're perfect in your own way."

"That's not it," I blurted out.

"What?"

I drew in a breath and it—it all just came out. "It's not just that I don't talk. I'm stuck."

"You're not stuck, Mallory."

"I am." I pushed off the bed and I began to pace. "I'm stuck and I can't get past that." My voice cracked and then I was talking faster, spewing out more words in a minute than I typically did in five hours. "Tonight was a first for me. It should've been fun and huge, and I didn't even like it. I didn't even experience it. I didn't try. Not really. I'm that lame."

"Mallory—"

"And you and I have always been this way. I need help. You... You're right there. I fall apart. You piece me back together. I don't even try to change that."

"What? Where in the hell is this coming from?" he asked. "That's BS."

I shook my head.

"And you are trying. You're in school. You're making friends. You're talking to people," he persisted. "You just had a setback. That's all."

It was more than just a setback.

"I'm scared of everything," I admitted, voice hushed. "Everything. My biggest fear is *forever*. That I will be like this forever."

He cursed. "That bastard did this to you. The way he treated you—"

"He treated you the same and you didn't turn out this way."

"I'm not perfect, Mouse. None of us are, but damn, I hate hearing you say this stuff, because I..." His sigh came through the phone, sounding bone-weary. "I don't know how to make that better."

Neither did I.

And maybe...maybe it wouldn't get better. Rider had said nothing lasted forever, but some things, some scars, ran too deep to ever fade away.

CHAPTER 28

Wednesday evening Ainsley messaged me on the computer.

You there, stranger?

I sent a quick yes. I'd barely talked to her since my party fail, too wrapped up in my own head to appreciate the stream of increasingly outrageous IMs she'd sent in the days that followed. Since that night I'd felt itchy and uncomfortable in my skin. I wanted to shed the layers but didn't know how or where to even start.

The feeling had lingered through the beginning of the week. I couldn't remember what was covered in class. Keira had asked about the party on Monday, and I'd lied, saying I'd come down with something. I knew Rider worried. We'd spent a few hours together after school on Wednesday, and I felt like I'd taken several steps backward. I was hyperaware of everything I did and said, which meant I said and did very little as we walked the Harbor. Rider watched me like he was afraid I'd break down at any given moment, which was probably what he expected.

He only held my hand and kissed me on the cheek when he left for the garage and work.

I'd stayed in my room since I got home, carving away at a new piece of soap. I couldn't touch the butterfly. It sat on the desk, half-transformed. Nothing I'd created with the new bars of soap looked right. I couldn't get the petals right on the bloomed rose. I'd accidentally broken the ear off the bunny I'd been working on, and the cat looked like something out of a Tim Burton film but not as interesting.

I wasn't concentrating. I couldn't concentrate. Maybe Ainsley could distract me. A new IM appeared.

Can I call you? I know you hate talking on the phone, but I want to call.

I straightened, frowning. For Ainsley to actually call meant something was up. Something more than just my not being in the mood to IM all week. Of course, I typed, and my phone rang a few seconds later.

"I know phones aren't your thing, but I just… I need someone to talk to," she said, her voice barely above a whisper. "And you're my best friend and I'm—" Her voice caught, and my chest squeezed. "I'm just really freaking out."

"Is…is it Todd?" I asked, moving my laptop out of my lap and onto my pillow.

Her laugh was cutting. "No. I wish it was just about him."

I folded my arm across my stomach. "What…what is going on?"

Ainsley's deep breath was audible through the phone. "You remember how I had to go to the eye specialist—a retina specialist? Because of what the doctor saw when I was getting checked out for new glasses?"

"Yeah, I…I remember."

"Well, I saw the specialist this afternoon and I…I don't even understand. I really just thought he was going to say something like *you have crappy eyesight* or *you have a mole on your eye.* Did you know you can have moles on your eyes? You can."

"I didn't know that." I chewed on my lower lip. "What did the...specialist say?"

"They dilated my eyes and then checked the pressure in them. It was a little higher than normal but not a big deal. Then they took images of my eyes—you know, when you have to stare at the *X* on the screen? And then they did another series of tests that were X-rays, I guess. They put iodine in me and then flashed all these lights in my eyes while they took pictures. It was really weird and it changed my vision to red and then blue for a few seconds." She took another deep breath. "And then the specialist finally came in and examined my eyes."

Ainsley cleared her throat before continuing. "He sat on his little stool, took off this head contraption that reminded me of something miners would wear, and he...he said he was pretty sure I had this thing called retinitis pig-ma-something-tosa, but he needed to schedule a field vision test to be sure. He also said there was swelling in my eyes. And I was like okay, so what do we have to do?"

"Okay." I clutched the phone tight.

"And he said for the swelling he was going to prescribe eye drops. Some kind of steroid. He made it sound like the swelling was pretty serious. Something called macular edema or something and that if the veins or something ruptured, it would be real bad."

Oh my gosh. "But the...the drops will help with that?"

"Yes." Ainsley's voice sounded strained. "I asked him how he was going to treat the retina thing and he said there wasn't anything he could do about that. There was no cure. And I was like okay, not a big deal, because I've always had less than perfect eyesight, but he was looking at me like he felt bad for me, and I didn't get it."

I had a really bad feeling about this.

"That's when he told me that I would most—I would most likely go blind or almost completely blind."

"Ainsley," I gasped, shocked.

"And they don't even know when it will happen, but it will happen. There are more tests they have to do, but he started telling me that I could either lose my vision from the sides or something called lattice vision and—" She cut herself off with a deep breath. "Okay. I'm not going to freak out."

"It's...it's okay to freak out about something like this," I reassured her. This was an official freak-out situation. "Are they sure it's really that?"

"I think so, Mal, I really think so. Even the assistant was looking at me like she wanted to hug me and I was just sitting there having no reaction at all. And I came home and it still hasn't... It hasn't sunk in. Like, am I going to wake up tomorrow blind? Do I have like a few weeks, a couple of years? I don't even know what to think. A couple of hours ago, everything was normal."

I pressed my hand to my chest. "Ainsley, I'm...I'm so sorry. I don't know what to say." And for once it wasn't because I was caught up in my head, but because I honestly didn't know what to say. This was a big deal. This was life-changing. "I hope...I hope they are wrong."

"Me, too," she murmured. "There is a chance, you know? They have to do a field test and they were mentioning some kind of genetic test to confirm, but no one in my family is blind. I don't know."

"Is there...anything I can do?"

"Find me new eyeballs?" She laughed, and for a moment, she sounded like her normal self.

When we said good-night a half hour later, I was still reeling from the news. I dropped my phone on the bed beside me and stared at my computer. Closing my laptop, I pushed it off the pillow and away from me. It slid to the middle of the bed, stopping as it reached my book bag.

"Oh my God," I whispered, closing my eyes tight for a moment.

Swinging my legs off the bed, I stood and started toward the door but stopped. I didn't even know where I was going.

Ainsley was going blind?

How was that even possible? How did you wake up one morning thinking everything was fine, that today would be like any other day, and then get told something like that?

I didn't know what to think.

Sitting down on the edge of the bed, I slowly shook my head. I had no idea what Ainsley must be going through, what she must be thinking. You took something like vision, no matter how poor, for granted. No one ever considered the possibility of not having it. Of not actually knowing what the color red looked like or how the sky changed at dusk. If I was her, I'd be panicking. I would be in a fetal ball somewhere, rocking—

I would probably never know what I'd do.

Because I wasn't going to lose my eyesight. At least as far as I knew.

My hands dropped to my knees as I stilled.

I would most likely never get shot in the back and lose my ability to walk. I would probably, hopefully never again experience what it was like to go to bed hungry at night, my stomach so empty it hurt. I didn't have to worry about everyone having low expectations of me anymore. I had Carl and Rosa, who cared about me deeply. I had great friends, one who was going through something serious, something that would change her entire life. I had Rider. I had all of these things because of the second chance I'd been given.

I thought about all the people who would never have the privilege of a second chance at *anything*.

I was lucky.

My life had been hard, but the past… It was a part of me,

but it wasn't me. I had a future, possibly a beautiful one where I wouldn't be a...a victim, and yet, when I got lost in my head or let what Mr. Henry did shape my decisions, I wasn't embracing that future.

I wasn't acknowledging everything I had.

That...that had to change.

And I thought, by realizing just that, becoming aware, I was changing.

CHAPTER 29

Rider grinned as he eyed the open bedroom door from where he sat on the window seat. I was sitting in the middle of the bed with my speech textbook open in front of me. We were supposed to be working on the next speech, one we were to deliver on someone who was important to us. I'd given my persuasive speech during lunch last week, which hadn't been hard to write though was still painful to deliver, but this one was giving me fits.

There were so many people I could write about. How could I just pick one? Taking a deep breath, I started writing again.

There are several important people in my life, people who have had a hand in changing who I am.

I stopped, sighing. It seemed obvious that I'd write about Carl or Rosa, but putting why they were important to me into words on paper was harder than I realized. I didn't want to go too deep into why they were so important even though Mr. Santos probably already knew part of it.

Rider pulled a sheet of notebook paper free, crumpled it up and then tossed it at me. I had no idea who he was writing his speech on. When I'd asked, he'd said he was going to write about Peter Griffin from *Family Guy*, and I was guessing—hoping—he hadn't been serious, because I doubted Mr. Santos would appreciate that.

I smiled as it landed among pieces of paper I'd painstakingly straightened. I knew without even opening it, it would be a drawing of some sort. This had become his habit over the last month, whenever we studied together.

I would study.

He would draw.

I would tell him to do his homework.

He would distract me in the best possible ways.

Things had been...different but the same in the weeks following the night of Peter's party. Ainsley's field vision test had confirmed what the doctor had diagnosed. She was losing peripheral vision—already lost about thirty percent without realizing it. The doc had told her she would still have several years of functioning vision and that with all the advancements in that medical field, there would likely be a cure.

Likely.

Ainsley didn't really talk about it. I wished she would, because I knew better than anyone that staying silent wasn't always the answer. There were some things you needed to talk about, and this was one of them.

Carl really hadn't warmed up to Rider, not even when he had dinner at our place at least once a week, but at least he hadn't interrogated Rider again. He'd graduated to silently stuffing his face during those meals while Rosa kept the conversation going. So that was a plus.

And things with Rider had been more than good.

They had been...new and exciting and fresh. Fun. And when I did something kind of crazy two weeks ago, he hadn't gotten mad or uncomfortable.

As seniors we had to meet with the guidance counselor to

discuss colleges and future plans, and while I'd been in the office, I'd picked up an SAT application. Not for me. I'd taken mine already. I'd picked it up for Rider. That same day, after school, I stopped at an art supply store and bought a generic, cheap portfolio. I'd given both things to Rider that night, after dinner, and he'd stared at them for so long, at first I feared I'd made a mistake. But then he'd smiled and thanked me.

I just wanted him to see that there were options for him and that he should be proud of his work. College shouldn't be off the table if he did want to go.

The next day he had taken me to the art gallery in the city where his painting still hung. And just as I had the day he'd first taken me to the abandoned factory, I found myself transported. Five feet tall and nearly as wide, the painting reminded me of the first one he'd shown me. It was a boy, but this time he wasn't looking at the sky. He was looking straight out, staring everyone in the face as they walked by, daring them not just to look at him, but to *see* him. I marveled again at the fact that he'd done this with spray paint.

Like before, it had been hard to look away from the painting, and even after we'd left the gallery, I couldn't forget the look of…*settled* hopelessness. The kind of look that said no one expected anything to change.

It stayed with me, even as I picked up the ball of paper Rider had tossed.

The first drawing he'd done while we'd studied was of the Baltimore skyline. I'd made him put it in the portfolio and his face was red the entire time. It was cute. There were at least two more lying on my bed right now that would be perfect for the book—the sketch of a sleeping golden retriever and the one he'd drawn of a mustang.

I carefully opened up the ball of paper. My mouth dropped open in amazement and I looked over at him. "You drew this in a couple of minutes?"

He shrugged a shoulder as he twirled his pen. "It was more like ten."

"Ten minutes? That's still unbelievable."

Awed, I lifted the piece of paper. In the time it had taken me to write a single sentence, he'd sketched me as I was right that second.

He'd captured the messy bun atop my head and replicated my profile as I stared at the speech I was working on. Brows lowered in concentration. I must've been biting my lower lip. There was even the freckle under my right eye. Every detail etched in blue ink. It was me, but it didn't look like me. This girl appeared older and more mature. The slope of the shoulders sophisticated. Sounded weird, but as I stared at the sketch, it was like seeing a different version of myself. A better version of myself.

Did I really look like that to him?

Perched on my shoulder was a butterfly. I thought that was a strange addition until my gaze lifted from the drawing and traveled to the desk. The butterfly carving that I'd started well over a month ago sat unfinished there.

It was finished in his sketch.

I laid the piece of paper on my textbook and carefully smoothed out most of the wrinkles. This one wasn't going in his portfolio. I was going to keep this forever.

"You like it?" he asked.

"I love it."

He chuckled, and when I glanced over at him, the pen was moving over his notebook. "Have you written anything for the speech?"

"Of course."

"You're lying."

"Maybe."

"Rider." I sighed.

He looked up through his lashes. "It won't take me that long to write something up. Besides, this is a better use of my time."

"How so?"

"The drawings make you smile," he replied with a grin. "Working on the speech doesn't do anything."

That...that was so sweet, I wanted to hug him tight, kiss him, too. "Working on your speech will make me smile, too."

His brows lifted and then he flipped his notebook closed. "I know what else will make you smile."

"What? You actually doing some homework?"

"Nope." He glanced at the door again and then rose. "I think me sitting closer to you will make you smile."

The boy knew me well.

He took a step closer. "I think holding your hand will make you smile."

I straightened as I watched him.

"And I think..." He sat on the edge of the bed and twisted his body toward mine. "I think kissing you will make you smile, too."

Oh, dear. I'd totally lost control of this conversation, but I liked it. The corners of my lips tipped up. "I think you're right."

"I know, but..." He placed his hand over mine and lowered his voice. "If Rosa comes up here and catches me making you smile in that way, it'll end badly."

"You're not worried about Carl coming up here?"

The right dimple appeared as he shook his head. "Rosa scares me more."

Laughing, I shoved his arm.

"What? She's pretty scary. Like badass scary," he replied. "She looks like she knows how to fight ninja-style."

"Ninja-style?" I laughed again. "I can confirm that...she does not know karate."

"That's a relief." Leaning over, he kissed my cheek. "It's about that time."

Unease curled low in my stomach. Party round two. It was going to be a very different party, not nearly as big as Peter's. It was just hanging out at someone's house, a guy from school that Hector and Rider played basketball with. Ainsley wouldn't be with us, but I was still nervous. What if I bailed again, unable to do it? What if I didn't talk to anyone? What if I was so worried about doing the wrong thing that I didn't even try?

He tilted his head to the side, eyes searching mine. "We don't have to go. We can stay here. Or go to the movies."

Staying here would be nice. Movies would be awesome, but what did that accomplish? I shook my head. "No. I want to go."

"Mouse..."

"I'm serious." I ducked my chin as I picked up the sketch of me and closed my notebook. Scooting to the edge of the bed, I stood and walked over to my desk. "I want to go to the party."

"It's not really a party," he said. "It's just going to be a couple of people hanging out at a house. Not a big deal if we miss it. There will be more."

Opening a drawer in my desk, I rooted around until I found the roll of tape. "We're going."

There was a pause. "Yes, ma'am."

I cracked a smile as I taped the sketch to the wall above my desk. "Wait here?"

His eyes were on the sketch. "Not going anywhere."

Walking out, I grabbed my makeup bag and took it to the hallway bathroom before I lost my nerve and ended up changing my mind. I pulled out the bobby pin and then ran a brush through my hair. I quickly retouched the makeup—lipstick, blush and added mascara. I figured the sweater dress and thin tights were good enough.

Rider was waiting for me like he said, and when I walked in, his gaze did a slow slide that left a wake of shivers. "I really love it when your hair is down."

My heart did a little skip at the word *love* and I told my heart to stop being stupid. "Thank you."

He rose and within three steps he was in front of me, lifting up a heavy strand of hair. "Such a gorgeous color now. Don't get me wrong, the orange was cute..."

I rolled my eyes. "The orange was not cute."

He ignored that. "I have no idea what I'd have to mix, color-wise, to get this shade, but I'm going to figure it out." Then he lowered his head and kissed the freckle below my eye.

I started to lean into him, but Carl's voice echoed through the house, and I figured that wouldn't be the best idea. "Let's do this."

On the way out, I grabbed my phone and a small purse. We headed downstairs to the kitchen, where I swiped my keys off the counter.

"You guys heading out?"

We turned at the sound of Carl's voice. "Yes."

Carl crossed his arms, his gaze fixed on Rider. "And where are you going?"

I responded before Rider could. "We're going to a friend's house."

"I thought you two were studying." Suspicion clouded Carl's tone.

"We were and we've finished." Which wasn't a lie.

He didn't look like he believed us, but before he could say anything else, Rosa entered the living room. "Neither of you have a jacket?"

"We aren't going to be outside for very long." I glanced at Rider. He was just wearing a thermal under his shirt. At least my sweater dress was thick.

He shoved his hands into the pockets of his jeans. "Thank you again for the sandwich, Mrs. Rivas."

Rider had thanked Rosa so many times for the ham and cheese sandwich she'd made us when he first came over that I was seriously starting to believe that he was really afraid of her.

Carl eyed Rider stonily. "Her curfew is eight."

"What?" My eyes widened as my grip tightened on the keys. "My curfew has always been eleven."

Rosa stepped forward, placing a hand on Carl's shoulder. "Make sure she is home before eleven."

"I'll have her back by eight," said Rider, and my mouth dropped open. Before I could say anything, he added, "I promise."

Carl's lips were pressed in a thin line, and I waited for him to thank Rider or something, but all he did was nod curtly. Anger pricked at my skin. Rosa was trying, kind of, but Carl wasn't. At all.

I reached down, wrapping my hand around Rider's. A muscle throbbed along Carl's temple, and I squeezed Rider's hand. I didn't say anything until we were outside, in the bright sunlight.

"I'm sorry about Carl," I said. "He's just…really protective."

"It's okay." Rider dropped my hand as we neared my car, and I knew that it really wasn't okay. "I understand."

I frowned. "Understand what?"

He lifted a shoulder as he snatched the keys out of my hand. "Everything."

★ ★ ★

The large, run-down industrial building across from the ancient row homes reminded me a little of Rider's abandoned factory. Windows were boarded up and the faded red brick was covered from the ground to the roof in graffiti. I knew it wasn't Rider's, because it wasn't nearly as beautiful, but it did create an odd combination of dull shades and bright, in-your-face color.

Rider pulled into a parking lot that was partially enclosed with high, chain-link fencing. Half the fence had fallen down, and someone had piled up the broken sections in one corner of the lot. The off-white pavement threatened to crumble beneath our feet as we walked out.

"Is it okay for the car to be parked here?" I asked. I'd never been to this neighborhood, but I knew it wasn't too far from where he lived.

Rider nodded as I dropped my keys into the purse. "No one will mess with it."

I wasn't necessarily worried about anyone messing with it. More like it getting towed away due to all the No Trespassing signs plastered everywhere.

Rider took my hand as we crossed the narrow street. "This is Rico's place. It's not the nicest, but we won't be bothering Mrs. Luna by hanging over here when she gets home from work."

My throat had dried as we climbed the wide steps. Rider didn't even knock. Just opened the door and we went right inside. Laughter echoed through the dark entryway and there was that rich, earthy scent.

"Hey, man," an older guy said. He was sitting in a recliner, a tall bottle in his hand. "What's up?"

"Nothing much," replied Rider. He squeezed my hand. The living room was full of people. My gaze darted nervously as Rider started to introduce me to the guys in the room. I recognized Rico, but I hadn't seen anyone else before.

"This is—"

"Mallory," a familiar voice said from behind us. Paige.

I stiffened as Rider turned halfway. "Hey there," he said as she handed him a cup. Not me. Just him. "Thanks."

"You're welcome." Her gaze flickered over me. "Nice dress."

I had a feeling that wasn't necessarily a compliment. She looked amazing, as usual, in skintight black jeans and a strappy tank top in a shimmery, silvery color. How was she not cold? Maybe it was because she was the devil.

The devil that spoke the truth.

"Thanks," I murmured anyway. Those were pretty much the only words she'd spoken to me since the day in the hallway when she told me I was going to break Rider's heart. I knew they still sometimes talked. I was okay with that as long as I didn't get dragged into conversations with her.

Paige arched a brow. She didn't just walk past us into the living room. She *sashayed*, swinging hips and all. She sat on the couch, in between two older guys who nodded at Rider. They were focused on the TV, their fingers flying over the game controllers.

"There's shit to drink in the kitchen." Rico nodded in my direction. "If she wants something."

"Cool." Rider tugged me around and we walked down the hall, into a sparse kitchen. Empty beer boxes were piled next to an overflowing trash bin. He placed the cup Paige had handed him onto the counter and then walked to the fridge. A sharp smell hit the air when he opened the door. "There's some Mountain Dew in here. That work for you?"

I nodded. "So does Paige hang out here a lot?"

He shrugged as he handed a can over to me then grabbed one for himself. "Sometimes. Rico's a friend of her family."

"You're not going to drink...what Paige gave you?"

"Nope."

For some stupid and most likely childish reason, I was happy to hear that. Rider curled his hand around the nape of my neck and lowered his head. When he spoke, his warm breath danced over my lips. "How are you doing?"

"Good," I murmured. "We just got here."

"I'm checking in, though." His head tilted slightly, and I shivered. "I'm going to do that a lot, and when you want to leave, you just tell me. Okay?"

"Okay."

He kissed me softly and then pulled away. I felt my cheeks heat as we walked back toward the living room. Rider stopped at the doorway. "Where's Hector?"

"Upstairs." Rico sipped from the bottle.

Rider glanced down at me. "Want to see what he's up to?"

"Sure," I said, trying to speak louder, but it came across as a whisper.

He smiled anyway and then led the way. The upstairs was slightly cooler than below, and Rider seemed to know where we were heading, because he went straight to the second door and rapped his knuckles off it.

"Yo" came the response.

"It's me. You busy? I got Mallory with me."

"Yeah, give me a sec."

There was a sound of something creaking and then a girl giggled. My brows flew up, and Rider winced. "Hey, we can come back," he called out, grinning at me. "Don't want—"

The door swung open. Hector was straightening out his shirt with one hand. We had so interrupted something. "Nah. No problem. Come on in."

"You sure?"

Hector nodded as he opened the door the rest of the way. A dark-skinned girl sat on the edge of the futon. She smiled when we walked in and gave a little wave.

A candle was burning on a dresser, and it reminded me of sugar cookies. I wondered whose room this was. Then again, it didn't really look like a bedroom.

"Have you met Rider?" Hector asked the girl, and she nodded. "Cool. Uh, this is Sheila and that's Mallory."

Sheila smiled. "Hi."

"Hi," I murmured.

Hector walked over to a dark red beanbag and plopped down in it. "So when did you guys get here?" he asked as we sat on the futon next to Sheila.

"Just a little bit ago," Rider answered.

Hector glanced over at me before continuing. "Everyone still downstairs?"

He nodded. "Rico and the guys are playing one of the 'Assassin's Creed' games. Looks pretty serious."

Chuckling, Hector reached up and snagged a clear glass off the small end table. "Sounds like normal. You guys planning to hang out for a while?"

"Maybe." Rider knocked his knee off mine. "We might catch a movie or something. Not sure."

"Sounds good. You catch the game earlier?" Hector asked, and as the boys started talking about a basketball game, I glanced over at Sheila. She was looking down at her phone, scanning what appeared to be Facebook.

There was so much I could say right now, so many questions I could ask. Options were limitless, but my tongue felt heavy. I started to look away, but stopped myself. That wasn't what I needed to do. I needed to *speak*. I needed to not do what I normally did, which was just shut down.

I forced my lips and tongue to move. "So...do you go to Lands High?" There. I did it. And I managed not to smile like a fool, too.

Sheila looked up. "No." She grinned. "I actually go to Howard University. I'm just home visiting for the weekend."

"Oh." Surprised, I glanced over at Hector, but neither of the guys were paying attention to us. "Um, what...what are you studying?"

She hooked a long leg over the other. "Education. This is my first year."

"That's...that's cool. Did you...always want to go into education?"

"Pretty much," she replied, and I was envious, because I wasn't sure what I wanted to do. Or maybe I was, but Carl and Rosa weren't exactly thrilled with the idea. "What about you? You planning college?"

I nodded as I set my soda on the floor. "University of Maryland. I'm not...sure what I'll study yet."

"You'll figure it out. There are juniors at my college who

still don't know what they want to do." Her phone dinged. "So you all go to the same school?"

I nodded. The conversation between us slowed and I focused on what the guys were talking about. They'd moved on from basketball to football, and I lost track of time. Maybe an hour passed when Hector rose and so did Sheila.

"We're heading downstairs," Hector announced, walking to the door.

"We'll be down in a minute."

Hector's grin was sly as he closed the door behind them. "Sure. Sure. Take your time."

I twisted toward Rider. "Why—"

I didn't get a chance to finish speaking. His mouth was on mine in a sweet, all-too-quick kiss.

"Proud of you," he murmured against my lips, and I smiled, because I knew what he was talking about. The small conversation I held with Sheila wasn't much, but it was a big deal. I was out of my element, but I hadn't just sat there, paralyzed.

Placing my hands on his chest, I smiled against his lips. "She seems really nice."

"Yeah." He kissed the corner of my mouth. "I'm pretty sure we totally interrupted them."

I giggled. "Yes. I think we did, too."

"We're such terrible friends." He cupped my cheek. "But you know what?"

"What?"

"I'm so going to take advantage of the fact that we're alone." He paused, and my stomach dipped like I was on a roller coaster. "What do you think about that?"

I lowered my hand to his knee. "I think...I think I'd like that."

"Good." He tilted his head. "Because I think I'm really, really going to like that."

Rider kissed me then, and it was slow and soft, and it warmed my blood. I didn't know how long the velvety, supple kiss went on, but after endless moments it changed, deepened. His tongue moved against mine, and I…I'd never been kissed like that before. Never felt anything like that before.

He made this noise in the back of his throat, and my heart was thundering in my chest as he leaned into me. Somehow, I ended up on my back and Rider was beside me on the futon. His hand slid down my arm, and it was just him and me. I wasn't thinking about this odd room or the people downstairs. I wasn't thinking about anything other than how he made me feel, how he kissed me, touched me, like I was something precious and invaluable to him.

My hands had a mind of their own, and I was touching him in ways I'd never done before. I tugged on his thermal and Rider immediately responded. He lifted up and reached around to the nape of his neck. Grabbing a fistful, he pulled his thermal and shirt off in one smooth movement.

I sucked in air as I got an eyeful of Rider shirtless. It was… Wow. Except for TV and movies, he was the first guy I'd seen bare-chested in real life. Carl didn't count, because that was, well, weird.

"You can touch me if you want," he offered.

I wanted.

Biting down on the inside of my cheek, I placed my hand on the center of his chest. Wiry hairs tickled my palm. I could feel his heart pounding. Slowly, I dragged my hand down, over the tightly rolled muscles of his abdomen. He jerked when my hand reached the band on his jeans. I drew my hand back, my gaze flickering to his face.

"It's okay." His voice sounded rough. "More than okay."

Touching him again, I slid my hand across his stomach, avoiding his jeans this time. I loved the feel of him. So much strength under soft skin.

Rider shifted back onto his side next to me and placed his

hand on my waist. Kissing me again, he quickly distracted me from my explorations. I got lost in the kisses and in the way my body was responding to them. Muscles low in my belly tightened. My head was spinning as his hand drifted to my neck and over my front, lingering in ways that caused my back to arch and my breaths to come quicker. Then he went lower, slipping his hand under the hem of the sweater dress and up over the thin tights.

His hand slid over my thigh and then between them. My entire body felt like it was on fire. Tension built deep inside. It was hot and tight and I didn't understand it. Unease curled low in my stomach as I gripped his arm. Some of the heat faded as my eyes fluttered open.

"Rider," I said, and he kissed me again, and for a moment, I got lost in that kiss, lost in what his hand was doing. It felt good, but I...

Oh, God, I wasn't ready for this.

"Can we...slow down?" I whispered, my hand tightening around his wrist.

His hand immediately stilled as he lifted his head. "Yes. Yeah." He cleared his throat as he eased over, drawing his hand away from me.

I squeezed my eyes shut against the sudden burn of tears. God. I didn't even know why I wasn't ready or if I should be. I had no idea, and now I feared—

"Did I hurt you?"

My eyes flew open. "What?"

He was staring at me intently. "Did I do something wrong?"

I couldn't answer. Nothing he'd done felt wrong. Quite the opposite.

"If I did, I really want to know. I promise I'll—"

"You didn't hurt me," I said. "I just... Why would you think that?"

He lowered his gaze. "I…I haven't done a lot of this." His cheeks flushed pink and my eyes widened. "I mean, I've done some stuff, but not a lot. I haven't…had sex."

For the longest moment I couldn't respond. All I could do was stare at him. "You're a virgin?"

One side of his lips kicked up. "Yeah. You sound surprised."

"I am. I thought… I don't know. You were with…Paige. I just assumed you had sex before."

"That would be a negative," he replied, picking up my hand. "You're looking at me like you don't understand how it's possible."

He could really read minds.

"It's gotten close, but I just never— I haven't wanted to go that far." He shrugged a bare shoulder.

"I haven't done it, either," I blurted out. "I mean, that's super obvious since…you're the first boy I've kissed, but yeah, I don't even know…what I'm saying and I'm just going to shut up."

Rider chuckled. "Don't. I love it when you ramble."

"Only you would enjoy that." I curled my fingers through his. "Do you want to…go that far with me?"

His lashes swept up and his eyes, with their greenish flecks, met mine. "Yeah. Yeah, I do. Someday."

Warmth swept across my cheeks as I whispered, "I…I want that, too. Someday."

The dimple in his right cheek appeared. "Then we're on the same page."

"Yeah." I lifted my head and kissed him. "I'm sorry about stopping. It felt good, but—"

"Mallory, please don't apologize." Rider sat up, pulling me along with him. "We can do whatever you want, go as far as you want and we will always stop when you want, no matter what. You feel me? There's nothing to apologize for and that's the way it should always be."

Oh my God.

Rider wasn't perfect, but he was damn close. Actually, he was perfectly imperfect. A giddy rush hit me, and I grinned at him.

"We should head down there, huh?" he asked, and I nodded. Rider picked his thermal up and pulled it on over his head, pausing to grin at me. "Sorry. I'm going to have to cover up. I know it's not fair."

I laughed as he shrugged on his shirt over the thermal. "It really isn't."

He pulled out his phone as he grinned at me. "Crap. My battery is about to die."

"I have mine."

"Cool. We can use yours later to see if there are any good movies out." He offered me his hand and I took it. The giddiness followed me on the way down.

Back in the living room, Rider sat in one of the plastic chairs catty-corner to the couch and pulled me down in his lap, curling his arms around my waist. I didn't see Sheila or Rico. It was then I realized we'd left our drinks upstairs.

"Nice of you all to join us," Paige commented as she looked over her shoulder.

Rider's arms tightened around me as Hector chuckled. *"Metete en tus asuntos."*

She shot him a dirty look as I heard the front door open. A few seconds later Jayden walked in. He saw us and smiled widely. "Yo! I didn't know you guys were here." He shuffled over. "Awesome."

"Hey," I said, smiling at him. The bruises had long since faded, and Jayden looked the way he did the first day I met him.

"We're probably leaving soon," Rider said. "Might catch a movie."

Jayden leaned against the wall as he looked around the room. "I see how it is. You figure you don't stand a chance with Mal-

lory now that I'm here to show her what a real man looks like."
He winked as Rider just shook his head. "Fine, leave. But no
dumb movie will be as entertainin' as the Jayden Show. And I⁻
don't charge admission."

Rider chuckled. "Whatever, man."

"Is Rico here?" Jayden asked.

"He was. Not sure where he's at now."

He nodded slowly as he shoved his hands into his pockets.
"What movie are you guys gonna see anyway?"

"I don't…know," I answered when Rider remained quiet.
An idea formed. "Do you want to come?"

Jayden blinked as if he was surprised. "Aw, that's sweet of
you, but I'm not good sittin' in a theater."

My brows furrowed. "Why?"

"Because he'd talk through it," Paige answered from the
couch. "He would literally talk through the entire movie."

"True dat," one of the other guys responded.

I grinned.

"It's true. You know, I like to add commentary every once
in a while," Jayden explained. "But for some reason people be
all upset over that."

"I can imagine," Rider replied drily.

"I like to think what I'm addin' actually enlightens the experience," Jayden said.

Paige snorted. "I don't think *enlighten* is the right word."

"My entire presence is enlightening," he replied.

Hector looked over his shoulder, eyebrows raised. "I can come
up with a few words that describe your presence. *Enlightening*
is not one of them."

Jayden grinned at his brother. "You know what they say."

"What?" Hector waited.

He winked. "Hate the game, not the player."

Hector shook his head as he squinted. "That don't even make sense in this conversation."

"That's because it's too highbrow for you," Jayden retorted.

His brother rolled his eyes. "Whatever. Did you fill out the application?"

Jayden nodded. "Yes, Dad. It's on the coffee table at home for you to take in tomorrow."

"Application?" I repeated, hopeful.

"Hector can't stand to be one minute without me, so I'm going to be workin' with him at Mickey D's," Jayden said. "Got to get a permit and stuff."

"Yeah." Hector laughed. "That's exactly why I want you working with me."

Happy to hear that he was doing something that his brother had been asking him to do, I smiled up at Jayden. "That's awesome." His gaze met mine. "Really," I repeated.

"Yeah." Jayden dipped his chin as his cheeks deepened in color. "Gotta start somewhere, you know?"

"It's a good…place to start," I told him, meaning it.

We ended up hanging out for another hour, and any earlier nervousness vanished with Jayden there, making fun of himself and cracking jokes in between messing with his phone. His texts were going off like crazy, and by the time we said our goodbyes and walked outside, I'd swear he'd sent about two dozen. Jayden followed us out, his fingers flying over the keyboard.

Rider draped his arm over my shoulders as we started across the street. "Any idea of what movie— Whoa!"

He yanked me back against a parked truck as a car roared down the street, seeming to come out of nowhere. There was a squealing sound and I caught sight of the passenger window rolling down.

Fireworks went off, the kind that snapped and popped when you threw them at the ground. Except they weren't fireworks. That sound. It wasn't—

Air punched out of my lungs as I hit the ground, a heavy weight settling over me. Horror seized me as my brain registered what the sound was.

It was *gunshots*.

CHAPTER 30

Tires peeled, kicking up loose gravel. Tiny pebbles sprayed into the air, pelting my cheeks. My palms stung from sliding across the asphalt, but the pain barely registered. I started to lift my head.

"Rider?" I whispered.

"I'm here." The weight shifted off me, and he said something else, but the blood pumping in my ears caused his voice to fade in and out. "Are you okay?"

"Yeah." Adrenaline coursed through my veins, pushing the disbelief aside. My gaze flew across the parking lot and then stopped on the person lying on his side. "Oh my God..."

Rider rose swiftly. "No. *No.*" He shot across the parking lot.

I froze, not believing what I was seeing. I couldn't afford to believe it. My heart stuttered in my chest. My stomach twisted painfully. Oh, God, this hadn't happened. This *wasn't* happening. These kinds of things didn't happen in broad daylight. They didn't happen right in front of me. They didn't happen to someone I knew. They didn't...

Those thoughts were so stupid, because it did happen.

That was Jayden.

That was Jayden lying on his side.

That was Jayden lying on his side with dark liquid pooling on the ground beneath him.

"Oh, shit. Oh, shit." Rider dropped to his knees beside Jayden. "Holy fuck. Jayden? No. Goddammit. *No!*" His voice broke on the last word and he shouted it again, the word ripping out from him, tearing through all the noise. *"No!"*

With shaky arms, I pushed to my knees and then stood. Swaying, I stumbled forward, my mouth moving, but there were no words.

Rider looked up at me, his eyes wide. He lifted his hands. The same dark substance covered his hands. I lurched to the side, pressing my palm against my mouth. Horror slammed into me with the force of a freight train, bowling me over. A million thoughts raced in my head as I looked around. People were gathering, coming out of the nearby row homes. Someone was crying. Screams still tore through the cold air. Everything was rushing around us but standing still at the same time.

I needed to get help. We needed help. I knew what to do. I reached for my phone as I heard sirens wailing. Help was already coming. I twisted back around, and Jayden was now lying on his back. I knew he didn't move himself, because I saw his eyes. I'd seen eyes like that once before.

They were fixed on nothing, dull and unseeing.

Oh, God. Oh, God.

Rider was touching Jayden's throat and he was shaking his head. The two blurred. I walked around Jayden's unmoving legs, my steps jerky. I knelt—fell to my knees beside Rider. I placed a trembling hand on his arm. He jerked as his gaze swung to mine.

Someone shouted and the small half circle of people broke apart as a tall form pushed through. Rider shot to his feet as Hector stumbled to a halt.

He took a step back and then doubled over, slamming his hands onto his knees. "No. No. No. That's not my— No."

Then Hector sprang forward. Rider wrapped his arms around his waist. "You don't want to see this, man. You don't—"

"That's my brother?" He struggled to get around Rider, voice cracking like a whip. "Man, is that my brother?"

Rider dug in, holding Hector back as he kept shouting, "That's my brother?" Over and over, he asked and each time it was like hearing the shots pop. "Aw, man, no. No. *No!* That's not Jayden. That's not him. That's not him on the ground!"

My heart caved in on itself. The blare of the sirens grew closer, drowning out everything except for Hector's broken, shattered voice, the sound of absolute heartbreak.

★ ★ ★

Red. Blue. Red. Blue.

Hours later, and I could still see the flashing, whirling lights. It didn't matter if my eyes were open or closed. I could still see them and the sea of blue uniforms that had swarmed into the street and the parking lot.

Everything had been a blur of questions and faces, and I didn't know how much time passed. Police asked me questions I couldn't answer. Then two men in suits were there, asking the same questions. I was separated from Rider, pushed back by the EMTs and then the police. The crowd had thickened, and it took me forever to get back to my car and find my bag. I'd tried calling Rider, but my hands were shaking so badly.

He'd found me, though, stalking out of the crowd. I'd cried out when I saw him and he moved to touch me, his hands hovering on either side of my face, but he didn't.

"I've got to stay with Hector," he'd said. "Go home and stay there."

"But—"

"Please, just get away from here. Please," he said again, his face leached of all color. "Just get away from here. Go home and stay there, okay? I'll call you when I can."

My heart had been thundering in my chest. "I don't want to leave you. Not right now—" I started to look to my left, where yellow tarp had been draped. "I—"

"Don't look. God, it's already too late, but don't look." He'd shifted, blocking my view. "Please, Mallory. Please get out of here."

That was the last thing I wanted to do, but he was begging me and I'd never heard Rider beg before, not even when he fell under Mr. Henry's fists. So I nodded, and Rider had kissed me then, a hard, almost brutal kiss that tasted like anger and fear. When he walked away, I wanted to follow.

But I got in my car and I drove home like he'd begged me to. In a numb daze, I parked my car and grabbed my bag. Feeling like I was walking through sand, I went inside and winced at the familiar, normal noises.

Carl was in the study, to my left, talking on the phone. Chuckling. Living. In the kitchen, I could hear water running.

"Mallory?" Rosa called out. "You didn't answer my text. Is Rider coming over for dinner?"

A dry, barely audible laugh rasped out my throat. Rosa was trying. She really was, but Rider wasn't coming over for dinner. I didn't respond. I dragged myself up the steps. I heard Rosa call my name again, but I kept walking.

Once inside my bedroom, I stopped in the middle of the room and turned in a slow circle. I saw everything, but didn't really see anything. I sat on the edge of the bed, forcing myself to take deep, even breaths as I rubbed my hands on my tights.

Pressing my hands to my face, I covered my eyes and opened my mouth. I screamed but there was no sound. It hurt nonetheless, ripping apart my throat.

I tried to process what just happened, but all I could think about was Jayden walking up to my locker my second day of class.

He'd tugged Paige's braid, called her a ghetto Katniss and then talked to me like he'd known me for years. All I could think about was Jayden in the car the first day of school. I could hear his laugh and if I breathed deeply enough I was sure I could still catch the earthy scent that clung to him.

I wouldn't see, hear or smell any of that again.

Gone. Forever.

I didn't understand.

He'd said he had different goals now and he was finally listening to his brother and Rider.

"Oh my God," I whispered.

"Mallory?" Rosa's voice was closer, at the top of the stairs. "You didn't answer..." She appeared in the doorway, her eyes widening. "Mallory!" She rushed into the room. "Dear God, what happened?"

I stared at her for a moment and then looked down. I yanked my hands off my legs. The tights were stained, soaked a dark red. "Oh my God..." I must've knelt in Jayden's... My stomach turned.

"Mallory." She clasped my chin with cold fingers, tilting my head back. "What happened to you? Your face? Are you okay?"

In a distant part of my brain, I realized that this was the most panicked I'd ever heard Rosa. She was always so calm and collected. Always so in charge, but she was touching me, smoothing my hair back from my face and she sounded like I felt inside. Out of control.

"Talk to me, honey." She knelt, grasping my hands and turning them over. The skin was raw and red. "Tell me what happened?"

I shook my head. The physical pain I felt was nothing. "I... Jayden is dead."

"What?" She blinked, and only then did I realize that she didn't know about Jayden. Not by name. "What are you saying?"

I met her dark gaze and the words tumbled out. "They shot

him. He was walking across the parking lot and they pulled up in a car and they just— They just shot at him—shot him. He was standing there and then he was gone." I shook my head. "I don't understand. They just drove up and started firing. He is—he was only fifteen, Rosa. He was…"

"Oh, God." She smoothed her hands down my arms. Several moments passed before she spoke. "How did this happen?" she asked as she lifted my hands.

"Rider. He…tackled me." I looked down at my scuffed-up palms. "My hands slid on the road." I swallowed, staring at the bright red scratches. "Pieces of rock were flying everywhere."

"You were with Rider? Where is he now?"

I shook my head. "He's with Hector. That's…that's Jayden's brother."

Rosa gently tugged me up. "Start from the beginning, and tell me everything."

As I spoke, her jaw hardened. She led me into the bathroom and turned on the tap. She had me sit and she was silent as she cleaned up my hands and cheeks, much like I had done the day Rider had come to the house. The same people who had hurt Rider had most likely been the ones who did this…who had killed Jayden.

The peroxide stung, but I sat still. At some point, Carl stuck his head into the room, but Rosa waved him away. When she was done, she gathered up the cotton balls and tossed them in the trash.

She knelt in front of me again. "Why don't you get cleaned up? Leave the tights in the hall. I'll throw them away."

I nodded.

Her gaze searched mine and then she hugged me tight. "I'm so sorry about your friend and that you had to experience that." She pulled back, leaving her hands on my shoulders. "I'm so very sorry. And I'm so very glad you're safe."

My lower lip trembled.

Rosa held my gaze as she rose and for the first time ever, I heard her voice shake. "This—this is why Carl didn't want you around Rider. This was why."

CHAPTER 31

Rosa's parting words echoed as I showered and quickly changed. The sweats chafed a patch of skin on my left knee, but I ignored it as I walked into my bedroom. Picking up my bag, I unzipped the side compartment and tried calling Rider.

No answer.

Opening up the text screen, I typed out: are you okay? The message zipped through and underneath it showed delivered. I waited. No answer. I turned sideways, brushing my damp hair back from my face. I shouldn't have left Rider. I should've stayed with him—with Hector. I couldn't have helped either of them, but I could be there for them.

Except I'd left.

I'd done what I was told, like always, and I left. I wasn't sure if leaving had been right or wrong. I glanced down at my phone and started to call Ainsley, but stopped. I didn't know how to tell her what happened, especially with everything she was going through.

I sat down on the bed and I didn't move. Minutes turned into hours. The sky darkened outside the window. I lay down, holding the phone close. My head was strangely empty except for a low buzz, like it felt when I had a head cold. I must've fallen asleep, because when I blinked, sunlight was cutting through the blinds. Tiny particles of dust danced in the streams. Mouth dry, I sat up and looked away. I stared at the closed door, knowing I'd left it open yesterday. For a few minutes I couldn't remember exactly why there was this horrible churning in the pit of my stomach.

Jayden.

My body jerked as I twisted at the waist, scanning the bed for my phone. There! It was between my pillows. I dug it out and hit the screen. No missed calls or texts.

Staring at my phone, I told myself that the reason Rider hadn't called or texted was that he was with Hector. Reassuring me wasn't his top priority. I understood that, but fear blossomed in the pit of my stomach, and nausea rose. Rider was okay. There was no reason for him not to be. The fear gave way to bone-deep dread.

I threw my legs off the bed and rushed out into the hall, into the bathroom. Closing the door behind me, I dropped to my knees and retched. Nothing came up. Not really. I dry-heaved until my ribs ached, and I sat there, breathing heavily.

Slowly, painfully, I stood and grabbed my toothbrush. Turning the water on, I brushed my teeth and then washed my face, wincing when the cleanser and hot water hit my cheeks. When I looked up, I saw my reflection. Tiny marks splattered my cheeks. Shadows were painted into the skin under my eyes. My hair was still a little damp from sleeping on it wet, and at the moment it was the color of wine, and going in every other direction. I pushed away from the sink and walked back into the bedroom. Each step felt immeasurably slow.

Nothing felt… Nothing felt real as I picked up my phone again.

"Mallory?" Carl called from downstairs. "Can you come down here?"

I clenched the phone in my hand and hurried down, finding them both sitting at the kitchen table. I slowed as I approached the island. They looked like they hadn't slept much the night before. His gray shirt was wrinkled. Stray hairs escaped Rosa's short ponytail, fanning her face like little fingers.

"Why don't you come sit down?" Carl advised gently. Coffee mugs sat in front of them and the scent was heavy in the air.

Sensing that this wasn't going to be a conversation I wanted to stick around for, I stayed where I was.

He looked at Rosa and then continued. "How are you feeling?"

I thought…I thought that was an incredibly stupid question.

"I know what you just saw was a lot to deal with. A lot, and Rosa and I both wished you would never have to experience something like that again."

Again?

Then it hit me. How could I forget? He was talking about Miss Becky. Besides the dull eyes, this was nothing like finding Miss Becky in her bed, long dead and cold to the touch. I didn't know the specifics, but her death had been peaceful compared to Jayden's. Her death was nothing like Jayden's.

"And we know that right now is a tough time," Carl went on, and I blinked, wondering if I'd missed half of what he'd said. "But this conversation can't wait."

"What…?" I looked between them as I placed my phone on the island. "What can't?"

"Rider." Rosa picked up her coffee mug. "We need to talk about Rider."

My brows flew up. "Why?"

"I think it's pretty obvious," Carl stated, his tone gentle but firm. "What happened yesterday—"

"Has nothing to do with Rider," I interrupted.

Surprise flickered across Carl's face and then was gone so

quickly I wasn't sure I actually saw it. "I'm going to have to disagree with that."

"Both of us are," Rosa joined in. "You would never have been anywhere near that neighborhood if it weren't for Rider."

"What's wrong with that neighborhood?" I demanded, and Carl raised his brow. "Yeah, it's not the greatest—it's not the Pointe or where Ainsley lives, but it's not the worst in this city."

"It's not a good place, Mallory." Carl folded his hands around his mug. "Now, I know you haven't seen a lot of this city, but we have. We—"

"I have seen the worst shit this city has to offer and it has nothing to do with the neighborhood." Anger flashed through me, bright as the sun, and I vaguely realized that I hadn't paused once while speaking. I was too—too *pissed* to care.

"Mallory," warned Rosa. "Language."

"My language? I saw someone get shot—" My voice cracked. "I saw a friend die yesterday and you're blaming Rider for this?"

"We're not blaming Rider," Carl replied. "We just don't think your friendship with him is the best thing for you right now."

"I'm not his *friend*." My hands curled into fists. "He's my boyfriend."

Carl muttered under his breath as he pinched the bridge of his nose. "Mallory…"

"What? You know he's my boyfriend."

"Yes, but…" He looked at Rosa helplessly.

"Look, honey, we of all people are not the type to judge, but Rider is not the kind of people you need to be involved with." Rosa set her mug aside. "That's what we're trying to say."

I stared at her, dumbfounded. "What *kind of people* are you talking about?"

"The kind who has no future. The kind who doesn't even care about the fact he has no future planned." Carl's tone hardened, and I flinched. Was that what they thought of Rider? "The kind that takes you to a neighborhood where fifteen-year-olds are shot in the goddamn street."

My mouth dropped open.

"Carl." Rosa reached over, placing a hand on his arm.

"No. We trust you to make smart decisions, but we don't trust him. We've been tolerant enough with this whole Rider business because we knew what he meant to you, but we are drawing a line with this." His cheeks flushed a ruddy color. "You could've been hurt yesterday or worse. That is unacceptable and I will not go through this again."

"It's not his fault!" I shouted.

Rosa blinked, taken aback. Not in the four years I've been with them had I ever raised my voice or talked back to them. "We know it's not his fault, Mallory, but that doesn't change what happened."

"Okay, let's talk about Mr. Stark." Carl's eyes flashed. "What is he planning to do once he graduates—if he graduates? Spray-paint cars for the rest of his life?"

My skin flushed hot. "What's wrong with that if he did choose it? He's good at what he does. And he is brilliant." I itched to pick up something and throw it. Not only because of what I was hearing, but because Rider did give off that impression to people. To everyone. That he didn't care, but he did. Now I was...I was pissed at them *and* him. "Rider has a future."

"He hangs out with people who—"

Rosa squeezed his arm, stopping him from finishing his sentence. Carl looked like he was about to throw up his hands. "I'm not trying to upset you, Mallory, but he's not good—"

"Don't say it." I lifted my hand and my finger trembled as I pointed it at them. "He made sure I was safe yesterday and he was there for me before you all even knew I existed. He was the only person there for me, and just because he thinks he's not cut out for college, you think he's not worthy?"

"*Mallory.*" Carl's eyes widened. "I know Rider has been there for you. I know what he did for you, and I'm not discounting that, but that doesn't change what happened yesterday. This isn't just about your past together, or about college. I know the kind of people he spends his time with. I know how these stories end."

I wasn't stopping now. A cap had blown off me. Pent-up emotion broke free. Everything that happened yesterday. Everything that had happened the last couple of months, the last four years—an entire lifetime. Tears burned my eyes. "Rider is good people. So is Hector. And so is—so was Jayden. Just because they don't have money or don't live in a house like this doesn't make them bad people."

"We know that." Rosa stood, shaking her head. "Neither Carl nor I come from money. You know that. It has nothing to do with money."

"Then what does it have to do with?"

"He's not good for you," Carl repeated.

"Why?" My voice became shrill to my own ears. "Just because I'm not agreeing with everything you all are saying? He's to blame for that?"

"You saw someone get shot and die because you were with him!" Carl's voice was as sharp as a blade.

"It's not his fault!"

"You can make better choices than this, Mallory. Smarter choices," he argued. "You have your entire life ahead of you, perfectly laid out. Don't throw it away. Don't throw away everything, because you're making a mistake."

I stiffened. No way did I consider Rider a mistake, but God, I was bound to make mistakes. It was going to happen. I wasn't perfect.

I wasn't perfect.

Something deep inside me clicked into place. Rosa and Carl knew I was far from perfect. They had to know I'd make mistakes. That I needed to make them. Wanting to be perfect for them no longer held the same power, because I couldn't be that. My shoulders straightened. "If it turns out to be a mistake, then…then I'm okay with it."

Looking away, he rubbed his palm down his face. "We never would have had to have this conversation with Marquette."

My jaw unhinged as I jerked a step back. Hurt rolled through me, fanning my anger like wind did to a fire. In the four years since they'd taken me into their home and their lives, I'd never heard them say something like that, at least to my face.

"Carl," gasped Rosa.

"I didn't ask…" I drew in a shallow breath. "I am not her. I will never be her."

He lowered his hand and then his head swung to where I stood. The color faded from his face. Regret filled his gaze immediately. "Mallory—"

"I'm not going to make her decisions," I said, hands shaking, and it all just came out again. "I don't want to spend the rest of my life in a lab. I don't want to do anything in the medical field. I'm not perfect like her. I don't want to be."

Rosa placed her hand to her chest. "Honey, we—"

Done.

I was so done with this conversation that I didn't even need words to tell them that. I didn't need to be lectured right now. I didn't need to hear anything they were saying. I needed to be with Rider—be there *for* him, like he'd been there for me so many times in the past. The rightness of that struck me hard.

It was *my* turn to take care of him and to be the strong one. The one who held it together so he could fall apart a little. I was not going to shatter and rely on anyone to piece me back together.

I was done.

Spinning around, I left the kitchen and darted upstairs. Once inside my bedroom, I slammed the door shut and then whipped off my loose shirt. I threw open a drawer and rooted around until I found a bra and then a tank top. I grabbed a hoodie and pulled it on over my head. I yanked my hair back in a loose knot as I walked over to my bed. Shoving my phone into my bag, I slung it over my shoulder and then pivoted. I headed out of my bedroom as I dug my keys out.

I took the steps two at a time and when I hit the foyer, Rosa appeared. "He didn't mean it."

"It doesn't matter." I walked straight to the door.

She followed. "Where are you going?"

"Out," I replied, my heart racing.

"Mallory—"

Opening the door, I stopped in the doorway and faced her. "I need to be there for him. Hector and Jayden are like brothers to him." Cold air washed over me and rolled into the house. "I need to go."

"You can't—"

"I need to go." My hand tightened on the knob as Carl appeared in the background. "I'm going."

Then I did.

I left the house knowing that Carl and Rosa didn't approve, knowing I was going to be in trouble.

Knowing that I was letting them down.

That I already had.

★ ★ ★

I'd tried Rider again, but the call went straight to his voice mail and the text I sent him didn't show delivered. I knew that most likely meant his cell was turned off. I tried not to let myself freak over that too much, because I was freaking about Carl and Rosa.

We never would have had to have this conversation with Marquette.

God.

God, that stung bad. It hurt. But it also hurt to know how they viewed Rider and even Hector and Jayden. Never did I think they'd be like that. I was so mad, so disappointed, that my knuckles ached from my grip on the steering wheel.

I couldn't think about Carl and Rosa right now. I'd deal with the fallout when I got home, and it would be a huge fallout, because I knew what I was doing was right.

And it was also wrong.

The first place I checked was the Lunas' house. I'd found a spot about two blocks down and jogged up the block, against the brisk wind whipping down the street. I saw Hector's Escort. People wearing bulky jackets and skull caps sat on the steps of the homes as I hurried past them and walked up to the front door. The autumn-themed wreath on the door had been replaced with evergreen and mistletoe.

Renewed anger hit me as I remembered what Rider had said about the school administration. That they saw certain addresses and then didn't even try. I never thought Carl and Rosa would be the same.

Sirens wailed off in the distance as I knocked on the front door, reminding me of yesterday. A shiver curled down my spine.

Heavy footsteps were heard inside and I tensed. The door swung open, and a tall, older man was standing there. He took one look at me and frowned. "Who are you?"

"I'm looking for—"

Another guy appeared behind him. I recognized him from yesterday. He'd been at that house, but I didn't know his name. "You're Rider's girl." He shouldered the other man aside. "You lookin' for him?"

I nodded. "Is…he here?"

"Yeah. Upstairs. The attic last I saw him." He stepped aside, letting me in. I swallowed hard as I looked around. The living room was crowded. I glanced back at the guy. "I'm so sorry about Jayden. I…"

His eyes glinted as he closed the door. "They ain't gonna get away with that. Aw, no. No way in hell they gonna get away with taking my blood," he promised, and I shivered again. The other man shook his head as this guy, who I was guessing was family, pointed to the stairs. "It's a little crowded up there."

I thought that was a little weird, because even though I hadn't been up in the attic, I was under the impression it was pretty big, but I turned and headed up the stairs, passing a very tall, dark-haired woman who was dabbing a tissue under her cheeks. I didn't see Mrs. Luna, but all I could think about was what Jayden had said to her before. That she wouldn't know what to do without him. My chest squeezed.

On the second floor I walked down the hall, past open doors. I didn't let myself look in, because I didn't want to see if any of them was Jayden's room. I couldn't see that—see his stuff. I walked past Rider's bedroom.

At the end of the hall, I opened the door. The narrow staircase was dimly lit, and there was a stale, earthy scent that reminded me of Jayden. Holding on to the railing, I made my way up and crested the top of the stairs.

Sunlight fought its way through the dusty attic windows, casting enough light that without the lamps on, I could still see.

And I saw.

I saw the mattresses and stacked pillows.

I saw the card table covered with bottles and cans of soda. And there was Rider's phone, on that table.

I saw the TV that wasn't turned on.

I saw the couch.

And my heart stopped and then dropped. Dropped like the stars falling out of the sky. My lips parted on a soft inhale. I'd found Rider. He was asleep, his head resting against the back of the couch. He wasn't alone.

My bag slipped down my shoulder and hit the floor with a thud.

Paige was there, curled up on the couch beside him.

CHAPTER 32

The sound of my bag hitting the floor didn't wake them. Paige stirred, though. She curled in more, pressing into Rider's side. Seeing that was like taking a punch to the stomach.

I couldn't believe what I was seeing.

For what felt like the hundredth time in twenty-four hours, I was absolutely dumbstruck, and my brain had a hard time catching up to what was happening.

I opened my mouth, but a sinking feeling cut me off as I stared at the two. Then my gaze cut to the table, to where Rider's phone sat. He hadn't answered any of my texts or calls. I'd believed it was because he was with Hector, and he was here, at home, but he wasn't with Hector. The punched-in-the-stomach sensation increased.

The guy's words from downstairs came back to me. *It's a little crowded up there.* Now I knew what he'd meant. Oh my God. Pain lit up my chest, and it felt so very real. Like my chest had been cracked right open.

As horrible as it was, I wasn't thinking about Jayden in that moment. I was thinking about the time Rider and I had spent together before we'd walked outside. How he'd held me. How he'd kissed me. Touched me. What he'd admitted to me.

And now he was here with her, asleep together?

I had to get out of there.

Picking up my bag, I wheeled around. I crept down the stairs, wincing each time the floorboards creaked. I had to get out of there before Rider woke up, because I...I couldn't deal with that right now.

Quietly closing the attic door behind me, all I could focus on was getting out of there and then? I didn't know. I couldn't go home. Not yet. I didn't know what I was going to do. I'd made it halfway down the hall when a door opened.

Hector walked out, scrubbing a hand through his hair. His body jerked when he spotted me. "Hey," he said, voice thick as he dropped his hand. "I didn't know you were here."

I glanced behind me and then refocused on Hector as I shut down the whirlwind of raw emotion swirling inside me. "I...um, I stopped to check on Rider—and on you. I am so sorry about...about Jayden."

"Me, too." His bloodshot eyes closed briefly. "The messed-up thing? I'm not—I'm not surprised, you know? Even after what happened with our cousin, I'm not surprised. He was making changes. Getting a job with me, but...but it was too late. He got in deep with people you just don't screw around with. I just thought... I don't even know what I thought."

I didn't know what to say and I didn't think there was anything I could say.

"He..." Hector's shoulders slumped. "He didn't deserve that. I don't care how much money he owed."

"No," I whispered, and I thought about the day in the garage and what Rider had said to Jayden. *You're going to get yourself killed.* Oh, God, Rider had been right. "He didn't."

He lifted a hand and scrubbed his fingers through his messy

hair. "I don't…I don't even believe the police will get them—the ones who got Jayden."

"They have to." My chest squeezed. I refused to believe anything else. "They will."

Hector nodded and the act looked like it took a lot of effort. "My *abuelita* is asleep. She's… They've got her sedated."

I still didn't have the right words, but innately I knew that this was one of the moments where there were none. Only action mattered in times like these, I realized. It was why I'd come over to comfort Rider. To just be there for him.

Except he'd obviously already had someone comforting him.

Stepping forward, I did the only thing I really could. I wrapped my arms around Hector and squeezed. He stiffened at first and then a sigh shuddered out of him. He folded his arms around me.

"Thank you," he whispered in a hoarse voice.

I nodded as I drew back.

Hector blinked rapidly several times. "So, um…" He cleared his throat. "You see Rider?"

A twisty motion in my chest threatened to steal my breath. "He's asleep. I…I didn't want to wake him."

"What? We can wake him. You came all the—"

"No. It's okay." I started to pass him. "I'll call him later."

"But—"

"It's no problem." I forced a smile as I stopped, facing him. "I'm…thinking of you."

A trace of a grin appeared on his lips and then he nodded once more before turning toward the attic door. I left then, hurrying out of the house as fast as I could without running.

Once I was in my car, I pulled out and I…I just started driving. My phone started ringing when I was about three blocks away, but I didn't look at it. I squeezed the steering wheel tight.

My phone rang again.

When it stopped, it dinged a few moments later, signaling a message was left, but I didn't look.

I just kept driving.

★ ★ ★

I didn't end up driving aimlessly. Thirty minutes later I found myself walking up to Ainsley's house after I left Hector's. Luckily, she answered the door...wearing cotton shorts, knee-high socks and an oversize hoodie.

Somehow she managed to still look cute.

"Hey, what are you...?" Ainsley trailed off as she eyed me. She snapped forward and grabbed my hand, pulling me inside. The toasty warmth barely eased my chilled skin. Tugging me toward the stairs, she called, "Mom! Mallory's here. We're going upstairs."

"All right." There was a pause and the TV was muted from the living room. "Do you two want some hot chocolate?"

Hot chocolate, she mouthed at me, rolling her eyes. "No, Mom. We're not ten!"

Hot cocoa sounded real good about right now.

"Are you sure?" Her mom's voice was closer and we were halfway up the stairs. "I have those tiny marshmallows you two like so much."

"Oh my God." And then louder, "Yes, Mom. We're sure."

"Just checking," her mom replied.

"Rather have some tequila," Ainsley muttered at the top of the stairs.

Her mom appeared at the bottom. "What was that?"

"Nothing!" Ainsley flashed a quick grin and then dragged me into her bedroom, closing the door behind her. "Jesus Christ, the woman has the hearing of a bat. And I don't know if bats have good hearing, but I think they do." She pushed away from the door. "What's going on? You look like you have the flu or something."

"I don't have the flu." I dropped my bag on the floor and then walked over to her bed, flopping face-first onto it.

Ainsley shuffled toward the bed. "Are you sure about that? I hope you are, because I really don't want to have to Lysol my comforter."

I cracked a grin and rolled onto my side. "Yes. I'm sure."

She ran the rest of the way and then jumped on the bed, causing me to bounce. "What's going on? And I know something is going on, because as long as I've known you, you haven't just showed up randomly." Her eyes widened. "Oh! Wait. Did you and Rider have a fight? Am I going to have to beat him up?"

My chest squeezed. "No. Not really."

"Not really?" She poked my leg when I didn't respond. "That doesn't tell me anything."

Sitting up, I grabbed a pillow and hugged it close. "I...I was going to call you yesterday, but you've got a lot going on."

Ainsley arched a brow. "I may or may not go blind, Mallory. That doesn't mean I have a lot going on."

I looked at her doubtfully. She might act like she wasn't stressing over her diagnosis, but the tightness of her mouth and the way she looked away spelled something totally different.

"Talk to me," she demanded.

Taking a deep breath, I told her everything, starting with what happened to Jayden yesterday, fighting with Carl and Rosa this morning and ending with finding Paige and Rider asleep together on the couch.

Ainsley's emotions were all over the place, much like mine. She hadn't met Jayden, but her eyes welled up with tears. "Oh my God, he's just... I don't even know what to say." She placed her hand against her chest. "How is Hector? Okay. That's a dumb question. How are you? You saw— Okay, that's also a dumb question." Springing forward, she smacked my arm.

I jerked, pulling back. "What was that for?"

"You should've called me yesterday!" she whisper-yelled.

"You went through an extremely traumatic event. You saw someone— God, I can't even say it. After everything you've been through, you see that happen?"

"Nothing...nothing that I've been through compares to what happened to Jayden." The back of my throat burned. "It's so... It's so senseless, you know? I don't care what he did or didn't do, it wasn't worth his life."

"No," she agreed as she wiped under her eyes with the back of her hand. "Do you know if the police have arrested the guy who did it?"

I shook my head. "I don't know. Hector...thinks they won't, but they have to. Everyone knew that...these Braden and Jerome guys were after...him."

Ainsley shuddered. "It's so horrible."

The burn in my throat didn't decrease, but the tears building in the backs of my eyes didn't fall. They never did. No matter. My tear ducts were defective.

I was defective.

"Poor Jayden." She folded her arms around herself. "Poor Hector. God, I can't even imagine what that's like. I don't want to. Do you know when the funeral is? Or is it too soon?"

"Too soon, I guess," I said, tucking a stray hair back from my face. "I didn't ask Hector when I saw him. I'm sure I'll find out. I'll let you know."

Neither of us spoke for a long moment and then Ainsley sighed. "Okay. Now this whole Rider thing."

The pressure in my chest clamped down like vise grips.

"I don't even know what to say about that." She shook her head. "I mean, it could be completely harmless."

I raised my brows.

Ainsley winced. "Hey, let's look at this logically for a moment. They had their clothes on, right?"

Oh, God. Immediately an image of Paige and Rider naked formed and I wanted to vomit. "Yes, they had their clothes on."

"Now, that doesn't really mean anything. When Todd and I had sex we didn't get completely naked and all it could've meant was that they put their clothes back on afterward."

I thought about what Rider and I had done yesterday while our clothing had remained on. Mostly. Wait. I refocused on what Ainsley was saying. "You think they had sex?"

"What? No. I mean, that's like the worst-case scenario. That in his grief and whatever, he hooked up with her." She stared at me. "Isn't that where your mind was going with this?"

"I…" Truth was, I didn't know what I was thinking. But I didn't believe they'd have sex after what Rider had told me the day before. My shoulders caved in. "I saw them and I just freaked. I don't know." I squeezed the pillow. "I just… I defended him to Rosa and Carl. Left the house to go to him—to be there for him, and he didn't even need me. He had—" My breath caught. "He had Paige, and he didn't answer the phone when I called or texted. He was with Paige, Ainsley, and yesterday we…we went pretty far and I—" Pressing my lips together, I cut myself off.

"What?" she asked softly.

I didn't want to say, because it made the hurting in my chest so much worse and it scared me so badly. Terrified me, because I knew what I was feeling was a big deal and acknowledging it made it true.

"You love him, don't you?" she said.

Squeezing my eyes shut, I forced a shallow breath. Yesterday the mere idea of falling in love, being in love, was as terrifying as it was exhilarating. Now it was just one of those things.

"Yes. I think I am." I opened my eyes and met Ainsley's stare. "No. I don't think I am. I know I am. I'm in love with him. I think I've been in love with him my entire life. And I love the grown Rider even more than I loved the boy when we were younger." My heart rate kicked up. "And that's scary."

"Damn straight it is," she agreed, one side of her lips curling up. "It's why I'm totes okay with whatever happens with Todd. I don't love him. I don't even know what that feels like, but I know it has to be scary."

I studied her for a moment and the knot expanded. "I thought Rider felt the same."

"Let's not freak out too much. Okay? We don't know what was going on there. They were asleep on the couch, not cuddled up—"

"She was pressed against him." Saying that made me feel sick, but I had to get it out of me and into the air between us. "He wasn't holding her or anything, but there was no space between them. None."

"That still doesn't mean anything."

My brows rose.

"All right, he's going to have to have one hell of an excuse for it, but we really don't know what was going on there. Paige is a friend of his and Hector's, right? She knew Hector's brother?"

I nodded.

"It could be harmless."

I wanted it to be harmless. And a part of me didn't. How crazy was that? But if it wasn't harmless, then it would hurt and it would suck but my life would go back to normal. I wouldn't have to worry about things like this. Or what Carl and Rosa thought of Rider. I wouldn't have to fight for him.

Or fight in general.

I squirmed, uncomfortable with where my thoughts were going.

Ainsley placed her hand on my arm. "Has he tried to call you since you left?"

I glanced at my bag. "The phone rang a couple of times, but I...haven't looked."

She stared at me like I had half a functioning brain. "You should look. Seriously."

"It's probably Rosa or Carl." But I slid off the bed anyway

and grabbed my bag, bringing it back to me. I sat and opened the compartment. I hit the screen and disappointment crashed into me. "It's not Rider's. It's an unknown number."

"Oh." She sighed heavily.

"Whoever it is left a message. Let me see who it is."

"Maybe Carl and Rosa hired a private investigator to find you."

Despite everything I laughed as I hit the message button. "That would be an excessive— Oh!" I stopped talking as I recognized the voice.

"What?" Her eyes widened as she rocked forward. "What?"

Shaking my head, I held my hand out as I hit Speaker on my phone. Both of us stared at it as Rider's deep voice filled the room.

"Mallory, this is Rider. I'm using Hector's phone. I forgot the battery was running low and mine died. Didn't even realize it. I'm charging it now. Shit. None of that matters. He said you were here. That you were in the attic. Why didn't you wake me up?"

There was a pause and Ainsley muttered, "Good question."

I shot her a look as Rider continued. "Hell. I know why. Mallory, call me. Try this number or try mine. Call me." There was the sound of a door shutting and then he said, "Please, Mallory. Call me."

The call disconnected and we both sat there, continuing to stare at it.

Ainsley was the first to speak. "Are you going to call him?"

"I..." Hope rose, sweet and sugary compared to the bitterness of disappointment and frustration.

"He said his phone was dead. That explains why he didn't answer when you called," she reasoned. "And he's never lied to you before, right?"

I shook my head. His battery had been low. I remembered that now.

"And he called, obviously right after you left," she continued. "That has to mean something."

I thought it did, but I honestly didn't know what to think anymore.

"Call him," Ainsley urged. "Give him a chance to explain himself." As I looked up at her, she smiled faintly. "I'm not an expert in the whole love thing, but if you love him, you'll give him a chance to explain himself. And you love him, right?"

My heart screamed yes.

"Call him."

CHAPTER 33

I didn't know what to do.

Well, I knew I had to go home and face the music, but when it came to Rider, I had no idea. I wanted to talk to him and I didn't.

Right now I didn't want him to have to worry about…about relationship drama. The boy he considered a brother had just been killed. He didn't need to deal with me and what was and was not happening with us.

But I was also scared of what he had to say.

Scared of how it would make me feel either way.

He apparently hadn't needed me.

I flinched. I hated that thought, because it was spiteful and it hurt. It clawed around in my chest, because when it came time for the script to be flipped, for me to be there for him, someone else had beaten me to it. The feeling sounded ridiculous, but that was how I felt. That was real.

And I felt like I failed somehow.

When I came home just before dinner, I expected Rosa and

Carl to be where they were, in the kitchen, waiting to pounce on me the minute I walked through the door.

That didn't happen.

The door to the library was closed, and I could hear someone moving around in the kitchen, most likely Rosa. I halted at the stairs, knowing I should just get this over with, go into the kitchen and face the music.

I hurried up the stairs instead and closed the bedroom door behind me. Pulling my phone out, I dropped my bag on the window seat. My phone had rung while I was driving. It was Rider, this time from his phone. He'd left a message again.

Knots formed in my belly as I lifted the phone to my ear and listened to the message. There was silence and then, "Dammit." He didn't say anything else. The message ended.

I sat on the window seat and stared at my phone. Stomach churning, I bit down on my lip.

I loved Rider.

Oh, God.

I was *in* love with him.

I knew that much was true. Love was the swelling, hopeful feeling in my chest every time I saw him. Love was the way I could forget about everything when I was with him. Love was the catch in my breath when he looked at me in his intense way. Love was the gasp he could draw out of me with the simplest of touches. Love was the way I could…I could be myself around him, know that I didn't need to be perfect or worry about what he was thinking, because he accepted me. And all of that?

Love scared the hell out of me.

I didn't want the heartbreak. I knew Rider cared about me, even loved me in a way one would love their childhood friend, but I didn't know if it was the same emotion I felt for him. Because there was a difference between loving someone and being in love. And he hadn't said he was in love with me. He'd said a lot and done a lot…to me, but those words had never been spoken. Seeing him with Paige hurt in a way I could barely put into words, a feeling I was so unfamiliar with. I felt sick and anxious, as if I was forgetting to do something, but there was nothing for me to do.

Heartbreak could only be worse.

I didn't want to lose him one day, and God, there were so many ways you could lose someone. I didn't want to disappoint him. I didn't want *him* to disappoint *me*.

Restless, I rose from the window seat and walked to the door. I stopped before I opened it. Where was I going to go? If I went downstairs, I'd have to face Carl and Rosa, so I retreated to my bed and I...

I didn't face them.

I didn't call Rider.

Like the Mallory of twelve years, I did what I did best.

I hid.

★ ★ ★

Today was going to suck.

That was all I could think as I dragged myself in the back entrance of Lands High. Jayden would not surprise me at my locker. He wouldn't randomly appear at lunch and flirt with the girls while stealing their French fries, and I imagined everyone would be talking about what happened on Saturday.

Every part of me ached as I climbed the stairs to go to my locker. The heavy sweater I wore did nothing to ease the chill settling deep into my bones. I'd hardly slept last night, and Rosa must have sensed that, because all she'd said at breakfast was to dress warm since it was supposed to snow. Somehow her tiptoeing around the events of yesterday had been scarier than her confronting me. Feeling like I needed a nap already, I started to open my locker door.

"Mouse."

My body jerked and then I whipped around. Thoughts scattered as I stared up at Rider.

He looked…he looked exhausted standing there. Dark shadows had blossomed under his eyes. His hair was messy, as if he'd been shoving his hands through it several times. There was a smattering of scruff along his jaw, and I wanted to rush toward him and wrap my arms around him. I wanted to hold him, because as those hazel eyes met mine, there was a wealth of sorrow in their depths.

I stood still.

Rider stepped forward, ignoring the person he cut off. "Can we talk?"

My heart pounded in my chest. "I have—"

"You have to go to class. I know," he said, stepping even closer. So close our shoes touched. "I couldn't wait until lunch. I mean, I will, but please give me a chance to talk to you."

I opened my mouth and I don't even know what I planned to say, only that what came out of me surprised me. "We can talk now."

"Now?" Relief flickered across his face. "You'll leave school?"

Nodding, I closed the locker and then faced him. I had no idea what I was doing. Last night I hadn't been ready to talk to him. I wasn't sure I was ready now, and leaving school was a bad, bad idea.

But I did it.

Rider studied me for a moment, like he didn't believe me. I didn't even believe myself, but we started walking. And we kept walking, right out into the cold air and straight to my car, going against the sea of students. No one stopped us. No one looked twice. We got into the car and I turned it on, cranking up the heat. I didn't let myself think about what I was doing or how much trouble I'd get into if the school contacted the house.

I looked over at him and realized then he was only wearing a black thermal and jeans. No jacket. "Aren't you freezing?"

His gaze roamed over my face. "I don't even feel the cold right now."

Looking away, I slipped the car into Reverse and backed out of the parking space. "Where to?"

"We can go to Hector's house," he offered. "No one is there right now. They're over at his aunt's."

I thought about his wording. "Why don't you...ever call it your house?"

He didn't answer and when I glanced over at him, he was staring out the window, his jaw locked down.

"Rider," I persisted. "You...you want to talk. Let's talk."

"I wanted to talk about what you saw yesterday," he replied.

The knots in my stomach doubled. "I want to talk about this first."

Rider kicked his head back against the seat and several moments passed before he spoke. "It doesn't... It doesn't feel like a home, Mallory. Not my home."

I focused on the road. "What does that mean? Your home looks like a home."

"Yours *feels* like a home. You're there. In the living room and in the kitchen. In your bedroom," he explained. "But I'm just sleeping in mine."

A sick feeling twisted up my insides. "Does Mrs. Luna... make you feel that way?"

"No." He sighed. "Of course not, but I'm not— I'm a foster kid, just one of the many Mrs. Luna took in. I'm not her grandson. God knows I'm not a replacement for Jayden, and no matter how much they make me feel welcome, I age out as soon as I graduate. I am not blood. I'm just another mouth to feed. I have to remember that. I always have to remember that."

I thought about what Carl had said yesterday and I understood that feeling, but I wasn't sure if Rider was giving Mrs. Luna enough credit. Or giving himself enough credit.

"It's not a big deal," he added.

"I think it is." I slowed with the traffic and glanced over at him. He was still staring out the window, tracing his fingers along the glass. I took a breath and then gave voice to thoughts I'd kept to myself. "I don't think...you realize how much Hector and Mrs. Luna care about you—how much Jayden cared about you. I don't think you believe you're worth it. It's the same with your artwork and art school—with college." My hands tightened around the steering wheel and certainty filled me. "You've given up on yourself before anyone else has a chance to."

Silence greeted me.

I could feel Rider's stare on me. Several moments passed. "That's bullshit, and kind of priceless coming from you. You gave up on me yesterday."

I started to defend myself, but I couldn't. I swallowed hard. "I know. You're right about that, but I'm also right."

"And how's that?" Challenge hardened his tone.

"Because I give up on myself on a daily basis," I admitted. My cheeks heated but I continued. "I know."

He sucked in an audible breath. "Mallory..."

I shook my head as I thought about all the conflicting emotions and needs and wants. "It's true. It's what I do. I don't mean to. Or maybe I do. It's...it's easier being scared of everything."

"How...how can that be?" His voice softened. "How can that be easier?"

My smile was faint. Suddenly, I really wished I was at home, with my head under the blankets. "You can't fail when you don't really try, right? You'd know that."

Rider cursed under his breath, and he didn't say anything after that. As I pulled into the parking spot a few houses down, I figured coming to talk was a bad idea, so I didn't turn the car off.

The click of Rider unbuckling his seat belt echoed. I looked over. "Maybe we should...we should talk later."

"What?" He paused with his hand on the door. "No. Not after what you just said. You're not giving up without even talking. Especially not after you just called me out for virtually the same thing."

Well, he had a good point there, but I hesitated.

"We're here. Okay? Let's talk."

The urge to run back to school or home rode me hard. I really couldn't even believe I'd left school and was sitting outside Rider's house—the house that didn't feel like a home to him.

"Okay," I whispered.

Rider waited until I grabbed my bag and got out of the car before he did, almost like he expected me to drive off the moment he stepped out. I followed him up the block, shivering as the wind lifted the hair off my shoulders.

The house was quiet as we walked in and it smelled more like pumpkin than apples this time. Before I could stop myself, I looked over at the wall behind the couch. Out of all the framed photos, I saw Jayden immediately. It was a Christmas photo, possibly from last year. He stood in front of a festively lit tree, smiling broadly at the camera while he held a Puerto Rican flag in front of his chest.

My chest grew tight, squeezing until I thought my heart would just stop. I couldn't believe he was gone.

My gaze crawled across the wall of photos, and I saw them—pictures of Rider mixed in with Hector and Jayden's, like he was family.

Because he *was* family.

I hadn't noticed them before, but Rider lived here. How could he not see that?

Rider didn't head for the kitchen. He made his way upstairs and I followed him up, into the bedroom he barely spent time in.

He flipped on the light. The first thing I saw was the copy of *The Velveteen Rabbit*. It was on his nightstand. I dropped my bag on the floor.

Rider sat at the chair in front of his neat, probably never-used desk. "My phone died sometime Saturday night," he began, and I slowly faced him. "Do you remember us talking about that earlier? It was down to ten percent before...before everything happened."

I sat on the edge of the bed.

"I wasn't ignoring your calls and I kept meaning to get someone else's phone to call you, but things were crazy. Some of the guys were trying to get everyone to go after Braden and Jerome, and I was trying— I was keeping Hector home, because I couldn't..." He cleared his throat. "I can't lose him, too."

"I knew you were busy. I didn't freak out over you not returning my calls. I...I came over because I wanted to be there for you. I needed...to be there for you. That's why I came over."

"I didn't know Paige was going to be here." His eyes met mine and he didn't look away. "I had no idea. I swear to you, I had no idea she was going to be here." He paused, his shoulders rising. "She was really upset. Paige has known Jayden and Hector for years. She and Jayden got on each other's nerves, but they cared a lot about each other."

I closed my eyes. I got that. I really did. I imagined brothers and sisters argued like they did. Jayden and Paige were a lot closer than Jayden and I had been, and despite everything, I felt bad for her. But none of that changed how I felt when I saw her and Rider.

"She must've fallen asleep after I did," he explained. "We didn't start out that way."

"I... She was curled up against you. Like you all have done it before," I said, voice low. "That freaked me out and I just left. I couldn't be there."

"It hurt you," he stated.

Lowering my gaze, I nodded. "I wasn't expecting it. I just wanted to be there for you."

"I wanted you there. I did," he said, and then rose. My gaze followed. He shoved his hand through his hair. "I wanted you there, but I also didn't want you around what was going down—

what could've gone down. You already saw what happened to Jayden."

"You saw what happened to Jayden, too."

"Yeah, but I…"

"There's no but. That wasn't… It wasn't easy for anyone to see. Especially not the person who was like a brother to him." I brushed my hair back from my face as Rider stopped a few feet in front of me. Having this conversation right now seemed wrong. "I don't want you focusing on us right now. Jayden—"

"Would understand that we need to straighten this out," he interrupted. "You mean everything to me, and when Hector woke me up and told me you'd been there? Fuck. My heart stopped. I'm sorry. Dammit, Mallory, I'm so sorry. We were talking about Jayden when I fell asleep. I hadn't slept all day and when I dozed off, not a lot of time could've passed before you showed up. It wasn't planned. And I swear to you, nothing happened between us. I wouldn't do that to you, and Paige knows better." He walked over and sat on the bed, his body angled toward me. "She knows how I feel about you. She might not be sending congratulations cards to us anytime soon." The half grin appeared and then disappeared. "But she knows."

My heart rate sped up. "How…how do you feel about me?"

"I think it's pretty obvious."

"Let's just say I need a detailed account."

His lashes lifted and his eyes met mine. "I can do that for you."

"Okay." I leaned toward him.

"I never once stopped thinking about you when you were taken away. Four years. All I could hope was that you were in a good place. Never expected you to walk into school. Didn't even allow myself to dream about that. And then you did, and seeing you blew me away. You were just like I remembered, but different. The hints of the girl I saw in you when we were younger were now right in front of me. The moment you said my name—the moment you hugged me I knew." Rider reached between us, folding his hand around mine. "I knew I'd fall in love with you and I did. I love you, Mallory."

My lips parted on an inhale. "What?"

"I love you, and not the kind of love we had for each other when we were younger, you know? Paige knows that. So does Hector. So did Jayden. I love you."

Oh my God.

I stilled as his words sank in, absorbed them as they traveled far, through my muddled thoughts, down into my skin and muscle, and all the way to the bone.

Rider Stark *loved* me.

I reacted without thinking.

Springing toward him, I wrapped my arms around him. Somehow, and I didn't even know how, I ended up on his lap, my knees on either side of his thighs. At first, I just held on to him, and he held me back. I wanted to cry. I wanted to laugh. I wanted to do a million different things.

I wanted to kiss him.

That was what I went with.

When I lifted my head and leaned in, he knew what I wanted and he gave it to me. His lips touched mine, and once again I was lost in him, in us. Our breaths mingled. Our hands moved.

And I wanted *this*. I wanted more of *this*.

The rightness seized me. Saturday I hadn't been ready but now I was. I didn't know what made me so sure, so *fearless*, when I'd been so hesitant two days before, but those days felt like an eternity. Maybe it was the events of this weekend, seeing what happened to Jayden. Seeing life just snuffed out. Something about that made me want to live, to experience everything. It could've been what happened afterward. Arguing with Carl and Rosa and realizing that I would make mistakes and that I wasn't perfect—that I couldn't be. There was something freeing about it. Finding Rider with Paige had forced me to face how deeply

I felt about him instead of avoiding it. Talking to him now and being open about everything. Hearing him say that he loved me.

Whatever the reason, I knew in every part of me that this right now, right here, was what I wanted.

I kissed him back, and I wasn't thinking about whether I was doing it right or not. I tasted his lips, touched his tongue as I slid my hands down his chest. I felt his heart pounding. My body moved over him, and the crazy, swirling sensations rippled over my skin. I slipped my hand under his shirt, awed when his entire body jerked as my palm glided over his bare stomach. I wanted to feel him, feel more.

Leaning back, I reached down and gripped the hem of my sweater. His hooded gaze followed my hands, and his lips parted as I lifted the material up over my head and dropped it.

"Hell…" His voice was thick, rough. "Mallory, you're…"

"What?" I whispered, feeling my body burn for two very different reasons.

"You're beautiful." His gaze dipped, tracking the lacy edges of the bra. "Never thought I'd see you like this. So freaking glad I have. You're so beautiful, Mallory."

My heart swelled so fast I thought it would lift me to the ceiling.

"But I think we…" His grip tightened on my hips. "We… we should stop."

Stopping was the last thing I wanted to do. Courage was buzzing through my veins. I pressed my hips down, and his groan shot a shiver of acute awareness through me. "I don't want to."

"Mallory." My name sounded like a prayer and a curse as his slid his hands up my sides. "We've both been through a lot. I don't want you to regret this."

"I won't." I rested my forehead against his. "I'm ready for this—for this with *you*." My fingers curled into his thermal. "I want this—I love you. I'm *in* love with you."

I don't know what it was exactly that I said that did it, but his hands tightened on my waist and then I was on my back, under him, and his mouth was on me. The kisses were hard and drugging and I knew what his kiss was saying.

Rider was ready, too.

CHAPTER 34

Everything sped up and then slowed down.

His thermal came off, and even though I'd seen him shirtless before, it didn't prepare me for seeing him like that again. He was all smooth, hard skin under my fingertips. His body was so different than mine. I was soft under his hands, but he appeared to be just as awestruck as I was. He explored. I explored. There were few words as first his jeans came off and then mine. The bra slipped down my arms.

I was nervous. My hands trembled. No one had ever seen so much of me, almost everything. The urge to cover myself was hard to ignore, but when his chest touched mine, and there was nothing between us, I wasn't thinking.

Everything was about feeling, and unlike before, there wasn't a bitter tinge of panic edging out the wonderful heat and curious tension. I was nervous. I didn't know what to expect, but it didn't drown the passion or make me want to run away. I rode it out as my hands moved lower, as his hands followed. Our bodies were moving against one another, restless and seeking. His hand slipped over my hip, his fingers following the band of my underwear. I shivered as my back arched. The sound he made curled my toes.

Using his elbows, he braced his body over mine. Rider kissed me deeply, thoroughly, as he pushed down. My leg curled over his. My fingers tangled in his hair. His mouth left mine as his lips coasted over my chin and then down my throat. My senses spun as he went lower, blazing a path.

"Shit," he groaned, lifting his head.

My eyes fluttered open, lips feeling wonderfully swollen. "What?"

"We…we have to stop." He moved up, cradling my face. Stop? I didn't want to stop. He made a rough sound, obviously thinking the same. "I don't have protection."

"You don't?" Surprise flooded me.

He rested his forehead against mine. "I'm guessing you don't, either."

I almost laughed. "Don't…all guys have condoms in, like, their wallets?" My face burned as I asked the question.

Rider chuckled. "God. I wish that was the case. I just haven't… Well, you know. I've never gone this far."

"I know." I slid my hand over his chest as I tried to get control of my breathing. "You didn't buy them when you…when you were with Paige?"

His gaze met mine. "I did. Once. Didn't use them." He turned his head, kissing the center of my palm. "Didn't really plan on this happening today."

"Me, neither." I bit down on my lip. Part of me wanted to forget about the fact that we didn't have protection, but that would be incredibly, well, reckless. Sort of dumb, too. Being responsible sucked, but if we couldn't do that… "There…there are things we can do."

His lips quirked. "Oh yeah, there are definitely other things we can do."

And we did some of those things. Things that we'd started

Saturday. And this time, when his hand slipped over my thighs, between them, I didn't panic. As the unfamiliar and nearly overwhelming feelings built inside me, I welcomed them, the unknown of it all. I touched him without fear of not knowing what to do, and I quickly learned, there wasn't much that I could do wrong with him. The only thing in the room that could be heard over my pounding heart was the breathy moans and deeper, rougher groans.

When it was over, I was shattered in a blissful, amazing way I could never have imagined. I could barely describe how it felt. It was like being pulled too tight, but in a very good way, and when all that strange, heady tension broke, it hit me in waves. It seemed to be the same for Rider, because when he collapsed next to me, he was breathing just as fast and heavy. Forever passed before I could speak.

"That was…" I rolled onto my side, facing him as I crossed my arms over my chest.

"Perfect?" he murmured, curling his hand around the nape of my neck. "It was perfect."

"Yes." I wiggled closer, fitting my head under his chin, and his hand slipped from my neck as he wrapped his arm around me. I couldn't even imagine what actual sex would feel like if what we'd just done felt that good. Then again, I figured sex, at least the first time, would probably hurt a little. And I was kind of glad that the first time I experienced something like this wasn't marred by even a moment of pain.

"Thank you," he said after a moment.

I lifted my head. "For what?"

He grinned a little. "For trusting me with this. For everything?"

My smile raced across my face. I snuggled in, closing my eyes. Every part of my body was relaxed, and I knew I could fall asleep until I heard Rider chuckle. I tipped my chin up and looked at him. "What?"

"I was just thinking." His cheeks pinked. "Man, this is going to sound cheesy, but I was thinking that this is the first time this room has felt like...*mine.*"

"No," I whispered. "That's not cheesy at all."

Rider brushed his lips across my cheek as he rose onto his elbow. "What are we going to do?"

"Now?"

"Yeah. You should head back to school. It'll be around lunch-time."

"What about you?"

"I think I'm going to head to their aunt's house. I want to be there today. I know they're going to start the whole funeral process."

The weight of grief returned. It wasn't like we'd forgotten about Jayden, but the pain had lessened during those brief moments. Feeling like I'd woken from a dream, I nodded. "If I'm lucky, the school hasn't called home yet. Carl and Rosa are already ticked off enough at me."

His brows lowered. "Why?"

It was hard keeping my gaze fixed on his face when he was sort of, kind of naked. I'd looked my fill, but I wanted to look more.

"Mallory?" He chuckled.

I was looking and I needed to focus. My cheeks heated. "They got pretty mad after I told them what happened Saturday."

The grin slowly slipped off his face. "That's understandable."

"Not really," I told him. "They...want me to stop seeing you."

His brows lifted as he sat up and swung his legs over the bed. He looked at the door, jaw hard. "Really?"

"Yeah, I got into a fight with Carl and Rosa," I explained as he rose, pulling up his boxers, and for a moment I got distracted by the stiff muscles along his spine. "What happened to Jayden wasn't your fault."

"But you saw that go down because I brought you to that

house." He swiped his jeans off the floor and then pulled them on. "That much is true."

I disagreed. "You didn't know that was going to happen."

Rider faced me, and I realized he held my bra. I flushed as he handed it over. "That doesn't change what happened." He looked away as I put it on. "How bad did the fight get?"

"I left the house. That's when I went looking for you." Scooting to the edge of the bed, I found my sweater and pulled it on over my head. When I stood, it fell to my thighs. "They were... just overreacting."

His gaze swung back to me and then did a slow slide, causing my toes to curl against the thin carpet. He didn't say anything as I found my jeans and pulled them on. I sat on the edge of the bed, worrying my lower lip as he finished dressing. "They just don't understand. It's like they expect me to make all these choices—choices they would make, choices Marquette would make, and I'm not them. I'm not her."

"They know you're not her." Rider walked toward the bed, stopping. I grinned when I saw his bare feet peeking out from the hem of his jeans. "They just want what's best for you."

"I know." I looked up at him. "Carl... He did say something that I really never thought he'd say. He said to Rosa that this—the whole fighting thing—was something he didn't have to worry about with Marquette."

"Shit," Rider muttered, running his hands through his hair. "He didn't mean that, Mouse."

I shrugged. Maybe he did. I'd been pretty malleable the last four years. "I never...I never disagreed with them over anything, you know. I owe them so much, so I always agreed with whatever they wanted. Whatever they thought best. Like they've been pushing this whole med school thing, and I don't want to do that. But I agreed to look at these pamphlets anyway. I don't even know why. I think I want..."

"You want what?"

"I think I want to go into social work." I waited for him to laugh. He didn't. I sat a little straighter. "It's something that makes sense to me. I could help people like you and me, but Carl had laughed and asked if I was being serious. He said I wouldn't make any money."

"Not everything is about money."

"Exactly."

"Money helps, though." He paused. "Carl seems like a good man. He was angry. People say stupid crap when they're mad." A muscle throbbed in his jaw. "But I…"

"What?" I asked when he didn't finish.

Rider opened his mouth and then shook his head. "We should get back to school. I don't want you to get into any more trouble."

I slid off the bed and found my socks. When I was finished, Rider was pulling a skull cap on. Tufts of hair curled along the edges. He was silent as we headed downstairs and out to my car.

Little balls of unease had formed in my stomach. I turned the ignition key and looked over at him. "Is everything okay?"

"Yeah. Everything's fine." He looked over at me. "Can you drop me off at their aunt's? It's on the way to school."

I studied him for a moment and then nodded. I needed to stop being paranoid, I told myself as I followed his directions to the aunt's house. Once there, I got out of the car and Rider met me on my side. He placed his hands on my cheeks and slid his thumbs along my jaw. Lowering his head, he kissed me softly, tenderly—a long kiss, one that left me breathless.

I didn't know what it was, but something about the kiss felt different than the ones we'd shared earlier. Something about it felt a little sad.

CHAPTER 35

As soon as I walked through the door, Rosa pounced. "Sit." All but dragging me into the kitchen, she gestured at a chair. Two mugs were waiting on the table, and I could smell the stick of cinnamon she always liked to place in her tea.

Taking a deep breath, I did just as she ordered. I didn't think the school had called since I'd made it to most of my classes, and I wasn't about to ask. As I waited for her to speak, I couldn't help but think the morning with Rider felt like forever ago. I was looking forward to reliving every detail when I next talked to Ainsley—I'd texted her earlier and it was a miracle her eruption of *squees* hadn't broken my phone.

"The first thing I want to say is that Carl and I love you," Rosa said. "We love you as much as we loved Marquette, and I hope you realize that. What Carl said yesterday was not okay. He was angry and worried about you. That's not a justification for his words. He owes you a big apology."

Placing my foot on the chair, I hugged my knee close to my chest. At least it didn't appear like the school had called. "I don't...want him to apologize."

"He needs to."

I shook my head. "I just want him— I want things to go back…" I trailed off, realizing what I was about to say. *I want things to go back to the way they were.* And that wasn't true.

I didn't want anything to go back to the way it had been.

"You're right," I said, lifting my chin. "He needs to apologize."

"And he will." She studied me. "There's something you need to understand about Carl. It's not my story to tell. I just hope you give him a chance."

I thought of some of the things Carl had said yesterday, things that made it seem like he had experience with what happened this weekend. I squeezed my knee. "I will."

"Good." She took a sip of her tea. "Carl and I talked a lot while you were gone yesterday, about you and about Rider."

Oh, I didn't like where this was going. Reaching over, I picked up my mug and took a drink. The warm liquid hit my throat, but it didn't loosen the knots in my stomach.

"In the four years since we've had you, never once did you raise your voice to us. You've always agreed with whatever we wanted, no matter what it was." She paused, and my eyes shot to her. Her knuckles were white as she placed her cup on the table. "You don't want to go to med school, do you?"

That came out of left field.

The immediate instinct was to assuage her concerns, to tell her yes, because I knew that was what she wanted to hear, but I…I couldn't do it anymore.

"No," I admitted quietly. "I don't want to do that."

Rosa closed her eyes briefly and then nodded. "Okay."

"Is it…is it really okay?" I asked, bringing up my other knee and circling my arms around both. "I know that's not what you want to hear."

"I've always been honest with you, Mallory, and I'll be honest now. It's not what I want to hear. A career in research will leave you set for the future, but it's your future." She exhaled roughly. "And the most important thing is that you're happy. Carl feels the same way."

I sort of doubted that.

She picked up her cup. "You've really been considering social work?"

Seeds of excitement rooted deep inside me. "Yes."

"Because it means something to you?"

I nodded.

"It makes sense." She lifted the cup to her lips. "With your past, it makes sense that you'd be passionate about making a difference, and I'm proud that you want to do that. It's not going to be easy for you."

The excitement rose swiftly even though Rosa was right. Pursuing a career in social work wouldn't be easy for me. I knew I would work cases that would be painfully similar to mine. I knew it would be a job I'd take home with me at the end of the day, but it would be a job I cared about.

"We'll support you, Mallory. I just want you to know that. Whether it be med school or social work or flying to the moon, we will support you."

A bit of weight lifted from my chest. "Thank you."

Rosa was quiet for a moment. "This situation with Rider—"

"I love him," I blurted out. Her gaze sharpened, but once I spoke the words aloud, I didn't want to take them back. "I love him. I'm not going to stop seeing him."

"Honey, I..." She leaned over, placing her hand on my bent knee. "I know you think you're in love, but you two have this past where it was just you and him against the world. I can understand why you might think you feel that way, after all that you two have shared."

What she said didn't sound crazy at all. Part of me could even understand it. "How do you know when you're really in love with someone?"

Rosa opened her mouth, but she didn't speak as she pulled her hand away.

"How did you know you were truly in love with Carl? How does anyone really know?" I shook my head. "I don't think you can...but I know how I feel right now. Maybe that'll change. I don't know, but don't—" I squared my shoulders. "Don't tell me that I don't know what I'm feeling or what to feel."

She sat up straight.

"Because I know that I feel strongly about him. I know that it *is* love. He...he accepts me, always has, but he doesn't expect me to stay the same, and when I fail at something in front of him, he doesn't make me feel bad about it," I said, trying to put words to how I felt. "He makes me feel good about myself, about *him*."

Rosa's eyes had widened as I spoke. "Okay," she said after a moment. "I won't tell you how you feel."

I was on a roll now, not stopping anytime soon. "I know he would do anything to make sure I was happy and safe, and trust me, he hates that I saw what happened on Saturday. Carl doesn't have to blame him for that. He already blames himself, but it wasn't his fault, and I hate—absolutely hate that what happened to Jayden has somehow become something about Rider and me. That's not right. That's overshadowing what happened to Jayden and that's wrong."

Her brows rose.

And I wasn't done yet. "I know you guys don't really trust Rider and you don't think he has a future, but what you don't know is that he's trying. He really is, and even if he decides he doesn't want to go to college, that doesn't make him less of a good person. That doesn't mean he doesn't deserve your respect. He's brilliant and he's so freaking talented. The last thing he needs is yet another person not believing he's worth the effort."

She looked away as she pressed her lips together. "I don't

think he's not worth the effort, Mallory. I just…don't know what to think."

My heart was pounding in my chest, a staccato of beats. "I just want you guys to really try—to try to see what I see in him."

Rosa smiled faintly. "We just want what's best for you and sometimes in wanting that, we mess up." Reaching over once more, she placed her hand on mine and squeezed. "We can try, honey. We will."

I closed my eyes. "Thank you."

There was a smile in her voice as she spoke again. "I don't know if you realize this or not, Mallory, but you're not the same girl we first brought home. That's a good thing." Her hand tightened on mine again. "That's a really good thing."

She was right.

I couldn't put my finger on the exact moment that I'd become a different Mallory. Maybe because it wasn't just one moment but more of a combination of hundreds, even thousands of them. It wasn't just going to public school or sitting with Keira at lunch. It wasn't the conscious decision to make myself uncomfortable by taking speech class. It wasn't just finally opening up about my past to Ainsley. It wasn't just the day I stood in the hall and looked past the meanness in Paige's words to the razor-sharp truth beneath. It wasn't just what happened to Jayden and seeing life snatched away.

And it wasn't just reconnecting with Rider, or falling in love with him.

It was *everything*.

It was making the decision to do things that frightened me. It was finding the courage that third day of school to walk up to Keira's table. It was giving a speech during lunch, and then another, even if I only had an audience of one. It was failing at Peter's party, but realizing that that was okay. It was accepting that my past would always be a part of me and a part of those who were close to me. It was finding something I was passionate about, something that made *me* happy. It was realizing that I didn't owe Carl and Rosa my life. That my love for them was enough. That I didn't have to become a carbon copy of their daughter. And knowing Jayden had changed me in ways I knew I would still be trying to figure out a lifetime from now. It was finding Rider again, and allowing myself to fall in love with him.

And it was knowing that I could still be…still be afraid of everything, but not letting that fear stop me from living.

The realization wasn't due to some kind of earth-stopping epiphany. It was subtle and slow, a combination of a thousand moments rolled into one, but as I sat at the kitchen table with Rosa, I knew it was true.

I'd changed.

★ ★ ★

Keira stared at her untouched plate. "I still can't believe it," she was saying. The table was quiet. "He was *just* here, you know? Last week he walked into this cafeteria and he asked me out on a date."

"While he stole my fries off my plate," Jo added. "And then offered to take me out on a date."

"He was always doing stuff like that." Keira let out a choked laugh. "It just sucks. There're no other words for it."

That much was true.

"I heard that the police picked Braden up yesterday afternoon," Anna said, keeping her voice low. "I didn't know Braden well, but he's, like, what? Eighteen? How can you kill someone when you're eighteen? That's just insane."

"How can you be killed when you're fifteen?" murmured Jo.

Keira and the girls didn't know that Rider and I had been there when Jayden was killed. Surprisingly, that wasn't something that had ended up getting out, and it wasn't something I was really willing to share beyond Ainsley.

It was strange seeing the lives that Jayden affected, knowing that he probably hadn't even realized how much he impacted others. And then there was the flip side; the people who knew only that some kid had died but who couldn't place his face. It wasn't that they didn't acknowledge the loss. It just didn't affect their lives. Today was just an average Tuesday to them. Wednesday would be no different. On Saturday they wouldn't be going to the funeral of a fifteen-year-old. In their minds, they still had forever.

But we knew better.

Forever was something we all took for granted, but the problem with forever was that it really didn't exist.

Jayden hadn't believed his days were numbered. He'd made plans, had other goals, and he'd probably believed he had forever. Ainsley had assumed, rightfully so, that she would always have her vision. She wouldn't have that, something most of us took for granted, for forever. Then there was me. I'd thought I'd be stuck the way I was for forever, always scared, always needing someone to speak up for me. I'd learned to cope with my fears, found my voice, and realized that Carl and Rosa would love me even if I wasn't perfect.

Forever wasn't real.

And I guessed, for me, that I was lucky it wasn't. But for others, I wished it was real, that they had forever.

Taking my seat in the back of speech that afternoon, I found myself staring at Hector's empty chair. When would he come back? I couldn't even imagine what he must be going through.

When Rider and I had been separated it had felt like he'd died. Those immediate months afterward had been lonely and never-ending, but I knew that Rider was still alive. My own pain and loss had been nothing like this.

Surprise flickered through me when I saw Rider walk into class. He and I had texted last night, and he'd said he'd be in class today, but I really didn't think he'd show when I knew he wanted to be there for Hector.

Rider still hadn't shaved and he was wearing the same clothes as yesterday. The dread from yesterday, when I'd dropped him off at Hector's aunt's place, resurfaced. Rider looked *wrecked*.

"Hey," I said as he sat next to me. The old notebook hit the desk. "Are you… God, it's such a stupid question, but are you okay?"

He nodded slowly as he glanced over at me. "Yeah, just tired."

But it was more than that.

"Can we get together after school?" he asked as the bell rang. "For a bit?"

"Yes. Of course," I said, smiling even though it wasn't real.

The dread I felt grew throughout class, and I only distantly listened to the upcoming speech schedule Mr. Santos laid out. I would have to give mine during lunch next Tuesday. Rider would do his on Wednesday.

I still hadn't finished my speech.

But I wasn't really focused on the example speeches Mr. Santos was giving. I was too busy noticing the fact that Rider didn't look me in the eye. Not when he sat down. Not when he looked over at me and not once during the class.

When the bell finally rang, I jumped in my seat, startled. I ordered myself to chill out as I packed up my bag. Rider waited at my desk, his gaze fixed on the front of the room.

"You ready?" he asked, his voice oddly flat.

My stomach twisted as I nodded, and I only managed a half-hearted wave to Keira on the way out. We didn't speak until we were outside, walking side by side under the overcast skies.

"Rosa and Carl won't be home for a while," I said, twisting my fingers around my keys. "You want to go hang out there?"

His brows furrowed and for a moment I thought he was going to say no. "Yeah, that's cool."

We didn't talk on the drive and my nerves were stretched thin by the time we headed inside. I dropped my bag by the steps. "Um, do you want anything to drink?" I asked, walking toward the living room.

"Nah." He followed slowly, stopping by the china cabinet to check out the soap carvings. "I'm good."

I dropped my keys on the island and went to the fridge, grabbing myself a Coke. A tremor coursed through my arms as I headed back to the living room. I sat on the couch and started to reach for the remote. "We could watch a movie or—"

"Actually, I want to talk to you."

"Oh." I toyed with the tab of my soda. "Okay."

He walked around the coffee table and sat on the couch—on the third cushion, putting an entire cushion between us. My fingers stilled on the tab. "I don't know how to say this," he said, resting his elbows on his knees. He slowly shook his head. "I really care about you, Mallory. I really do."

Oh, God.

I put the soda on the end table before I dropped it. "I really care about you. I...I love you, Rider."

His jaw flexed. "Yesterday was a mistake."

My lips parted on a sharp inhale. I didn't hear him right. There was no way I heard him right.

"It wasn't that I didn't enjoy what...what we did. I do—I did, but this can't go on. We can't get together. Not like this," he said in that same flat tone. "I'm sorry."

For several moments all I could do was stare at him. I tried to process what he was saying, but the pounding blood in my head made it difficult. "I...I don't understand."

"We can't be together," he repeated, still not looking at me. A crack fissured my chest, and I sucked in air, because it felt so real, a line of fiery pain. "We can be friends, but that's...that's all."

"I don't want to be just friends with you," I blurted out as I jerked forward. "You said you loved me. Just yesterday." My voice caught as the knot expanded in my throat. "Like a little over twenty-four hours ago. I don't understand."

He placed his palm to his forehead. "I do love you."

"Then why are you saying you don't want to be with me?" I put my hand on the couch, grounding myself, because it felt like it was moving. Like the entire world was trembling. "That doesn't...make any sense."

"I just can't be with you. It's over."

Then the strangest thing happened. An odd, almost suffocating feeling of relief hit me. It was over. I could just go back to the way—

I stopped.

Everything stopped.

That wasn't me anymore. I didn't give up and give in just because it was easy. I wasn't *her* anymore.

"This is for the best, Mouse."

"Don't call me Mouse," I snapped as fury flooded my system, overtaking the welling hurt and washing it away. "I am not Mouse. That girl doesn't exist anymore."

Rider recoiled as if I'd slapped him. "Mallory..."

"No. Don't look at me like I've hurt you." I rose from the couch, hands curling into fists. "You need to give me a better explanation than just because. You owe me that."

He lifted his chin, his eyes bright as he finally looked at me. The shadows beneath them were deeper, darker. "Don't you get it?"

"No. Obviously I don't."

Rider stared at me for a moment. "You deserve better than me."

My mouth dropped open.

"And you shouldn't be fighting with Rosa and Carl because of me. They took you in, gave you the world, and I'm not going to come between you," he said, and I think he kept talking, but I really wasn't hearing him.

You deserve better than me?

Wasn't that the same thing Paige had said before she said the opposite? It *was*.

"Are you serious?" I cut him off. "Are you really serious right now?"

He swallowed. "Yes, Mou—*Mallory*, I'm serious."

I laughed, but there wasn't any humor to the sound whatsoever. "So let me get this straight. You're breaking up with me because it's what's best for me. Because you don't want to come between me and Rosa and Carl?" There were no pauses in my words now. "It's because of what happened this weekend."

Straightening, he raised his hands. "It's more than that, Mallory. You and I—we aren't the same. We used to be, but not anymore. You're going in one direction and I'm staying the same. That's how it's going to be."

My hands unclenched. Funny. For the longest time it felt like everyone around me was going places while I sat, immobile and stuck, but this whole time I really had been moving and it had been Rider who wasn't.

"You're so wrong," I breathed.

His brows shot up. "Seriously?"

"Yeah. Seriously."

His cheeks flushed pink. "You know what we used to be? We were just discarded trash. That's how we were treated. There's no prettying up that shit. Our fucking parents didn't want us. Or maybe they just died in some tragic car accident or couldn't keep us. Who knows? I asked. Do you know that? No answer. No one cared enough to find out. And Miss Becky and Mr. Henry? We don't even have to talk about that mess," he continued, eyes flashing. "And the group home I was in afterward? They tried—the staff. They really did, but they couldn't keep their eyes on everything. By the time Mrs. Luna came around, what the hell was the point?"

I paled. Whoa. I was not expecting all of that.

He wasn't finished. "You got out of all of this. I didn't. What you have is real. I don't have that. I'm just pretending."

I flinched. "I don't understand. Hector's family is good people. How can you say that I got out and you didn't?"

"It's not the same. I'm just temporary. It's nothing like what you have with Carl and Rosa."

Staring at him, I shook my head. "That is utter...bullshit."

He blinked. "Did you just cuss?"

"Yes. Yes, I did, because that's bullshit," I repeated. "Hector's family cares about you. I don't know Mrs. Luna that well, but it only took two minutes around her for me to see that she thinks of you as one of her boys. They all care about you. They don't treat you any differently, or like you're a burden to them."

Rider said nothing.

"Or do they?" I demanded. "Do they treat you like a burden?"

The muscle along his jaw throbbed. "They don't, but—"

"But nothing!" I shouted, and he jerked again. It was probably the loudest I'd ever spoken in my entire life, but dammit, disbelief and frustration beat at me. "They love you, Rider. And they need you now, more than ever. Hector just lost his brother. Mrs. Luna is burying her youngest grandchild—a boy who once told me you were a second brother to him. Yesterday you said you wanted to be there for them, but how can you when you refuse to acknowledge that you're their family and they're yours?" I took a breath but it went nowhere. "You know what I said to you yesterday? It's true. So damn true. You gave up on yourself before they even had a chance!"

"Mallory—"

"And you're doing it to us! You're giving up on us before we even get started. And worse yet, you're using me as an excuse. You're going to do what you always did—protect me when you shouldn't have."

"This isn't like before," he stated quietly.

"Yes. Yes it is. You have no sense of self-preservation." I took a step toward him, but stopped. If I got close enough, I might beat him with a throw pillow. "I always thought you had taken on this role as a knight in shining armor, but I was wrong. You're just a martyr."

He looked like I had picked up a throw pillow and beaten him with it.

"What is it with you, Rider? You are so freaking smart and so damn talented, but you—*you*—" I raised my hand and pointed at him "—you don't try, and the moment something becomes hard, you run. You give up. That wasn't the Rider I knew growing up. You were a fighter back then, but when it matters most, like with your damn life, you just give up."

"I don't…"

"You do." Tears clawed their way up the back of my throat as I stared at him. God, this wasn't fair. This was so damn unfair. "I sat in this kitchen yesterday and I told Rosa that I loved you. I told her not to tell me how I felt and begged her to give you a chance. She promised that she would. And now you're standing here telling me that what you have isn't real. You can't just say that about your foster home. It's also about me—about us. You're saying what we had was never real."

Rider grimaced as he closed his eyes.

I sucked in a shaky breath. "Did you ever fill out those SAT forms I picked up for you?"

He didn't answer.

"Did you?"

"No," he whispered.

My heart shattered. "The boy that you keep painting—the one at the warehouse and at the art gallery? That boy is you, isn't it?"

Rider didn't say anything.

"It's not you from the past," I whispered. His handsome face blurred. "That's still who you are."

He closed his eyes.

"And you know what? This whole time I've thought I was the one who was messed up. That I was the one who walked away from that damn house damaged and screwed up. I thought it was *me*." My voice broke as I backed away. "And it wasn't. It was you. It's always been *you*."

His gaze rose to mine and the pain in his eyes was a punch to the gut, because he was doing this to himself. And God, that hurt more than anything else. This was on him. Not me.

It was always on him.

He put that weight on his shoulders; he found guilt and responsibility wherever he could and he hugged that mess close. This wasn't me giving up on him. This was always him giving up on himself. It struck me then, and it took everything to swallow down the sob.

"You're stuck," I whispered.

Rider stiffened.

"It's true." I smoothed my hands over my hips. "You've had years—eighteen years of feeling this way. No conversation is going to undo years of feeling like you're nothing, of ignoring all those around you telling you that you do matter. The Lunas couldn't fix that. Oh my God, I can't undo that. I can't fix that. I would've tried—" My breath caught again. "I would've tried, because I love you, I love you so very much, but you have to be the one to change it. Not me."

"Mallory." He stood and took a step toward me.

"No." I held my hand up and tried not to see how it shook. "You—you need to leave."

He blanched. "I'm—"

"Please. Just leave. Go." I could feel my face start to crumple. "There is nothing else I can say. Go."

Rider hesitated, and for a sweet, hopeful second, I thought he was going to ignore me. I thought that maybe something I said reached him, triggered something in him and he was going to fight for us, for him.

But he didn't.

He turned and walked toward the door, and in a daze, I followed him. I wanted to keep following him. I wanted to scream at him. I wanted him to see what I saw in him, what I knew Rosa and Carl would see if given the chance. But I didn't, because how in the world could I fight for him when he wouldn't even fight for himself?

So I did what I never thought I would.

I closed the door on Rider.

CHAPTER 36

My chest was a hollow, empty shell.

Okay, maybe I'm overreacting a tad, I thought as I stared at the ceiling of my bedroom. But that was how it felt since I'd closed the door on Rider yesterday. I'd holed myself in the room. I didn't go to school Wednesday. Lame, but I just couldn't do it.

The last couple of days had been too much. Every high and every low that could happen had been experienced. Love. Loss. Love. Loss again.

I needed a break. I needed quiet time. So I took it.

That was something I'd learned from my time with Dr. Taft. When things got overwhelming, when you were stressed and stretched too thin, it was time to take a breather. He was all about mental health days. I remembered him ranting once about how if someone coughed, they were given time off from work, but if someone was mentally fatigued, they were expected to suck it up.

I'd told Rosa I wasn't feeling well, and considering she didn't take my temperature or force cold meds down my throat, I figured she knew that what kept me in bed wasn't something she could treat.

My chest ached. It felt empty, but the emptiness hurt. I hated that Rider had done this right now, when he had to be hurting so deeply over the loss of Jayden and I couldn't be there for him.

Clutching the pillow to my chest, I rolled onto my side and squeezed my eyes shut. I finally realized that I'd changed and at the same time I discovered that Rider hadn't.

I curled my knees up against the pillow as I thought back to the first day of school, to the first time I'd seen Rider. I replayed all the times we'd hung out and the things we'd told each other. The signs had been there. I'd noticed them then, but I didn't know how deep the scars ran in Rider. I'd been so wrapped up in everything that I had going on and in how Rider was making me feel. Could there have been something I could've done weeks, months ago?

I wasn't sure.

It had taken four years for me to begin the process of changing and even though I wasn't the same girl I used to be, I was still a…a work in progress. Rider hadn't even taken the first step.

Keira texted in the afternoon, asking if I was okay. I let her know that I wasn't feeling well and then dropped my cell on the bed beside me.

Tomorrow.

Tomorrow I would get up and go to school. I couldn't stay in bed forever. Saturday I would go to Jayden's funeral, and I would be there for Rider if he needed someone to talk to. I couldn't not do that, but that was as far as I could go. I was willing to fight for us to be together, but it couldn't be one-sided. Rider would have to fight, too.

And he had chosen not to.

My eyes were damp, but the tears didn't fall as I whiled away the day in bed. The sun had begun to set when there was a quiet knock on my door before it opened. I sat up as Carl walked in, wearing pale blue scrubs.

"How are you feeling?" he asked, stopping a few feet from the bed.

Part of me wanted to lie, because I wasn't sure if I had it in me to talk to Carl, if that was what he wanted to do. I didn't. "Yeah, I'm feeling better."

"Up for a little company?"

I nodded and then pushed myself up so I was leaning against the headboard. I brought my pillow with me, cradling it to my chest.

Carl sat on the edge of the bed, his upper body angled toward me. "It's been a long week, huh?"

I nodded once more.

"And we're only halfway there," he mused, smiling slightly. He turned his head away and I noticed the gray around his temple was spreading, peppering the side. "You going to go to school tomorrow?"

"Yes." I cleared my throat. "That's the plan."

"That's good. With the holiday break coming up, you don't want to get too behind," he said, hooking his leg over the other. "I know you talked to Rosa Monday, and I would've talked to you earlier, but the hospital has been a little crazy. With the cold weather and improperly used kerosene heaters, I've had back-to-back surgeries." He looked over at me and a moment passed. "But I've been wanting to talk to you. I need to apologize for what I said."

That inherent need to tell him it was okay was hard to ignore, but I did it. I waited in silence.

"Rosa and I know you're not Marquette. We didn't adopt you to replace her," he began. "The moment we decided to adopt you, you became our child, just as important as Marquette and every bit as amazing as she was."

My chest tightened, so I held the pillow close.

"We're your parents, and parents...they mess up. I know mine did. It's inevitable, and I messed up on Sunday. I said something out of anger and frustration that I shouldn't have said. And I'm sorry. I know it hurt your feelings and upset you, and I am truly sorry for that."

Pressing my lips together, I nodded as I willed the pressure in my chest to go away. It seemed to expand instead. "I forgive you," I said, and I did.

"I'm happy to hear that." He smiled again as his gaze met mine. "Rosa told me what you told her about Rider, and I want to say that you're right. I really wasn't giving him a shot."

Rider was the last thing I needed to talk about. "We don't—"

"No. We do. Hear me out, okay?" The genuine request in his tone had me snapping my mouth shut. "I have been entirely too judgmental of Rider. I've let my own biases and experiences get in the way and that's not right."

I thought about what Rosa had said yesterday about Carl having his own story to tell.

"I had a brother," he said, surprising me. "His name was Adrian. He was only two years older than me. The city wasn't like it is today, but there were problems back then. The violence in these streets is nothing new and just like now, it has always touched too many lives. For some, more intimately than others." He scrubbed his fingers through his hair. "It wasn't always guns. Sometimes they had knives and baseball bats, anything they could get their hands on, and sometimes it was just their hands. Anything, even fists, can be deadly weapons."

Oh, man, I had a feeling where this story was heading and I felt sick.

"Adrian was always in trouble. He dropped out of school when I was a freshman. To be honest, I don't even know what he was doing. We were opposites in a lot of ways, but he always seemed to have money and I knew enough to know it wasn't coming from anywhere good. Back in the seventies, jobs were already beginning to dry up and there was little opportunity left behind," he explained. "Either way, I remember Adrian being at home on a Wednesday. I remember my mother upset and crying. And I remember our father telling him to leave. Not sure what happened exactly and my parents never really talked about it. I think they blamed themselves. If they hadn't asked him to leave, he'd still be alive kind of thing."

Carl tipped his head back and sighed. "He was killed about a week later. Baseball bat to the head. It wasn't a wrong place or wrong time. We don't know what he was killed over. The police had suspected drugs, but they really hadn't looked into his death too hard. Adrian was just another kid they were scraping off the streets."

"That's...that's horrible." Did they think that when they were called in for Jayden? I already knew the answer to that. I just didn't want to think it, and that didn't say very good things about me.

His dark eyes glinted. "Adrian made some bad choices. Just like I imagine this young friend of yours had. Doesn't make it any easier to deal with. And that doesn't stop anyone from wondering about what could have been if a life hadn't been wasted."

"Oh my gosh," I whispered, staring at him. "I didn't know."

"You wouldn't. It's something I haven't had a lot of reasons to talk about." He paused, his expression thoughtful. "Or maybe I should've found some reasons."

But there had been hints over the years, things he'd said that suddenly made sense. "I'm sorry."

"It was a long time ago, but thank you." He reached over, patting my blanket-covered leg. "When Rider came along, I couldn't help but think of Adrian. He reminded me of him— the carelessness in the way he approached life, as if he just didn't give a damn."

I lowered my gaze, hating the truth of those words. I wasn't sure if Rider gave a damn about himself or not. I used to think he did.

"And with what happened to that young boy, it really hit home. I let my own experiences get in the way. I don't know about Rider. Maybe I'm wrong. I hope I am, and according to what Rosa told me, I probably am."

My eyes met his, and I knew what he was saying, and I didn't have the heart to tell him it didn't matter anymore.

His gaze held mine. "I'm going to try. There are going to be times when it seems like I'm not, but I will be. I want you safe and I want you happy. You're smart enough to make good choices. I forgot that."

Oh, gosh. Oh, man. Tears stung the backs of my eyes.

"And there's something else I wanted to tell you. I know I've been on you pretty hard about going to med school. I was wrong about that, too. Rosa said you really wanted to look into social work, and I should've listened when you first brought that up," he said, and I let go of the pillow I was holding on to for dear life. "I think it's an admirable path, and with that right there, you proved that you will make smart choices. I see that now."

Several seconds passed where I was frozen and there was nothing but his words repeating over and over.

Then something cracked inside me, and it was a good shattering. I sprang forward and wrapped my arms around Carl's shoulders, nearly knocking him off the bed.

He caught himself and me, and he hugged me back. For the first time in years, the knot in my throat didn't get stuck. Emotion didn't choke me. The tears didn't fade away. They broke free.

CHAPTER 37

The butterfly was taunting me.

I stared at the sketch Rider had drawn of me the day Jayden had been killed—no, he hadn't been killed. He'd been *murdered*. There was something about that word that made it hard to think and speak, but I forced myself to label what happened to Jayden correctly. He hadn't died like Marquette from a tragic, natural cause. He hadn't been killed in an unexpected car accident. He'd been murdered in a senseless act of violence, like Carl's brother.

My gaze drifted to the butterfly soap carving and then back to the sketch. One was complete. One wasn't. Closing my eyes, I turned away as my mind floated back through the long day at school.

Rider had looked a mess in class and had barely murmured hello, and it was like there were a million miles between us. At the end of class I had thought he was about to say something to me, but he had changed his mind. All he said was goodbye and then he'd left.

Keira had noticed the difference between us immediately and it didn't take much for her to figure out that Rider and I...that we were no more. "It might just be what's going on with Jayden and stuff. You're not asking for my advice, obviously, but…don't give up, Mallory. Anyone can see you belong together."

I knew that Jayden's murder had taken a heavy toll on Rider, but that wasn't the only thing he was dealing with.

What was wrong with Rider was something that not only ran deep, but also was etched into his bones and ingrained into the fibers of his muscles.

I didn't know what could change the way he saw himself or if anything could. All I knew was that it took years for me to get where I was today and I still had a lot of work to do.

As much as I wanted to hope that change was possible for Rider, I knew it wouldn't ever happen until he was ready.

And he wasn't.

★ ★ ★

"We need to talk."

My back stiffened as I stood in front of my locker Friday before lunch. Nothing good ever followed when Paige said those words. I had no idea what she thought we had to talk about, but I closed the locker door and faced her as I started to shove my speech text into my bag. I stopped when I saw her.

Paige's eyes were puffy and red. Her hair was slicked back in a low ponytail, and the sweats she wore were a size or two too large. She took a deep breath and her shoulders squared as she stared down at me. "You and I don't really get along and we only have, like, one thing in common." She stated what she thought was the obvious, but we had more in common than she realized and maybe that was why there wasn't a hint of animosity in her tone. "And that's Rider."

I tensed.

"I don't know what the hell is going on between you two, but I think it's pretty fucked up that you pulled this crap after what happened with Jayden."

My mouth dropped open. "I pulled this crap?"

A flicker of surprise shot across her face. Probably because those four words spoken to her were without a moment of hesitation. She quickly hid it, though. "Don't play stupid. You broke up with Rider right after he watched his friend—a friend he considered a brother—die."

Was I living in an alternate universe? "I didn't break up with Rider."

"Bullshit." She lowered her chin, eyes narrowing. "He was already miserable with what happened to Jayden and now he's freaking depressed as all hell."

Confused beyond belief, I shook my head. "I don't know what Rider told you, but I...I didn't break up with him."

Paige laughed with derision. "I know you're lying, because the last thing he'd do would be to dump his *precious* Mouse."

My brows rose.

"God, do you know how often he talked about you over the years? How perfect and kind and sweet and smart you were? To me? You know, the girl he was with until you came back into the picture?"

I wondered how rude it would be if I smacked her upside the head with the book I held.

"So I know it's bullshit. He would never do it. You did it after coming to the house Sunday and finding us asleep on the couch," she accused. "Nothing happened between us. Not that I wouldn't have been thrilled if something did."

My eyes narrowed, and my hands clenched around the book. It was a really thick book.

"I knew you would break his heart. He loves you and—"

"If he told you I broke up with him, then he's the one who's lying." Angry, I shoved my book into the bag and yanked the zipper up. "I didn't break up with him because of Sunday...or for any reason, because I didn't do it. Look, I'm sorry if you believe that. The last…the last thing I'd ever want to do is hurt Rider and I didn't. He broke up with me."

Disbelief crept into her face as she stared at me. "He didn't tell me you broke up with him. I just assumed it was you since I knew—or I thought—he wouldn't do it."

"Well, you assumed wrong." I started to walk away, because admitting to Rider's ex that he'd dumped me wasn't exactly brightening my mood.

Of course, she stepped in front of me. "Why did he end it?"

Jaw aching, I cast my gaze to the end of the hall. It really wasn't her business, but out of frustration, I spoke the truth. "Because he thinks it's better that way—for me. That I can do better than him."

"That's…that's stupid."

"Agreed," I muttered.

"Like that's super stupid." Paige paused. "And you're going to let him believe that?"

"Let him? I tried, but I can't change the way he thinks about himself."

"You should try harder," she fired back.

"It's not as simple as that," I told her. "You…you know what he's been through, right? He's told you…some stuff. That crap he has in his head is there deep. I can tell him a million times that he deserves the world, but he has to believe that. Not me."

Paige blinked.

A teacher stepped out of a classroom, frowning when she spotted us by my locker. "You two need to get where you're going, which is not this hallway."

Paige rolled her eyes as she turned away from the teacher. "You need to try harder," she said again, backing away. "If you really cared about him, you would."

I said nothing as Paige pivoted around and walked in the opposite direction. Try harder? As if it was that simple.

★ ★ ★

It was an absolutely beautiful day, and I didn't know if that was fair or not for a funeral.

Part of me thought that the morning shouldn't be so lovely. I wasn't sure if Hector or Mrs. Luna wanted to see the sun shining so bright. Or maybe the gorgeous day helped remind them of the beauty of the world. Maybe some kind of meaning could be attached to the cloudless sky. I didn't know.

This was the first funeral I'd ever attended.

Ainsley had met me at the Lunas' church and we'd stood in the foyer for quite some time before the service started. My feet, mainly my toes, were pinched in their black dress shoes. Shoes I'd never worn before. I'd borrowed them from Ainsley since I realized at the last minute I didn't have the right pair to wear with the wool pants and black blouse.

I hadn't seen Hector or Rider. Not until the doors opened. The first thing I'd noticed was the chairs, and even though I didn't want to look, my gaze had traveled the wide aisle and the maroon carpet up to the vases and bundles of flowers, to the casket.

The casket was open.

And I could see just the tip of Jayden's nose and the smooth slope of his forehead. Ainsley and I veered toward the back of the room. I couldn't go closer. I didn't want to see Jayden like that, because I knew that was how I'd forever see him.

As people began to file in to the pews, I saw Hector and Rider. They were up at the front. Both were pale. Hector's grandmother was already seated, her back to us, her posture heavy.

Rider was dressed much like Hector. White dress shirt tucked into trousers. I don't know how long I stared at them, but Rider turned suddenly, and with unnerving accuracy, his gaze collided with mine.

I sucked in a sharp breath as we stared at each other from

across the room. Neither of us looked away for several moments, and then Hector spoke to him. Rider turned, and I closed my eyes, exhaling roughly.

"Are you going to talk to him?" Ainsley asked in a quiet voice.

"No." I twisted my fingers around the strap of my purse. "I mean, if he wants to talk to me, I will, but...I don't want to create any drama. No one needs that right now."

Ainsley leaned into me. "Do you think it would cause drama?"

I shook my head. "I don't know, but I'm...not willing to risk it."

The room was quickly filling up, and I saw Keira and Jo sit in pews opposite us. They couldn't see us and it wasn't like I was going to yell Keira's name.

The service started with a pastor reciting verses from the bible and when he began talking about death, my attention roamed to the casket. Lifting my hand, I wiped under my eye with my palm.

I didn't understand how this could happen. How someone could kill another person in cold blood, and over what, exactly? A couple hundred dollars? The fact that I couldn't comprehend such an act showed, despite my upbringing, how incredibly privileged I was. These were things that I didn't have to worry about, not in the way others did.

My gaze moved to where his family sat in the first three rows. Rider was sitting next to Hector, and I wasn't the only person watching Jayden's brother. So was Ainsley. The moment I saw Hector's face start to crumple, I wanted to get up and hug him. I didn't give good hugs, but I wanted to at that moment, because his shoulders shook and he broke.

When the service drew to a close, I waited until most of the room had paid their respects before I approached Hector. It didn't seem he saw me as he leaned down for my awkward hug. It was like he was there, but not, and when I spoke to him, he murmured back words I couldn't understand.

Saddened, I turned and came face-to-face with Rider. I took a step back, startled, and was about to sidestep him when I stopped myself.

That wouldn't be the right or the kind thing to do.

Rider didn't speak as I turned back to him. I rose up and wrapped my arms around him. I squeezed tight, putting everything I couldn't say into the act. He didn't hug me back. Maybe I moved away too quickly. Maybe I shocked him. Maybe he just didn't want to.

I settled back onto my feet and looked up at him. There were a thousand things I could've said to him in that moment. I didn't know why, out of everything, I said what I did. "Jayden told me once, after the day in the garage, that he looked up to you and Hector. I...I just thought you should know that *was* real."

The skin around his eyes and mouth tightened. I did something else I didn't really think about. I stretched up once more and kissed his cheek. I felt his sharp inhale, and with one last look at him, I turned.

Ainsley was waiting halfway up the aisle. She hadn't come up with me, but her gaze was focused on where Hector stood with his grandmother.

"I want to talk to Hector real quick." Ainsley hugged me quickly. "I'll call you later?"

I hugged her back. "Okay."

I didn't see Keira or Jo in the mass of people as I walked out of the church, and I wasn't sure if what I'd said to Rider had helped or hurt. The only thing I knew as I walked to my car was that the bright glare of the sun was still there and the deep blue sky was still spotless and endless.

Walking into my room when I got home, my gaze landed on the unfinished butterfly sitting on my desk. As I stared at the half-transformed carving, I thought about everything I had said to Rider, everything Paige had said to me, and I knew there was something else I needed to do, something I needed to prove to myself.

I grabbed my notebook and pen off the desk and walked over to my bed. It was time to write my speech, and this time I knew what I wanted to say.

CHAPTER 38

I was not going to be sick to my stomach.

If I repeated the mantra enough, maybe it would come true. I'd been on the verge of hurling all day Wednesday, but at least I wasn't the only one. Keira's lunch sat untouched next to mine, her face pale as she read her speech over and over under her breath. The paper rattled in her shaking hands.

I took my seat in speech with no memory of how I'd gotten there. As if through a tunnel, I saw Paige come in. She'd been out yesterday, as was Rider and obviously Hector.

I took out my paper and smoothed my hands over it as I focused on taking deep and even breaths so I didn't pass out.

There was a good chance I was going to pass out.

Just as the tardy bell rang, Rider strode into class and my heart lurched in my chest. I wasn't expecting him to be here.

Oh my word, I was so not expecting him to be here for this.

My hands trembled as I dropped them into my lap. Paige's eyes followed him as he headed toward the seat between us. Her smile was sad, and I didn't know if he returned the gesture, but then he sat and looked over at me. He'd shaved and his clothing wasn't wrinkled. His hair was a mess, though, like always.

I hadn't seen him since the funeral on Saturday.

I hadn't heard from him.

And I couldn't think about that right now.

Rider's gaze trekked over my face. "Hey."

"Hi," I whispered.

His lashes lowered as his shoulders tensed. "Do you think—"

"All right, class." Mr. Santos clapped his hands, cutting us off. "We've got a lot of speeches to get through today, so we need to get started. So, welcome to speech number three—The Person Most Important to Me, one of my favorite of the year. I hope that in writing about someone who's influenced you, you've learned a little something about who you are. And I hope by delivering your speech here today, you'll remember to cherish the person you're telling us about. Because as we were reminded of recently..." His gaze flickered briefly to Hector's empty seat. "Life can be all too brief."

Whatever Rider was about to say to me faded to the background as Mr. Santos called the first student to the front of the class. Then the next student went up. Then Keira, who gave her speech clutching the podium. By that point I'd scooted to the edge of my seat, prepared to either make a mad dash for the door or fall out of my chair.

On her way to her desk, she threw me a thumbs-up. I tried to smile, happy that she'd gotten through it, but I was currently doing everything to keep myself from running from the class. Next to me, Rider was braced on the edge of his own seat, his posture a strange mirror of mine.

"Leon Washington, the floor is yours," Mr. Santos said. "I'm sure we're all dying to know about the influences that have molded you."

I didn't hear a single thing Leon said. People were laughing, though, and Mr. Santos looked like he was considering early retirement, so I wished I'd been able to pay attention.

"Mallory Dodge?" Mr. Santos called from his perch on the edge of his desk. His eyes were kind as they met mine, as kind as they'd been when I'd come to him at lunch yesterday with my odd request. "You're up."

I heard Paige's sharp laugh of surprise.

I didn't remember standing, but I saw the shock on Rider's face as I stepped around my desk. Halfway there I realized I didn't have my paper, and I had to go back and get it. My face was hot. Someone, a guy, chuckled. He sat in front of Paige.

Paige kicked the back of his seat.

Perhaps I had passed out and hit my head, because I couldn't believe she'd done that, but no one else laughed—or if they did, I didn't hear them over the sound of the blood rushing in my ears. I made it to the front of the room and turned, standing before the chalkboard and behind the podium.

My gaze roamed over the class. Half weren't even looking at me. They were staring into their laps or at their desks. Or their eyes were closed. That left the other half. Who were definitely looking at me.

I glanced at Keira and she grinned, sticking up her thumb again.

"Anytime you want to start," Mr. Santos said.

Nodding, I tried to swallow. I saw a sea of faces staring back at me. The seal started forming in the back of my throat.

Someone coughed.

This was…this was horrifying. Tears started to clog my throat. I looked to Mr. Santos for…for I don't know what, and then I was staring at the class again.

Out of all the faces, my gaze landed on Rider's, and he…he *nodded*. I could practically hear his voice in my head. *You can do this*. And then it became my voice. He was right. I was right. I could. It would be painful and probably embarrassing—no, not embarrassing, because only I controlled whether or not I was embarrassed. And I could do this. And I wouldn't be embarrassed. Even if I was, just a little, it didn't matter in the big scheme of things. This speech wasn't forever. Being embarrassed was not forever. None of this was forever.

But trying was.

Living was.

My gaze fell to my paper and the seal slipped down my throat.

> Some people have one person who's important to them. Who's influenced them more than anyone else. Our assignment was to write about that one person, but as I wrote this speech I realized that I couldn't pick just one. And when my story ends I hope you'll understand why, but for my story to make sense, I need to start all the way at the beginning.

Mouth dry, I didn't look up at the class as I started again with the hardest three sentences I'd ever written or had to speak out loud.

> When I was a little girl, I used to hide in my closet. The space was dust-covered and dark, and it smelled like mothballs. But it was my sanctuary from the monsters outside. When I got older and I would have to hide, I used to fantasize that I lived in a house where the closets trapped all the monsters and where I would be safe in my bed. That I lived in a house with parents I could look up to and admire, and one day they would become the subjects of a speech I wrote about how they changed my life for the better. I didn't live in that kind of house. But the monsters I hid from shaped who I've become by teaching me that kindness and love are things that should be given freely. They taught me who I never want to be. That's why they're important to me today.
>
> Two people adopted me when I was almost thirteen. They didn't see a frightened child who didn't speak. They saw a daughter,

their daughter. They dedicated every spare moment to erasing the bad memories and beating back the nightmares. They opened up doors that had never been available to me before, and believed in me. They proved that love and kindness can be given freely and without expectation. They taught me to trust and that I no longer need to be afraid.

When I was homeschooled I met a girl who had never had a problem speaking or meeting new people. At first I was envious of her openness and friendliness. Meeting people and making friends was something I wasn't good at. We were polar opposites, and I never expected that one day she would become my best friend. She proved that you can find your best friend when you least expect it. And recently, she has influenced me by not taking what I have for granted.

The really tough parts were coming up, so I took a brief pause and inhaled slowly before continuing.

Just a few months ago, I met a boy who was kind to me even though he didn't know me. He always had a smile, and charm to spare. I didn't know this boy well, but his influence is possibly one of the greatest, because he has taught me to take nothing for granted, but most important, to have a smile for a stranger. He offered kindness when I needed it most, and I hope to do the same for others.

The last important person in my life has been there since I can remember. He lived in the house where the monsters roamed the hall. He kept me safe when they got too close. He read to me when I was too scared to sleep. Because of him and all that he sacrificed to make sure I was safe, I'm able to get up every morning in my own bed. Because of him, I have a second chance at life.

Stopping, I took another deep breath and glanced up, half expecting most of the class to be asleep. Some were. Only a few. The rest of the class stared, their faces a blur. I saw Paige. Shock was etched into her pretty face. I saw Rider, and he... His lips were parted and he was sitting rigidly in his seat, his arms limp at his sides.

I forced myself to continue.

But the reason why he is important to me is that he proved that helping those who need it, even if they think they don't want help, was worth the risk. He has shaped who I am today because he was the first person to recognize that I had a voice worth listening to.

Some people have one person who influenced them more than anyone else. I learned while writing this speech how glad I am to have many. That it's a series of people and events that shape who you become. I learned that even monsters could have a positive impact. I learned that there are people out there that will open their homes and hearts for nothing in return. I learned that strangers could be tolerant and kind. I learned that those who are always helping others help themselves last. Most important, because of all of them, I learned that I could do what I thought was impossible—that I can stand here today.

The room was quiet, and I wasn't sure if that was a good or bad thing.

Mr. Santos cleared his throat. "Thank you, Mallory."

Gazes followed me as I walked back to my seat. Keira looked like she was seconds away from crying as she shot me a huge grin. Even Paige stared as I sat.

I looked over at Rider.

His face held the same expression he'd worn the entire time he sat through my speech, knowing what no one else other than maybe Paige realized—that it was about him. He looked thunderstruck.

And I...I could've floated right up to the ceiling.

I'd done it.

Pressing my lips together to hide a stupid smile, I faced the front of the class. I'd done it. Holy crap, I'd really gotten up in front of the class and given a speech. I'd stumbled over words and there had been a lot of awkward pauses, but I'd done it. Tears, the good kind of tears, burned the back of my throat. I wanted to dance and shout. It took everything I had to sit there through Laura Kaye's speech without jumping out of my seat and screaming.

Mr. Santos called on me when the bell rang. I dared a quick peek in Rider's direction as I gathered up my stuff and walked to the front of the class.

Mr. Santos smiled as he clamped his hand on my shoulder. "You did really good, Mallory."

My heart was pounding. "I…I did."

He nodded. "I just want to let you know that I know how hard that was for you, especially with such personal subject matter. I'm proud of you."

I swallowed hard. "Thank you."

"Now I expect you to be up here for every speech," he said. "Do you think you can handle that?"

Could I? I didn't know, but I did know I would try. I nodded.

"Good." He patted my shoulder. "Have a good evening."

I murmured something along the lines of "You, too" as I turned around. Rider was already gone, and despite everything that had gone down between us, that surprised me. A lot. I'd thought he would've hung around to congratulate me, because he, of all people, knew what a big deal this was. But he was nowhere in sight.

Walking out of the class, I told myself I wasn't going to let his disappearance burst my happy bubble of accomplishment. It sucked that he wasn't there, but…but what I'd done today was more important, and I knew just how I wanted to celebrate it.

As soon as I got home from school that day, I went straight

up to my room and dropped my bag on the floor by my bed. I opened the drawer on my desk, pulling out the supplies. I picked up the half-complete butterfly and took it over to the window seat. Sitting down, I finally finished the carving.

It was fully transformed with delicate wings spanning out on either side of its small body. I'd even added a tiny smile below the indents for eyes.

I placed it back on my desk, just below the last sketch Rider had done of me, and then picked up my history text. I had an exam to study for.

★ ★ ★

"Mallory?" Carl called. "Can you come downstairs?"

Shoving the index card into my history text to mark my spot, I flipped the book closed and scooted off the bed. My sock-covered feet hit the floor. It was too early for dinner that night, so I had no idea why I was being summoned.

I tucked a loose strand of hair back behind my ear as I went down the steps. Carl was standing just inside the living room. Rosa was standing beside him, but my gaze was glued to what he held in his hands. It was a small, rectangular package wrapped in brown paper.

My steps slowed. "What is that?"

"It's for you." He held out the package.

I stared at it for a moment before reaching out to take it. "Um, why?"

Rosa leaned into Carl. "It's not from us, honey."

"Oh." I turned the light package over. There was no writing on it, and the brown paper reminded me of a shopping bag. "Who's it from?"

"Why don't you just open the package?" Carl advised.

Huh. Good idea. I slipped my finger under the edges and peeled off the tape. The paper came right off and the moment I saw what was underneath, my heart leaped into my throat.

It was a copy of *The Velveteen Rabbit.*

Not the old copy Rider used to read to me, but a shiny new one. A blue hardcover edition with the rabbit standing up on a small, grassy mound.

The brown packaging slipped from my fingers and fell noiselessly to the floor. There was a piece of paper sticking out of the pages. With trembling hands, I carefully opened the book. The thin slip of paper was nothing more than a torn sheet of notebook paper, but a large section of print was highlighted in blue.

"What is REAL?" the Velveteen Rabbit asked the Skin Horse one day. "Does it mean having things that buzz inside you and a stick-out handle?"

"Real isn't how you are made," said the Skin Horse. "It's a thing that happens to you. When a child loves you for a long, long time, not just to play with, but REALLY loves you, then you become Real."

"Does it hurt?" asked the Velveteen Rabbit.

"Sometimes," said the Skin Horse, for he was always truthful. "When you are Real you don't mind being hurt."

"It doesn't happen all at once," said the Skin Horse. "You become. It takes a long time. That's why it doesn't happen often to people who break easily, or have sharp edges, or who have to be carefully kept. Generally, by the time you are Real, most of your hair has been loved off, and your eyes drop out and you get loose in your joints and very shabby. But these things don't matter at all, because once you are Real you can't be ugly, except to people who don't understand. But once you are Real you can't become unreal again. It lasts for always."

Rider had drawn a line from the last sentence to the margin, where he had written, It lasts for forever.

"Oh my God," I whispered hoarsely. Squeezing my eyes shut, I held the book to my chest. Those highlighted lines were *everything*. They summed up how I felt, how I'd changed. None of it happened all at once, but once it happened, it couldn't be un-done. And it happened because I was loved. By Carl and Rosa, by Ainsley and even Rider, but most important, by myself.

Carl cleared his throat. "I think you should open the door."

My eyes flew open and my gaze shot to them. "What?"

Rosa nodded at the door with a small curl of her lips. "Go on, honey."

I stood there for a moment and then I whirled around. Rac-ing to the door, I turned the handle and yanked it open. My breath caught.

Rider was on the stoop and he turned slowly. He was wearing what he had in class earlier today. His hands were shoved into the pockets of his jeans. He wore an actual sweater for once, a thick wool one in navy blue.

His gaze roamed over my face and then to the book I still held to my chest. "I'm real."

Those two words. *I'm real*. No one else might have gotten the significance of them, but I knew they meant the world. Tears clouded my eyes as I stepped back and to the side, holding the door open for him.

Relief flickered over his face and he walked in. I closed the door, unable to speak, and not for the typical reasons.

"Keep the door open up there," Carl advised, and then he pivoted on his heel and walked into the kitchen.

Rosa smiled at us.

Looking at me, Rider waited, and I nodded. He followed me up the stairs to my bedroom. I left the door open. Sort of. There was at least a one-inch gap between the door and its frame.

Rider went to the window seat and he sat. His weary gaze followed me. I walked to the side of the bed facing him and sat on the corner. A tired smile pulled at his lips. "I don't know where to start," he said.

"Anywhere," I whispered, clutching the book as hope and wariness warred inside me.

He lowered his chin. "I guess I'll start with the speech. That was... It was beautiful. The words, what you said, what you meant? But the fact that you got up there and did it was the most beautiful of all those things. I mean it, Mallory."

"Thank you," I whispered.

"I...I wanted to talk to you before class, but I'm glad I heard that speech first. Because I knew you were right before, but now I know it even more."

I took two breaths.

"You were right about what you said about me, about how I see myself and others, you were right. I don't give other people a chance to give up on me. I never really thought of it that way before, but you were right." He dropped his forearms to his knees. "It's weird. You know, what you said to me at the funeral, about Jayden and that being real? I... God, I could only say this to you, because you understand, but I didn't feel real. In some ways, I still don't."

"I do understand." I held the book tighter. "I totally do."

His lashes lifted and his eyes pierced mine. "I know. Both of us were that damn rabbit." He laughed roughly. "I was sitting in that funeral on Saturday and I...I was thinking about everything. Thinking about how fucking unfair it was that Jayden was in that damn casket and something hit me right then. I've been living like I didn't have anything. No family. No opportunities. No one who really cared if I was here or not, and I was looking at Jayden, sitting next to his brother and his grandmother and I..." His voice cut, and my chest squeezed. "Jayden had a family. He had opportunity. You know? He had plenty of people who cared about him being here, and yet, he still ended up dead in the damn streets."

Rider shoved his hand through his hair. "And I'm here. I'm so damn lucky, because I haven't been careful. Henry could've easily killed me."

I sucked in a sharp breath. He was so right there. Many times I'd thought Henry was going to beat him to death.

"When Henry's friends would come...after me, I used to think I did something, you know? That it was somehow my fault—"

"What? That wasn't your fault, Rider. None of that was."

"I know, but sometimes my head gets... It gets messed up." He paused. "And when I was in that group home, I didn't care. I got in older, bigger kids' faces. I got the shit knocked out of me multiple times, and I didn't care. By the time Mrs. Luna came along, it felt too late for me. She tried. She really did— still does, and I've done so many stupid things that should've ended my life."

I hated hearing that. It scared me to death.

"Jayden makes one or two bad mistakes, and he's dead. Me, I'm still here." He dropped his head back and sighed. "I'd been given opportunities others hadn't and I've been wasting them, and now I have to really wonder if it is too late."

"It's not," I whispered, truly believing it.

His throat worked on a swallow. "After the funeral, I went home and I picked up that book. I...I started reading it. Don't even know why, but I got to that part, and I... God, it hit me, you know? The truth of those damn words the Skin Horse spoke. Being real could hurt. Being loved could hurt. That's what...what living is all about and the opposite is unimaginable."

Lowering the book to my lap, I smoothed my palm over the hard, glossy surface as I thought about the Skin Horse's words. They could be interpreted in so many ways. To me, they were all about letting go of the fear of being imperfect. Accepting that it was okay to be wanted and needed and loved, to be heard and seen.

Rider and I were a lot like the little boy and the rabbit who wanted to be real. Both of us spent so long relying on only each other. We'd been tossed aside, unwanted. And we wanted nothing more than to be cherished, treasured and loved. We wanted to feel real. Both of us were afraid of the opposite. To some the opposite was death but to me—to us—it was being stuck forever. Never changing. Never seeing ourselves or others around us differently.

"I do," he continued, voice gruff. "I do care. I don't want to be like this forever."

My gaze rose to his.

"I broke up with you because I thought it would be better that way. That you would eventually find someone who has their shit together, who has a future and isn't stuck. Things were—are—messed up in my head. I'm trying, really trying, to change that."

I stilled.

"I know you may never forgive me for hurting you. I can understand that. I can also understand if you don't want to have to deal with me while I'm trying to do better, be better, but I...I want to be the person I think you deserve."

Oh, my...

"I want to be the guy with a future, with his shit together and who has hope," he admitted, scooting toward the edge of the window seat. His gaze met mine and those beautiful eyes carried a sheen that tore through my heart. "I want to be the guy worthy of your love, and I swear, if you'll have me, I'll do everything in my power to be that man. I'll never stop trying. Ever."

Oh, my, my...

"And I want you to know that I heard what you said in that speech," Rider said, his voice scratchy. "I might've saved you all those years ago, but now you've saved me."

My heart stuttered and then sped up. I reacted without thought. Placing the book on the bed, I launched myself at Rider just as he came off the window seat. We collided. I folded my arms around him as we went down onto the floor, me partially in his lap and his arms tight around my waist, his face burrowed against my neck. I felt a tremor run through his body and then he shook in my arms. I held him tighter as he broke into pieces, and years of holding it together shattered. I held him through it all.

Then it was *me* who put Rider back together.

EPILOGUE

The remote was right there, taunting me from where it rested on the thick cushion of the ottoman, next to the tray that held two glasses and a bowl of barely touched pretzels. All I would have to do was sit up a little and stretch. I could grab it and I wouldn't have to watch any more of this basketball game.

Sitting up and stretching wasn't exactly doable at that moment, though.

A heavy arm was curled around my waist, and if I moved too much, I'd wake Rider and that was the last thing I wanted to do, especially when he'd been so exhausted the last couple of days. The shadows deepening under his eyes every day the last two weeks worried me.

He'd been pulling a lot of hours at the garage on a custom paint job he'd finished up on Thursday. After school yesterday I'd gotten to check it out, and like every design of Rider's, it had been amazing. Mind-blowing. I still had no idea how he could take paint and spray it on *any* surface, designing something so amazing and intricate.

This custom job had been on a car the owner raced at one

of the tracks near Frederick. On the hood, Rider had painted a dragon, complete with detailed green-and-purple scales. Reddish-orange flames erupted from the dragon's gaping mouth and crawled along the front side panels.

I'd snapped a picture of it with a real camera, to add to Rider's ever-expanding portfolio of work. Like before, he had acted weird about it, as if he still didn't know how to process recognizing his own talent.

I still had no idea how he didn't see that, but he was getting better at it. Like so many other things, like me, it was a work in progress.

Rider had told me a few weeks ago that sometimes he opened up the photo book we'd picked up together at the craft store and just flipped through the pictures of his work. His cheeks had been bright red when he admitted it. I'd thought the reaction had been adorable. Sometimes we sat and looked at his art together, and he blushed then, too.

But the custom job wasn't what had Rider worn out to the point that he'd fallen asleep the minute his head had hit the throw pillow on the couch.

This morning had been a big deal for him.

He'd used up every spare moment of the last several weeks preparing for the SATs he'd taken this morning. A smile inched across my face. Studying for the exam wasn't something he'd ever thought he'd do. His taking the exam had probably shocked the entire school administration into stunned silence. Well, except for Mr. Santos.

A goal was scored, and the crowd on the TV cheered. Or was it a point? A basket? I really had no idea. Why couldn't I have telekinetic powers? Moving things with my mind would be *awesome*.

Glancing down at where Rider's hand was lying on my lower stomach, I welcomed the dipping sensation. The fluttering feeling that occurred every so often with Rider wasn't something that faded with time. I didn't think it was ever going to.

Blue paint was smudged along the inside of his middle finger. He never seemed to get all the paint off his fingers.

I tilted my head back and looked to my right. The fluttering turned into a thousand butterflies bouncing between my ribs as my gaze coasted over Rider's striking face. Feeling a little like a creeper, I continued to check him out. A lock of dark brown hair, the color of coffee, fell across his forehead. Thick lashes, much darker than his hair, fanned his cheeks. His full lips were slightly parted.

It seemed strange now that there was a point in my life, a point that lasted for several years, where I sincerely believed I'd never see Rider again. When lying like this, in his arms, was a fantasy I hadn't even allowed myself to dream about. Now it was a reality.

Life was weird.

"If you take a picture, it'll last longer," he murmured.

My eyes widened as heat poured into my cheeks. "What?"

Lashes lifted slowly, revealing eyes that seemed to be neither completely brown nor green. "The picture will last longer than you staring. Then you can have a picture to cuddle with at night, when I'm not with you. You can hold it close. Squeeze it tight."

I rolled my eyes as my lips twitched into a grin. "Whatever."

"Uh-huh." Lifting his arm, he stretched it above his head as he yawned. "When are Carl and Rosa getting here?"

I glanced at the pale gray wall clock. "Probably in an hour."

"Good thing I'm awake instead of drooling on you as they walk through the door."

"Yes," I said seriously. "Good point."

Rider smirked, but joking aside, neither Rosa nor Carl would be thrilled to come home and find us snuggled together on the couch. It wasn't like they expected Rider and me not to get, well, close to one another. But they were still…adjusting to my relationship with Rider. It was another work in progress, and they were coming along. They were trying, and that was so much better than their being afraid of what they originally believed Rider symbolized.

Plus, it helped that Rider was becoming more serious about his future, and studying for the SATs had helped endear him a little to goal-oriented Carl. Winning him over completely was harder, but I could tell Carl was beginning to respect him. He was starting to see him as more than a boy with no future who was going to lead me down the wrong path like the Pied Piper of Hotness, but their walking in on us all wrapped up together probably wasn't going to help matters. I started to sit up.

Rider's arm tightened around my waist and he rolled slightly, shifting me under him. My hands lifted to his shoulders, and when I looked up, my heart stuttered at the sight of his half grin. "Where you going?" he asked.

"Up." My fingers closed, gathering the material of his shirt. "Carl will…kick you out of the house…if he finds us like this and you don't even want to know what Rosa will do."

"True." He dipped his head, running his nose over mine. "Rosa still scares me."

I giggled.

"You think that's funny, but she really does." Tipping his head to the side, he kissed my cheek. "I'm convinced she knows how to deliver as much damage as possible with a single punch. She's a doctor. She knows things."

Laughing again, I tried to picture Rosa punching anything and failed. I patted his shoulder. "You'll be okay."

"I might need you to protect me." He kissed my other cheek again.

The corners of my lips curved up. "I…I can do that."

This time his lips brushed my temple. "Sorry about falling asleep as soon as I got here. We haven't been able to spend a lot of time together, and the first time we do and I'm not studying or working on a car, I sleep on you."

I kind of liked him sleeping on me. "It's okay. You've been… working hard. How do you think you did?"

Rider lifted his head. "I think I did pretty good. Only a few questions really threw me."

Thrilled to hear that, I smiled. "Are you excited?"

"I guess. I mean…" He trailed off, brows knitting. "There's still a lot that's got to fall into place. I have until June to get the form in for financial aid, but it's going to be hard getting in with my grades this late in the game. I'd have to have blown the SATs out of the water."

"But you have spring. If you don't get into the fall semester, it's…not over," I reasoned. "Before you know it, you'll be at College Park with me, studying visual arts."

"You're right." A wicked little grin tugged at his lips. "I think we should celebrate." Pausing, he waggled his brows at me. "We have fifty minutes now. I only need, like, five of them."

"Oh my God." I laughed, shoving at his shoulders. "You're terrible."

"I'm not terrible." His eyes met mine, and the flutter was back, deeper and more dizzying. "I'm in love."

Oh, gosh. My heart swelled like a balloon, and all I could do was stare at him for several seconds before I managed to whisper, "I love you, too."

"I know." Rider lowered his mouth to mine, and the kiss scattered my thoughts. I was still shocked that a kiss had that kind of power, that when his tongue touched mine, I could forget everything in the world.

The kiss ended all too soon. Rider shifted off me and sat up, lifting my legs so they were in his lap, and I sort of lay there, arms lax at my sides as I stared at him. A goofy smile split my lips, and I didn't care. I was thinking about how we could utilize the remaining fifty minutes.

"How're things with Dr. Taft?" he asked as he shifted his legs, spreading them a little. "I didn't get the chance to ask you yesterday."

Huh? I started to frown. I was over here thinking about getting back to kissing and other stuff, really nice stuff, and he just mentioned my therapist's name?

Rider smacked my leg lightly and chuckled. "Focus."

I narrowed my eyes at him, but focusing was hard when my body felt like I'd been out lying in the sun. "It was...good. We talked about how I was feeling and how I was...handling stress."

I'd started seeing Dr. Taft once every two weeks again. Mainly because I felt like I needed someone who wasn't a part of everyday life to just...talk things out, because I still had work on myself to do. It had been really depressing at first, because it had been two years since I'd spent time in his office. Like I'd somehow gone back into the past instead of progressing forward, but Taft drilled something into my head that was so important. Something I'd already known, but really needed to understand.

The past never went away and it was not designed to do so.

It would always be there, and it should be acknowledged. Dr. Taft insisted that attempting to erase the past would only lead to a crisis in the future, and he was right. My past could not be surgically cut out of me. It couldn't be removed from Rider. What happened to Jayden couldn't be forgotten.

My past was a part of me and it molded who I was today, but it was not the sum of who I was to become. It did not control me.

Rider leaned over and found my hand. He threaded his fingers through mine and squeezed. "I don't want to lose you."

Pressure clamped down on my chest and I squeezed his hand back. I thought with Jayden dying, it had Rider on his toes. Having mortality smack you in the face would do that. "You won't."

"Good." Rider smiled as he tugged me up into a sitting position. His other hand cupped my cheek, and he kissed me once more, sweet and soft. He pulled back just enough so that his warm breath danced along my lips. "I think I want to kiss you again."

"I'm more than okay with that," I told him, and I smiled.

Truthfully, I was okay with…with myself. I wasn't a hundred percent, and that was okay, because *I* was a work in progress. There were moments when things felt too much, like the other day when I had to stand up and deliver another speech. There were other situations, especially when I thought about the fact that I'd be in college in less than a year. Or when I found my mind wandering to Jayden. Death was frightening and over-whelming. Sometimes, when I thought about what Ainsley was facing in the future, I stressed out for her.

I still had a lot of work to do and that was *my* work to complete and it was my voice that needed to be heard when I needed to speak. No one else. It was me who had to carry myself over the finish line, and all I needed to remember when I felt like not trying was that that feeling wouldn't last forever.

Forever.

I used to believe it didn't exist. One word had terrified me as a child and haunted me. But now I knew, in many small ways, that it was real, but it didn't scare me anymore. Forever wasn't the little girl cowering in the closet. Forever wasn't the shadow sitting in the back of the class. Forever wasn't doing what I thought Carl and Rosa wanted instead of what I needed to do with my life. Forever wasn't believing I was some kind of re-placement daughter and that I was letting them down. Forever wasn't being the one who needed protection.

Forever wasn't pain and grief.

Forever wasn't a problem.

Forever was my heartbeat and it was the hope tomorrow held. Forever was the glistening silver lining of every dark cloud, no matter how heavy and thick it was. Forever was knowing mo-ments of weakness didn't equate to an eternity of them. For-ever was knowing that I was strong. Forever was Carl and Rosa,

Ainsley and Keira, Hector and Rider. Jayden would always be a part of my forever. Forever was the fire-breathing dragon inside me that had shed the fear like a snake shedding skin. Forever was simply a promise of more.

Forever *was* a work in progress.

And I couldn't wait for forever.

★ ★ ★ ★ ★

ACKNOWLEDGMENTS

Writing a novel that dealt with childhood neglect and abuse and their long-term effects meant I would be delving into a world a lot of people may find it hard to look closely upon. A world where some want to believe that what Mallory and Rider suffered are complete works of fiction. It wasn't easy to equally represent all the good in the services designed to protect our children while recognizing that some have and still do slip through the cracks of an underfunded, overworked and understaffed system.

Some have asked why I chose to set *The Problem with Forever* in Baltimore. I grew up not too far from the city, and I almost always try to have books take place in areas I am well familiar with, and I'd been to Baltimore more times that I can count. But I believed the city itself is more than just a backdrop to the story. In a way, the city is also a character, which, like Rider, Mallory, Jayden, Ainsley, Hector, Keira and the other characters in this novel, is full of beauty and hope, yet has often slipped through the fingers of our nation.

The Problem with Forever was not an easy book to write. Mallory was unlike any character I'd ever written, but as I realized at the end of the book, there is a bit of "Mouse" in all of us. So there are several people I need to thank who believed in this story and helped bring the book together.

Thank you to my agent Kevan Lyon for supporting *The Problem with Forever* and being the awesomely awesome agent that she always has been. This book would've never happened if it was not for Margo Lipschultz and the entire team at Harlequin TEEN. Thank you to Mallory Dodge and Rosa who let me use their names.

There were a few people who were of special help to *The Problem with Forever*. A special thanks to Ashlynn King who read a very, very early partial and didn't want to gouge her eyes out with a rusty spork. I guess I should thank her mother, Tiffany King, at this point, because she adeptly dubbed this book one of my horcruxes even though the last time I checked I didn't commit a great evil. I think. Another big thank you to Vilma Gonzalez for also reading an early draft and not laughing outright in my face and having so many ideas on how to make this a better book. I cannot forget Damaris Cardinali, who helped me with all the Puerto Rican in *The Problem with Forever*, and didn't lose her patience with me when I was losing patience with the fact that you can say one thing three different ways in Puerto Rican. Thank you to Jen Fisher who helped with a lot of the homeschooling information, and who has always read early and been honest about her feels…or lack thereof. A big thank you to Danielle Ellison, who helped me come up with the perfect title in Twitter DM style.

A special thank you to you, the reader. Nothing that I do would be possible without you and your support.

And thank you to Margery Williams for writing *The Velveteen Rabbit*, a book I hated and loved at the same time as a child. I think all of us, at the end of the day, just want to be real and want to be loved.